Strivers Row

During the 1920s and 1930s, around the time of the Harlem Renaissance, more than a quarter of a million African-Americans settled in Harlem, creating what was described at the time as "a cosmopolitan Negro capital which exert[ed] an influence over Negroes everywhere."

Nowhere was this more evident than on West 138th and 139th Streets between Adam Clayton Powell and Frederick Douglass Boulevards, two blocks that came to be known as Strivers Row. These blocks attracted many of Harlem's African-American doctors, lawyers, and entertainers, among them Eubie Blake, Noble Sissle, and W. C. Handy, who were themselves striving to achieve America's middle-class dream.

With its mission of publishing quality African-American literature, Strivers Row emulates those "strivers," capturing that same spirit of hope, creativity, and promise.

BETWEEN
BROTHERS

BETWEEN
BROTHERS

a Novel

C. Kelly Robinson

VILLARD • NEW YORK

All rights reserved under International and Pan-American
Copyright Conventions. Published in the United States by
Strivers Row, an imprint of Villard Books, a division of
Random House, Inc., New York, and simultaneously in Canada
by Random House of Canada Limited, Toronto.

VILLARD BOOKS is a registered trademark of Random House, Inc.
STRIVERS ROW and colophon are trademarks of Random House, Inc.

This work was originally published by
Against the Grain Communications

LIBRARY OF CONGRESS CATALOGING-IN-PUBLICATION DATA
Robinson, C. Kelly, (Chester Kelly)
Between brothers : a novel / C. Kelly Robinson.
p.   cm.
ISBN 0-375-75772-4
1. African American college students—Fiction. 2. Children—Services
for—Fiction. 3. African American men—Fiction. 4. Community
centers—Fiction. 5. Washington (D.C.)—Fiction. 6. Male friendship—
Fiction. 7. Young men—Fiction. I. Title.
PS3568.O2855 B47 2001
813'.54—dc21   2001025840

Villard Books website address: www.villard.com
Printed in the United States of America on acid-free paper

24689753

First Strivers Row Edition

Book design by Mercedes Everett

For Kyra

ACKNOWLEDGMENTS

There are so many people to thank at a time like this, and I've only got so much space. First I give honor to God for bringing me through a tough self-publishing experience and allowing me to meet so many supportive readers and fellow writers along the way.

Thanks to my wife, Kyra, for hitting the pavement with me to sell our books and for agreeing to go into a little debt along the way. To my parents, Chester and Sherry Robinson, thanks for setting a great example and providing ongoing friendship and guidance. To my brothers and sister—Russell, Barrett, and Shelli—thanks for egging your crazy big brother on. I'm also grateful for the support of my extended families, the Alfords and Robinsons.

Thanks to my agent, Elaine Koster, for your professionalism and for sharing your knowledge. Thanks to Melody Guy and the entire Villard/Strivers Row staff for the vote of confidence. Let's get more books into the hands of college students and "twenty-somethings."

Thanks to the fellow authors and writers who have provided unselfish advice and encouragement, via e-mail or in person: Timm McCann, William July, Kimberla Lawson Roby, Victor McGlothin, Lolita Files, Tracy Price-Thompson, Tonya Marie Evans, Brandon Massey (the next Stephen King), Phil Cargile, Dr. Frank Dobson, Troy Martin, Karen Miller, Daryl Green, Greg and

Devivia Morris, Parry Brown, and Jamie Walker (HU in the house!). I also owe thanks to the African-American Online Writers Guild and to my heroes at the National Stuttering Association.

Finally, big thanks to the bookstores and book clubs who gave me a chance as a self-published author in 1999 and 2000. Special thanks to Toni Birdsong and Wilberforce University, the Omega Missionary Baptist Church family, Peggy Hicks and TriCom Publicity, the Howard University Bookstore, Janet Mosley and Tenaj Bookstore (Ft. Pierce, Florida), Emma Rodgers and Black Images Book Store (Dallas), Dr. Jawanza Kunjufu and African-American Images (Chicago), Robin Green-Cary and Sibanye Books (Baltimore), Jack & Jill of America (Dayton, Ohio), and the Phenomenal Women Book Club (Houston). To everyone who has shown support or interest, you are not forgotten.

BETWEEN
BROTHERS

Prologue

Sheryl Gibson's heart simmered as she met Nico Lane's cold, narrow stare. She would never forget the hopeful, engaging eighth-grader he had once been, but the sight of him this morning nearly drove those days from her mind. She breezed past him into her office on the second floor of Ellis Community Center, trying to hold on to the fading memory of that promising child. Gritting her teeth, she opened the rickety blinds of the window over her desk and turned to face him. "Nico, I have a busy day ahead of me. What do you want?"

Picking carefully at a piece of lint on the right sleeve of his navy blue blazer, Nico strode toward Sheryl and helped himself to the sunken wooden chair opposite her desk. "Sheryl, you didn't even give me a chance to say how fine you're looking this morning." His eyes burned with restrained glee as they danced up and down her wrinkled red pantsuit. "You know, I just realized I haven't been here in a while. It's impressive, the way the place has grown. I just stopped down in the basement. You can fit hundreds of kids in that dance studio, and how big is that pool? You've done quite a bit here, my sister."

As Nico stroked his smooth, oval chin, Sheryl shook her head. With his baby face and multiracial heritage, Nico, now twenty-six, drew constant comparisons to Tiger Woods, a sinister, bulkier version. The boy was a living, breathing contradiction; his articulate phrasing and proper English made him sound like

Bryant Gumbel, but he wasn't fooling anybody. Word on the street was Nico was the most feared dealer in D.C.'s Shaw community. Sheryl had heard last week that he was now officially off the street. As an investment banker of the drug world, he oversaw trades of street dealers and remitted the receipts to the men near the top of the food chain, those who likely worked hand in hand with the DEA and CIA.

As she eyed her unwelcome visitor, Sheryl's mind whirred in anger and confusion. This man had spent years of his youth at Ellis, winning Knowledge Bowl competitions, science fairs, and math contests. And what had he done with it? Used it for exactly what she and the Ellis volunteers had hoped he would avoid.

She fixed him with a glare. "You remember Tommy Benson, one of the boys you tutored in algebra, before you stopped coming around?"

Folding his hands in his lap, Nico smirked. "Sheryl, save the guilt trip. I know Tommy was found with a hole in his head last night." He sighed innocently. "Word has it he had fallen in with the wrong crowd. Shameful." Apparently sensing that Sheryl's patience was shot, Nico matched her weary stare. "Let me get to the business at hand. You know I was born in the projects that border this land. I appreciate what Ellis has done for this community. The academic programs, the free swimming classes, the basketball, all this stuff kept me and my boys off the street when we were coming up."

"Not that it did much good in your case." Sheryl crossed her legs and impatiently tapped her desk. She refused to let Nico have all the fun.

"Come now, Sheryl, stop and think about what you're saying. I'm one alumnus of Ellis who pays *all* of his bills on time. *I* don't get nasty calls from my creditors. Can you say the same thing about Ellis?"

Annoyed, Sheryl waved a hand in front of her lightly perspiring brow. D.C.'s spring weather, unpredictable as always, was unseasonably warm for March. She would have to go buy herself a fan this evening; there was no room for one in Ellis's budget.

She knew she must look a mess. The stress of the last few weeks, since the center had lost the majority of its funding from the D.C. government, was taking its toll. Although she had turned more than a few heads in her day, she knew her maple complexion, broadly sloped nose, and jutting cheekbones were losing their luster. She had enough on her without being taunted by Nico Lane. "Nico, the center's financial status is none of your business. What is your point?"

Chuckling, Nico stood and extended his arms toward her in a gesture of invitation. "Sheryl, I want to make life easier for you. You've put your blood, sweat, and tears into this place for more than fifteen years, and for what? So brothers like me can still wind up selling crack and brothers like Tommy Benson wind up using it. And now, to add insult to injury, the mayor had to discontinue your funding. I read, you know. I know the District was responsible for about seventy-five percent of your budget. Exactly how do you plan to make up the shortfall, sister?" The final word was a violent stab to Sheryl's heart.

She put on a brave face. "For your information, we're getting a lot of interest from private donors. In addition, we've hired former councilman Rolly Orange as our business manager, and we've got four Highland University students raising money from the private sector. I expect we'll have a solid base of private capital in the next six months."

Nico twisted his mouth into a frown. "Sister, please. Don't try to snow me. I know damn well that in this day and age smaller government is in vogue. That means free-market enterprises like the Annenberg Center are supposed to pick up where dinosaurs like Ellis will leave off. If the *Post* is to be believed, Ellis's doors should be shut right now."

Sheryl's heart pounded. Nico had to go and mention that damn Annenberg Center, the recreation club funded by a group of Fortune 500 corporations and their nonprofit foundations. She had fumed over the infamous editorial in the *The Washington Post* last week, the one that lauded Annenberg for its innovative design and suggested that Ellis and other urban centers be closed and folded into Annenberg. Wishing she could leap across the desk and strangle Nico into submission, Sheryl pressed her right thumb and forefinger together and recalled her *Acts of Faith* reading for the day. She had to stay in control. "Nico, a corporate behemoth like Annenberg could never serve the children of Shaw the way Ellis can. Everyone knows that."

"Sheryl, you and I both know that's neither here nor there." Without looking at her, Nico abruptly reached into his jacket pocket and retrieved a gold-trimmed, leather checkbook. The room filled with the obnoxious smell of cowhide. He pulled a Cross pen from the other pocket. "I believe in being real, Sheryl, so I'll be blunt. Ellis Center is cutting into my business. Every few weeks I get calls from my street dealers, asking me to help pull back recruits who drop out after they get involved in activities at Ellis. I admit, I'm impressed. Before you took over, back when I was little, kids who came here usually still ended up slangin' rocks or using 'em—it just took a little longer. But, you, you . . . there's something different about what you've taught these kids. Some of my dealers have actually had kids tell them that *they're* stupid for dealing, that they should come here and find out about all the positive things they can do in life! Can you imagine that?"

"Nico, get out. I'm calling security." Sheryl reached for her phone. She didn't like where this was going.

Startling her, Nico reached across the desk and slammed the phone down before she could dial. His eyes were filled with the uncontrolled hatred she'd seen on young Nico's last day at the center—the day after his long-lost father sent him away and told him never to come around again. As Nico squared his jaw, the vernacular of the street began to seep into his voice. "You didn't let me finish. Ellis's days are numbered, one way or the other. I suggest we both save ourselves a world of trouble. It works like this. You take this check I'm about to write you. Fifty thou should hold you while you resign from Ellis and search for a new job, right? I know you need the money. Your daughter got herself knocked up, your husband pulled a disappearing act a few months ago, I know things are tight. Just take the check and help yourself to some happiness, Sheryl. You've earned it."

As Nico clamped his hand over hers, Sheryl stared back in disbelief. Her nostrils stinging at the sharp smell of his Polo cologne, she stared through Nico and fixed her gaze on the wall opposite her desk. She was not going to dignify this with a response. She let her eyes and the twist of her neck—along with a barely audible "Humph!"—do the talking.

Meeting the hate in her eyes with his own, Nico released his grip from her hand. Before Sheryl could utter the epithets that had built up inside, he staggered back from the desk and swiped his derby hat from her wooden chair. "It was worth a try, wasn't it? Guess I'll have to take other measures." Huffing and puffing like a humiliated child, he swaggered to the doorway of her office before flicking a white business card toward her desk. "If you change your mind, use the cell-phone number on there. That's the one for my Mercedes, the S350. Bye, Sheryl. And I do mean good-bye."

As Nico slammed the door shut behind him, Sheryl stood to her aching feet, folded her arms across her chest, and closed her eyes in desperate reverence. *Lord*, she prayed, *if I ever needed you, I need you now*. Trying to collect herself, she turned and faced the sunlight streaming through her window. She stared out at the white steeple of Highland University's Founders Library and sighed. Maybe, she thought, the young men on that campus—Brandon, Larry, O.J., and Terence—could be the difference in the uphill battle Ellis Center faced. The community would be counting on them.

1

CHOIRBOY

"Brandon, you twenty-one . . . and you ain't got no kids?" Little Pooh Riley's wide eyes bugged out as he searched his mentor's face for an answer.

Seated a few feet away from his favorite student, in the front of the basement classroom off the center's busiest hallway, Brandon Bailey shrugged. "Pooh, how many times I gotta tell ya," he said, smiling, "you don't *have* to start making babies when you turn sixteen."

"Mmm-mmm, I don't know 'bout that," the saggy-faced cherub said, shaking his head feverishly. "My momma say all most men do is make babies and leave. She done already told me I'll do the same thing, by the time I'm fifteen."

"Fifteen!" Brandon slapped a hand over his mouth as the class rocked with laughter. *Slow your roll, don't rub the boy's face in it,* he reminded himself. "Uh, Pooh," he said, choosing his words carefully as he held up a hand to quiet the other twelve boys in the class, "next time you talk to your momma, tell her about me."

Pooh ran a fidgety hand over his classic Washington Bullets jersey. "Aww, I don't know about that, Brandon, you a little young for my momma!" The other nine-year-olds erupted in another fit of amusement, some of them cupping their mouths and hooting toward the front of the classroom. "Brandon gon' get some booty! Brandon gon' get some booty!"

"All right, that's enough." Brandon kicked his miniature plastic chair aside and stood, stretching his sinewy legs and smoothing his beige Dockers slacks. "Pooh—all of you, for that matter—my point is you don't have to make babies at any age. Most of my classmates at Highland? We're waiting until we graduate college and get good jobs before we bring children into the world. You can, too."

Anthony, a lean, gawky hood-in-training, sat up in his seat and twisted his neck skeptically. "My granny say all men is dogs and any who ain't are *punks*. Gay, in jail, or married."

Brandon felt his heart surge self-defensively. "Your granny? How . . ." It occurred to him he probably didn't want to go down this road, matching wits with a grandmother who was probably younger than his own mother. He reminded himself: he was here, as he was every Monday, Wednesday, and Friday afternoon, to teach these boys basic math and pray that his "positive example" rubbed off in some way. It was just so hard to see any progress in them some days.

He had nothing to prove to them. By now, Brandon's applications to Duke, Northwestern, Ohio State, and Johns Hopkins were all signed, sealed, and delivered. Each application had been packed with the envy of every Highland premed student: stellar recommendations from two arts and sciences deans, spanking GPA and MCAT scores, and mentions of his strong medical lineage (Pops, Brent Bailey, as well as Grandpa, Willie Bailey, continued thriving private practices). His admission to med school was money in the bank.

Yes, he thought as he closed the class with one last word problem and dismissed the boys to the courtyard for afternoon break, Brandon Bailey had done quite well for himself these past four years at Highland. So why had the ill-conceived ideas his students had about manhood bothered him so much just now? Could it be, the thought asserted itself as he wiped the blackboard clean with a moist paper towel, his growing unease about the legacy he was leaving on Highland's social scene? "Legacy," he said to the empty room as he tossed the limp towel into a round metal can near the doorway, "*what* legacy?"

Even now he couldn't believe it; in two months he'd be leaving Highland University behind. The nation's top-ranked HBCU (historically black college/university), Highland was the one place where amazingly beautiful sisters of every hue were a moment-by-moment fact of life. How lovely the sight, day after day: nothing but allegedly ripe-for-the-picking, deliciously desirable, fiercely intelligent black queens. Whether he wound up at OSU, Northwestern, Duke, or Johns Hopkins, he'd never again see such a selection. All that opportunity, he thought, and what did he have to show for it? He had let four years at this oasis pass him by without finding Ms. Right. Everyone knew the first reason you attended an HBCU was to grab yourself a mate.

How had he, Brandon Bailey—high school star defensive back, future physician, a guy told more than once he looked like Theo Huxtable with body—how had *he* managed to emerge romance-free from a campus with a three-to-one female/male ratio? His mother, Barbara, and every other woman in his family constantly reminded him how great a catch he was. That had to be more than familial bias, didn't it?

He swept the silly questions from his head, shut the heavy wooden door of the classroom, and strode down the hallway to the nearest exit. Thrusting the door open, Brandon searched the courtyard for his boys. The circular space, covered in craggy concrete and hemmed in by Ellis' aging brick walls, was a rowdy place today. The boys and girls, ranging in age from three to twelve, were scattered across the courtyard, running, tossing, pinching, screaming, and taunting like mad. Four other counselors and a security guard crisscrossed the area, damping the groups playing too hard and bringing order to the few kids dangling at the fringes. Brandon walked over to where Pooh and several of the boys were running around. He took Pooh aside so they could talk.

He looked to his left and right, trying to respect the boy's privacy. "Hey, your mother doing any better?"

"Not really," Pooh said, his eyes suddenly aimed at his shoes. "Some strange dude been comin' over a lot, man. A Japanese-looking guy, Nico."

"Well," Brandon said, "are you afraid this Nico's going to hurt your mother?"

"I don't know. I just know he always talk in hushed tones, acting real serious. I stay out of his way as long as he don't be touchin' her."

"That's best," Brandon said. "Listen, Pooh, don't forget. Any time you wanna talk, I'm here—"

"Excuse me, everyone!" Sheryl Gibson had taken center stage in the courtyard, her hands cupped around her mouth like a megaphone. Brandon noticed the wrinkles in her red pantsuit and the weariness in her eyes. Her condition reminded him that Sheryl, and the center in general, needed so much help. This private-donor campaign had to work. He'd been up most every night the last few weeks coordinating a Highland alumni pledge drive for Ellis, but there was only so much time.

"Listen, everyone," Sheryl said as the counselors herded the children toward the center and instructed them to take seats on the cool concrete, "we have two Highland students here today to give you some information about the field trip next week. Yes," she said, shaking her head at a counselor giving her grief from a few feet away, "this *will* be a short trip. You're just going to go across the street and get a full tour of the campus. But you have to have your parents' permission to leave Ellis's premises. These ladies are going to pass out the forms and tell you more about the trip." She stepped forward and motioned into the crowd behind her. "Monica?"

A young woman stepped forward and began speaking in a smooth, confident voice. Her athletic figure, trim but rounded in all the right places, was nestled beneath a flattering Guess jeans ensemble. "Boys and girls," she said sweetly, "let me tell you about a special place, a land called Highland . . ."

From his perch near the back of the courtyard, Brandon gulped like an embarrassed child. Panic crept up his shoulders as his face grew dewy with sweat and the gallop of a crazed horse beat within his chest. Monica Simone! The woman he'd worshipped from afar since his first days at Highland had invaded

Ellis, his private sanctuary, a place where he could selflessly serve and be free from the vagaries of his lonely nights. Again Brandon was reminded he was not your stereotypical brother, the sex-crazed, verbally adept hound that TV and movies portrayed every chance they got. No, Brandon's rapping skills came straight from Dear Old Dad, and even today Pops was the first to admit he'd been no Bobby Brown in his single days.

As Monica completed her presentation and the kids rewarded her with a round of frantic applause, Brandon felt a burning in his chest and tried to gather his nerves. Monica rendered him as help-less as a child suffering his first crush. He watched her turn toward Sheryl and make conversation for a moment. By the time he'd leaned over and grabbed up his Highland backpack, Monica was a foot away, making her way through the shrinking crowd as the kids were rounded up for Sheryl's comments. His chest still heav-ing anxiously, Brandon checked his watch and realized he was a few minutes late to meet someone. Should he even bother speak-ing to her?

"Hey, Brandon," Monica said, flashing a polite smile and paus-ing as his eyes met hers. "You're a counselor here?"

Caught in the thicket of her caramel complexion, flowing ebony mane, and soft cheekbones, Brandon was a deer in Mon-ica's headlights. His mouth refused to work. His mind swam in an alternate reality, one where he imagined the ways he would meet her every need, calm her innermost fears, and stoke her heart's most passionate desire, if she would only let him. *Oh, if only*, he thought . . . What could he say to her, when the stakes of every word, every flirt, were so high? His legs planted into the court-yard's cement ground like two stubborn iron poles, Brandon swallowed carefully. "I, uh, yeah, I do work here, with the eight-and nine-year-olds. Math," he said, the last word coming out with a squeak. Why couldn't a love jones endow him with some cool for a change?

Seemingly unaware of his sudden difficulty with words, Monica twirled a lock of her hair around her right index finger. "I think the things you all do here are great. I plan to sign up and teach one of the business classes next year. Figure I may as well share the marketing knowledge HU's taught me."

"That's admirable," Brandon said, noticing his voice had regained its bass but was sounding too deep now. His mind pushed him forward. *Come on, now, say something charming . . .*

"I'd better go," Monica said, shifting her weight slightly and tucking her notebook under her arm. "Bye now."

Returning her smile and wondering if her wave was as coy as he hoped, Brandon watched Monica walk off and felt his mind fill with thoughts no Christian boy should entertain. He had it bad. As the gallop in his chest slowed to an exhausted limp, he realized he had missed yet another golden opportunity. Monica was gone. On the scoreboard of his heart, paralyzing fear had scored yet another touchdown, and Brandon hadn't even scored a field goal since high school. Since Brandy.

He ran a hand over his forehead, ran back to the center of the courtyard to slap hands with Pooh and the other boys, and bolted through the front hallway until he came to the main entrance. His cousin Bobby Wayne, a fellow Highland senior and also premed, was leaning against the inside wall. His arms were crossed impatiently, but his eyes, the same wide, piercing ones that Brandon and most every member of the Weaver side of the family had, were dancing with mischief.

"Okay, first of all," Bobby said, straightening the legs of his Levi's, "you're late. I have to get downstairs and teach my class at four *sharp*, man. Now *I'm* late. You got the dang clippers?"

Brandon sighed and reached into his backpack, producing his best pair of Wahl hair clippers and slapping them into Bobby's palm. "There. You just make sure you clean 'em good before bringing 'em back. I ain't got time to be picking your dandruff out of my stuff."

"Oh, ha, very funny." Bobby rolled his eyes. "I got another beef with you, cuz. I just saw Monica walk out of here, without my love Tara of course." Bobby had been in hot pursuit of Monica's best friend, Tara Lee, since sophomore year, to no avail. Brandon had never told Bobby, but he was pretty sure his cousin had had a good shot until he'd opened his mouth; Bobby had beat him out in the girls' "Looks" polls in high school back in Chicago, but he'd also been consistently voted Class Clown. His goofy ways never failed to sabotage his game.

"The question is," Bobby continued, stepping toward Brandon and blocking the door, "did you rap to Monica? You know we've only got so many months left in the year."

Brandon shook his head and removed a pack of Snackwell's vanilla cremes from his backpack, preparing for the trek back to campus. "Look, Bobby, Monica's not exactly known for being the most spiritual woman on campus. You know I need a woman who's strong in that area."

Bobby snatched a cookie. "She's a churchgoer, ain't she?"

Chomping on a cookie as he spoke, Brandon waved a finger at his cousin. "Bobby, there's some of everything up in the church. Look, I can tell when a woman is at my spiritual level and when she's not. What are you laughing at?"

Bobby was shaking his head, which was neatly framed in with a professional box fade. A smirk was plastered on his coffee-bean complexion. "Boy, life as the Choirboy must be great! If I had your powers of perception, life sure would be simple. Imagine, to know through osmosis whether a girl is right for you or not, just by lookin' at her! No need to call her or talk to her. Why risk rejection anyway?"

Brandon gave his cousin a playful shove. "Forget you, man. I couldn't understand half of what you said anyway." He and Bobby liked to razz each other about the newfound ethnicity they'd adopted at Highland. Granted, no one would be mistaking them for Tupac or Snoop Dogg, but they'd come a long way. Back in the suburbs of Chicago, their private schools and white middle-class subdivisions had left them with mannerisms and styles of dress the city kids dubbed "white." Even some at Highland had initially questioned their authenticity freshman year. Not two weeks into that first year, Bobby had rushed into Brandon's dorm room one afternoon with a look of pain across his face.

"Brandon, do I *stand* white?"

Resting in a rickety chair near his window, Brandon had squinted in confusion. "*Stand* white? Exactly how would one do that?"

"I don't know," Bobby had mused. "Tara told me I carry myself like a white guy. Now I've heard that I 'talk white,' even 'dress white,' but 'stand white'? She said the way I lock my knees and hold my back erect looks like 'white guy' posture. Are real brothers supposed to stand with their knees bent and their hands on their nuts? I don't get it."

Neither had Brandon. That had been the first of many times he'd suggested Bobby release his fascination with Tara. Any sister who couldn't love a brother the way he was, "standin' white" or not, was not the Right One.

As Brandon opened the heavy front door and stepped out into the fading sunlight draping Ellis' front steps, Bobby continued to pick at him. "You know and I know that you haven't tried rapping to Monica 'cause you are *scared*! Be a man, just admit it."

Brandon paused in the doorway and grimaced. "Well, I have such an encouraging example in you, Bobby. Tara's never even given you one ounce of dap. Why would I wanna be like you—spend my life getting shot down?"

"Ah, so it's like that, cousin? Well, I know one thing. When *I'm* kickin' butt in med school next year, I won't be losing one bit of sleep about what *could've* happened if I'd let Tara know how I feel. What you got to say to that?"

"How about this? Let's just agree it's nun y'on—none of your business. I gotta get over to the library, man."

Bobby stepped forward. "All I got to say is, man, don't let this year get away without makin' some moves, even if you fail. Stop beatin' yourself up over Brandy—"

"So you know," Brandon said, shaking his head and looking away, "you're officially over the line now."

"Whatever, Holmes. I better go. My class is calling me."

Brandon's pursed lips matched his rueful tone of voice. "Yes, it is. I need to go myself, get some studying in before tonight's Black Impact meeting."

"Oh, really," Bobby boomed, "well, you have fun now! I thought you had joined me in self-imposed exile from the Disciples! You know, it's that group that has you scared to ask out a girl like Monica in the first place."

Brandon stepped through the doorway and let Bobby catch the door. "Terence finally agreed to attend a Disciples meeting with me, man. I think it might be good for the brother."

Bobby frowned. "What's the real reason you're going?"

Brandon shook his head again. "Well, I have been drafted to do some fund-raising for Ellis. You know the Disciples' backers have deep pockets."

"Yeah," Bobby said, releasing the door handle, "the question is what will they want in return. Good luck!"

Turning on his heels, Brandon hopped the steps, tore across the busy thoroughfare, and stepped onto Highland's hallowed ground.

Focusing his thoughts on his upcoming studies, he crossed the expansive concrete diamond separating Just Hall from the ivy-covered brick steps of the Highland Undergraduate Library. The sun was just beginning its descent, a faint orange glow hovering above and to his right. As Brandon approached the steps, he shot off several "What's up?" nods to assorted friends and acquaintances milling about in the afternoon crowd, and he slowed to slap a few hands. Students of every hue, height, weight, and style filled the diamond, and in his eyes they were all beautiful. Dreadlocks, Afro puffs, extensions, S-curls, box cuts, fades, skin-tights, ponytails, naturals, bobs, weaves—they were all here. They were attired in Polo, Hilfiger, Versace, Claiborne, Karl Kani, Sears, J. C. Penney, and every regional bargain-basement chain. The varied visions of black folk merged into one enthusiastic, ambitious whole. Highland was a vibrant sea of Afrocentric-flavored diversity; Brandon couldn't imagine attending college anywhere else.

He walked through the central sliding glass door leading into the library's lobby. The main floor, jam-packed with book stacks, computers, and furtive groups of earnestly whispering students, was a buzzing cauldron of social activity. Some work was getting done, but it was in very gradual increments. Anyone who was anybody couldn't count on getting five minutes of study in without someone walking up and starting a conversation.

Planning to seek a hideaway on the less popular basement level, Brandon was distracted by a table near the front door. Seated there were Larry Whitaker, Mark Jackson, and Ashley Blasingame, huddled in deep and animated conversation. Ashley, her black suede CiZi jacket and vinyl pants drawing immediate attention, sported long, flowing locks of feathery hair that were professionally primped and styled. Her unblemished oval face, outlined with high cheekbones and colored with a sunny beige complexion, completed the picture. Even on a campus boasting the entire spectrum of black beauty, Ashley never failed to catch Brandon's eye. Seated next to her, his friend and housemate Larry looked like exactly the type to pull a woman of her beauty (which he had, shortly before the end of last school year). Tall and tan-complected, with a fine grade of "good" hair, Larry tired of being told he looked like Will Smith. "Fresh Prince ain't even in my league," was always his brusque reply.

"What's up, people?" Brandon rolled up on the group, even as he felt his study time slipping away.

"The future doc himself, what up, man?" said Mark, a five-foot-ten, solidly built wrestling champion with a high yellow complexion and a near-bald haircut. Larry and Ashley were feverishly consuming a copy of the *Highland Sentinel*, which was spread in front of them.

"Just tryin' to squeeze in a few minutes of study before a meeting," Brandon replied, noting the look of consternation on Larry's face. Something was obviously up.

Seemingly realizing he had left his boy hanging, Larry leaned back from the paper and acknowledged Brandon's presence. "Choirboy, what's up, man?" They exchanged the secret housemate handshake, slapping hands, following with a quick grip, sliding their fingers against each other's palm, and closing with a quick snap of the fingers. Nothing special, but it made for some good male bonding.

Now Ashley finally deemed Brandon worthy of recognition, issuing him a weak smile. "Hey, Brandon."

Larry rubbed his eyes and sighed. "Man, we're just sitting here trippin' off the latest Sheila Evans work of art."

Brandon hadn't seen a copy of the *Sentinel* this week. "Oh, Lord, what has she done now?"

His trademark cockiness oozing between the lines, Mark piped up with a quick summary. "Seems Ms. Sheila has fired her latest round of editorials designed to give the *Sentinel* endorsement to our opponent, the good 'Rev. Jackson.' She got some nerve, man, claimin' that our boy here is a member of the Young Republicans chapter, that he was on the administration's side of the big student protest last year. She's got him misquoted, misplaced, you name it, it's just ugly. But she'll get hers."

Brandon was intrigued but remembered his need to get a few minutes of study in before the Disciples meeting. He turned to Larry, adjusting his backpack. "I'll have to pick up a copy of the paper. I'll find out more about your response tonight. By the way, we need to rap about that Ellis Center meeting. You'll be home tonight, right?"

Casually, Larry leaned over to his left, resting his weight against Ashley's silk blouse. "Well, you know that depends on what Ms. B here has to say . . ."

Delivering a mock smack to the side of Larry's head, Ashley interrupted. "Brandon, if he's home tonight, I'm sure he'll let you know."

Brandon laughed good-heartedly and stepped toward the elevator. "Peace, people." Turning to take a last glimpse of the picture-perfect couple, Brandon sighed, trying to repress a gnawing sense of regret. He had no concept of what life at Highland was like with a fine lady by his side. He was starting to think he'd never know that pleasure, at Highland or anywhere else. It had been four years since he'd been with a woman, and even then he and Brandy had stopped just short of the line, in the name of preserving his virginity. In the end, where had standing by his principles gotten him?

When the elevator doors popped open, he stepped forward and tried to drown the thoughts cluttering his mind. Maybe the boys at Ellis and their mothers were right. Maybe all men were really dogs, and he, with no woman and no kids, was less than a man.

A punk.

2

SMOOTH OPERATOR

"You'd think the brother could have shown a little more interest," Mark said indignantly once Brandon was out of earshot. "Is he going to be helping you out with this campaign, bro?"

Leaning forward, Larry chuckled. "Brandon believes in the power of prayer over politics, Mark. I don't view him as a political tool; he's my friend. When I see him back at the house he'll wanna hear all the gory details. Like it's any of your business anyway? Who are you now, the thought police?"

A faked grimace crossing his face, Mark winked at Ashley. "Boy, don't you know I am your campaign manager? My one and only job is to see to it that you are elected to the presidency of the Highland Student Association—nothing less, nothing else. That job includes sizing up those around you. That's my only reason for prying. You sho' 'nuff sensitive today. Ashley, take this boy home and give him something to relieve that dam of stress he's built up."

Clearly amused but too proud to admit it, Ashley leaned back in her chair and saluted Mark with her middle finger. Hints of a stifled smile seeped around the corners of her perfect mouth.

Larry was glad he'd chosen not to live with any of the brothers in his closest circle of friends. Mark was the best friend he had at Highland, and as close to a kindred spirit as he had ever known, but he'd always known his ability to tolerate Mark's antics would not survive their sharing the same house. Besides which, Ashley had made it clear to him last summer that she wouldn't stand for his sharing a house or apartment with Mark. She knew all too well of Mark's reputation as a man-about-town, and she also knew how many girls he and Larry had in common.

"Larry, no man of mine has ever even thought about going back to an old girlfriend once they've been with me. So don't even think of living with Mark. You and I both know he'd have a constant parade of your ex-playthings going in and out, at all times of the night. I don't play that."

Larry had found Ashley's protective instincts somewhat amusing. He hadn't been involved with anywhere near the number of women Mark had. He had *very* high standards, at least where the physical realm was concerned. Any woman sharing Larry's bed, from his first encounter as a ninth-grader up to the present, had fit a carefully defined profile: feathery, shoulder-length hair; a well-developed, firm frame free of any noticeable body fat; and a beige or lighter face that made men lose their minds. Anyone who couldn't make a living as a professional model need not apply. With Ashley he'd outdone himself. His own father, the man who taught him the criteria by which to choose a woman, had gone green with envy the first time he met Ashley. Larry knew he had a good thing, so he'd let Ashley have her way regarding where he could live. The price was worth it to have a woman who made the perfect trophy.

"Shall we get to the business at hand?" Rolling up the sleeves of his denim Calvin Klein oxford and checking the time on his gold Wittnauer, Larry tried to put an official tone into the crackle of his fluid tenor. "I was ten damn points behind Winburn in the latest election poll, and now I've got an editor who's out to spill my political blood. Sheila knows I was a member of the Young Republicans in name only; hell, we all make sacrifices in the name of networking. She also knows I chose to refrain from the sit-in at the administration building because President Billings is a former business associate of my father's. Everyone knew I was with the protesters in spirit! Come on, I helped broker the final agreements between Kareem, Tasha, and Billings."

"Baby," Ashley interrupted him, "you know the truth makes no difference to that girl. She crafted this precisely so all the facts are true, even though the implication is obviously false."

"It's a classic case of the unfounded negative political attack," Mark groused. "Throw enough mud against the opponent, and pray something sticks. But this one's coming right back at her, Larry. Check this out!" Mark thrust a printed sheet of paper at his friend, hot off the press from his Compaq laptop. Larry was unable to stem the tide of a grateful smile as he read his friend's articulate, straightforward, and savvy prose. Mark's words stabbed back at each of Sheila's accusations, reasserting truth after truth, then offering his own conclusions.

"Oh no, you didn't!" Larry groaned at the section where Mark implied that Sheila was suffering a "sour grapes" complex following her own defeat in running for the presidency last year. After changing a few words for maximum impact and softening a couple that bordered on the obscene, Larry hurled the memo back at his manager with his signature of approval.

"Guys, I am so sorry I'm late." Janis Kelley, student president of the school of business and a tight ally of Mark and Larry's, snuck up on them and seated herself before they realized she was in their midst. "I've read the editorial, Larry, and I think you're best off not responding at all. Anyone who cares enough to read Sheila's article is just as likely to be at the debates. You know that's where the real election is decided, at least as far as public forums go. I don't see how her remarks deserve to be dignified with a response."

"Well, try that on for size," Larry said as Mark slid his letter in front of Janis. As she read it her face registered some of the same emotions Larry had experienced a few moments earlier. "I think Janis has a point," Larry said. "People know what's up, right? Maybe we go with this letter and just leave it there."

"I agree," Janis said. "Go with the letter, let Mark be the Bad Cop. It puts the truth out there forcefully, but anyone offended by it will be able to separate Mark's personality in it from yours. What ever did you *do* to Sheila Evans in the first place, babe?" She

smiled playfully at Larry, her pert little pug nose shining innocently.

Smacking his lips in defiance, Larry threw his hands in the air.
"You got me, J. She's had it in for me as long as I can remember."

"I can hazard a guess," Ashley said, her green eyes dancing
with mischief. "Penis envy. She knows she'll never get yours or
anyone else's!"

After enjoying a good belly laugh, the team reviewed Larry's
current platform and debate strategy. There were two other serious contenders in the race, only one of whom Larry was particu-
larly concerned with.

The noncontender, Winston Hughes, was an ambitious junior
political science major. He was known for his staggering intellect,
outmatched only by his complete lack of personality. In public forums such as the upcoming campaign debate, the boy radiated the
warmth of a block of ice. Coupled with his inability to match his
ties to the Sears suits he always wore, Winston's lack of charisma
spelled certain death in Highland's image-conscious political
arena.

The opponent who kept Larry awake at night, the one he
knew Sheila Evans was laboring to put into office, was David Winburn. Winburn was affectionately known campuswide as Rev.
Jackson, due to his obvious desire to be Generation X's Jesse. He
stood six feet tall, almost even with Larry, and cloaked his lanky
frame in professionally tailored suits and loud ties. He had a large
rectangular head, a deep maple complexion, wide eyes, sparkling
white teeth, and a well-groomed mustache processed with the
same S-curl juice he used on his hair. Winburn's image had graced
so many campaign posters for the past four years, he was almost
a household name around campus. Larry knew that face even better than most, because it haunted him every time his head hit a
pillow.

He and Winburn had entered Highland with the same class,
lived in the same dormitory, even traveled in the same social circles. Larry had won the presidency of the school of business at the
end of freshman year, while David stormed into the same office in

the liberal arts college. From there Larry served in the HSA cabinet while David served as student representative to the university's board of trustees. Everyone who'd known them had expected this year's Battle of Titans over the HSA office. Larry, for his part, had absolutely no intention of losing. His father's urgent motto raced across his mind as he wiped David's face from his mind: Whitakers Don't Lose.

In exactly the way he knew Winburn was doing with his own campaign team, Larry and his friends always reserved a healthy chunk of time to dissect their key opponent's major assets and liabilities. In the arena of policy, they had decided to focus on Winburn's cozy relationship with the university administration, and the role that allegedly played in several decisions he made as undergraduate trustee. Mark was the lead soldier on Operation Pull the Covers Off.

Full of bravado, Mark briefed them on his latest mission. Last night he'd wooed Shannon Moon, a former girlfriend of David's, sweet-talking her as she'd crossed campus and getting her to agree to an impromptu date. The night had ended at El Cerrito's in Georgetown, where Mark had filled the girl with quesadillas, margaritas, tequila, and more margaritas. By the time her tongue was completely loosened, she'd given him an earful of allegations about David's stewardship as university trustee: an agreement to "go along and get along" on the most crucial issues of interest to students, in return for a few amenities, such as the snazzy new Accord he'd started sporting that year. Supposedly Shannon had access to memos and other documents to back it all up.

If he felt a prick of conscience at the manipulation of an innocent sister, Larry waved it aside in the name of political ambition and let Mark continue. Sometimes he wondered if the price of following in his father's footsteps as HSA president would be worth it. He banished the thought: of course it would. It hadn't served Larry senior too poorly, had it? His father had gone from running a student body to spearheading a multimillion-dollar business enterprise. For Larry, the HSA presidency was just the next rung toward the top.

It occurred to Larry that the revelations about David's political deals were far from surprising. Winburn's alleged actions were far from heinous; in fact they sounded like the bargaining of a natural politician, if that was a good thing. But Larry knew this would mean jack to the average Joe Student, who would find Winburn's abdication on important policy issues entirely inexcusable. This was a good thing; at this point Larry would take every edge he could get. Twenty minutes later he clapped his hands loudly. "My brother and my sisters, thanks for another productive war room session. Let's get outta here!"

Mark eyed Ashley and Janis as they began gathering their things. "Word, word. Larry, can I, uh, talk to you privately for a minute, bro?"

"What you need, man?"

Mark heaved himself back from the table. "What say we rap outside by your car? The ladies can meet us out there in a minute."

In a few seconds the men had gathered their briefcases and windbreakers and were on the brick walkway outside the front lobby. Larry walked to the curb and set his leather satchel near the front of his Lexus. "What's up, man? What crazy woman you messing with now? I gotta bail you out again?"

Mark cut his eyes at his best friend. "Nothing like that. Look, I gotta be real with you, Larry. I don't know if this thing about David's misdeeds will be enough to save your ass."

"Why not?"

"Five letters, Larry. E-l-l-i-s. You got to get off your soapbox, money."

Larry wriggled his neck and squinted. "Wha? What are you talkin' about, Mark?"

"Larry, come on. This thing about adding a campaign promise requiring all Highland students to perform community service at Ellis or one of its affiliate centers, if you're elected president? You really think folks want their time infringed on like that?"

Larry leaned gently against the gold gloss of his ride and crossed his arms. "Mark, I believe we all gain when we give something back. Plus, the more I can circulate Ellis's name and get people interested, the better. You know why I treasure institutions like Ellis, man."

"Yeah, yeah, yeah, I know. Aunt Rae."

"Damn right, Aunt Rae." Larry smiled at the sound of his late great-aunt's name. It had been Aunt Rae, his grandmother's sister and a popular baker in north Chicago, who had taken him and his younger sister, Vera, to the Rosewood Community Center every summer when they would visit for several weeks. Larry's grand-parents, Chaney and Lola Whitaker—a family physician and an interior designer who still lived in Hyde Park, folk of old money who behaved like it—had taken them in each summer but always made sure they saw some "real life" through Aunt Rae's eyes.

Larry would never forget the sense of belonging the Rose-wood staff instilled in the kids there, many of whom hailed from single-parent homes and had seen nothing but the armpit of life. Every summer he'd gained from Rosewood, learning the latest fads (which he'd quickly taken back home to the Cincinnati sub-urbs and coopted in order to solidify his "cool" credentials), but it was the spirit of the kids, and the way the center fostered that re-silience that stuck with him. As long as those images were fresh in his mind, Larry couldn't let Ellis Center fold. There was too much good to do.

He patted Mark on the back and yelled over the roar of a pass-ing truck. "Mark, playtime is over where Ellis is concerned. They need a hundred and twenty-five thousand bucks to meet their next loan payment, by September first. The bank's already given them several extensions, but these guys are not saints. Ellis has to deliver this time, or the doors could be closed."

Mark choked back a phony sob and put a hand to his chest. "Larry, just remember I play to win. All this time you're spending trying to save Ellis—the schmoozing with local CEOs, holding fund-raising banquets, it's all very cute, but it ain't gonna win no votes. Highland students want you to deliver in three areas: finan-cial aid, housing, and security. They don't need you to tell them that in addition to working their way through school, staying in broke-down dorms, and studying their asses off, they gotta log eight hours a month minding somebody else's bad kids."

Larry sighed in relief when Ashley and Janis rolled up, interrupting Mark's rant. He smiled lazily in Mark's direction and decided to fight this battle later. "Player, I appreciate the sentiment. Now good night."

He slapped hands with Mark and placed an arm around Ashley. He would worry about his poll standings in the morning. It had been a long day; right now he needed to let his spirits be lifted by the revelations about Winburn. No matter how temporary it might be, he was going to enjoy the feeling. He would chill at Ashley's downtown apartment, watch the Wizards game against L.A., then blow off steam in exactly the way Mark had suggested earlier.

A good woman was the best form of stress release going.

3

SINISTER MINISTER

Ten blocks west of Highland's campus, the Light of Tabernacle Missionary Baptist Church family was kicking its Wednesday-evening service into high gear. The congregation was proud of its new home, a month-old stone-and-glass structure on a five-acre lot. Just a year ago the ground beneath them had been awash in beer bottles, syringes, and cigarette butts. The church's new sanctuary and Christian-education center now employed four additional people, all of them local residents who had previously been homeless or on public assistance. This self-proclaimed "small-town church in a big city" was slowly but surely moving into the big leagues.

At the front of the crowded sanctuary, a platform stage rose ominously from the sunken floor, towering over the congregation. In the center of the pulpit sat five high-backed chairs draped in cushy red velvet. In front of the center chair, in which Pastor Otis Grier reclined, stood a solid marble column from which arose a glass lectern and a bank of silver-tipped microphones. Whenever Grier or one of the associate ministers climbed the short stone steps that led up to the lectern, they were immediately reminded of the awesome nature of their calling.

The Reverend Oscar Jarvis Peters, Jr., lovingly known as O.J. to most, sat to Grier's right. Winking at his pastor, O.J. matched Grier's pace and bopped his head to the rhythm of the youth choir's raucous performance. Seated on an incline of six rows with ten chairs each, the young people were driving the church mad with their rendition of Kirk Franklin's "Melodies from Heaven." Although O.J. still marveled at how little Kirk had somehow managed to do the unthinkable—his music enthralled everyone from the jeep-hoppers out in the street to the old folk in God's house—he was growing a little tired of this particular tune. He swore that every church he'd visited in these last few months had sung that dang song at some point in the service.

Carl Shockley, the director of the choir, was a reedy young man of average height, a member of the Highland University Gospel Choir and a classmate of O.J.'s in the liberal arts college. Despite persistent rumors about Shockley's personal life, O.J. admired the vigor with which the young man pushed and prodded his choir. Large beads of sweat cascaded down Shockley's beaming face, several of them coming to rest just above his thin, crusty lips.

"You betta sang that one mo' time!" he exclaimed.

The choir let loose with its final line:

"MELODIES FROM HEAVEN! (Pause) RAIN DOWN ON ME! RAIN DOWN ON ME!"

Now Carl ushered in the close. "MELOOOOODIEEEES!" he piped, spurring the choir to respond.

"MELODIES FROM HEAVEN! (Pause) RAIN DOWN ON ME! RAIN DOWN ON ME!" As Carl shushed the choir into silence, congregants of every age and gender burst from their seats. O.J. knew they were praising God for another day and for the talent of their teenage choir.

O.J. smiled as the time for the evening's sermon arrived. Pastor Grier, a tall, bald-headed man whose beige complexion was muddled by a faceful of razor and acne scars, rose to address his congregation. As the overhead lights bounced unfavorably off Grier's blemishes, O.J. thanked the Lord for his own baby-smooth, cocoa-brown skin. Combine that with his heavily waxed head of waves, courtesy of Dax, and O.J. knew he was pretty. Grier was his mentor and a great role model, but the man was no sight for sore eyes.

Grier eyed the crowd enthusiastically. "Did I hear somebody

say they wanna praise him?" A buzz of "Yessirs" swept across the sanctuary.

"Er, uh, wait a minute," Grier said, smacking his lips and rolling his tongue around in the back of his mouth. "I don't think you heard me, chu'ch. I said, you ought to get up and praise your Lord right now!" As a wave of applause and hallelujahs began to fill the air, Grier pressed on. "You just heard a choir full of your own chil'ren stand up and praise the Lord our God, asking to be filled with his spirit! Not, mind you, selling drugs—"

A deep, rippling note of emphasis went up from the church organ.

Grier continued. "Singing about 'freakin' "—again the organ hummed—"stealin' from the corner store, or from the local bank, fo' that matta—"

The third ring of the organ brought the audience to its feet, once again filling the sanctuary with shouts of joy. "You oughtta be praisin' him for these young folk, for your jobs, for this new sanctuary, for all the things he brought you through!" Grier ceased his oratory long enough to take in the adoring, pumped-up crowd. Clearly satisfied that he had lathered up the people for his pupil, he set into his introduction.

"Bringing you the Word tonight will be one of my *prized* associates!" Hearty laughs greeted Grier's playful tone of voice. "No, no, y'all know I don't play favorites among my ministers, but, when it's their turn to preach, I believe in turning the spotlight up! This young man has been a real find for the ministry of this church, a preacher's son himself, a man of the people about to receive an English degree from *the* Highland University, and, soon enough, to be admitted to Dallas Theological Seminary for his master of divinity!" A rush of *Mmm*'s, *Well all right*'s, and *You go, boy*'s met Grier's proclamation. O.J. wished again that Grier would stop announcing his interest in seminary like it was a secure fact. He had yet to be admitted to one seminary. "Give the Lord a hand of praise and encourage our brother, O. J. Peters!"

Shaking Grier's hand as he rose from his seat and ascended the inspiring steps, O.J. smoothed his satiny black robe and

stepped to the lectern. As he sucked in the smell of burning can-
dles and Afro Sheen that permeated the sanctuary, O.J. knew he
was home. The black church was the office from which he would
build a lifelong career, one that would someday bring him his own
Mercedes and BMW, a beautiful wife, and a fancy house outside
Atlanta, probably in good ol' Buckhead. For a moment he let himself bask in the silent adoration of the congregation. As always,
the moment of peace filled him with memories of his late mother.
Momma, you'd be proud of your baby.

As the audience waited reverently on his first word, O.J.
gripped the podium, ready to start the show. He'd stayed up too
late with his "Freak of the Week" the last couple of nights to craft
a new sermon for this service, but he'd been inspired this afternoon. On the fly, he'd worked up a revised version of his message
from Mt. Vernon Baptist's revival last month. Far as he could recall, no one from Light had been in attendance that night; a few
new sprinkles, and this would come off as a completely different
message. The Lord was good.

"Praise the Lord, saints!" Almost five years into his preaching
career, O.J. was free of the nervous mannerisms and tentative
openings of most preachers his age. To keep his concluding remarks from sounding stilted, he decided to open in the singsong
cadence he loved to close with.

"Well, uh, church, giving honor to the Lord God and our Savior Jesus Christ, I just wanna let you know that I stopped by
tonight with a word! A word from who, ya say?" O.J. paused long
enough to ride the wave of adoring encouragement the congregation lavished on him. They were eager for his next words, just the
effect he lived for. "The Lord talked to me last night and told me,
he said, O.J., someone at Light is hurting! Someone just had some
disturbing news brought their way! Maybe a loved one is ill.
Maybe a wayward child got their rusty butt locked up in jail.
Maybe it was something as simple, God forbid, as hearing a fellow
member is bad-talkin' you behind your back! But that would *never*
happen here." O.J. grinned mischievously as a ripple of laughter
washed through the sanctuary.

"But seriously, my brothers and my sisters, you may right now be in the midst of a trial, something that makes you feel like you're dying a slow death. Well, the Lord told me to stop by and deliver you the following message: he can give you life after death, no matter how difficult the experience or the trial may be. He specializes in life, and he's an expert at overcoming death. Please join me in turning your Bibles to the following Scripture . . ." Like a veteran clergyman, O.J. eloquently read and then began to interpret his 1 Kings passage. With a seamlessly smooth delivery, he broke the essence of the words into easily understandable morsels, making the audience feel the Holy Book had been written especially for them.

Twenty minutes later he was lubricating the congregation to the breaking point, evidenced by the swooning and swaying of women, young and old, as he huffed and puffed toward the climax of his message. In his wildest dreams as a pudgy preteen, he'd never imagined he could have this effect on women, godly or otherwise. Even as he leaned hard into the microphone and raised his right hand heavenward, he couldn't stop the thought that crept through his mind. *Some of these same women wouldn't have given my chunky behind the time of day a few years ago. But I'm showing 'em, that's for sure. No woman says no to O. J. Peters anymore.*

He pressed forward, knowing the climax was near. "God has an answer for your trouble! He showed how well he overcomes death when he let Jesus lie in that grave Friday and Saturday before raisin' him up on Sunday, oh, that marvelous Sunday! Jesus died that horrible death so that we can live today, regardless of the trials! In him, we can overcome anything!" Swept away with enthusiasm, O.J. grabbed the microphone from the lectern and began to croon a baritone version of "His Eye Is on the Sparrow," slaying the few remaining members who had kept their composure.

Minutes later, thunderous applause filled the sanctuary. O.J. descended the steps back to the main platform, pumped his fist heavenward, and collapsed into his plush chair. The high he got from delivering the Word was second only to the rush of romantic passion. Maybe he'd never be anything more than a C student, and he'd certainly never be respected for his athletic abilities, but one thing he knew: no one could touch him when it came time to perform.

After the service, O.J. stood in line with Pastor Grier and the other associates, receiving the gratitude and prayer requests of members as they made their way past the clergy. He stood between Grier and the Reverend David Archibald, Grier's official right-hand man. Archibald didn't seem to care much for him, but O.J. was in the dark as to why. He had no ambitions of ever taking over the reins at Light of Tabernacle; he knew his father's home church in Atlanta would be ready and waiting for him when he got out of seminary. Pastor Peters, Sr., had already seen to that. Maybe he needed to assure Archibald of this. He was tired of the judgmental glances and frowns the little man would shoot his way when he thought O.J. wasn't looking.

"Rev. Peters, thank you for the inspiring message. God sho' is blessing you, boy," said Sister Myrna Phillips, one of the most senior members of the body. Though her back was bent at a forty-degree angle, the radiant inner beauty and peace that shone on her cardboard-colored complexion was always what struck O.J. most powerfully. Life had not dealt this woman a fair hand in his book—widowed, abandoned by her second husband, and preceded in death by her only daughter, this saint continued keeping on. It was people such as this who reminded O.J. there were real lives that needed the encouragement he and his colleagues provided. Pastoring wasn't entirely a game.

"Sister Phillips, thank you so much." O.J. leaned down and wrapped his arms around her. "How are you feelin' this week? You're lookin' just as lovely as always!"

"Thank you, baby, the Lord's been good," Mrs. Phillips responded. "Keep me in your prayers."

O.J. flashed a wink at the elderly matron. "Only if you promise you'll do the same for me. God bless!"

"Reverend, you headed for the seminary, huh?" Anticipating Grady Wells' infamous viselike grip, O.J. tried not to wince as he took the man's hand. A mailman with more than ten years of faithful service under his belt, Wells was not quite thirty years old and could have passed for O.J.'s age. Despite a salary that was far from staggering, Wells appeared to be a confident leader and provider for his wife and their four children, ages one to nine. "So when you become the reverend doctor, try not to forget us peons at the little church, okay?"

Jovially slapping the bigger man's back, O.J. laughed his comment off. "Hey, Grady, you know and I know a minister ain't nothin' but a servant. We all got our own ministry, you know. I'll never forget where I came from 'cause I'm always gonna *be* where I come from—God's church!"

"I heard that," Wells exclaimed. "Seriously, bro, we're all proud of you. Now I hear you even working to help save the Ellis Center!"

O.J. beamed. "I'm just doing my part. Someone's got to keep that place open. The harvest is plenty, but the laborers are few, my brother!"

Wells clamped a taut hand onto O.J.'s shoulder. "Well, you keep servin' in God's name, O.J. We need more role models like you. Whenever my oldest boy, David, fights me about staying up to do his homework and make the grades I demand, I point to you. I tell him, 'You hear how Rev. Peters talk so good and powerful, even though he even younger than your daddy? That's 'cause he is educated, about to graduate with a college degree, and then earn one from a seminary!' Keep up the good work, young blood, little ones are looking up to you."

Flattered, O.J. whispered his thanks and turned to his right as Wells began his customary banter with Pastor Grier. The sight of the next person in line made him want to crawl under the communion table. Keesa Bishop, a short honey dip with an attractive and healthy figure, was dressed in a stonewashed denim jacket, matching knee-length skirt, and a mock turtleneck. The short brown locks of her fresh perm complemented her perky but plain facial features.

O.J. was not in the mood to appreciate the new do. For the last five days since he had kicked her out of his bed, Keesa had taken to harassing him. Although he'd made it clear that their relationship was over last Friday, she had left a total of six messages on his voice mail since then, insisting he return her calls. She had not shown up at service on Sunday, much to his relief, but now, suddenly, here she was in front of him.

"Good word, Rev," she said, shooting him a crooked smile that was obviously painted on solely for the pastor's benefit. The glare of the four gold earrings in each of Keesa's ears threatened to knock O.J. off his feet.

"Thank you, sister, thank you," he replied, shaking her hand for appearances' sake and turning his attention to Odessa Carp, who stood behind his former lover. O.J. could feel his right hand shaking. He'd never been confronted in church by a woman he'd wronged. Most of the time they had enough sense to respect his need to keep business and pleasure separate. He knew Pastor Grier would never tolerate a minister who had women chasing him down in front of the congregation. He prayed Keesa would keep stepping and keep her mouth shut.

"Oh, O.J.," Keesa said as she took Grier's hand, "we *will* talk before you leave tonight. I'll be waiting by the door. I hope you don't think you can ignore me forever, boy." Whether she was aware of it or not, the twist of her neck, in plain view of Pastor Grier himself, was unmistakable. O.J. felt a small bead of sweat form on his forehead. *Has this girl lost her mind?*

Pausing midshake, Pastor Grier looked from Keesa to O.J. with a playfully amused expression. "I'm stayin' out of that one!"

Cracking a phony smile at Grier's quip, O.J. turned and grabbed Odessa's hand as if it were a life preserver. "How's my favorite girl?" he oozed to the little biblical scholar.

The eleven-year-old's eyes met O.J.'s, reverence brimming in her voice. "I enjoyed your message, Reverend. What was the text again? I want to take it home and share it with my mommy and her boyfriend."

Amazed again at the little girl's maturity, O.J. relaxed and plunged into an exposition of the scriptural texts from his message. He would do whatever it took to wait Keesa out; he'd deal with her on his own terms and no one else's. It was time for Keesa to recognize he had a reputation and a future ministry to protect.

Keesa had been a pleasant diversion once, but she was *not* going to ruin his career.

4

BOOTSTRAPPER

Terence Davidson was having a bad dream. It was Pledge Night in early September, and he was a freshman again. He and four of the other thirty-three pledges of the Gentlemen of Quality Social Club were several blocks from campus, braving the harrowing labyrinth of streets surrounding Highland. Their heads shaved skin-tight, their bodies clothed in faded blue jeans and white Fruit of the Loom T-shirts, Terence's group of "little bros" raced through one block after another in a state of panic.

Tonight was the big scavenger hunt, and Terence's group had been scampering through Highland's hood—the Highland Grille up the block, the General Highland statue near Alabama Avenue, even the banks of the reservoir near Children's Hospital—all in search of items chosen by the "big brothers" of GQ. They'd located as many as they could find before realizing they were running late for the check-in at Johnson Hall. The last team to arrive could forget the prize of GQ membership and all they believed it would bring: access to campus leaders, in-crowds, and of course, women.

As they hurtled toward Johnson, an off-campus dorm deep in the heart of Briar Hollow, the project-packed community bordering Highland, Terence and his bros shouted at one another with growing impatience and unease. Already Terence's mind was full of the nightmares he knew the others shared: endless push-ups as punishment for their tardiness, blistering verbal abuse, and finally, humiliation in front of Johnson's finest coeds.

By the time they rounded the corner of Twelfth and T, two blocks away, Terence felt his wind growing short but refused to show it. He smiled wearily as Kelvin James sped past him. "They gonna make us look like punks," Kelvin sputtered, his feet flying. "It ain't about getting there late, y'all!"

"We almost there now," Terence gasped. "Move your legs and shut your mouth, man." The sudden backfire of a car down the block silenced him. He shrugged it off and tried to forget how stupid it was for five Highland students to be on this street, at this hour. Johnson's neighborhood of decaying row houses and miniature projects was the worst of any off-campus Highland dorm. An after-dark sojourn through here was a legendary unwise move: the only folk traversing this terrain at night were ill-informed freshmen or overconfident upperclassmen.

As they crossed another block, diving into the heart of Briar Hollow, Terence felt his chest pump with a new anxiety; fear was seeping in. Imagine, him: a brother who'd spent his formative years in the nearby Shaw community, in his granny's rented two-bedroom row house. He had plenty of experience in these hoods. As the grunts and groans of his bros closed in on him, though, Terence knew what was different this time. He wasn't surrounded by the most reliable aides: far as he knew, all of these other dudes were from one-light small towns or cushy suburbs. Even his boy Brandon Bailey, whom he'd made fast friends with a couple weeks back, was turning white with fear. These brothers couldn't handle themselves in Briar Hollow. What were they doing?

"Oh, freak!" Brandon paused under a dingy street lamp, checking his watch, and the others stopped too. "We're late. It's two after ten!"

Panicked, Kelvin desperately pointed a high-yellow finger to his right. "Look, if we cross over and cut through there, we'll save two blocks and come out right at Johnson!"

Terence followed his friend's gesture and winced at the small elementary school halfway down the block. To its right sat a large, weed-filled yard that stretched over to Johnson Hall's block. Terence knew it would save time, but he also noticed the series of idling cars lining the block in front of the school. Standing beside the autos—cracking jokes, smoking blunts, and imbibing forty-ounce Red Bulls—were a group of neighborhood residents. For a moment Terence felt more at home than he had so far in his first few weeks at Highland. Here were some down-to-earth, unpretentious folk, just bein' themselves, damn what the rest of society thought. They were almost his homies, after all. He canceled that thought when he noticed their suspicious glares. Who was he kidding? To these folk, he wasn't Terence from around the way; he was just another faceless, uppity Highland student.

He played with the idea of protest before letting his pride take over. "A-all right, let's do it, fellas! Follow me!" He put his chin down and charged toward the school-yard entrance, dodging the sidewalk straddlers.

"Damn, ya could say s'cuse me, spoiled brats," came a predictable reprimand from a whiskered man with beer sopping his patchy beard.

Near the yard entrance, a spike-haired sister squatted on a cement staircase. She eyed Terence and yelled at the top of her lungs, to no one in particular. "Who these muthafuckas?!"

The heavy smell of marijuana stung Terence's nose and eyes. It was no more pleasant to him today than it had been when his younger brother, Biggie, started using it. Expelling the rank air from his lungs, Terence sensed a growing restlessness in the crowd. As Brandon and Kelvin pushed ahead through the opening of the ten-foot chain link fence surrounding the yard, the night lights overhead glanced off their shiny noggins.

"Who you little shits think you is, comin' on our territory!" A teenage boy dressed in a loud Nike sweat suit sneered and began to run alongside Terence, hatred filling his eyes. Terence pumped his muscled legs, which had propelled him to glory on nearby basketball courts, and decided to play deaf. A few more yards, and they'd be out of harm's way. No need to provoke the silly-ass brother by answering his trash talk.

"Hold up, nigga, I got somethin' for 'em!" The threatening voice, which came from behind Terence, was loaded with malice.

Terence's eyes grew wide with shock. "Brandon, get down!"

His warning was too late. Brandon's pace was cut short as a forty-ounce projectile glanced against his bald head. He had been leading the pack, but the sensation of blood oozing from his right temple stole his fire, leaving him wobbling in place and clutching at the mushy wound. The other bros, clearly out of sorts, continued past their fallen comrade, ducking and weaving to save their own lives. From behind, Terence heard the cock of a gun barrel. "Go on, y'all," he yelled, wondering if they even heard him. "I got him!"

He sped over to Brandon, who had dropped to the ground, and grabbed his arm, barely slowing his stride. "You want your momma to get a call in the middle of the night? Get the hell up!" Before he had even finished the sentence, Brandon was at his side and matching Terence's pace with ease. Neither one dared look back. They were almost through the yard when a shrill ring pierced Terence's eardrums.

With a start, he awoke from his afternoon nap. He reminded himself: that's in the past now. Though he'd survived his share of moments more harrowing than that night, those events recurred in his dreams every so often. He didn't view the dreams as nightmares so much as reminders of the trials he and his boys had survived to make it this far. They were going to beat the odds, and a dream like this one drove that truth home. As Terence rubbed sleep from his eyes, he heeded the shrill purr of the cordless Motorola on his chest. He pressed the flash button, feeling morning breath caking his gums. "Um, yeah."

"Terence Marshall Davidson, is that you answering the phone, like some ill-mannered slob?" There was no mistaking the crunchy voice of his granny, the woman who had almost single-handedly raised him.

"Oh, uh, hey, Granny, this is me. I'm sorry if I sound ignorant, I just woke up. An unplanned nap." Without opening the blinds or flicking on his desk lamp, Terence clumsily stood up, stepping into the nearest pair of size-thirteen Grant Hill Filas.

"Now look, boy, you know I raised you better than that. What did I teach you, Terence? A man should always behave as if he's at least one step higher up the ladder than he really is. When you do that, you'll never stop advancing."

"And I believe you, Granny. Come on, this is your prized grandbaby here!"

"Don't I know it. Look, baby, I had to sneak away from the social hour so I could make this call, so I have to be quick. I just wanted you to know I'm workin' on a way to get you some tuition money. I know those financial aid people been getting rude with you, and Granny's not gon' sit by and see her baby mistreated."

His hands on his hips, Terence stopped dead in his tracks. "Granny, how many times I gotta tell you, your money's no good where I'm concerned? You got to trust me when I tell you my job is paying me plenty. I can handle my bills. 'Sides, you get to movin' your savings around, and the Manor might try to put you out for lack of assets. Granted, you could always move in with me, but I don't think you really wanna do that—"

"Oh, baby, stop that nonsense. Granny would never burden you with putting her up, at least not till you make your first million and get you a little mansion! But I am gonna get you some money now—"

Not that it mattered, but Terence was shaking his head insistently. "Granny, anything you send me, I'm sendin' back."

"I'm calling your bluff. Terence, my concern for you didn't end the day I got sick, or the day you started college. So you look for the money. Anything that lightens your burden is worth my trouble. But I got something else I need to tell you."

Suddenly realizing that he was supposed to be up on campus right now and that he'd overslept, Terence gently prompted. "Uh, Granny, what is it?"

"Well, I was reading this article in *Essence* yesterday. Actually, it wasn't a full article, but one of those inspirational passages by the girl who used to run the magazine, you know the one. Real pretty girl, I think her name is Susan something. Anyway, baby, it was titled 'Embracing Commitment.' I'm mailing you a copy today. I think you need to show it to that Lisa of yours."

Rolling his eyes as he could only do over the phone, Terence gingerly opened the blinds over his desk. "Okay, Granny." The problem was, Lisa was not his right now, but there was no point arguing that fact with Granny. She had pegged Lisa as a heart-breaker from Day One, not that her prediction had helped free him from Lisa's spell. "I'll be looking for it in the mail. I need to go, Okay?"

"I'll let you go, baby, but don't forget your granny's words. You are so special, son, pulling yourself up by your own boot-straps like you have. That's what's so important about that work you're doing at the community center. You having any luck get-ting those bean-pie boys to support the center?"

"Granny, they're the Nation of Islam. Ellis needs their support as much as the church's. The Nation be takin' care of business. Don't sell them short."

"Whatever, child. My point was, you got to pull some more folks up with you. When I think of how many boys who grew up on our block are dead or in prison, it breaks my heart. You're doing so much better, Terence, but you still have some learning to do. Read that *Essence* article. One day you'll appreciate my overflowing wisdom! Love you, baby."

Setting the phone down and clicking on his desk lamp, Ter-ence checked his watch. He'd gotten off work early from Tech-notronics today, decided to treat himself to a rare nap before going up to campus to attend the Disciples of Christ meeting with Brandon. From there he would be attending a business dinner with his mentor from work, Jerry Wallace. He remembered, through the groggy haze clouding his thoughts, that the Disciples meetings started at seven; his plastic neon clock told him it was 7:58. And he had told Jerry to pick him up at Highland's front gate at 9:00 sharp. Brandon would never let him hear the end of it, but there was no point trying to make the meeting now. He had to get dressed and make it up to campus in time to meet Jerry. He picked up the phone and punched in a number. On the third ring, the owner of the cell phone picked up.

"This is Larry."

"Larry, what's up, Big Dog?" Terence sank back into the tempting cushions of his squeaky twin bed.

"Is this Terence?" Larry's voice was jovially indignant. "Boy, I told you not to make me waste my valuable cell-phone batteries taking calls from my housemates. You can talk to a brotha anytime."

Terence came fully awake as he traded quips with his friend. "Yo, I need you to stop over at the Student Center and tell Brandon why I missed that Disciples meeting." This was the third time he'd wigged out on Brandon's invitation, despite the fact that Brandon had attended a recent Nation of Islam meeting with him. Terence wasn't a member in good standing, but he still believed the Nation did more before 9:00 A.M. to help the community than the average Baptist church on the corner.

Larry chuckled. "Bro, you know I got no place up in the midst of the People of God. Make up an excuse and tell Brandon yourself."

Terence hee-hawed conspiratorially. Larry had to be the most slang-using Buppie he'd ever known. "Come on, Dog. They have a break at eight. Just stop over and let him know, so he doesn't spend the next couple of hours cursin' me."

"I got you covered, T. I'm in the midst of a big strategy session now. I'll check you out later, awright?"

Terence clicked the flash button on his phone and stretched out his long right arm, resting the phone on the rickety wooden table a few feet from his bed. Activating his *Marvin Gaye's Greatest Hits* CD on his Emerson boom box, he decided playtime was over. Because he was putting himself through school by working a lucrative internship at Technotronics, Terence could only attend classes Tuesdays and Thursdays, meaning those days were packed full of electrical-engineering classes. This very night he was going to have to write a paper and review for two exams. But that would have to wait until he returned from tonight's dinner.

Dragging his six-foot-two frame through his doorway and taking the few steps required to reach the bathroom, he bent over the miniature porcelain sink and turned on the sputtering spigot.

He splashed cold water onto his Pepsi-colored face and the shiny pate of his clean-shaven head. The sounds of Marvin's "Trouble Man" percolated throughout the hallway, helping to clear the fuzzy clouds blocking Terence's thoughts. The weight of what he had to accomplish in the coming weeks hit home. In addition to completing his latest project at Technotronics and passing his course load for the semester, Ms. Simmons, Highland's financial aid director, would require his attention.

He had lied to Granny about his financial status; he was one step away from financial ineligibility. He shuddered involuntarily as he hung his red washcloth on the towel rack next to the sink. To think that witch Simmons held his future in her miserly hands made him crazy. He had to stop thinking about it. Granny was always reminding him that his father, Tony, who'd died in prison, had had chronic high blood pressure. Terence had no desire to worry himself into an early grave. He had won Ms. Simmons over so far, and he would have to keep employing the Davidson charm until he could earn the rest of his tuition money at Technotronics. But he knew time was running out. If he didn't get his back tuition paid off by the end of the year, Ms. Simmons had made it clear he could forget registering next fall. He stared blankly into the mirror and admitted to himself what he was going to have to do.

An hour later Jerry Wallace pulled up to the red brick front gate of Highland's campus. Terence was waiting faithfully, dressed snappily in his only full suit, a J. Riggings pinstripe he had purchased over Larry's bougie objections. He tugged at the tight collar of his Van Heusen white oxford and wiped the last few beads of sweat from his forehead. He had made the eight-block walk from LeDroit Park in five minutes despite being dressed like he was going to church, but it had come at a price. He hoped he didn't look too rumpled.

Rolling down the driver's side window of his burgundy Lincoln Navigator, a high-end jeep that drew immediate attention from the other students lining the front gate, Jerry winked at Terence. Even from several feet away, Terence's nostrils tingled at the new-car smell emanating from the Navigator. Leaning out the window, Jerry yelled over the roar of house music flooding the street. "Hey, Terence, my man, hop in. We've gotta beat Burton there if we wanna keep our reps up!" A millionaire vice president of Technotronics, an upstart software engineering firm and a current darling of Wall Street, Jerry was as self-assured as could be expected, even in a neighborhood most thirty-two-year-old white men would find intimidating.

As Terence peeled off a warm smile and climbed into the passenger's seat, he and Jerry made small talk. Terence wasn't sure if it was simply Jerry's personality or the security he had of being wealthy enough to retire, but Jerry had seemingly taken a genuine interest in Terence's career from the first day of his internship three years ago. Assigned to be Terence's mentor, Jerry regularly treated him to fancy lunches and even social gatherings at his lavish home in Alexandria, where he would clue Terence in to the politics of Technotronics and suggest new technologies he should include in his studies. Jerry was the first white man Terence had known who acted in a way that took his mind off skin color. Terence still didn't grant the man complete trust, of course. Truth was, Jerry looked a hell of a lot like one of those sneering, snotty white boys at his private grade school, the ones who had rained racial epithets on him until he had flexed a few muscles and sent them scurrying into their dark corners like sprayed roaches. He wasn't going to forget that stuff overnight.

White man or not, though, Terence figured he was too desperate to be proud. It was time to seek Jerry's help with his financial problems. Boldly, he laid out his situation for Jerry and asked if the company might provide an advance on his future salary, so he could pay down his Highland bills.

"Terence, I would love to help ya out," Jerry replied. "But we're only allowed ta offer advances to full-time employees, and ta be honest, it's rarely done even for them." A native of Boston, Jerry had a salty blue-collar accent belying his current status in life. "How much do you owe?"

Terence felt his eyes slide to the floor of the luxury jeep. "I owe back tuition of three thousand dollars, and I have to come up with another four thousand to pay for this spring semester."

"Lordy!" came Jerry's anxious reply. "Terence, what type of

advance would you be looking for? An advance on your first year of full-time employment?"

Terence bit his lip in frustration as Jerry whisked his SUV around Dupont Circle. The glaring lights of the CVS pharmacy and the hip eateries surrounding the circle aggravated his percolating headache. He was not in a mood to appreciate the meaty Scot's attempt at humor. "I just know I need to get a major down payment on the balance before the director of financial aid cancels me." He cursed himself for using such obvious slang in front of Jerry. *Good job, Terence; just encourage the man's stereotypes, why don't ya.*

Showing his concern, Jerry asked how Terence had managed to make it so far with unpaid tuition balances. Checking his level of trust, Terence told him how inefficient Highland's financial aid office was, how they managed to bungle students' loans and grants on a daily basis, something to which he had fallen victim plenty of times. The only positive was the fact that Annabelle Simmons, the director, happened to be a distant family friend, and had agreed to play dumb regarding his unpaid balances, up to a point at least. He didn't mention that her help had come with an embarrassingly high price tag. But Terence was refusing to go *there* with her anymore. A brother had to retain some pride, broke or not.

"How about this?" Jerry smiled in a reassuring, fatherly manner as he guided the Navigator to a curb near the four-star Prime Cut Restaurant on M Street. "I'll ask Burton if we can give you an advance of five hundred a month. Maybe that could keep your director friend happy for now."

I need the money right now, not parceled out in small-ass pieces, Terence thought. Jerry was offering him a Band-Aid for a gaping, festering wound. *Damn.* How was he going to get out of this hammerlock? Just last week he'd been harassed again by old high school friends trying to bring him into their street operation.

"A couple deliveries a week, T. Two, three hours of your time at best, nigga. You could clear a few extra Gs a week, bro. Think about it." Terence had told them to get out and go to hell, and now he felt like telling Jerry Wallace the same thing. Wishing he could be honest, he turned toward his mentor and forced a smile as he shook Jerry's clammy hand. "Thanks, Jerry. I really appreciate it."

Jerry grinned and climbed out into the street, quickly circling the car and meeting Terence at the curb. "You just make sure you do a kick-ass job on the Reveal project. You're the star intern of your class so far. Keep making me look good, OK? Oh, by the way, let me know this week if you're up for an Orioles game next month. I'm taking some of the execs in a couple weeks, and thought it'd be good exposure for some of the interns and new hires."

As they ducked under the awning of the restaurant, Terence frowned to himself. Another outing? Wasn't tonight enough for a while? Corporate America really demanded more of you than nine to five. He wanted to tell Jerry he had better ways to spend his time, but he knew a have-to when he heard one. "Sure, I'll let you know tomorrow." As Jerry slapped him on the back and they stepped into a smoky lounge filled with Technotronics employees, all of them lily-white residents of suburban Virginia, Terence gritted his teeth and reminded himself to turn on the charm. Just two hours, he told himself, and then he could return to his normal world. Maybe the monthly advances could hold Ms. Simmons off for the rest of the year. He'd try not to worry about that tonight, but he'd still have a ton of work waiting for him. And once he got that straight, he'd have to spend yet another night in bed without Lisa.

Terence tried to remind himself to be grateful for the small things. Sometimes that was all that kept a brother going.

5

MILITANT CLOWN

On Friday morning Rolly V. Orange, former D.C. council-man and man-about-town, cruised down Alabama Avenue and observed the Ellis Community Cultural Center from the spring warmth of his black late-model Cadillac. The center beamed down at the campus of Highland University from a grassy perch atop a quarter-mile slope. Awash in slowly chipping red brick paint, the aging structure proudly bore the stripes earned by twenty years of service to its beleaguered community. To the left of the towering three-story structure sat a swimming pool surrounded by dilapidated plastic furniture. An entrance on the east side of the building led to a regulation-size basketball court with recently replaced backboards and thick cloth nets. Plastered across the faded blacktop of the court was the center's motto: Lifting As One to Lift All.

Orange pulled his Cadillac into one of the few available spaces left on the block in front of the center. Hoisting his rotund frame from the car, he lumbered up the front steps and entered the lobby. Turning to his left, he entered Conference Room 105, a wood-paneled study where Sheryl Gibson sat at a maple-colored round table. Orange nodded politely and took a seat in a wooden chair with plaid cushions that had seen better days.

"Sheryl, how are you?" he said, noting her freshly permed head of curls, her maroon blazer, and the new sheen of her skin. It seemed she had survived yesterday's board meeting with more poise than he had. He wondered how long she could hold up.

"This is such a battle," Sheryl was saying. "I can't tell you how much I appreciate having you aboard, Rolly. We have to get the private sector energized. I just spoke with President Billings at Highland. It's official; they can't provide any more financial support this year. They've been helpful, granting college credit to students who serve as volunteers, but the university's own recent financial woes have dried up their well for now."

"Not to worry," Rolly said, patting Sheryl's hand and stilling the flip in his heart. "I have quite a Rolodex, Sheryl, don't forget that. I will get Ellis onto the radar of some of these VIPs."

Sheryl smiled at her old friend, hoping he didn't realize some of her glow was amusement at his outfit. A tall, pear-shaped man with a prodigious belly that usually threatened to break through the quivering buttons on his shirt, Rolly was attired today in a draping kente-cloth outfit with vivid hues of red, black, and green. Sheryl imagined her friend thought it gave him an air of authenticity, but in reality it made him look like a militant circus clown.

In hiring Rolly as Ellis's business manager, Sheryl was hoping for the best, but it didn't take a genius to see her friend was still recovering from his fall from grace. He insisted on denying the aging process, his round head flanked by Jheri-curled locks, though the top of his cranium was clean as a baby's bottom. He needed some work, but Sheryl had faith in him. This man had managed multimillion-dollar budgets and helped D.C. realize countless dreams. Rolly Orange still had it, she was sure; with her emotional support, he would organize the center's affairs and fill its coffers.

Sheryl tore her eyes from Rolly's outfit and put a hand to her chin. "Rolly, about last night's board meeting . . ."

A fleeting look of irritation danced across Orange's face. "Don't tell me about it. I still can't believe the impudence of those Highland kids—"

"They mean well," Sheryl said. "Larry and Brandon are new to the board. They were just trying to get an understanding of all the accounts we're using to record the donations and grants as they come in."

"I passed around clear summaries of each account's balances, along with explanations of the accounts' purpose," Orange huffed. "Our investments are earning a good return, they could see that. It's not my fault that most of them are restricted to use for specific programs and capital projects. I explained how we exhausted our reserves refurbishing the playground, pool, and basketball courts in preparation for the summer's programs. If they can't understand why that only leaves us with the monthly interest earned on our mortgage bonds to pay off the bank loans"—Orange emitted a brief sigh and locked eyes with Sheryl—"I felt disrespected, Sheryl."

"Rolly, you know I took up for you. I made it clear that I back your decision to put the Highland contributions into the new investment pool that you're structuring. I know your expertise and your network of contacts can help ensure that the money they raise earns a maximum return, for the long term benefit of the center."

Orange stood, walked to a low couch a few feet away, and collapsed into the cushions, sitting with his hands behind his head and his eyes on Sheryl. "But that wasn't enough for them, was it?"

"I backed you, Rolly." Sheryl shook her head and began flipping through her planning notebook. "I made them back off. Don't be so sensitive. They're just young men learning leadership skills and finally getting a chance to give something back. They're not a threat to you. We're all in this together."

"You're right." Orange checked his watch and grimaced. *Not already.* "Sheryl, can we talk about this week's fund-raisers after lunch? I forgot I was supposed to call a representative from the NAACP at ten."

"That's fine," Sheryl said, looking up momentarily. "I have a teleconference in a few minutes myself."

Orange heaved himself up from the couch and barreled back down the hallway, heading for his office, a cramped space with linoleum-tile flooring and the scent of Raid. The place had to be sprayed weekly to keep roaches and rats away. How far he'd come, Rolly V. Orange. From councilman, a man with the ear of Jesse, Marion, Eleanor, and every CEO in town, to . . . this.

How had this happened? He knew better than to ask that question. The beginning of the end had been a bottle of the wrong Scotch, one he had grown far too fond of. Then there had been Angela's illness, lupus, a shot from out of nowhere that still puzzled him. She was alive, but so fragile in more ways than one now. The rage simmered within him.

He took a seat at his metal desk and shuffled papers absent-mindedly before grabbing at the rotary phone to his right. He'd memorized the number by now, after refusing to call for several weeks. He'd thought he could be strong, thought he'd tell the Kid where to go, the way he'd done most every time he'd approached him at council meetings. But after his run-in with those kids last night, young men with everything in front of them, questioning his judgment as if he was a nobody, a has-been at the tender age of forty-eight . . . Orange gripped the phone receiver and shut the thoughts out.

"Nico," he said when a voice answered on the other end. "We need to talk. Where can we meet?"

6

MINDS OF THEIR OWN

When the fellas sat down in their living room to review Ellis business, as they did every Saturday morning, Larry was a little preoccupied. He stewed in silence as the others bantered idly about who had the hottest date last night, what club was jumping, and who was seen with whom. He couldn't stop reading and rereading Sheila Evans's latest editorial attack in the *Sentinel*. Damn if she wasn't accusing him of improprieties in his position as financial adviser to last year's HSA president. It was a bunch of lies about him steering some homecoming contracts to vendors with ties to his father's business, complete falsehoods. But someone was bound to believe this stuff. He didn't need to lose any more points—he was still trailing Winburn by ten.

"Larry, you look like you got something on your mind," O.J. said, snapping him from his trance. "What up?"

Larry folded the paper and shook his head, ready to get down to business. The conversation turned serious and each housemate gave an update on their fund-raising progress. Brandon was concerned about the Disciples of Christ's willingness to help. They seemed troubled by the close ties between Ellis Center and the local Nation of Islam chapter. The Nation, on the other hand, had encouraged Terence and asked for a couple of weeks to look at their budget before committing to specifics. O.J. was just getting started but was ready to hit churches from the heart of Northwest D.C. to the bottom of Southeast. For his part, Larry had riled up a few thousand with phone calls to wealthy alumni but had lists of people he hadn't reached yet.

Once the issue of fund-raising was covered, Larry began complaining about their most recent meeting with the Ellis Center board. "I wouldn't follow Rolly Orange across the street," he said, huffing and puffing. "Why does a woman as sharp as Sheryl pay that fool any mind?"

"Look, you know the sister's got a lot on her these days," O.J. piped up from his perch on a beanbag in the center of the floor. "She just got divorced in the last year, and now her daughter's pregnant. That's no small load to carry while running a center with a well that's gone dry."

"Don't get me wrong, fellas, Sheryl's all good," Larry stressed, "but I can't condone sittin' by and letting Orange run rampant with the money. I don't know if the rest of that board is clueless or in collusion with him, they supported his plan so quick. Come on, somebody's got to serve as a check on this mug."

"I hear ya," Brandon said from his reclined position in a black lounge chair near the bay window. "Maybe we should move the rest of our money."

"Brandon, what are you sayin'?" Terence whipped around from the other end of the couch. "You gonna take your contributions away from Orange & Company?"

Larry shook his head eagerly. "If I hear my boy correctly, he's suggesting we stop putting our fresh contributions into the Ellis Center accounts, where Orange can put his grubby hands all over them. Am I right, Choirboy?"

His eyes shut, Brandon tipped his head back against the lounger's leather. "To my mind, we're under no formal obligation to put our contributions directly into Ellis's hands. Look, we've already got pledges of fifteen thousand bucks. That's not exactly Monopoly money.

"Until we get some comfort about Orange, we can set up a savings or money market account, one that would require one of our signatures, as well as Sheryl's, for any withdrawals. That way, the contributions are technically placed under the center's control, without sacrificing our right to see that the funds are handled responsibly." For a few moments, the men sat in silence, considering the weight of the step they were about to take.

"I'm with that, brother," O.J. bellowed. "The board would be hard-pressed to argue with such a setup. It might even make them rethink their choice to follow Orange like sheep being led to the slaughter."

"I'll get my banker on the phone, if that's okay with everybody." Larry's authoritative tone gave their gathering the air of a formal business meeting. "He'll get us an account set up, and we can have all donors send the checks directly to a bank lockbox. Let's hook up again for an update meeting next week."

7

MO' MONEY, MO' PROBLEMS

T he next Saturday morning, Larry sat up in Ashley's bed and planned his escape. Her four-poster queen-sized bed creaked slightly as he rose from the champagne satin sheets and delicately placed his right foot on the cushy carpet below. As he swung his torso to the left and sprang to his feet, the bed emitted another faint warning that he feared would alert Ashley to his movement. He wasn't trying to step out on her, he just wanted to get the day moving. It was almost eight o'clock, and he had to brush up on Ellis Center's history before his brunch with Raheem Ramirez, a local venture capitalist and frat brother of his father's. There was no way he was gonna get Ramirez to part with some dough if he couldn't effectively sell the center's accomplishments. Once he had wined and dined Ramirez, he had to swing by the house and pick up some campaign brochures and posters. Mark had insisted they spend at least three hours every weekend making the rounds of the dorms. The latest poll still showed him almost ten points behind David Winburn.

Grateful that he had taken to keeping a few outfits at his woman's apartment, Larry eased open the door to her walk-in closet and stepped inside. Ashley had neatly arranged three of his suits and several shirts and khakis on the right side of the space. For a moment he paused and laughed softly. No college student needed to live like this. Granted, the closet in his room at home in Cincinnati was at least this big, but that was different. He was perfectly happy with his current digs in D.C.—tasteful, spacious enough, but within the price range of his more middle-class housemates.

As he toyed with which Hilfiger combination to throw on, Ashley's velvety voice floated through the cracked closet doorway. "Laaawrence," she drooled her pet name for him, "what are you doing?"

"Just chillin', deciding what I'm gonna wear today." He stepped out and observed his rising beauty. "Once I figure that out, I need to boot up your Compaq and do some job-search business on the Net, before I meet Ramirez."

Ashley raised her delicate arms over her head and yawned. "Why do you even bother job searching, Larry? You've got boatloads of contacts who'll hook you up."

"But I never know when I might miss out on the best opportunity just 'cause I don't know somebody. Ash, you know I believe in leaving no stone unturned. Whitakers never settle for second best."

"Suit yourself," she replied. Larry watched his woman as she emerged from the bed, dressed only in a black silk lingerie short set. As she draped her tall, lithe figure in a silk robe covered with a light floral pattern, Larry recalled how aggressively he had removed all of that clothing just a few hours earlier.

Noticing the effect her movements were causing, Ashley met his eyes, a smile of knowing naughtiness on her face. "Are you thinking nasty thoughts? I would have thought I wore you out last night."

"Oh, there's always more where that came from." As he stared across the room, Larry thought of rushing her, but before he could complete the thought Ashley retrieved a large black comb from her porcelain-white dresser and began teasing her long locks before the mirror.

"Some days I just don't know what to do with this mane. Maybe I'll just go to Lucien's next week and have it all cut off, put it into short waves or something."

Disappointed that the opportunity for a last-minute groove had passed, Larry taunted her. "You, of all people, with a short cut? Why, babe, how ever could you lampoon the hair of every other girl on campus if you had none yourself?"

"Ha-ha, you missed your calling, Eddie Murphy," she said, not breaking a stride with her comb. "Sometimes I just get tired of being high-maintenance."

"I'd have to be a fool to touch that one," Larry said, snickering.

"So how are we doing this thing with our parents tonight?" Ashley had raised the subject Larry had been pushing from his mind for the last few days. Tonight would be the equivalent of D day for this couple: finding out if their parents could coexist in peace. This was more of a concern for Larry and Ashley than for most. Anytime the only son of a millionaire entrepreneur and the little girl of a thriving bond trader were interested in hooking up, sparks were bound to fly.

Lawrence Whitaker, Sr., was both Larry's role model and a thorn in his side. Following in his own father's footsteps, Larry senior had taken control of his father's businesses twenty-five years ago. After spinning off or closing those that were unprofitable and focusing on a core of grocery-store and electronics retail chains, Larry senior had built the businesses into the $350 million operation they were today.

As a child, Larry junior had been unable to escape his identity as the son of the man who owned Whitty's Electronics and Lola's Grocery Stores. As a heartbreaking preteen, he'd even been subjected to the ridicule of serving as a chipper spokesperson in local TV and radio ads. *Shop at Whitty's, we'll save you pennies.* Well-meaning senior citizens and smart-ass kids throughout Cincinnati taunted him with that line to this day.

Perhaps some of that early usurping of his identity had led to Larry's resistance to taking over the business. Larry senior was, of course, adamant about the idea, even though he acknowledged the value in Larry's working elsewhere first. But he was not open to turning the company over to anyone other than Larry junior or Vera. And with Vera in self-imposed exile working as a missionary in Russia for the next two years, Larry knew he had been targeted as the prime candidate.

Although Larry had modeled himself after his father for most of his life, he figured his parents had raised him too well: his ambition had outgrown theirs. Larry senior had run his consortium of businesses from the same gleaming corporate tower in Blue Ash, Ohio, for the past twenty years. Sure, he had a beautiful office with plush carpet, antique furniture, and a few modern amenities like the wet bar and home entertainment system, but he went to and from the same office day in and day out. Larry could not relate. The taste for the finer things in life, which his parents actively bred in him, was calling him to the world of high finance, not his father's world of union battles, manufacturing snafus, and humiliating negotiations with snobby bankers. Oh, no, Larry was going to *be* one of those snobby bankers, arranging multimillion-, even billion-dollar deals and walking off with a nice little cut that would be more than most people earned in a lifetime.

Despite his mother's occasional criticism of his passion for the almighty dollar, Larry didn't view himself as money-hungry. He simply believed in evolution. His father was a multimillionaire; he would be a billionaire. And he would never get there running Whitty's or Lola's, fine businesses though they were. When he had first reached the point of making an official decision about the family business last spring, it had been Ashley who encouraged him to go for the green. He was pretty certain he'd made that decision of his own will, and not just because that had been the first night they'd gotten busy. Regardless, he had decided to keep his decision from his father until he graduated next year. A peaceful relationship with Pops meant he got to keep his Lexus, talk to his baby sister, Laura, on a regular basis, and hit senior up for extra bones for his own as well as Ellis Center's needs.

Responding to Ashley's question about the dinner, Larry squinted at his clothing selections and scratched at his mound of uncombed curls. It was about time for another haircut, maybe a shorter fade this time. "Your folks want everybody to meet them at The Four Seasons, right?"

"Yeah, you know Daddy's a member of the club they have on the penthouse floor there. Have you cleared it with your dad?"

"Yeah, yeah, sure," Larry said, chuckling. "You shoulda heard his 'tude when I first mentioned your father's proposal. In Cincinnati, he ain't used to being one-upped. There's plenty of middle-class black folk there, but he's always been one of the wealthiest ones around. Usually he's the one inviting folk to his exclusive clubs, understand. But I think he recovered from the shock."

Ashley's smile was patronizing. "Come on now, your father's sophisticated enough to know that a New York bond trader lives in a different world from most other businesspeople."

Larry was a little perturbed by this comment. He resisted the urge to ask if that made his father chopped liver, and hit the floor to do a few quick push-ups before turning on the computer. "Anyway, their flight gets in around one this afternoon," he panted in mid-push-up, "they're gonna call me when they get settled into their room at the Hyatt, and we can pick them up on our way over to Four Seasons."

As he continued pumping, Ashley came and stood over him. "You know, I wish I could be meeting your real mother first."

Satisfied that he'd knocked out enough reps to maintain his physique, Larry rolled back on his elbows and looked up at the ornate light fixture overhead. "Yeah, I know. She promises she'll get out here before the end of the year, and she wants us to spend a weekend at Hilton Head with her and Bill sometime over the summer." The mere thought of his mother "spending weekends" with anyone other than Larry senior still made him queasy, so he quickly moved off the subject of Bill. "Anyway, the paper is planning to send her to D.C. more often to cover the latest scandals, so she's looking to size you up over the course of several visits."

Tired of playing with her hair, Ashley headed for the closet, the intoxicating scent of Victoria perfume trailing behind her. "Well, I welcome her critiques," she said, overconfidence dripping from her tone. "I'm sure your mom and I will hit it off."

Thankful that her back was turned, Larry treated himself to a fleeting smirk. He was working gradually to prepare his mother for Ashley ahead of time. Nothing characterized the difference between his parents more than the initial reactions each had when he first flashed a picture of his new girlfriend last year.

His father had been uncouth as always. "Good God, son!" Larry senior's mouth had come dangerously close to hitting the floor. "What you trying to do—put your old man to shame? *I'm* supposed to be the mack up in here! My partners see you with this fine thang, they gonna ask me why I've never landed a piece like that!" Larry had spent the next few minutes fending off impolite and relatively private queries about Ashley's anatomy, as well as the particulars of her sexual performance. Not exactly the type of conversation he cared to have with his dad, though he'd always known Larry senior was no prude. He wondered sometimes if his father would ever get tired of the player's game. The man was almost fifty years old, but his attitude toward attractive women hadn't evolved a bit.

Larry's mother, Mona, on the other hand, had not been so impressed by Ashley's photo. Last summer, as they sat in her office at the *Cincinnati Enquirer,* she had fixed him with a skeptical gaze. "Larry, does this girl have anything in her head?"

"Mom, that's not fair. Grandma could have asked Dad the same thing about you when you were in college."

Mona's eyes had turned suddenly quizzical. "Oh, really? Says who?"

"Mom, I've seen your high school and college photos. Obviously, for my own psychological protection, I can't elaborate, but there wasn't much difference between you then and Ashley now."

"Aw, boy, hush," Mona had said, a slight blush coming over her. Larry had never been a fool. Since grade school, he had grown accustomed to the rude remarks of peers who found his mother to be uncommonly attractive.

"Regardless of what *I* looked like, I was about something. Is she?" Larry knew what she meant. His mother had come from a working-class family and worked to put herself through college. While she had always been fashion-conscious enough to play up her natural beauty and draw the eye of someone as picky as

Larry senior, she had never been the primped, prepped princess that Ashley was. Besides, she knew of her son's early tendencies to date women based on style instead of substance. Of course, he hadn't been all about style. They had to be giving up some play, too.

But Larry had decided last year that he was ready to outgrow his days of judging women based on cup size, body-fat percentage, and hair texture. For several months before he and Ashley first hooked up, he had purged his life of one-night stands and shallow relationships. He was still no saint, but he had already grown tired of the player's game. The life of a player had yet to satisfy Larry senior, who was already stepping out on Amy, his second wife. And as much as he admired his father in the business arena, Larry was determined not to end up like his father when it came to his treatment of women. Larry had stumbled across his father's affairs several times in high school, so much so that he was almost relieved when the old man finally announced he was trading the mother of his children in for a new model. At least there was no need to pretend anymore. Now he could care less if his father played around on Amy; the girl had known from jump what she was getting. Once an adulterer, always an adulterer.

Larry was ready to start settling down now, and Ashley was as good a prospect as any, at least on her good days. Of course, he wasn't sizing her up for an engagement ring quite yet. With her tastes, he wouldn't be able to swing an acceptable ring for her without depleting all of his upcoming summer earnings or taking a chunk out of his trust fund. Besides, he wasn't ready to choose a wife yet; Ashley was the first girl he'd ever even considered in those terms. But Larry wanted to at least get into the habit of monogamy. He was afraid if he waited until he was married to try being faithful, he'd end up like Dear Old Dad.

Ashley broke his introspection, yelling up to him from the mahogany staircase. "Babe, I'm booting up the Compaq for you! You can get started on that while I go fix a little breakfast." She shared the two-floor luxury apartment with Jill Jones, a blue-blooded classmate and sorority sister. Jill traveled a lot on the weekends and usually stayed at her boyfriend's during the week, so Larry and Ashley were used to having the place to themselves.

Searching the customary Web sites, Larry started accessing his routine daily information. He'd not had time to check the stock market listings yesterday, so he was pleasantly surprised with most of the results. The Dow Jones was up five percent, and some of the sectors in which he was most heavily invested had driven the climb. Whipping open his stock-summary spreadsheet in Excel, he updated the key stocks' prices and checked the summary calculation.

"Ash, my portfolio appreciated eight percent yesterday!" An 8 percent appreciation on a $250,000 portfolio was no small matter. Ever since his mother had urged Larry senior to let his son manage a portion of his stocks, Larry had taken to the responsibility like a kid in a candy store. Sure, today's gains could quickly become tomorrow's losses, but he knew that in the long run his efforts would bring a return well above what the bank down the street offered.

"That's nice, dear," came Ashley's patronizing reply. She didn't enter into the kitchen very often, which made her weekend ritual of fixing breakfast for Larry somewhat endearing. That was why he was letting her make him a meal before his brunch with Ramirez; and, he didn't want to be sidetracked by hunger while he tried to plead Ellis's case. That said, right now he wished she could forget the food and show some interest in his financial-management skills. Sure, her professionally managed portfolio was probably ten times the value of his, but at least he knew what was happening with his. Ashley relied on quarterly reports and an annual face-to-face with her father's financial adviser, some guy with J. P. Morgan. This wasn't right, and Larry knew it; how many people, given the privileges he and Ashley had, would treat their own trust fund like the immense blessing it was? It was time for him to do his duty as Ashley's man and help her take more responsibility for her fortune.

Pausing to take her to task, Larry descended the towering

staircase to the first floor. Ashley stood inside the contemporary white kitchen, its high glass chandelier and gold-rimmed cabinets and sink reeking of overindulgence. "When's the last time you made a strategic decision about the makeup of your portfolio?"

Seasoning the large omelette simmering over the stove, she turned a suspicious eye his way. "Larry, have you ever considered the fact some of us have other things we prefer to do with our time? Remember, I'm going to be the lawyer someday that helps you bankers and businessmen protect your money. I'll always hire somebody else to handle my investments."

"I'll never understand how you can be so cavalier about money that your father and his ancestors busted their butts to earn for ingrates like you and your spoiled cousins." Larry hadn't meant to start an argument, but his indignation at Ashley's indifference to the weighty fortune that lay at her feet was too strong to suppress. "You wanna practice corporate law, right? You know how much insight you could get into business matters by managing your own investments?"

Rolling her hazel eyes, Ashley placed a well-manicured hand on her hip. "Larry Whitaker, what do you think you can possibly tell me that my father hasn't already told me a thousand times?" The flash of impatience in her eyes told him his weekly breakfast was in danger of being pitched if he kept up his line of questioning.

"Ashley, I just believe in always giving your best, regardless of where you are in life. You got to understand, the money in the Whitaker family ain't as old as yours. My great-grandfather grew up on a former slave plantation, never moved off the estate. But he and my great-grandmother taught their kids to reach for life's best. That's how my grandfather built a dual career as a physician and entrepreneur."

Ashley leaned over her simmering omelette. "Larry—"

"Hear me out, please? My grandfather never forgot where he came from or how he got out of it: hard work. He never let my father rest on his laurels, and that's why my parents have always forced me to be responsible for the money they've devoted to my future."

"So I'm *irresponsible* now?" The twist of his lady's head told Larry he'd be lucky if she even finished preparing his omelette. "Fool, please. *You* are the problem here, Larry. If you're going to be with me, you're going to have to learn how the truly wealthy in this country live. You think JFK, Jr., was studying the minutiae of stock market fluctuations when he was in college? Hell no, he was enjoying life and doing the type of things most black people don't even dream of doing, like spending a year studying and traveling overseas, experiencing the finer things in life, meeting VIPs from coast to coast, and, when time allowed, deciding what he wanted to do with his life. When you come from a family with money like mine, the wealth *allows* you the freedom from fretting over nickel-and-dime fluctuations in asset values. You get to *enjoy* life!"

Taken aback, Larry tugged at his left earlobe violently. "Well, well, here we go again. It was inevitable. You're the princess, I'm the pauper. Damn, Ashley, it's so easy for me to forget. I sure am glad you keep me in my place."

"I am not ashamed of the truth, Larry. Your father is in the top five percent of the black upper class, but mine is probably among the top ten black wage earners, period. This is only a contest if you make it one. Baby, you have to understand what it's like to grow up wealthy beyond most people's dreams. That's the only way that you'll get rid of this habit of judging people. You know, if you had taken my advice and moved into that condo with Jeffrey Kemp and George Clemmons, you might be better able to relate to the other half."

"Those pseudo-Negroes are stuffed shirts, way ahead of their time where I'm concerned," Larry bellowed, his face cracking at the thought of living with the two blue-bloods. "They're always primping over their Jaguars, sampling the latest wines, caviar, and going on skiing weekends with their blond playthings. No thank you, this brother likes to keep it real." Larry paused and took a look around Ashley's ostentatious apartment. "Well, most of the time. My crib is a nice place, but it's in the hood, and my house-mates are good brothers who know who they are." He scooted closer to Ashley as she slid the omelette onto a plate. "No shame in my game."

"You know, I've never understood why you chose those guys in the first place. I know your and Brandon's fathers are friends from their Highland days, but why would you want to stay with *any* of them?"

"Oh, so now that I've insulted your work ethic, you insult my friends. Fine, Ashley. I chose housemates that weren't tight friends because I've seen too many friendships end when folks try to live together. And all these brothers are cool, in their own way."

"Fine, Larry, it's your life. You don't mind the fact that Terence's brother could bring his gangbangin' cronies up in that house and do God knows what, or the fact that nobody can enjoy sex in the house for fear of offending Brandon's old-fashioned ass. And we all know it's just a matter of time before one of O.J.'s dumb-ass little whores comes after him, straight out of *Fatal Attraction*. It's hanging with the crabs at the bottom of the barrel that keeps those of us with money from being able to fit in with the rest of the upper class. I don't know when you'll learn that."

Scooping up his plate with one hand and balancing a plastic pitcher of orange juice in the other, Larry decided to let the shots slide. When Ashley got started on a tear like this, it wasn't worth fighting back—that just made it worse. "Ash, you do your thing, I do mine. I'm gonna eat and scoot to make that meeting with Ramirez." As Larry turned to leave the kitchen, Ashley grabbed her plate from the counter. He could hear her vigorously scraping her omelette into the gilded trash can. He set his juice and omelette on the glass coffee table, hearing the slamming of the refrigerator door, kitchen drawers, and pans Ashley had used to prepare breakfast. Determined to eat in peace, he grabbed at the stereo remote and drowned out her nonverbal tirade with the After 7 CD that had served as the soundtrack for last night's love session. As the Edmonds brothers' voices filled the apartment throughout the night, Ashley had called out his name with the worshipful ardor of a saint on Sunday morning. Now she was probably busy creating names for him that could be spelled in four letters or less.

A few hours could sure change things.

8

PRIMARY COLORS

F ive hours later, in the blacktop parking lot outside the Highland Student Center, Mark Jackson reclined in the driver's seat
of his candy red Mazda Miata, his head snapping in time to the
rhythms of the latest Blackstreet jam. For anyone within half a
mile of the vibrating auto there was no mistaking the boom of
"No Diggity."

Larry pulled up alongside Mark in his Lexus, not bothering to
get his friend's attention. Mark was in his own world. A pair of
Ray-Ban sunglasses masked his eyes as he pretended he was Teddy
Riley himself.

"And this is who you entrust your campaign to?" Dressed in a
loud olive suit and black wing tips, O.J. laughed heartily as he
climbed out from the passenger side of the Lexus. Brandon and
Terence emerged from the backseat as Larry circled around to
Mark's window, rapping loudly as the writhing man pretended to
be oblivious to his surroundings. Then Larry gave a conspiratorial
nod to his housemates. "Fellas, let's wake the fool up, shall we?"

Immediately catching his boy's implication, Terence positioned himself behind the rear bumper of the Miata. In seconds
O.J. and Brandon grabbed ahold and began to help lift the back of
the gleaming machine off the pavement, as Larry rocked it from
the front. Feeling the back of the car rise, Mark whipped off his
Ray-Bans and removed his key from the ignition, bringing the
sounds of Blackstreet to a sudden halt.

A mock frown twisting his face, Mark emerged from his cocoon. "You niggas must be out your freakin' minds!"

As the men stepped back from the Miata and slapped hands in amusement, Larry stopped Mark in his tracks. "Mark, need I remind you, my campaign manager, that we are in the parking lot of the *Student Center*?" Larry's tone was jovial but carried an undercurrent of annoyed sincerity.

"Ah, damn, you right." Mark placed a hand on the roof of the Miata, calmly closing his door. Larry knew Mark hadn't really been upset at their prank, but if anyone passing by had heard him use the dreaded N-word, it could be turned around on Larry for Winburn's political gain. More than a few past HSA candidates had been embarrassed in the past over stray comments or actions. Larry's stomach curdled as he remembered the way the student body booed Ian Roberts off the stage last year, when he'd admitted to calling his girlfriend a bitch in the heat of the moment. No way was he going out like that.

The posse of young brothers made their way up the central staircase of the Student Center and wound around to the large conference room at the north end of the top floor. Inside were enough blue plastic chairs, arranged in neat rows, to seat all fifty-five of Larry's campaign team members. Before the chairs sat a rectangular fold-out table, draped with a LARRY WHITAKER: THE PROMISE decorative cloth. Ashley had paid a pretty penny to have that and numerous other advertising vehicles designed by a tailor she had used back when she lived in Manhattan. Larry admired the rich blue and gold colors, which conveniently matched Highland's. Ashley could go overboard sometimes, but there was nothing like going overboard in style.

Most of the campaign workers had already arrived and taken seats, though they continued to mingle and socialize. Ashley and Janis stood in front of the table, updating the list of attendees. Mary Corkley, campaign secretary, was seated at the table, wildly flipping through a manila folder, searching for her copies of the meeting's agenda. The other occupant of the table, Chuck Dawkins, was the campaign's unofficial bouncer. As always, Dawkins was dressed for war, his bulky frame draped in a pair of army fatigues and a white cotton turtleneck. A six-feet-five linebacker for the football team and a former roommate of Mark's, Dawkins was a faithful running buddy to both Larry and Mark. Everyone on campus knew he was more than willing to express that loyalty by embarrassing, even physically harming, anyone who attempted to crash these campaign meetings. Larry and Mark had barely entered the room when Dawkins bolted from the table and stomped their way, his clunky Timberland boots slapping against the thin carpet.

"Hey, dudes," Dawkins said, in the flat tones of his native Minneapolis. He gripped Larry by the shoulder and glanced between him and Mark. "Guys, we got trouble."

Larry pursed his lips in annoyance. "What now, Chuck?" Dawkins tended to be quick on the draw; he could find evil in the most innocent gesture. Larry doubted this was anything serious.

"It's this," Dawkins said. He stepped back and fished deep into the right pocket of his fatigues, until his hand emerged with a neatly folded sheet of printer paper. He held it out toward Larry and Mark. "This was in the campaign's mailbox this morning. Read it, then tell me whose ass I gotta kick."

Larry grabbed the sheet, unfolded it, and held it down so Mark could read as he did. The note was typed in a large, bold font that took up the entire middle of the page.

Whitaker: Our neighborhood ain't your playground. Back up off Ellis Center and mind your own Silver-Spoon business. Don't think you ain't being watched.

Larry met Mark's eyes, which had grown to twice their normal size, and yawned. "You know," he said, stretching his arms overhead, "Winburn and company have lost their minds. What kind of stupid-ass scare tactic is this?"

Dawkins began pacing, his hands on his hips. "You think Winburn did it? Cool. I'm gonna go find that little—"

"Chuck, Chuck," Larry said, waving him off. "Forget it. We're grown folks here. Best thing to do is ignore this nonsense."

Mark crossed his arms and followed Larry over to the front

table. "You really think that's what this is? Larry, nobody wants you to play savior over this community center. The student body don't care, and the community sure don't appreciate a spoiled brat like you." As they took their seats, he lowered his voice. The crowd had quieted in recognition of their arrival. "At least leave Ellis out of your speech for now," he whispered.

"I got you, chief," Larry said, surveying the crowd. More than fifty of the plastic seats were occupied, so it was time to begin. He swept his eyes over the crowd, taking in the diverse constituency before him. He noted the presence of some of his long-lost running buddies from freshman year, several members of current and past HSA administrations, acquaintances that he knew only from a few classroom conversations, people who were really just friends of friends, and even, to what he knew would be Ashley's dismay, a handful of his past romantic conquests. No one could say he didn't know how to treat women, even when it came time to return a relationship to the land of platonic friendship.

Taking his seat at the center of the table, Larry met Mark's eyes, intuitively signaling it was time to begin. Dressed in a maroon Perry Ellis casual suit and a pair of leather sandals, Mark sprang to his feet. The crowd's mixing and mingling came to a sudden halt.

"We'd like to begin, people. Let me thank you for taking time out of your busy schedules to help fulfill the promise of our candidate for Highland Student Association president, Mr. Larry Whitaker!"

ᘔᘔᘔ

As Mark began to rev the crowd up, Brandon eased into a seat in the back row. Having avoided Highland's political circles as if they were hell itself for his first three years here, he was still a little uncomfortable at these types of events. Not helping his unease was the fact that Monica Simone was sitting three rows up and two seats over. Brandon knew that Monica and Tara had run with some of Larry's crowd in the past, so he had no reason to be surprised to see her. That still didn't stop his heart from galloping all over again. Sinking into his seat, he accidentally locked eyes with the woman sitting one seat over. The sister, her face partially covered by the bill of her white Detroit Tigers baseball cap, was working valiantly to make herself invisible. In fact, Sheila Evans, editor of the *Highland Sentinel,* had scooted so far down into her seat that her shoulders were parallel to the armrests of her chair.

Deciding to have some fun, Brandon leaned over and tapped Sheila's left shoulder. "Hey, how'd you get past Chuck Dawkins? You know you're not welcome here. Your editorials have been all over Larry's back."

Turning her rich brown face, which was free of any trace of makeup, Sheila looked at Brandon like a kid caught with her hand in the cookie jar. "Now, look, I am completely in my rights to be here. I know you, right? We had an English class together or something. Look, friend, I already had this discussion with Dawkins."

"Oh, really?"

"Yeah, the big lug tried to put me out like he did those punk freshmen, but I set him straight. Told him I am a professional, impartial journalist, and he had no cause to keep me from covering this campaign."

Brandon smirked. "And he bought that?"

"Let's just say he was swayed by my promise to highlight his bouncer act in the *Sentinel,* if he didn't treat me like he had some sense. I may not be a fan of a corporate wannabe like Whitaker, but I'm here as a reporter, not an editor. When I write my editorials, I can speak from the heart. Today, I'm just recording the five W's for the Highland public."

"The five what?"

"When, where, who—never mind." Sheila paused as Janis completed her treasurer's report. Clearly amused at the proceedings, she turned again to Brandon. "Look at Whitaker. So smug, so full of himself. *Knows* he's fine. Had a silver spoon lodged in his spoiled mouth from Day One. If I hear one more woman on this campus include him in her top five most desirable men, I'll be sick. That's not what this university needs."

Brandon was enjoying this. "Oh, I agree. The brother's revolting. Can't stand him myself."

"Look at the way he handles himself. Some sisters say he reminds them of a young Harry Belafonte, though I think the Will Smith comparison is probably apropos. Unfortunately, as I've found the hard way, *pretty* usually also means *prick*."

Brandon licked his lips with glee. This woman must be short a few friends, to be sitting here spilling her feelings about Larry to a virtual stranger. Looking toward the front of the room, he admired Larry's poise. This was a man who relished having the eyes of the entire room fixed on him. His photogenic, clipped smiles and winks at various audience members were tailor-made to impress, and they were clearly hitting their mark. Larry was a natural-born politician and charmer. And Sheila Evans was fooling herself if she thought she was impervious to his charms.

Brandon leaned into Sheila's left ear as Mark called Larry to address the audience. He noticed that she smelled like fresh toothpaste. "Sister, I hear every word you're saying about Larry. By the way, I'm Brandon Bailey." He extended his right hand. "Larry and I are housemates." A rush of triumph swept over Brandon as Sheila's face flushed with a hint of red.

Up front, it was time to whip the troops into action. Larry removed his Ralph Lauren jacket and began to roll up the sleeves of his Eddie Bauer oxford. "My brothers, my sisters, those of you who know me, and I would hope that includes everybody, know that I am first and foremost a businessman. What things are important to a businessman, you ask? I'll give you my vision of a successful business: one that puts out a good product, on time, at the most efficient cost, with the maximum return to its shareholders." Pausing and whipping his slender frame around to the front of the table, Larry accelerated his rate of speech. "Now, don't go silent on me, people." As the crowd shifted and buzzed in reaction to his change in style, Larry pressed forward.

"What's a good product for a historically black college? I'll tell you. A well-educated graduate is the best product an HBCU can produce. A graduate who has been given the technical skills, the historical knowledge of his people, and the high quality service of this school's administration. Why? Because this person will go out into that real world and do two things. *Succeed*, and *give back!*"

"Well, all right!" From the midst of the crowd, O.J.'s churchy response rang like a bell. The crowd erupted in a peal of laughter.

Obviously amused, Larry paused for a laugh of his own before resuming his message. "Sounds so simple, doesn't it? But it's not! We all know it! Every person up in here can tell a horror story about the way the administration has jacked them over in one way or another. If it's not financial aid, it's housing, or lack thereof! If it's not a lack of course options in your chosen field of study, maybe you're just tired of seeing your favorite teachers fired because they haven't published their work in five journals this year!" Some members of the crowd were on their feet now, their appreciation for Larry's insights made clear.

"Ladies and gentlemen, as we go forward into the campaign, I assure you I am a realistic leader. We can't do everything in one year. But we *can* lay the groundwork for future administrations, which, if done right, will leave them no choice but to follow in our footsteps. Are you with me?"

The resounding *"Yess!"* nearly knocked Larry off his feet. "Well, all right, I'd like to take a quick minute then to talk about my key platform policies. You've all received a detailed copy of the platform, to which you can refer while you're out spreading the good word. I think there are three policies we want to stress today as we go around." Larry was now enunciating every word clearly, using the King's English in the way he instinctively did whenever it was time to get down to serious business. By the time he was finished summarizing his platform, the crowd teemed with the blind enthusiasm of an Amway meeting. They were ready to go out and sell Larry to every student on Highland's campus.

"Okay, I need everyone to pay close attention as I read off the teams for the dorm visits!" Having summarized the platform brochures and scripts that the campaign workers were to use, Mark barked out the team assignments with the rapid-fire pace and energy of a drill sergeant. The partners were to trade off, going from door to door and taking turns serving as the key spokesperson. The teams had been assigned so as to show the authenticity of Larry's student support; all people who were known to be close friends or associates were separated, so that Larry's supporters would not appear to be one big clique. Team by team, Mark read off the names of the workers, who met up front to gather their materials before setting off on their assigned mission. Brandon couldn't help but chuckle when the first pairing turned out to be Terence and his ex-girlfriend, Lisa. Lisa had broken Terence's heart too many times to count, and here she was at his side again.

As a frustrated Terence exited the room, Brandon shifted in his seat and hipped Sheila to Larry's antics. "Hey, Sheila, check this out. Larry matched my boy Terence up with—"

Up front, Mark's green eyes danced as he read the next pairing. "Brandon Bailey and Monica Simone."

Brandon's brain processed the words in slow motion. Surely he hadn't heard right. This damn fool did *not* set him up to go out campaigning with Monica. As Monica, dressed in a wine-colored silk pantsuit, rose from her seat and floated to the front of the room, Brandon remained glued to his chair, his brain nearly shutting down.

Mark was obviously in on the joke. "Ahem, Mr. Bailey, paging the future Dr. Bailey." The entire room collapsed in laughter as Brandon wobbled out of his seat.

Brandon realized Larry had backed him into a corner, and now he had a choice. He could keep doing what he'd done for years, and cower in the heat of love's glare, or he could bare his claws and attack the challenge before him. He reminded himself: She's not Brandy.

Brandon arched his back and stormed to the front of the room. Arriving at the front table, he wiped his palms on his navy blue Dockers and eyed Larry like a calm cat scoping a scampering mouse. He wanted to tell Larry where he could go with his matchmaking attempts, but he couldn't do that with Monica literally standing on his heels. That only left one option.

His mustache glistening with nervous moisture, Brandon turned toward Monica. "Monica Simone. Gee, I couldn't have gotten a better partner if I'd picked you myself." He emphasized the last few words, slyly cutting his eyes at Larry.

Smiling and brushing a wavy black lock out of her right eye, Monica placed her left hand on her hip as Brandon grabbed a stack of brochures and a couple of scripts from Mark, who was grinning like the Cheshire cat.

Monica met Brandon's eyes as he turned from the table. "Well, this'll be an opportunity for us to talk for once. Seems like we normally just say 'Hi, bye' while your cousin Bobby pesters my best friend. You'll have to tell me about the *real* Brandon Bailey."

His mouth set with courageous determination, Brandon inhaled deeply as he turned toward the exit. "Well, why don't we set a date and time to do that right now? Monica, what say I take you out sometime?" Too far gone by now to be deterred by the look of shock that invaded her face, Brandon headed for the door. "Don't feel pressured to give me an answer now. We've got work to do first. Larry, we'll be back after we've gotten you a few hundred votes, all right?"

Before Brandon could escape the room and the snickers and glares of those who had overheard, Monica raised her voice a notch. "Hold up, hold up, what is this about?" Her hands were on her hips and her right foot was planted solidly into the carpet. She didn't exactly seem flattered by his approach.

Frozen in place, Brandon looked helplessly at Larry and Mark, who were feigning complete ignorance as they handed out materials to other volunteers. Brandon was on his own, and he felt like he was up a very long, cold creek. "Uh, what do you mean? I asked you out, Monica. *Capice?*" *Capice?* Why the heck did he say that? Black men didn't say *"Capice."* He was screwing up, bad.

Monica's captivating eyes were full of fire. She walked over to where he stood, just inside the doorway. "Let me hip you to something, brother." Her sharp but proper New York accent sounded like a cross between Salt-n-Pepa and Robin Givens. "Women don't appreciate being put on the spot. If you wanna ask me out, you keep it between me and you." Her stare was full of indignation.

This is exactly why I should stick with girls from the Disciples, Brandon thought. What was her major malfunction? He'd psyched himself up for this, and now she was ready to crucify him. It was time to stop giving a damn. "Excuse me, Ms. Simone, but it just so happens that I've got a jones in my bones for you. Now, you don't have to like it—fact is, you don't have to give a crap. But Larry set us up as partners because he knows how I feel about you. He thought I'd wilt like an old flower. I asked you out when I did to prove him wrong, and to make sure I didn't talk myself out of doing it. How's that sound?"

The fire in Monica's eyes began to die down. She tugged at a lock of hair near her right temple. "Well, that helps explain, but I don't like having my business out in public, Brandon. Maybe I was too defensive. Let's talk about this after we cover our route for the campaign."

Feeling his oats for having defended himself, Brandon swaggered toward the door with Monica in tow. "Deal. But I do want an answer."

As the pair made their way out into the hallway, Larry sighed with pride. He had led Brandon to water, and the boy was at least trying to drink.

His needling of his housemates complete, Larry worked with Mark to clean up the extra brochures and materials. He'd had his fun; now it was time to get out there and start selling. There was only one question counteracting his upbeat mood: Who had really sent that note?

9

PLYING THE FAITHFUL

A few hours after Larry's campaign meeting, the Interfaith Alliance annual church service concluded. The Reverend Joseph Batiste, pastor of Phillips Temple CME Church, a medium-sized congregation in the Deanwood section of Northeast D.C., was rightfully proud of the service his church had hosted. Apparently secure in his manhood and unconcerned with the impressions of the women flooding the fellowship hall, Batiste unzipped his black pastoral robe and allowed his healthy belly to protrude past the metal zipper. His graying, closely cropped hair still glistening from the sweat induced by his emotional performance just minutes earlier, he leaned against a wall near the buffet table. One of his deacons was preparing a plate of collard greens, hot cross buns, barbecued chicken, and potato salad, all of which were known to be his favorites. Once that hot plate was placed in his hand, he would sink gratefully into one of the plastic chairs lining the metal fold-out tables that congested the spacious hall.

As he received the steaming repast, Batiste pointed a stubby finger at O.J., who stood a few feet away in the growing buffet line. "Peetahs!"

Deep in conversation with an attractive coed from the Union Methodist Young Adult Choir, O.J. hoped Batiste would be satisfied with a smile and a wave. He could talk to the old man once he had gotten through the line and obtained the unsuspecting honey's phone number.

Batiste was having none of that. "Why you standin' in line, son? One of my members will get you some food. Come here, I got to put a bug in your ear!"

Called out in front of the burgeoning crowd, O.J. excused himself. Straightening his Chess King tie, one of many items he'd snapped up at a going-out-of-business sale last month, he smiled warmly at the young beauty. "Michelle, I hope we can continue this conversation later." He smiled, hoping his interest was not too overt. Some Christian sisters were actually scared off by that. The knowing glint in Michelle's eye suggested his interest was reciprocated. It *would* be on.

Striding over to Batiste, O.J. shook the pastor's hand vigorously. "Pastor, you all put your feet into this evening's service! It was beautiful. As a representative of Light of Tabernacle's clergy, I can assure you Rev. Grier will model his stewardship of next year's service on the job you've done here."

His eyes fixed on the heaped plate before him, Batiste responded in the lilting accent of his Caribbean heritage. "Son, please, you and I bot' know it was all de Lord's work."

O.J. met Batiste's eyes reverently. He knew this was no false humility on the minister's part. The native West Indian sincerely credited Christ for working through him. He was completely devoid of ego, a rarity among the preachers O.J. knew.

"O.J.," Batiste continued, "I want to tank you again for taking part in de service. Your testimony and song put a hurtin' on these people, brother. I'm sure you've been told dis before, but you have a real gift for de ministry."

Uncomfortable with such overt flattery, O.J. folded his hands together, thankful that a deacon had emerged with a plate of food for him. "Well, the Lord is good, and here's a perfect example right here." As O.J. bit into a candied yam, he artfully continued the conversation. "Let me thank you for the opportunity to minister, Pastor, as well as the chance to make that appeal concerning Ellis Center. I've already had ten or twelve people tell me they'll be mailing checks to the lockbox account we've set up with the center's board."

Deeply involved in his own meal, Batiste swallowed a piece of chicken and slapped O.J. on the back. He paused to acknowledge a few of the other visiting ministers who continued their way through the buffet line. "It's my pleasure to see de center's mission advanced. Did you know my associate, Rev. Webster, grew up in dat Shaw neighborhood? He swears by Ellis, say he'd be dead or in jail now if he hadn't been tutored and exposed to some culture through dat place. Matter of fact, dere are several families here at de church who live in dat area and send deir children dere on a regular basis." Glancing at the two ministers approaching them from across the room, Batiste cocked his head and scooted closer to O.J., lowering his voice to a whisper.

"I don't know if you're aware, son, but dere are rumors about de stability of de center, and I'm not just speaking about de financial foundation. I hear dat de Nation of Islam is planning to set up a Fruit of Islam division there, dat would train those innocent kids up as Black Muslims. Do you know anything about dat?"

Squaring his shoulders, O.J. let out a deep sigh. Even Batiste had fallen into the web of innuendo the center's detractors had spun. "Reverend, now that Ellis will no longer be funded by public money, they are taking this as an opportunity to infuse limited religious concepts into the course and activity offerings, but no one religion will be favored. If you know what I mean." O.J. winked at Batiste, a knowing smile on his face. "You see, the center recognizes that Christianity as well as other religions each offer some valuable lessons, and now they will be able to allow some facets of those religions in. But there will be no formal endorsement of any one, and more importantly, the majority of center administrators *and* board members are either Christians or heathens, so it's only natural that the gospel will rise above the noise created by any other religions."

Leaning in towards Batiste and balancing a hot cross bun between his right thumb and index finger, O.J. dropped what he hoped would be a calming revelation. "Quiet as it's kept, sir, I've been teaching them kids Bible lessons for the last two years, even while they were publicly funded. If that ain't proof of Ellis Center's *true* bias, I don't know what is."

As Pastors Welby and Davis joined the table, O.J. saw the flash of light from Batiste's smile and felt assured his remarks had hit home. Every time he was onstage, he came out a winner.

"Ah, gentlemen," Batiste greeted the ministers. "Have you met young Rev. Peters from Light of Tabernacle? He and I have been discussing ways in which we clergy can help raise some support for de Ellis Community Center. Why don't you tell dem some of the reasons we need to help save dis institution?"

Nearly an hour and two mountainous plates later, O.J. felt the heavy hand of Tony Powers, the assistant director of the Highland University Gospel Choir, on his shoulder. "Sorry to interrupt you, gentlemen," Powers said, "but I have to get back to campus. O.J., you about ready to go?"

His ears grating slightly at Tony's loud, raspy baritone, O.J. thanked the ministers again for their advice and support regarding Ellis Center. "I'll be giving Pastor Grier a full report on the service, I'm sure he'll be in touch with each of you shortly."

Batiste saluted him with a plastic cup of Kool-Aid. "O.J., don't be a stranger, son. Perhaps we can have you back to bless us with a word in de near future."

"That would be my honor, sir. God be with all you brothers. Have a blessed week!" O.J. hopped from his seat and followed Powers toward the back exit of the fellowship hall. As Powers wound his tall, athletic frame through the gradually emptying building, he drew one glance after another from the young ladies—an attractive range of teenagers, college students, and young adults—lining the back wall.

They were near the door when they were accosted by Michelle, the young woman O.J. had scoped out in the buffet line. She placed her hands on her slender hips and tapped her left foot impatiently. "So are you going to call me, or do I have to call you?"

O.J. met her green eyes, admiring her high-yellow complexion, short haircut, and healthy, Coke-bottle-shaped figure. He did some quick math. She'd said she was a member of her church's youth choir, right? He hoped she was over eighteen. He'd have to confirm that before they went out. He knew he needed God's grace, but even grace would get him only so far if he ever committed statutory.

Reaching into the pocket of his jacket, he whipped out a business card. "All my numbers are there: home, church, and pager. Will you write your number on the back of another card for me?"

Grabbing the card without removing her eyes from him, Michelle began writing her information. "By the way," she said, turning slowly toward Tony, "several of my friends were wondering if you're seeing anybody. Your choir's performance caused quite a stir up in here."

"Well, it sounds like the interest is in something other than my choir, so I'll have to decline respectfully." Despite Powers's pious response, O.J. sensed that his friend could not resist the curiosity caused by a longing to return to his old ways. "Uh, just for my four-one-one," Powers said sheepishly, "could you point out which friends asked about me?" Michelle discreetly pointed to a tall, well-built ebony beauty with a face plastered with makeup, a short and sweet tan-faced honey with prodigious cleavage, and a mocha-colored waif whose exquisite outfit and hairstyle failed to mask her youth. Powers sighed, seemingly reminding himself of his loyalties. "Tell them I'm spoken for, but very flattered."

O.J. climbed into the passenger seat of Powers' well-worn Honda Accord and looked at his friend. Indignation was all over his face. "Tony, you wanna tell me how you passed up all that good stuff just now? Brother, I could take the tall one off your hands!"

Powers exhaled and let out a good belly laugh. "Peters, don't you ever get enough, boy? The Lord giveth and the Lord taketh away, you know! You keep givin' your stuff away to every woman, he bound to take it eventually!"

Leaning forward in his seat as Powers exited the parking lot, O.J. refused to let the statement stand. "You got your nerve, fool. You bug the juice out of me, tryin' to act high and mighty. How many members of that gospel choir have you slept with? Hmm?"

Powers arched his eyebrows in pain, his eyes focused on the road ahead. O.J. already knew the answer to that question. The first year Tony had been in the choir, he had attempted to stay the straight and narrow, until he had slipped into bed with a fellow choir member. The pressure of two years of abstinence had been released with the force of a Mack truck, and the boy had been unable to stem his desire ever since. He had carried on three carnal relationships with choir members over the last three years and in his lowest times had even bragged about the encounters to O.J. Now it was clear Powers regretted having admitted his vices to his old friend.

"O.J., if you wanna play Drudge up the Past with saints," he said, "you'd never take advice from any of 'em. We all live in glass houses where sin is concerned. I ain't trying to judge you, I'm just suggesting you modify your lifestyle, brother. Trust me, I know how much more peaceful life can be when you have just one woman, a godly woman, in your life."

"A godly woman that you shackin' up with."

Powers frowned. "I never said Stacy and I were perfect, now, did I? But at least we're faithful to each other, we ain't spreadin' ourselves all over the campus and the city, like a lot of the other choir members, or *you*."

As they rolled past the freshly blooming trees of Gallaudet University's campus, O.J. bristled at the implication. "You don't know a thing about who I spread myself to, Tony, so don't even play that." O.J. knew he was a player, but he believed in discretion. He never knew when he might need the help of a pastor who expected ministers to actually live what they preached where sex was concerned.

Obviously upset, Powers pressed the argument. "You don't know *what* I know, O.J. How about this? I know whose baby Keesa Bishop is carrying!"

For a moment O.J. lost his sense of reality, his head swimming as the phrase echoed repeatedly. What in the Lord God's name was Powers talking about? Keesa had said something about an "urgent situation" in her latest message on his machine, but he'd blown her off. Certainly she had moved on to someone new in recent weeks. Some other poor sap was the father, if she was really pregnant in the first place. Certainly he wasn't the father. Was he? Shaken to his core and filled with a smoldering anger, O.J. grew silent, fixing his eyes on the road as Powers neared his house.

Apparently sensing he had crossed a line, Powers attempted a peace offering as he pulled up to the curb. "Brother, if what I've heard is untrue, I apologize for throwing it in your face. I ain't mentioned it to anyone else. If it *is* true, well, God help you. You need anything, let me know."

Already intent on calling Keesa, O.J. slid out of the Accord without a word, slamming the door with enough force to send it to the shop. As Powers revved up his Accord and wheeled off, O.J. turned his key in the lock of the front door, curses cascading from his lips. This was not happening. He felt like a character in a bad soap opera. It was time to deal with Keesa.

She was *not* going to jack up his career.

10

Whipped

U pstairs in his room, Terence slid off his Washington Redskins windbreaker and opened his closet door. Overhead
hung a Nerf basketball hoop, sagging low after years of avid use.
On the front of the door was a door-length poster of Michael Jordan in action. Terence wondered what his boys would say when
they realized Lisa was here.

Although he had tried his best to treat her cold as ice while
they had made the rounds of the dormitories for Larry, her luminous smile and soothing voice had won him over, and he had
ended up accompanying her to dinner at the Georgia Avenue Cafe
just off campus. By the time they'd finished their meal, it had almost been dark, and she had created some lie about the shuttle
bus to her off-campus dorm being out of service, meaning he
should walk her home or back to his house. A willing fool, he had
seen through her ruse and played right along, figuring Brandon or
Larry might be able to give her a ride home later.

He watched her circle his room before landing on his raggedy
twin bed. He and Lisa had come so far. In high school they had
been the Couple Most Likely to Succeed. Like most of their peers,
they had come from humble means, but both had worked hard to
graduate at the top of their class. They had actually battled down
to the last week for the salutatorian title; she had won by a hair. He
had been a starting forward on the basketball team, she had been
head cheerleader. Most important to many of their classmates,
though, their successes hadn't changed them. Terence had never

varied from his trademark image: a near-bald haircut, a clean-shaven upper lip, and a wardrobe consisting of blue jeans and sweat suits, all of which looked suspiciously alike. The boy was known for keeping it real, and that would never change.

Lisa had always been round-the-way as well. Although she never claimed to be a beauty queen, she was one of the most desired girls at Cardozo High and had always attracted the attention of other boys. At five feet six she was dwarfed by Terence, but her firm, well-rounded build and meticulous perm made her appear taller and more striking than she would have otherwise. What always captivated Terence more than anything was her chocolate brown face. Her cute pug nose and wide, inquisitive eyes gave her a childishly innocent aura. Of course it didn't hurt that she had what his boys referred to as "nice back" either, but when he had fallen in love with this woman, it had been for her brains as much as her beauty. His feelings for her hadn't changed, either, but today he'd made himself a promise. She was not going to seduce him and make him forget all that she'd done. No diggity for Lisa, Terence promised himself.

"Ooh, is this CD any good?" Lisa had moved over to his stereo. Terence eyed his new Isley Brothers CD. "Oh, yeah, it's straight. I would've thought you'd have bought that joint by now, what with all that extra scholarship money you have."

A momentary look of concern passed through Lisa's eyes. "Terence, you know scholarships don't put extra money in your pocket, they just pay the bills."

Terence picked up his Nerf basketball and began batting it from hand to hand, regretting his little jibe. The last time he had thrown her out, they had argued about whether or not he was still harboring envy over the scholarship, for which she had beaten him out when they both decided to attend Highland. Without one of Highland's rare merit scholarships, he'd been plunged into the world of need-based federal loans and grants that continued to make life a living hell.

"My bad, let's try a different subject," he said. "How are your job interviews going?"

Lisa smiled. "Well, a pleasant subject indeed. Chevron just

made me an offer to start as a chemist at one of their operations in San Francisco next fall."

"That's hittin'! Would you really go all the way out there?"

"I wouldn't rule it out. The money they talkin' sounds awfully good."

Terence let loose a sheepish smile. "You mind if I ask how much, just out of curiosity?"

"Try somewhere north of thirty-five thousand."

Terence moved closer to the bed, leaning against the maple wood dresser adjacent to Lisa. "Oh, rhe-he-hea-eally," he said, twisting his voice into a corny Jim Carrey impression. "I'm scared of you, girl. You go! I'll bet there's more offers out there still, too, huh?" It was times like these, seeing her field job offers, that he wished he'd done a four-year major like chemistry. Engineering required too much work to cram into eight semesters.

Meeting his eyes after pretending to be embarrassed by her accomplishments, Lisa cracked another smile. "Well, Merck's offering a little less to work at its headquarters in Jersey, and I've still got several other promising interviews in the pipeline."

Terence smacked his lips as he sank a Nerf shot into the distant net. "Mmm-mmm, so you gonna have to hook a brother *up* when you start collecting them big checks."

Leaning back on the bed, which wasn't exactly foreign to her, Lisa rested her head on top of her palms. "Speaking of money matters, are those idiots in financial aid treatin' you right yet?"

"You don't wanna hear the half of it," Terence said, waving his hand dismissively. He tried to avoid the subject of Ms. Simmons around Lisa as much as possible. There were aspects of that relationship that he would be taking to his grave. "I'm workin' on it. They harassing me about not being able to register next year if I don't get this bill paid up once and for all. I got a small advance from Technotronics, plus Jerry Wallace, my mentor there, called Ms. Simmons on my behalf, you know, assuring her that I will have the money to pay off my bills once I start working for them full-time. So financial aid's backed off a little, but they're still coming down on me." Terence knew Ms. Simmons' promises to cut him some slack could be trusted about as far as he could throw her, but he didn't feel like dwelling on that right now.

Lisa screwed her face into a frustrated frown. Her full-ride scholarship had inoculated her against the vagaries of the financial aid office, and even after four years Terence understood why she couldn't relate to that special brand of misery. "I don't understand, Terence. Don't they know you have a Pell Grant that's supposed to cover all your tuition? Why do you keep coming up short?"

"Well, every year it's somethin'. This year the story was that I filed some forms after the deadline, meaning my grant was reduced fifteen percent, leaving lil' ol' me to make up the shortfall. And you know how the story goes; they never have to register me again, as long I have an overdue balance."

"I guess you owe Ms. Simmons a little gratitude for not throwing you overboard, but you need to set her straight."

Terence tried to choose his words carefully. "Well, she and I had a long talk about her attitude toward me a few months ago. She agreed to stop meddlin' and just mind the store. Since then, the only communication I get from her is my monthly statement, along with some ominous handwritten notes." *And you'll never know exactly what she asks for in return,* he thought.

Chuckling to herself, Lisa sprang to her feet, facing Terence head on. "That lady is a character. No wonder she's been knocked out by more Highland parents than anyone can count."

"The only question is who will knock her out next, not if or when," Terence replied, his eyes caught deep in Lisa's. He had promised himself he would not let her have him so easily.

Interrupting their flow, the shrill purr of the phone demanded his attention. Reluctantly, he tore his eyes from Lisa and jumped over the bed, landing at his desk. As he pulled the phone to his ear, he bit his lower lip, aware of who the caller was even before hearing his voice.

"This is Terence."

"T, whaz up, nigga? This Biggie!"

"Biggie, what's happenin'?" Terence acknowledged his brother with a defeated sigh, sinking into the black leather chair at his desk while rolling his eyes at Lisa. He had never hidden his feelings for Biggie from her. He had only recently stopped trying to be his brother's savior.

"Nuttin' much, dog. Just figured it was time for my monthly check-in with my big bro. You know, a brother needs a good role model these days," Biggie said, snickering.

Wiping his hand over his face, Terence dispensed with the inane jokes. "How is the baby doing? That's what I wanna know."

There was a momentary pause on the line. "The baby, nigga, is just fine. You need to stop by Adrian's house and see her again sometime, she lookin' just like me, dog, though I'm still partial to my little Dwayne."

"They're both your children, Biggie, they deserve equal treatment." It disgusted Terence sometimes that although he knew he himself was not ready to bring a child into the world, his irresponsible little brother had already taken that liberty twice.

"I know, I know, but I be seein' Dwayne's momma more often than Adrian. She don't be talkin' all that crazy mess about committin' to a relationship, settlin' down, you know? I can just kick it with her. Hell, she done already had kids by two other Negroes since me."

Terence looked at Lisa and rolled his eyes. "Whatever."

"Hey, look," Biggie said, "you still involved with that Ellis Center, man? I ain't tryin' to freak you out, but I been hearin' Nico Lane and 'em want it shut down. I heard anybody who tries to get in their way's gonna get a cap busted in their ass. You know what I'm sayin'?"

"Nico Lane? Biggie, are you working for that fool again?"

"A brother do what he gotta do. Don't worry about it. You just watch your ass."

Terence bit his lip. Biggie was out of his mind, talking stuff about Ellis. The center might not be popular among the local dealers and gangbangers, but they knew Ellis couldn't keep all the kids from their grasp. Biggie was probably high, spewing a bunch of marijuana-aided nonsense. Unable to bear his brother's annoyance any longer, Terence cleared his throat. "I'm gonna have to check you later, man. I got company."

"Company?" He could hear the start of hiccupping laughter in Biggie's voice. "You can't say who it is, can you, nigga? Well, let me see . . . if it was a bro, ya'd just say so, and if it was a new honey you'd probably fess up on that, but that would never happen. No, my bleedin' heart, do-good bro has eyes for only one lady. You got that trick Lisa up in there, right? Just how many other brothers is she gonna have to do before you give up on her?"

"Dammit, Biggie, you had to go there!" Terence stomped his feet as the rage he had fought to hold back finally unleashed itself. "Don't you *ever* disrespect Lisa or any other woman in my life like that again, do you understand? Now get off my damn phone. I said I'd call you back." *Punk-ass drug dealer,* Terence fumed, *who does he think he is, talkin' to me like that?*

Laughing hysterically, Biggie adopted a mock tone of obedience. "I'll leave you kids alone now, Terry. Remember to put that jimmy hat on tonight! Wouldn't want to ruin that sterling future career of yours! Later, nigga!"

His eyes still burning with rage and exasperation, Terence punched the flash button. Dammit, why couldn't he have some supportive family other than Granny, families like Brandon and Larry's? Brandon's brothers were like his hanging partners, and his parents were his trusted friends. Larry's parents had helped plan every aspect of his life, and his father had provided him with every advantage possible. And what did Terence have in his family?

A mother who had damn near dropped off the face of the earth.

A father he had only met once, when Tony made a desperate visit to his elementary school playground and interrupted Terence's playtime with friends. He'd choked out something about how Terence was "his boy" and roughhoused with him for a few minutes before stuffing a Rawlings cowhide football into his arms. Terence had grinned wide, until he'd realized his father was trudging off toward a police cruiser parked nearby. He never saw

Tony again, but he still had that football. Terence's brain ached with the question that haunted him every few months. *What did I do?*

As Lisa walked toward him, he trained his boiling eyes her way. He didn't feel like talking about Biggie or his parents right now, least of all to her. "Don't ask."

Her eyes full of what looked like sympathy, Lisa placed her arms around his waist. Terence realized she had started up the Isley Brothers CD; Ron Isley's soaring falsetto filled the room. The song was "Let Me Cry," but Terence didn't exactly feel like crying right now. As Lisa bore her soft, warm body into his, he could smell the Rapture perfume that he'd purchased for her a few months back. He wondered if she had worn this scent on purpose today, planning to win him over. Before long, such suspicions were far from him. Everything was familiar again—the curve of her fleshy lips, the peachy smell of her hair, even the warm heave of her bosom against his aching midsection. As he surrendered to the call of his body, he made one self-defensive statement, hoping to protect his ego.

"You realize this don't necessarily mean anything?"

The flame in Lisa's eyes told him his plea was falling on deaf ears. "I know."

11

CLASH OF THE TITANS

Nico Lane opened the back door of his Mercedes and flashed a calm smile at the dumpy white man waiting at the curb. "Mr. Hollings, please join me. There's plenty of room."

From his place next to Nico in the backseat of the Mercedes, Rolly Orange sucked his teeth impatiently. He wanted to get this little hobnob over ASAP. He'd told Sheryl he was going to a doctor's appointment, so he had plenty of time before he was due back at Ellis Center, but he was still uneasy. He'd driven clear across town to Anacostia, where Nico had picked him up before driving to a secluded lot behind Saint Elizabeth's Hospital. But what if one of those punk Highland kids was suspicious of him? Orange didn't like chancing these types of meetings in broad daylight. Relieved that they'd finally picked up Hollings, Orange told himself to relax. He leaned over to make eye contact with Hollings as Nico sat between them like an inconspicuous matchmaker.

"Mr. Hollings, pleasure to make your acquaintance. Nico has told me quite a bit about your, uh, abilities." Orange tried hard to keep from making eye contact with the private detective. He prayed the man would not be tempted to tell anyone a former councilman was riding around with the top dealer in Northwest D.C. "I understand you have contacts on the Highland campus, that you can keep tabs on and research the habits and patterns of some troublesome elements there."

His jaw set in resolution and his eyes staring straight ahead,

Hollings exhaled softly before responding. His breath filled the car with the smell of stale cigar smoke. "Anything, anyone you need tracked, I can do it. Nico knows my work. Who you need me to watch?"

Orange handed a thin manila envelope to Nico, who slowly slid it over to Hollings. "You'll find the names, addresses, and Social Security numbers of four men we think may get in the way of a project Nico and I are working on," Orange said. "I need you to get back to me with every important detail of their lives, things like—"

"Where they live, how often they're there, how they're doing in school, who they're screwin', what their family situations are, and what's most precious to them. I leave anything out?"

As Orange scratched his head in admiration, Nico placed a hand on each man's shoulder. "I love it when a plan comes together. Orange, Hollings here will get all the four-one-one we need. You can cease your silly little harassment of the boys for now." He turned toward Hollings and winked. "You'll get a kick out of this—Rolly here sent a threatening letter to one of these kids and has a couple other scare tactics planned. They're child's play, though. I need you to get us a real game plan."

Hollings stared ahead, his eyes impassive. "Check."

Nico smiled widely, showing all his teeth. "All right then. Rolly, get back to Ellis Center and keep finding ways to lose money. Hollings will handle the kids."

☙❧☙

It was Saturday evening, and Lawrence Whitaker, Sr., was perturbed. Fiddling with his Saks Fifth Avenue tie from the passenger seat of Larry's Lexus, he was reaming his son for rushing him. They were running late for their date with Ashley's parents.

"Sorry, Pops," Larry replied as he careened the Lexus through the crowded intersection of Pennsylvania and Twenty-first. Larry senior had been complaining since Larry picked him up from the Hyatt Regency on Capitol Hill, and it was getting old. But Larry wasn't letting Pops get to him; the Terence Trent D'Arby in his CD player was a welcome distraction. "Ashley and I have had our hands full today, between my networking meetings regarding the community center, a campaign meeting, and a ton of other deals. I gave you the wrong time for tonight's dinner."

"Never mind that now, you guys," Amy Whitaker chirped from the backseat, where she was holding a polite conversation with Ashley.

Larry stole a glance at his stepmother in the rearview mirror. His father finally had what Larry senior considered the ultimate in a trophy wife: young, nubile, and, most important, white. If Larry had seen Amy on a street, one stranger observing another, he'd have pegged her as a fashion model, or maybe a classy *Sports Illustrated* girl. With her flowing blond mane, thin lips, slight hips, and shapely breasts, she could pass for Heather Locklear. Larry had never been given a straight answer regarding her age, but he knew she couldn't be older than thirty-five, which would make her at least twelve years younger than Larry senior.

Larry had decided in recent years that Amy was a pretty good person. He supposed that was why he rarely thought of the day he first met her six years ago, when he'd accidentally walked into his father's office and found the two of them half-dressed and using his father's massive teakwood desk as a makeshift mattress. Larry hadn't exactly been surprised to catch his father in a compromising position. Even Amy's color hadn't thrown him off. He'd always figured Larry senior's preference for light-skinned sisters would eventually translate into white women.

He was surprised now at how rarely he thought of that day, or of the subsequent months during which his parents had divorced. In truth, he had never thought of his parents as having a real marriage; it had always been more like a congenial arrangement. Perhaps that was why he was able to keep from hating Amy the way he felt he should. If it hadn't been her, it would have been someone else.

As he came to an abrupt halt at a stoplight, Larry tried to escape his father's rants by bringing his stepmother into the conversation. "Amy, are you gonna take this old man around town and see the sights after dinner tonight?" He was actually happy she'd come along. He was counting on her to keep his father and Ashley's dad from making a complete mess of the evening.

"Well, Larry, you know me," Amy said, her pleasant, airy voice wafting through the car. "I have to do it up wherever I go. Your father and I have reservations for a midnight cruise tonight, and tomorrow he's taking me shopping at Hecht's and every other store of my choosing. Aren't you, dear?"

Finally taking his mind off his hundred-dollar tie, Larry senior gruffly acknowledged his wife's ribbing. "Yes, I'll be spending all of my children's inheritance on you before we're through, my love."

"All right, Pop, I wanna know the real scoop. How're my sisters doing?" They were nearing The Four Seasons now, and Larry wanted to get some real conversation in before the mutual inquisition kicked into full gear.

"Laura is just a gorgeous little angel, as far as I can see, but I'm obviously biased," Larry senior declared.

"She loves the birthday gift you got her, Larry," Amy offered. "That little rocking horse stays by her bed, and she guards it like a jealous lover. She doesn't even ride it that often, but some nights when I walk by the room, she's just sitting there on it, smacking it around, saying, 'Larry, Larry, Larry!' I asked her the other day why she likes it so much, and she giggled and said, 'Larry gave it to me.' That's all that matters to her."

Against his will, a smile of pride welled up and burst across Larry's face. Laura was probably the most confusing little person in his life. Six years earlier, his father's choice to leave his mother for a younger white woman had bordered on a criminal offense in his mind. When Larry senior called him freshman year to announce that he and Amy were expecting a child, Larry had barely registered any emotion. He had not expected to love this mixed child, had figured it would only be a tangible reminder to his mother of the rejection she had suffered.

Then he had seen little Laura during his spring break, just a month after she was born. He still remembered her new-baby smell, her unjudging, trusting eyes, and her crinkly little smile.

They had been soul mates instantly. Even now, as her features were taking a more pronounced shape, her resemblance to Amy becoming clearer every day despite her swarthy complexion, Larry could look at Laura and judge her as his baby sister, and that alone. She could make him forget the realities of racism, the delicate difficulties inherent in interracial dating, and his mother's challenging new life as a single woman.

"What about my other sister?" He hadn't heard from Vera since she had written him from Kiev almost three months ago. He was always promising to write her more often, but the hectic pace of his life these days just wasn't allowing much time.

"She called the other day for money, which I didn't think she was allowed to do." Larry senior wore a quizzical look on his face. "I think she's homesick but too proud to admit it. Fortunately she'll be back in the States in a couple more months. I don't know how my child wound up over behind the Iron Curtain, trying to tell people about *God*. She sure didn't get that idea from *me*. My parents sheltered us from religion, until we were old enough to make rational decisions about which one to follow."

"Oh? And which one have you chosen, Dad?" Larry had heard this bull before. His father liked to brag about how enlightened he was for never following any one religion, unlike the sheep who sat in churches Sunday after Sunday as a simple matter of habit. Larry didn't happen to think this was anything to brag about. As far as he was concerned, both he and his parents were happy heathens, too shallow to be concerned with what would happen after life on earth.

Larry senior coughed into his hand and reached for a handkerchief before responding. "Well, smart-ass, I have decided that I'm not up to par for any of the organized religions, how's that? No one can do the things I've done in the business world and truly follow the tenets of the Bible, Koran, or that crazy concoction those Jehovah's Witnesses use."

"Leopard never changes his spots, right, Pops?" Father and son laughed boisterously, slapping hands loudly as Amy and Ashley looked on in amusement.

"Aren't they just adorable?" Ashley said to Amy. "Things

rarely get this animated around the Blasingame household, even on family vacations." A tone of slight concern seeped into her voice. "I hope they tone it down some when we get to The Four Seasons. I don't know if my parents could handle this much irreverence."

Looking out the window, Amy smiled widely. "Well, we're here now, hon, don't worry. My husband is a master chameleon, and your boyfriend didn't fall far from the tree."

Five minutes later, the foursome emerged from the glass elevator and stepped into the lobby of The Four Seasons' penthouse floor. Near the elevator stood a tall, high-yellow man in a pepper gray worsted suit and a short, almond-skinned woman holding his hand.

"We are so glad to see you," Bartholemew Blasingame intoned smoothly.

"Larry Whitaker, Bart. Pleasure to meet you." Larry senior snapped out of his Midwestern ethnic vernacular and into the official business tone that he reserved for whites and his more stuffy black business contacts. "This is my wife, Amy." From her position cradled under Larry Senior's right arm, Amy extended a hand to Mrs. Blasingame.

"You must be Bonita. It's so nice to finally meet you after hearing so many great things about you and your daughter," Amy said.

Cracking a guarded smile, Bonita Blasingame took Amy's hand but made immediate eye contact with Larry. "I knew my little girl had good taste. You are a *handsome* young man."

As Mrs. Blasingame grabbed Ashley's hand and pulled her out in front of the party, Larry trailed behind his father and Bart. He was accustomed to flattery, but Bonita's tone rattled him. She had spoken without the sparkling touch of humor that usually went with such a remark. Instead she sounded oddly passive, almost as if she were sizing up an attractive car instead of a person.

The party engaged in small talk as they took their seats at a round table near the center of the club's ornate dining room, which was decorated with antique furniture and art. A stuffy senior waiter with a hangdog expression took their orders from menus with no prices listed on them, and then the men were ready to begin battle. Cupping his silver-handled pipe in his right hand, Blasingame crossed his legs and began the oral exercise. "So, Larry, how is business?"

Enjoying a chance to lay out his accomplishments, Larry senior let loose with an anecdote-filled, irreverent summary of the odyssey of his businesses, pausing long enough to allow fluff questions from Ashley and Bonita. Having heard his father's self-congratulatory tales more times than he could count, Larry tuned out by honing in on the soft sounds of the jazz quintet in the far corner. The harpist was especially talented.

Several long minutes later, Larry senior concluded, "Anyway, I figure when you've got profit margins as fat as mine, strong cash flow, and well-managed debt, why would I ever consider taking my company public? All that would do is open me up to the intrusions of shareholders, the SEC, and even more bankers than I have clogging my phone lines today."

Blasingame narrowed his eyes. "Exactly why are the bankers clogging your phone lines these days?"

Momentarily breaking eye contact, Larry senior leaned back in his seat slightly before continuing, his legs artfully crossed in front of him. "Ah, I'm gettin' calls from people claiming to have potential buyers for my business all the time now. They don't believe a black man can expand a multimillion-dollar business without selling out to the powers that be."

Blasingame stroked his bearded chin, making no effort to conceal skepticism. "Well, if your company is as solid as you say, with profit growth, strong cash position, and low debt, who wouldn't want to take it over? I'm working right now on a major bond offering by a Fortune 100 retail company in California. You know why they're selling some billion dollars' worth of Class C bonds right now? They're snapping up every sound, medium-sized consumer retail chain they can get their hands on, given certain criteria, of course. In fact, yours sounds like it would be an appetizing target. You say you're in grocery and electronics, right?"

"Now hold up, Chumpy." Slipping into a bit of Ebonic slang,

Larry senior leaned forward in his chair and planted an elbow on the white tablecloth. The message was clear: he was not amused. "Whitaker Holdings' businesses are not, never have been, never will be for sale! What do you think I'd do, deprive my boy here of the chance to take over his pop's company someday, and support your daughter in very comfortable fashion, I might add?"

Tipping his head to the left, Bart chuckled respectfully. "Sir, you'll have to excuse me for being a believer in the free market. If your businesses are as well managed as you claim, it seems only proper that someone with deeper pockets buy them, make you a truly wealthy man, and then expand on that foundation to build them into nationwide chains or franchises. You don't think you could take the cash windfall and start up some new businesses? Aren't you up for the challenge?"

His courage called into question, Larry senior wound around to a different tack. "You know, I think it's best we respect each other's differences, Bart. We disagree philosophically. Let's just agree we each serve a vital role in this nation's economy. I add value to consumers' lives by bringing them tangible products and services, at an efficient and affordable cost. *I* enrich people's lives. Along the way, I provide qualified individuals with stable employment, enabling them to support their families and contribute to society." He paused for dramatic effect. Larry had seen his father do this millions of times.

"You, Barty, on the other hand, serve a role by helping the rich get richer, and that's not *all* bad. You take a company selling bonds for cash to support its operations, guide it to a buyer looking for a return on investment, and take a fat fee out of the difference between the buying and selling price. Granted, you *really* add no value—the buyer and seller could interact directly if they wanted to—but you fulfill the psychological need that each has for a 'professional.' " Larry senior held up his hands and wiggled his index fingers to accentuate the sarcasm behind his remark. "All in all, I'm sure, an honorable calling in its own right."

As his father's cheesy grin clashed with Bart's stoic glare, Larry could feel his heart leap into his chest. These *were* two grown men, right? His father's skin was too damn thin sometimes.

Moving to divert attention from the damage, Amy turned to Larry. "Larry, have you told the Blasingames about your involvement with that community center? That certainly sounds like a worthwhile endeavor."

Eager to cool off the simmering egos at the table, Larry stopped pretending to eat his dinner salad. "No, I haven't had a chance to mention it to them. I don't know if Ashley already has—" The vague roll of her eyes signaled that she hadn't. What the hell was her problem? She always acted like she was too good to keep up with his Ellis Center activities. Of course she hadn't told her parents anything about it. "Well, my housemates and I are working to help keep a community center located near campus from closing. The place has a rich history of helping the local children and teens overcome the obstacles they face living in that part of town."

"You mean the obstacles they face as black folk in America." Larry senior's quip, coming from a man who didn't have a militant bone in his body, was clearly designed to scrape its way under the Blasingames' sensitive skin.

"Ah, Pop," Larry said, placing his hand on his father's shoulder, "we all have obstacles, but when you grow up in an underprivileged, crime-riddled environment like Northwest D.C., you need special help to understand all this country has to offer."

"Oh, I agree totally," Mrs. Blasingame replied in her patrician tone. "Too many people of color seem to think that a little melanin in the skin is an excuse to start crying racism. Anything that a place like that can do to keep children from developing that victim mentality is to be applauded."

The hangdog waiter arrived with the entrees, and Amy reached to continue this positive bent of the conversation. "What kind of programs does the center run, Larry?"

As the smoky smell of his charbroiled filet mignon wafted to his nostrils, Larry steeled his rumbling stomach long enough to respond. "They really have one of the most comprehensive curriculums I've ever seen. For children ages three to twelve, they have a year-round evening program that bolsters their students' daytime educations, which leave something to be desired. They offer courses in reading, spelling, mathematics, science, literature, Afrocentric history, and business and entrepreneurship."

"They're able to convey some of those concepts to children that young?" Bart Blasingame fixed Larry with a dubious glare.

"As the children get older, yes. Some of my peers in the school of business volunteer as instructors in the entrepreneurism class. This year they're teaching a class for the twelve-year-olds and one for teenagers. Each child's project is to design their own business. The best projects will be funded for actual implementation. More than a few of these students in the past have gone on to form their own companies. I met a guy at a board meeting who attended the center in the early eighties and now owns a chain of local hardware stores."

Larry senior elbowed his way back into the conversation. "That's not all, is it, son? You see, I know, 'cause Larry talked me into making the first significant private contribution the center's received in a few years. They have some summer programs that have literally kept kids out of gangs and pulled other knuckleheads out. They work with local churches, the Nation of Islam, and politicians to bring diverse resources to these kids. I'm a booster."

Halfway into a bite of his grilled salmon, Blasingame made no attempt to acknowledge Larry senior's speech. Larry shook his head as his father continued to push.

"So what do you say, Blasingame? I've already given my boy in excess of twenty thousand big ones to help save the center, now that they've lost so much public funding. Certainly a man of your means would want to show some community activism and meet my contribution level. Can I have Larry put you down for twenty thou?"

Running his fingers through his well-gelled mound of hair, Blasingame allowed a smirk to rest on his face. "Whitaker, I could write your son a check for twenty thou out of my petty-cash account right now if I wanted to. Let me suggest that you never challenge a man who has a bigger wallet than you."

"That's about all you got bigger than me," Larry heard his

father mumble under his breath. He dug his elbow into his father's fleshy side. Speaking audibly now, Larry senior leaned in toward the Blasingames. "There's no need to make this a contest, Blasingame. I just thought you'd like to show some support for your daughter and the man in her life. Forget it."

Sighing out of apparent frustration, Bart returned to his meal. "I'll have my accountant get a financial package from the center and determine if it would be a wise donation." He paused to glare at Larry before reaching for his silverware. "I'll get back to you, son." Larry decided not to hold his breath waiting on Blasingame's donation.

12

THE KID IS NOT MY SON

It was several hours after Tony Powers dropped him off, and O.J.'s massive Pioneer stereo system bubbled with the soothing sounds of the Reverend James Cleveland. From his gray plaid futon sofa, which he had set up in the middle of the floor, O.J. admired the monstrous technological wonder, which included a turntable, an equalizer, a six-disc CD player, and two speakers. He had saved and invested all through his first three years at Highland for a setup such as this. If there was one thing a man of God needed, it was a quality sound system to blast his holy harmonies.

Just above the stereo, perched on a shelf built into the wall, sat O.J.'s thirteen-inch Zenith TV. On-screen, with the sound muted, Keith Sweat was bumping and grinding his way through another video, promising the joys of the flesh. O.J. wondered when Keith's next CD would be out; he had to get that, Keith was his boy.

The phone was screaming beside him, but he couldn't decide whether to answer it or not; he was still praying for some peace after Tony's revelation about Keesa. But he knew it was time to confront her and quit running. On the sixth ring, he opted to be brave and pick it up.

"O.J.?" The husky voice was warm and familiar.

"Dad! Hey, man, what are you doing?" This was the one person who could bolster his spirits right now. Maybe the Lord had heard his prayers.

"I'm wondering if you're ready to come home for my twentieth anniversary service, that's what I'm doing. You know it's just a few weeks after your graduation."

It was hard to believe it had been twenty years since Rev. Peters, his wife, Myra, and his infant son had come to serve the Mount Moriah Baptist Church of Atlanta. He was just a couple of years out of Bible college at the time, and his qualifications had been questioned. By the third year of his reign, though, his powerful preaching, careful financial management, and active networking on behalf of the church had won him enough fans to ensure lifelong employment, the ultimate goal of many black preachers.

O.J. laughed at his father's question. "Man, you know it would take Jesus himself to come back and take me away to keep me from bein' there. Besides, if I don't make it, who'd give the keynote sermon?"

Rev. Peters laughed heartily. "I figured you were still comin', but I know things are heating up with graduation, your own ministering, and the seminary thing. Heard from any schools yet?"

"Well, they've been better, in all honesty. I got a rejection notice from Trinity Seminary on Wednesday. They trippin', man, saying my grades were questionable, and—get this—they questioned my commitment to service, you know, witnessing and outreach."

"What!" O.J.'s father sounded disgusted. "How could they question that, O.J.? You're an associate minister at a respectable church, traveling and preaching all over town. Plus you do volunteer work at that community center."

O.J. shook his head in mutual exasperation. "I don't see it, either. I guess I just gotta wait and hope that Dallas, United, or Walker comes through for me. Guess it's a case where I gotta let go and let God."

"Amen, son. God will take care of it. You know, I pray for you every day, thanking our Father for the gifts he's given you, and trusting you'll be responsible with them. Son, as you show yourself faithful to God, which I know you have, he will in fact direct all your paths. Stand on that!" The pastor was slipping into his preacher's tone.

"You betta say that, Dad." O.J. rubbed at the side of his head. "I try to remind myself that all things work together for the good of them that love the Lord. When it's time for me to attend seminary, he'll open a door." A thought pricked O.J. as the words rolled off his tongue: *Do I really buy that?*

Pastor Peters sighed in agreement. "That's faith, just like God wants, son. Never forget, I am proud of you. Your momma would be, too. Matter of fact, I believe she is. I know she hears my prayers for you. Sometimes I feel like God lets her comfort me and answer my requests in his stead. The Lord really blessed us with you."

Hesitant to touch on the subject but unable to resist his curiosity, O.J. interrupted his father. "Dad, at the anniversary celebration, will there be any recognition of, well, you know." The silence of empty air hung between them as O.J. searched for the right words.

"Son, there *will* be a speech to honor your mother's memory. I didn't even have to suggest it. Sister Parker and Deacon Smith are heading up the anniversary committee, and they pulled me aside months ago and let me know of their plans. They've even got a separate write-up for the church program, summarizing her life and accomplishments. It's taken care of. All you need to do is come with an inspired word, preach, then relax with me and enjoy the festivities."

Satisfied, O.J. relaxed fully into the futon, closing his eyes. His father updated him on the church's building-fund progress, prompting an argument about what O.J. viewed as the "stingy spirit" of most black congregations. Ever the optimist, Pastor Peters refused to join O.J.'s tirade.

"I just get tired of black folk's attitude toward preachers," O.J. insisted. "First, they want you to take some ridiculous vow of poverty, like a call to the ministry should mean you have a lower standard of living than someone 'called' to the business world, or law, or medicine. That don't make no sense. If I'm entrusted with guiding souls to Jesus, I think I'm entitled to *more* than some layman. They don't do nothing but work to support themselves and their own families."

"O.J., you and I have had this conversation many times, son," his father replied. "I felt the same way myself when I was a young preacher starting out. And it is true that some folk have unrealistic expectations of us, and are too stingy to financially support the church, but you know what? If I'm as close to God as I say I am, I should have faith that he can help overcome those obstacles for me, *in his own time,* of course."

O.J. sighed. Another argument that would get neither one of them anywhere. "All right, Dad, you always add a new perspective. God bless you, man. I'm gonna get off and let you go out and have some fun tonight."

"Son, you know I ain't had no *fun* in quite a while. Since I broke up with Sister Johnson, I haven't really met anybody I hit it off with. And I've learned the hard way the follies of shallow relationships. That's probably the only good thing about my hitting an age where lust for the flesh is starting to slacken off."

Now thoroughly uncomfortable with the subject his father had thrown on the table, O.J. rushed to close the conversation. "Well, Dad, I gotta be out."

Rev. Peters injected the standard phrase he loved to inflict on his son. "Son, remember, if you're treatin' yourself to the desire of the flesh, I at least pray that you are being *safe.* God bless."

As he hung up the phone, O.J. rose, breathing quickly. Now that he had been pumped up by his father, it was time to knock out the unpleasant task that awaited him. Pacing the floor with the long white cord of his phone trailing him, he punched in the seven digits. She better be home. He didn't feel like playing phone tag.

"Hello." The voice sounded almost angelically pure. A stranger might actually be fooled, O.J. thought.

"Keesa, this is O.J.," he said, his mouth tightening.

"Ohh! Now you can call me, huh? What happened? Did Tony Powers do just what I expected? He blabbed off to you, didn't he!"

Gritting his teeth, O.J. tried to sound light. "Keesa, a brother's been unbelievably busy lately. I don't have time to return phone calls immediately." He began pacing through the jumble of textbooks, Bible-study lessons, and party fliers that littered his floor.

Keesa wasn't sounding very peaceful. "I seem to remember telling you we needed to talk at church last week, before your punk ass ran out after service."

Throwing his arms in the air at the sound of profanity, O.J. was indignant. "See, why do you have to be like that, sister? I'm callin' you tryin' to show some respect, and you have to go and get ugly. Lord Jesus!"

"I just found out I'm two months pregnant, *Oscar*," she said, using his formal name like a deadly weapon, "and you, of all people, know I didn't get this way by myself."

"How long have you known?"

"About two weeks. I'd been late for a while, and when I started throwing up, my roommate took me to the campus health center, where I got the lovely news. *That* was why I harassed you for so long, not because I wanted your sorry tail back. You got some responsibilities to live up to."

"Okay, okay, slow your roll. Let's do some math here."

"There's no math to be done, O.J. You're the only guy I been with in the last year."

O.J. felt his voice rise to a new level. "What do you think I am, Keesa, some kind of fool? I didn't want to tread on this territory, baby, but your reputation precedes you. We only dated six months; you gonna tell me—"

"I'm gonna tell you what, nigga?"

"You're gonna tell me six months was time enough for you to run off all the other brothers used to havin' their way with you?"

For a moment O.J. thought she had hung up on him. Maybe his bold telling of the truth had intimidated her into admitting that she had no idea who the father was. Those hopes were dashed as he heard a faint, haunting laughter come through the receiver.

"Is *that* the best you can do? Mr. Preacher Man, Man of God, God's Vehicle? I've heard pimps and dealers give more sophisticated defenses than that shit! I knew you were a sorry ass, but, damn, is that really all you've got?"

Thrown off balance, O.J. fished for a way to calm her. He tried to imagine what some of his heroes in the clergy or the gospel-music industry would do. He had heard plenty of horrid tales from Grier and other ministers in both D.C. and Atlanta, men who had weathered storms that resulted from their voracious appetites for women. Back-door payoffs, offers of employment, scholarships to attend school, even luxury apartments complete with a monthly allowance—all these had been used by ministers he knew to pacify pregnant or spurned lovers. It was time to come up with his own bag of tricks.

"Keesa, you're a sophomore this year, right?" O.J. paused as a loud bang shook his window. He assured himself it was someone's car backfiring; there hadn't been a shooting on this block for almost six months.

Keesa's tone was dismissive. "What's it matter?"

Assuming that meant his guess was correct, O.J. pressed forward. "I realize that if you have this baby, whoever it is, you're going to want to do your best to complete school in a timely fashion. You're working a couple of jobs and going part time to UDC, you're gonna need some help."

"Is there an offer on the table?" The bile in her voice was starting to intimidate him.

"I know one of the trustees at the church is the comptroller of UDC, Harvey Benton. I bet I could place a good word with him to push you as a top candidate for a full scholarship next year. Your grades have been pretty good."

"Oh, really now?" She was beginning to sound interested.

"If I could deliver on that, Keesa, would you be willing to let the issue of paternity lay?"

"Could I put your name on the birth certificate?"

Stifling a laugh, O.J. tried to making his tone genuine and soothing. "Now, what purpose would that serve, Keesa? I can't be identified as the father of an illegitimate child. I've got a pastoral career to build."

"Oh, please, I know plenty of well-established ministers with a walk-in closet full of skeletons!"

O.J. clenched his jaw and extended a finger heavenward. "You're right, but you must understand, I'm at a tender point in my development. The very accusation of immorality could keep some ministers from inviting me to preach at their churches or take part in their seminars and conferences. Those types of events are a major source of income."

"Look, Rev, I'm sorry to be screwin' up your business, but that don't mean jack to me. If I can't claim a father for this baby, no other payoff is gonna do. You know how screwed up it was for me, growing up with my momma's name? Made me feel like the man who could make me wouldn't claim me. I won't have that happen to my child. It's *my* fault I'm in this situation, not this baby's."

Pursing his lips and pulling on his ear to relieve the tension building inside, O.J. made one more lap around his room. "Well, I've offered all I can, Keesa. You always knew we weren't serious; we had the understanding it was not exclusive. I pray you make a mature decision about this. I'll be here when you're ready to agree to my terms."

"Well, don't hold your breath, you phony, hypocritical, no-good—"

O.J. slammed the receiver down. Any more of that woman and he'd have to let Satan have his way with him.

Hurling himself onto his futon and loosening his tie, he turned his eyes toward the clock at his bedside. Eight-thirty Saturday evening. He decided to take a catnap, trusting that could help relieve some of the stress. He expected calls from Carla Grier, the pastor's daughter, as well as Angela and Sylka tonight—not to mention the possibility of his new friend Michelle. Sighing, he stared at the ceiling. It was time to decide which one to spend the evening with. He didn't have the energy to go creepin' tonight.

13

GOOD MEN ALWAYS LOSE

As Sunday-morning worship was wrapping up at Mount Zion AME Church, Brandon stood in the crowd near the back of the sanctuary, shaking hands with Dr. Adam Brinks.

"Thanks again for your cooperation, Doctor. Ellis Center will be more than grateful to utilize your services."

"It's not a problem, son. I've performed free physicals at my daughters' schools for years, so why not donate that service to a place like Ellis?" Brinks eyed his wife and two young daughters. Brandon could tell the girls were growing restless, ready to get out of their Sunday dresses and into their playthings. "Well, my little ones are giving me the evil eye; I better run. Give me an update when you know the dates they want me there, and make sure to have your daddy call me! We Highland alums don't stay in touch like we should!"

"I'll do that, sir," Brandon said as the portly physician turned the corner of his pew. A Highland graduate who had studied alongside Dr. Bailey in many science classes, Brinks had been the first person to invite Brandon to Mount Zion AME. Brandon had eventually joined under Watchcare, meaning he was a temporary member until he moved out of D.C. Their conversation this morning capped a profitable week. Counting Brinks, four influential members of Zion had agreed to provide Ellis with volunteer services, including medical, legal, and accounting help, thereby saving the center thousands of dollars in fees. Reduced operating expenses would be every bit as crucial to the Ellis Center's survival as fund-raising.

Satisfied that he was accomplishing his objectives for the center, he scanned the oak-paneled sanctuary for a sign of his cousin Bobby. He spied him directly in front of the pulpit, in the midst of a small group of Highland students. Bobby was talking with Kelly Grant, another friend and member of the Disciples of Christ. A short and shapely sister with a deep almond brown complexion, Kelly cut a pleasing image that snagged Brandon's eye, almost making him forget they hadn't talked regularly for several weeks now. For a moment, he regretted telling Kelly that their relationship was over, after she'd finally admitted that she'd never let him out of her friend zone. Maybe it was time to rekindle what had once been his best friendship with a Highland woman.

Then he noticed Kelly's companion, a tall, lightly muscled man with a well-groomed beard and a close-cut fade. Brandon recognized him immediately but couldn't match a name with the face. It didn't take a genius to figure out why Kelly was with him. As his heart began a slow slide toward his bowels, he realized he may as well face the music. He couldn't wait on Bobby forever.

Striding up to the group, Brandon wore a smile that was an unspoken lie. "Good morning, saints," he greeted them warmly.

"Hey, Brandon," Kelly said, her eyes resting on his.

Straining to appear nonchalant, he observed Kelly's new hairstyle, a bob that accentuated her soft features. She'd never dolled up like this when he had taken her out. It was obvious Kelly was about to officially break his heart, and he could do nothing but stand firm and take it like a man. A good, "nice" man.

Her eyes still boring into his, Kelly placed a hand on the shoulder of her companion. "Brandon, have you met Scott?"

In a flash Brandon recognized the brother. Scott McKnight, the Highland basketball sensation who had broken the school's record for career points scored as well as rebounds in a single season. Scott McKnight, the brother he had once heard boast about having more girls on campus than any brother in the school's history. Yes, Scott McKnight, the man who had once been notorious for never stepping foot inside a church.

Now he and Brandon stood face-to-face, and there was no mistaking why. A few months ago the Highland community had been aghast when McKnight irreparably injured his knee in an intersquad game. Since that time, Brandon heard McKnight had conveniently found God and was even starting to attend some Disciples of Christ meetings. Now he was coming to church with the one good Highland woman Brandon had ever dared to pursue.

"What's up, brother?" McKnight grabbed Brandon's hand and squeezed it aggressively before Brandon could recover from his momentary trance.

"Oh, yeah, pleasure to meet you, man." He decided not to fawn over McKnight in the way he figured Bobby already had. "We're glad to have you visit, hope you come back." *Without Kelly, that is.*

"Well, I've always heard so much about Zion," Scott replied, "and when Kelly and I were talking last week, she reminded me that I've been claiming I'd visit for 'bout a month now. I figured it was time to make good on my promise."

Brandon offered up a token inquiry. "Did you enjoy the service, then?"

McKnight grinned like a kid who'd found his first candy store. "Oh, brother, it was truly a blessing. The way Pastor broke apart 1 Corinthians 12:9 was divine, wasn't it?"

Nodding absentmindedly, Brandon looked at Kelly as McKnight carried on with a heartfelt exposition of the sermon. He could see it already in her eyes, the admiration at the sound of a man waxing eloquent over Scripture. How odd; a lifetime of walking with God had not given him this skill, but McKnight had come in off the sidelines and in no time acquired the lingo and mannerisms the black church rewarded in its saints. Two more months and McKnight would have a minister's collar around his neck.

Kelly met his eyes again. "Well, we'd better get going. I have to get back and study for my Spanish final. Brandon, are you going to the Black Impact meeting this week?"

"You know I haven't been a regular attender lately." Brandon no longer cared that his tone was short.

"Well, you know you're always welcome. Stop by sometime. We should talk and catch up."

Talk to your new boyfriend, you got nothing to say to me, he thought. "You know my number. Hey, Scott, nice to meet you, bro. I'll see you guys around." Shaking hands with Scott and waving to Kelly, Brandon turned to pull Bobby away from a new conversation he had started with one of the assistant ministers. "Brother, some of us have to get home and take care o' business. You comin'?"

Hearing the impatience in Brandon's voice, Bobby stopped in the middle of his punch line. "You mind if I finish this sentence?"

"Meet me out front, two minutes." The words were barely out of Brandon's mouth before he turned and shot up the aisle. Seeing Kelly with her basketball beau had ruined a fine morning. Now he remembered why his love life at Highland had been so desolate. When he wasn't avoiding a white-hot sister like Monica Simone, he was getting dissed by a "good girl" like Kelly. If he was a drinker, Brandon would have been ready for a good, stiff Scotch or two, or three. As it was, he'd have to make do by venting to Bobby. Life as a nice guy was so lame.

Minutes later, as Brandon slammed the driver's side door and turned the key in the ignition, Bobby leaned against the passenger door, looking perplexed. "Uh, Brandon, did you get anything out of the service today?"

"Why would you ask that? Of course I did. The Word went forth, the youth choir's selections were excellent, and I did get an enlightened understanding of that text from Corinthians. No complaints this way." Hoping to soothe his bruised ego, Brandon turned on his CD player, and the car filled with the bass-heavy rhythms of Commissioned. He fast-forwarded to "King of Glory."

Bobby wasn't satisfied. "So why were you lookin' constipated when you bullied me into leavin' with you?"

"Bobby, didn't you see who Kelly was with?"

Squinting and twisting his mouth into a phony frown, Bobby tapped his finger on the dashboard. "Gee, I don't know. Whatever could you mean?"

"You know darn well what I mean. The same woman who

told me that she couldn't date me because it would interfere with her 'focus on God' suddenly has time to date the Most Desirable Man on Campus."

Bobby sighed. "Maybe they're just friends. She may be taking this as an opportunity to witness to him, you know, exposing him to some good preaching."

"Please. Neither one of us is stupid enough to believe that. Even if her motives are pure, I'll lay money his aren't. I've seen it enough to know the routine of some of these brothers. When hittin' the clubs and talkin' foul to the girls on the street stops workin' for them, they put on their best sheep's clothing and cruise the churches and Christian groups. And some of these women seem to enjoy falling for it!"

Bobby shook his head. "Brandon, you've been close friends with Kelly since freshman year. There was a time when you two were joined at the hip. You gonna tell me, as well as you know her, that you'd expect her to fall for McKnight's act, if that's what it is?"

As they arrived at a red light, Brandon turned to meet his cousin's eyes squarely. "Let me state this as clearly as I can. Yes. *Hell* yes."

Shaking his head as Brandon returned his attention to the road, Bobby slapped the dashboard loudly. "Look, you ain't saying nothin' new, you know that. We figured out a while ago that sisters lie when they say they want a good man. What they want is a reformed dog, someone who they gotta tame or keep tame. So until guys like us go out and screw everything with two legs, develop a drug addiction, or join a gang, we need not apply where some sisters are concerned. "

Now Brandon was amused. "Who are you to be so hypocritical? Fool, who just called me last week crying in his soup because Jolene never even bothers to return your calls, after you poured your heart out to her last month? You didn't sound so sanctimonious then."

"I did *not* cry over Jolene," Bobby replied defensively. "I cried over Tara, a long time ago. For the record, I was hurt over what I knew to be a fact. I took that woman out, showed her a nice time, told her I was interested in being more than friends, and she said she only saw me as a 'bud.' The only problem is, now she won't have anything to do with me. When I catch her, she's always sayin' we should hang out, but she never follows through."

Brandon frowned. "It's called the brush-off, my boy. Trust me, I know it all too well."

"I know that, fool. That's why *I'm* being logical when I feel hurt over Jolene's rejection. When Kelly gave you her brush-off speech, at least she was sincere about maintaining the friendship. So you've had time to get over it. Now you gettin' all twisted up just because she shows up at church with some guy. The least you can do is wait until you see them kissin' or somethin' before you go off the deep end."

"I'm sick and tired of waiting on all these *good* women to appreciate me, Bobby. If I hear one more tired sister claim that there are no more good brothers or that all men are dogs, I don't know if I can be held responsible for my actions."

Shifting from his devil's advocate role, Bobby sighed. "I know that's the truth," he said wistfully. They rode in silence, contemplating a hard truth: too many sisters liked bad men, and there was no escaping the fact that Brandon and Bobby were good, for better or for worse.

Brandon broke the silence. "You know what I found in my old trunk the other day when I was cleaning it out?"

"You not gonna really make me guess, are you?" Bobby's voice was one big taunt.

"How about this. My freshman year I sat down and made out a list of things I planned to accomplish by the time I graduated from Highland. You wanna guess what was on said list?"

"Let's see. Graduating summa cum laude?"

"Yes, and you know I got that one down already. How about another?"

"Get accepted into a top med school?"

"Yep, and I just got my first admission letter from Duke last week, as you know. Come on, try another."

Bobby ticked numbers off on his fingers. "Brother, you had to have somethin' down there about the Disciples of Christ. We were both sold out to them back then."

"Well, it was kind of related. I had the goal of sharing my faith, witnessing, whatever you call it, to at least one hundred people. I passed that milestone last fall. Not that I've rested on my laurels since, mind you. I pray for my housemates every day."

A smirk leaped across Bobby's face. "Even O.J.?"

Brandon paused. "Even O.J."

"Well, I bet I know the fourth milestone. I don't suppose it involved a soft, warm, attractive member of the opposite sex?"

"A girlfriend. It sounds like such a childish term now. I wanted to have a relationship with a serious girlfriend by the time I graduated, hopefully someone with marriage potential."

"Well, you've passed *that* test with flying colors," Bobby replied cynically.

"Hey, nobody can say I haven't tried. That's specifically why I quit the Disciples, so I wouldn't feel pressured not to ask girls out. I'm no smooth operator, but if you count Kelly, Nikki, and Melba, I've approached several of the spiritually mature sisters I've been attracted to. Unfortunately, they never choose to reciprocate."

"You know you're preaching to the choir, right?" Bobby let loose with a deep, throaty laugh that helped lighten the melancholy they were fighting. "I've probably hit on, asked out, or harassed ten times that number of women, and what do I have to show for it? Tons of unreturned phone calls, several Let's Be Friends speeches, more than a few Fake Boyfriend stories, and a pair of pants with broken zippers from that date I had with Alisa Morgan."

"I warned you that girl was fast, man," Brandon said, chuckling. "If you'd listened to me, you wouldn't have found yourself running out of her apartment with your pants around your ankles! That was too hilarious!"

"You put yourself in that situation sometime, you won't find it so hilarious. Hell hath no fury like a woman with a frustrated love jones! That girl was ready to tear me limb from limb."

Brandon was grinning at the memory of Bobby's rendition of

the encounter. "She almost stole your born-again virginity, eh? Did you ever explain to her why you wouldn't sleep with her?"

"That was a tough one, man. At the time, I panicked. I made up a story about coming out of a recent breakup, not feeling ready, or some bull crap. But hey! I told Alisa about my faith recently. She said our talk helped her understand what happened between us, and we're cool again. I just won't be going over to her place by myself anytime soon."

"Well," Brandon said, biting his lower lip, "at least it ended with some civility. It could have been another Brandy situation."

Bobby inhaled deeply. "Come on, man, why'd you have to go there? What happened to Brandy wasn't your fault, man. Just because you slipped and—"

"Never mind," Brandon said, shaking his head. Why had he brought that up? He had to move on. "Forget it."

He whipped the Altima into the parking lot of Sarah's Soul Food Cafe, a favorite haunt of many Highland churchgoers. The recently renovated two-story structure sat on a corner lot a few blocks from campus. It was surrounded by a grove of transplanted evergreen trees that made it appear an oasis in the midst of the declining community. Most Sunday afternoons Brandon, Bobby, and some combination of their friends could be found here, downing fried okra, black-eyed peas, fried chicken or catfish, and sweet-potato pie.

The two switched over to small talk as they waited in line and paid. Bobby changed the tenor of the conversation as they took their seats. "You know, while we've been having a pity party about Christian sisters, I've been letting you off the hook, brother. What's this I hear about you being out on campus with Monica Simone yesterday?"

Popping a forkful of catfish into his mouth, Brandon began chewing and wondered if he could avoid the subject if he kept chewing indefinitely. It was so complex. Images, many of which he had confided to Bobby, flooded his brain.

Brandon had experienced two major unrequited loves at Highland. There was Kelly and then there was Monica. If Kelly had broken his heart, he'd so far denied Monica that opportunity. Where Kelly appealed to the Christian, wife-seeking male in Brandon, Monica called out to his red-blooded, hormone-driven side. He remembered the first time he saw her, freshman year, as clearly as if he had kept a Polaroid.

He and Bobby had been kicking around in the cafeteria one night with some brothers whose names they could barely remember now when she'd glided past his table. She immediately caught his eye, her jet black hair glinting in the fading sunlight. Her face, with its smooth caramel complexion and striking opal pupils, had won him over, and her trim athletic figure, replete with round, sculpted hips and a carefully restrained bosom, had held the interest.

He had told himself that night that the infatuation would end just like all the others. He had regretted not talking to her that first time and again on their next few encounters, until the failure to approach her became second nature, as involuntary as a baby's burp. Then he would spin himself into sanity with a good spiritual rationalization. By denying himself the challenge of chasing Monica, he would reason, he'd be storing up treasures in heaven, resting solely on God's intervention to hook him up with the right woman at the right time.

Monica, however, had proven to be the exception. Three years after that first night, she was still the only woman who could give him a mild heart attack; a white-hot, numbing sensation that started in his loins and sliced its way up through his stomach, into the pit of his chest. He supposed this was because he wanted her yearning for him to be comparable to his own, though he didn't really consider that possible. After their time together on the campaign trail, though, Brandon "Choirboy" Bailey was questioning three years' worth of assumptions.

Bobby cleared his throat, interrupting Brandon's reverie. "Excuse me, man, but I'm not hearin' any scoop. What up?" He hadn't touched the food on his plate yet, his curiosity displacing the hunger he had complained of moments ago.

Brandon put his fork down and folded his hands in front of

him. "Nothing to tell, B. I guess Larry called himself pulling a fast one on all his housemates, putting us all with someone who we either liked or disliked with a passion. I guess O.J. actually got the worst deal; you should have seen Sonya Loritts hanging over him, like she'd landed her a husband!"

Temporarily distracted, Bobby guffawed at the image of O.J. and Sonya. "O.J. a husband! That'll be the day!"

"Anyway, Monica surprised me. You know, she was warmer than I would have expected. She immediately struck up a conversation, asking me about my plans after graduation, talkin' about her own ambitions to go to grad school after she works in corporate America a couple years, the whole nine. We even tripped off you and Tara's friendship, but you don't wanna hear about that."

Bobby's interest was piqued. "What exactly did you two trip off of?"

"Nothin', man. She was just laughing about some of the tricks you and I used to pull back when you were tryin' to rap to Tara, that's all." Brandon decided not to mention the condescending tone Monica had used when talking about Bobby. She had made it clear, with a simple look, that she didn't think his cousin had a snowball's chance in hell of winning Tara over. But she hadn't exactly been sending Brandon the same message about his chances with her.

"So, come on, give it up," Bobby said, eyes widening. "Did you get any juicy facts? She seein' anybody right now? Is she interested in you? She saved? More importantly, she *is* a virgin, right?"

The cousins' uproarious laughter caused the nearby patrons to turn pointedly in their direction. Brandon and Bobby both had long given up on finding unplowed soil among the women of Highland.

"I don't know where she stands spiritually, man, you know I never have. I know she goes to church at Metropolitan—we talked about that some yesterday. You know, she's givin' the old standard 'I know I should go more often than I do, I need to do better' line." Brandon mimicked Monica in a falsetto.

"Like you cared. You were probably too busy trying to keep from messin' up your pants."

Fixing his cousin with an amused frown, Brandon continued. "I don't know, man, I really feel like we hit it off. I guess I had always comforted myself about her by telling myself she was some mean-spirited sex goddess who'd do nothing but bring me down spiritually. Now I feel like she's a real person, you know, with feelings and faults like everybody else. Maybe she feels she's ready for a good man in her life."

Furrowing his brow as he set down a forkful of sweet-potato pie, Bobby leaned forward, his tone growing excited. "Do you realize what you're saying? Is there an echo in this place, 'cause you sound like you've gone and found some nerve. You're gonna ask out Monica Simone!"

"What did I have to lose? None of the 'good women' want me, and who's to say Monica's bad just because she may not be at my level spiritually? I never thought I'd say it, but maybe it's time for a little missionary dating. It seems to work for the sisters in Disciples of Christ, not to mention most sisters in the church. Why shouldn't I give it a try?"

Leaning back and patting his well-fed midsection, Bobby let loose with a toothy, ear-to-ear grin. "My boy, so how you gon' do it? What creative method will you use to kick this off?"

A sheepish smirk on his face, Brandon prepared to return his tray, signaling Bobby to do likewise. "No method required this time, Hoss. I was all about carpe diem yesterday, asked her out before she knew what hit her! By the time we got done trippin' yesterday, *Monica* actually suggested next Friday. I guess there is a God. She says she's bringin' Tara and suggested I grab you. Are you down?"

Setting his tray into the metal rack near the exit door, Bobby couldn't contain his excitement, oblivious to the curious stares of the crowd. "Hooo! My boy! Of course I'll be there! I got to see this!"

Hooting and hollering like frat boys, the two stepped onto the front sidewalk and began shoving each other congenially. "You did it!" Bobby shouted. "You are *there,* man, with *Monica.*"

As he caught sight of his car, Brandon stopped and balled his fists. "What the . . ."

Something sticky and red dripped from the hood of his Altima. Brandon waved Bobby off and stepped to the windshield, where a sheet of notebook paper was jammed beneath a wiper. He snatched it up, shook off the excess ooze, which looked frighteningly like blood, and opened it. The words, scrawled in smeared pencil, made his brow grow hot with anxiety.

> Boy,
> You Ain't From Here
> You Ain't Gonna Change Here
> Leave Ellis Alone

14

CONSPIRACY

Monday afternoon, the last week of March. From the massive tinted window that stretched the length of the far wall, William "Buzz" Eldridge had a spectacular view of the Mall, the shimmering green lawns that separated the Lincoln Memorial and the U.S. Capitol.

"Damned eyeglasses aren't worth a piece of crap," the aging man rasped to the empty room. The vivid hue of the grass testified to the coming of spring, but the beauty of the sight was marred by Eldridge's blurry vision. He told himself, again, that his failing eyesight was the simple progression of age. It was not a valid measure of his ability to save his struggling business. This plan to get rid of the Ellis Center would work, clearing the way for the apartment complex he had proposed. And the erection of such a key piece of property, in a blighted area like Shaw, would finally satisfy the stingy councilmen denying him access to the riverfront project. He was going to get a piece of that if it killed him.

It was five o'clock now, and the Washington Park Hotel, which his brother-in-law Cecil had recently purchased, was still crammed full of conventioneers, lobbyists, and journalists busy schmoozing, wheeling, and dealing. A perfect time for Eldridge and the men he was meeting with to slip unnoticed into a bare conference room on the sixth floor.

Eldridge wasn't too worried about being seen with Rolly Orange, who was still as respected as a public figure with his obvious foibles could be. Hell, in a town where Marion Barry could smoke crack and emerge unscathed, Orange was a choirboy in the eyes of the local press. What filled Buzz with dread was the specter of some novice reporter from the hood spotting him meeting with the Kid, Nico Lane. If any wind of his alliance with Lane made its way to the officials administering the riverfront project, the deal would be shot and Buzz would have to close up shop. With his business just one step from bankruptcy, Buzz coveted the river-front project in the way he had once longed for a young woman's embrace. Without the millions of dollars in business his company would earn as a developer on that project, he would have no choice but to shut "his baby" down. Closing up shop was not an option. Not for a man who had worked himself to the edge of an early grave in order to leave a legacy to his four children. That was the only reason he was subjecting himself to the antics of these two black goons.

Just as he checked his watch and noted that his associates were two minutes late, several loud bangs shook the oak door of the conference room. Clenching his fists, he squared his shoulders and prepared to do battle.

Rolly Orange was waiting on the other side of the door. "Buzz, sorry to be so dramatic, but I had a reporter following me up here," he explained as Eldridge whipped the door open. His face dripping with sweat and his body emitting the strong scent of English Leather cologne, Orange rushed into the room, continuing his monologue all the while. "Little whippersnapper thought she smelled a story, probably thought I was here"—he paused to take a deep breath, his large stomach heaving—"here to meet a hooker or somethin', but I reminded her there are conference rooms on every floor of the building, and I was here for a meeting regarding a political issue. I think I charmed her into letting me be, but you can never be sure, so I didn't want to be out in that hallway too long."

"Your talent for the world of intrigue is amazing, Orange." Nico Lane, dressed in a beige designer suit and shiny leather loafers, was literally on Orange's heels. As the shorter, younger man entered the room, Eldridge and Orange both unconsciously deferred to his sniping remarks. "This is the last time we are meeting over here, do you understand? Eldridge, I thought all real estate developers knew how to organize shady meetings! What kind of fifth-grade hijinks is this? It's a wonder we didn't have a damn camera crew follow us up here!"

As Nico slammed the door shut, Eldridge's mind turned to his children. He could not disappoint them. Nico Lane was an experience to be survived and endured, not enjoyed. "Well, perhaps we should try to find a hotel or restaurant in a less public section of town."

"Hotel or restaurant my ass, Buzz! No, we'll be meeting at one of my apartments over in the hood from now on. Most reporters are too frightened to be over there in the first place, and no one else will recognize either one of you. Unbelievable!" A small vein on his right temple pumped almost imperceptibly. Nico removed his coat to reveal a well-toned physique. "What kind of world do we live in, when a crooked entrepreneur and a dirty politician can be so naïve? I should be doing this by myself." Afraid to further incur the gangster's wrath, Orange and Eldridge pretended to observe their surroundings as Lane ripped a chair out from underneath the table and deposited his five-feet-ten frame within.

From his seat at the head of the table, Eldridge took the silence as an opportunity to get down to business. "I suppose we need to update one another on the progress of our mission to close Ellis Center. Judging from my notes at our last meeting, we agreed to a three-pronged strategy. I agreed to use my contacts with local businessmen, the chamber of commerce, and Mayor Williams to get some positive word of mouth flowing about my Develcorp Living Complex. Mr. Orange outlined a plan to sabotage the center's program structure and current funds, as well as the cash streaming in from those damned college students." Eldridge trailed off as he pretended to search for a note of anything Nico had promised to do besides funding Orange's salary and living expenses. Nico had forbidden Eldridge or Orange to even mention his name in the meeting notes.

"When I have news to report about what I'm doing, you'll hear it," Lane snapped. "Right now I want to hear what you two gentlemen have accomplished these last couple of weeks." He leveled his narrow eyes in Orange's direction.

Eldridge couldn't help but pity the obese man as he wiped his brow and leaned forward in his seat. Rolly Orange had come a long way from his days running the city council. Here he was reporting to a drug dealer half his age, looking like some timid schoolchild who had lost his homework assignment.

"First, the good news. You'll both be pleased to know I am effectively in charge of all business activities of Ellis Center, after just two months. Sheryl Gibson is a tireless worker, and her lifeblood keeps the programs running, even in this tough time."

"You're gonna move me to tears with your tribute, Orange," Nico said. "Get the hell on with it."

"Well, the good news is she's the only one left on the board or in the administration who really gives a damn. Most of the administrators left when the budget cuts came down, and aside from the Highland students and the few clergy on the board, the other trustees are too caught up in their own lives, or in the past, to keep up with the finances and daily realities of runnin' the place. As a result, Sheryl has turned to me to keep the place propped up."

Eldridge frowned. "What exactly is she doing all day while you're ransacking the offices, Orange?"

"Oh, she has her hands plenty full," Orange responded. "To save money, we had to lay off several program administrators, so Sheryl spends every evening from four until eight overseeing the students and instructors in each of the four age groups. It's not uncommon for her to have to substitute-teach in some classes, because on any given night there's a volunteer who can't make it in. In the morning, she helps the kitchen prepare breakfast for the preschoolers, before she sits down to revise the budget, which changes on a daily basis. Not to mention all the fires she has to put out, dealing with impatient creditors, problem children, and, worst of all, their parents. That leaves me to pay the bills that can be paid, invest the cash, and deal with all the filings required to keep the center operating and certified."

"Responsibilities, all of which you are carefully botching?" Lane's temporarily patient tone sounded like that of a slightly irritated parent.

Orange rebelled in his own way by taking time to fill his glass with ice water from the crystal pitcher in the middle of the table. "The center is operating at a deficit. When I first came on board, monthly losses were running around three thousand dollars. This month we will record a deficit of twelve thousand plus."

"That's what we like to hear," Nico said, flashing his first smile of the meeting. "Has this information been communicated to the banks and other creditors?"

"You have to understand, Nico, I have to tread softly in my communications with outside parties. They expect me to stand up for the center, paint the best picture possible. Anything less would be a fiduciary violation and might draw suspicion. No, I've been holding off the banks, promising that our financial statements will be much more attractive once we use the new contributions we've received to pay off our overdue loans, notes payable, and vendors."

"So they can probably guess that you guys are in violation of the debt covenants underriding your credit facilities." Buzz was starting to relax now, the sordidness of the center's financial state becoming more clear in his mind.

"If they've taken Accounting 101, they can," Orange chuckled. "They take away our credit facility, they rob us of the ability to operate, they know that. There's no way we could raise enough contributions to pay off our debts *and* do all of the renovations the center desperately requires. But no bank wants to be painted as the bad guy, so they're willing to give us a little time to come up with cash to reduce our debt and meet the covenants."

"And your job is to see to it that as few contributions as possible come in. Where does that little wrinkle stand right now?" Looking as if he were ready to leap across the table if the answer didn't satisfy him, Nico bore his eyes into Orange's greasy face.

Fiddling with his hands, Orange set his jaw firmly and pushed ahead. "Everything was progressing fine until those damned college kids came aboard. Who would have thought four spoiled Highland brats would think they could single-handedly save Ellis? Neither Sheryl nor any of the other board members have raised the type of money these kids have. One of them's daddy, some businessman in Cincinnati, even made a twenty thousand dollar donation last month."

Eldridge felt his eyes bug out. He'd always known that there were wealthy, successful blacks in the country, despite the familiar, comforting negative images the media provided on a regular basis. Even so, to hear of a black man throwing down more money than he himself could spare right now made his blood boil. He had to rebuild his business; his children should never face the shame of being outdone by a minority.

Nico looked ready to come over the table. "Twenty thousand! What are you doing to flush that money down the toilet, Orange?"

Orange steeled his back and met Nico's eyes head-on. "Don't go off just yet, Nico. This Whitaker guy's donation was by far the largest. One of the other kids has been working with his father to raise money from influential alumni, and in total they've raised about ten thousand. Then there have been miscellaneous corporate, church, and Islamic donations that total another fifteen thousand or so. Counting anything that's rolled in since I prepared this report yesterday, they're probably at fifty thousand right now. Now, I admit it, that is enough to cause concern. Fifty thousand could pay off the largest outstanding vendors and one of the smaller loans. That wouldn't bring the debt covenants into compliance, but it might be enough progress to encourage the bankers to show some leniency. So I know we have to get rid of that money."

"Orange, I've had to take very few lives since I was initiated into the Rocks twelve years ago." The glint in Nico's eyes added to the chilling effect of his remark. "I've always been ambitious, aggressive, and intelligent, but never bloodthirsty, you know? Even when I tracked down that crooked Japanese lobbyist who fathered me and then tried to deny child support to my mother, I just had

Bobo give him a good ass-whippin'. If I was a monster, I'd have his neck snapped on the spot. But I felt no emotion where the man was concerned. All he did was contribute some wayward sperm; he means nothing to me. And I've always said that *when* I kill, it can only be for one of two reasons: business or love. Now, ain't no love between any of us here, so that only leaves business. You know what I'm speakin' about, Orange?"

As Buzz ran his bony fingers through his silvery hair, Orange's professionally groomed mustache began to glisten with the moisture of a thick sweat. "Nico, you act like you're talkin' to a man that's never dealt with a killer before. How do you think I kept a council seat for a decade and a half? I've wheeled and dealed with every player in this town, including some of the very gangbangers and dealers you cut your teeth under. So this intimidation act can cease right now, far as I'm concerned. What good am I gonna do you dead? You want to keep the center from infringing on your business, *let me do my job.* Otherwise you may as well just burn it down and hope no one traces the trail back to your yellow ass." Now planted firmly in his seat, Orange was almost shaking, the tone of his voice indicating he was tired of playing whipping boy.

"Gentlemen, I think we need to remove the emotion from this discussion," Buzz interjected, hoping to avoid a confrontation. "Rolly, why don't you explain how you'll dispense with that fifty thousand?"

Easing back into his seat as he continued to eye Nico, who was now feigning disinterest, Orange continued to lay out his plan. "Approximately thirty-three thousand is in a savings account at Nationwide Bank. The donors have been promised that their monies would be placed into a restricted fund limited to payment of principal and interest on the center's loans, and a second fund limited to repayment of vendor obligations. I have managed to delay the establishment of the escrow accounts for these restricted funds, arguing that we must wait as long as possible to pay any of the debts, because to do so will invite immediate scrutiny. We have to build up more contributions first."

Eldridge raised a bushy eyebrow. "Does the board have any

idea that most of the loans and credit facilities will be called within the next couple of months?"

"No clue. The official word from U.S. Bank, which holds the majority of our notes and loans payable, is that we have until September 1. That gives the board a false sense of security that they can raise considerably more money in the intervening months. In order for that angle to work, we're depending on you, Buzz."

Eldridge sighed. He had called in a big favor to his old college classmate Marvin Burns, a lending vice president at U.S. Bank. The coincidence of their friendship had been a priceless advantage when he and Nico had first discussed their interest in the center's demise. The loans were offically due on May 1, and the bank would be free to call them at their discretion as of that date. "I've got it handled. Marvin has already informed the responsible loan officer to call the loan on May 15, with only two weeks' notice. By May 1, there'll be no way they could raise the cash in time."

"And even if they did, what they thought they had will be gone, right, Orange?" Nico's ominous tone added weight to what sounded like a flippant observation.

Orange pursed his lips and reclined slightly in his chair. "I'm going to have an emergency meeting with Sheryl tomorrow and urge her to authorize the placement of the thirty-three thousand into a futures contract I've set up with our friend Tracy Spears. You know Tracy is a master of creative accounting. He'll make the money disappear in no time. Then all we do is have him explain the technicalities of futures and their high risk to Sheryl, which should thoroughly embarrass and demoralize her, ensuring her resignation. After mine, of course. Tracy will route the money back to us exactly one month later."

"I don't hear you mentioning the other thirty thousand, nor the subsequent monies that are bound to flood in," Nico said, eyeing Orange the way a teacher scrutinizes the class clown just before his biggest trick. "Finish your story, please, before I have to lose my couth."

Orange's eyes pleaded for patience. "Our fears have come true," he said, holding out open palms. "The kids have cut me off,

Nico. They came to Sheryl a couple weeks back and gave some song and dance about a joint money market account into which all their contributions go now. Now those funds can't be accessed without three signatures—mine, Sheryl's, and one of the little punks'. I'm pretty sure I can talk Sheryl into placing those in the futures fund, too, but I don't know how to get the students on board."

"I have an idea. Why not kill them? I think that would remove the issue of their approving the withdrawals." Despite the wicked smirk on Lane's face, Eldridge shuddered, certain that the suggestion wasn't just a pipe dream in Nico's mind. He was having no part of murder, he told himself. He had found the line he would not cross to shore up his business.

Seeing the increasingly pallid tone of Eldridge's skin, Nico reached out to his right, slapping the man on the back so hard that he almost jumped out of his seat. "I'm just foolin' around, Buzz. Even Rolly knows that's not how I operate. What we do is neutralize them, military-style. They are the enemy, and thanks to my friend Mr. Hollings, we do know our enemy well, don't we, Orange?"

Without answering, Orange reached into his briefcase, pulled out two thin manila folders, and slid one to each of his partners. "Everything you ever wanted to know about Brandon Bailey, Larry Whitaker, Terence Davidson, and Oscar 'O.J.' Peters. I'm not sure what else to do about them. Hollings's efforts so far have failed to scare them off. We've escalated the tone of the notes, you know, gotten real ominous about what could happen if they keep this up."

Scouring through the folders, which included a photograph and bio on each student, Nico froze as he came to Terence's. "Orange, are you trying to make my day?" Nico raised his head and met Orange's confused stare. "Terence Davidson, Biggie's older brother. I'll take care of this one. I dangle his little brother's life in front of him, he'll dance to my music. Who's next?"

Eldridge fixed his gaze on O.J.'s bio. "This Peters kid sounds like a real piece of work. I'm not exactly religious myself, but it sounds like he thinks he's some freak combination of Billy Graham and Billy Dee Williams. I don't suppose that all the women in his life are acquainted?"

"I wonder if his mentor, the great Pastor Grier at that Light of Tabernacle Church, is aware that O.J.'s messing with his own daughter?" Nico was fascinated by the details of O.J.'s life. "I can't imagine he'd be too happy to see that get out."

Apparently feeling he should contribute something, Orange continued to peruse Brandon and Larry's records. "Maybe we can throw some roadblocks in the way of the Whitaker brat by leaking damaging information about his affiliation with the center. Fear regarding his run for Highland president or his job search might make him back away. This Bailey kid, I don't know what we can dig—"

"We have enough," Nico said with a wave of the hand. "We have all we need to get to Whitaker, the sinister minister, and Terence. They fold, this Bailey dude will too."

Seeing the glee in Nico's narrow eyes, Buzz relaxed for the first time since the meeting had begun. This should be child's play, he told himself; these boys weren't ready to take on three savvy men heavy in experience with the ways of the real world. A few weeks more, and the Ellis Center would be history.

15

SPONTANEOUS SPARKS

"Did we tear that joint up or not!" It was Tuesday afternoon, and Mark was ecstatic, half an hour after his and Larry's financial-policy class had ended. Their group had completed its capstone presentation for the year. Both their classmates as well as Professor Kinsey had been knocked off their feet by the quality of their analysis.

"How'd you like Margaret Ray's attempt to trip us up with that question about debentures?" Mark was as pumped up as he had been in high school after a football or wrestling victory. "We wrecked shop up in there!"

As they walked down the sidewalk toward the headquarters of the *Highland Sentinel,* Larry sucked air through his teeth, adjusting his Ray-Bans even though he knew he didn't really need them today. The sun was fighting a losing battle with the clouds and would probably be completely submerged in minutes. "I'm as relieved as you are, boy. If we get the A Kinsey seems to be leaning toward, we are in there! We can take that as our final grade and do nothin' but show up these last five weeks. Thank God for one more load off my back."

Mark slapped his partner on the back. "And now you get another one off. You've been fretting over this interview with Sheila for nothin', man. That girl recognizes now, she's been pretty evenhanded lately with her editorials. Don't get me wrong, we both got to watch our backs in there, but I'm not expectin' any foul play, know what I mean?"

Stretching his arms heavenward to relieve the lingering tension he had built up before class, Larry slapped Mark back as they climbed the short wooden steps to the crumbling two-story brick structure. "We'll see, G. We'll see." He hoped this could be a peaceful interview. All the campaigning and glad-handing he'd done the past few days had bought him only one additional point in the poll released this morning. He needed every break he could get. This was no time to have a knock-down-drag-out with the editor of the *Sentinel*.

As they entered the cramped lobby, dimly lit by a dust-caked overhead lightbulb, Mark and Larry found themselves face-to-face with Ms. Sheila Evans herself. She was dressed in her trademark getup—a thin blue hooded sweatshirt over a white T-shirt, a pair of loose-fitting Levi's, and solid white Nike tennis shoes. Her chocolate-colored hair was pulled back into a ponytail, and she wore a flowery headband. Roughly Ashley's height, which meant she towered over Mark but still looked up to Larry, she had the long-and-lean look of a track athlete. Larry wondered again if an attractive woman might be hiding under the plain guise Sheila presented to the world. He knew a lot of sisters who had been wronged by bad brothers reacted by trying to make themselves less desirable; maybe that was her story.

"Gentlemen, you're right on time. Please follow me and we'll get this interview conducted in a timely manner." As she turned and headed toward a cubbyhole of an office in the far right corner, Mark turned to Larry and began to mock Sheila's professional tone, mouthing "follow me" and imitating her long-legged gait. Stifling a laugh, Larry gave his friend a poke in the ribs.

As Sheila climbed through the piles of books and stacks of paper that blocked her way to the rickety seat behind her desk, the men helped themselves to the two wooden chairs that faced her. "Well, let me thank you, Larry, for taking the time to do this interview. The *Sentinel* is committed to giving each candidate an opportunity to express his views in an unfiltered format."

"So why not just publish a prepared statement?" Mark insisted on playing devil's advocate.

Sheila slipped him a mild frown. "Mark, for the record, the other candidates agreed to interview on their own, without their manager present. I don't object to your presence, but if there are problems with the format, they should have been discussed before now."

Placing a hand on his partner's shoulder, Larry leaned forward, crossing his legs in front of him. It was time to be the perfect picture of restraint and manners. "Mark, I'm satisfied with the interview format. And Sheila, I do appreciate your allowing his presence. You might understand there are a few ruffled feathers in my camp after some of your recent editorials."

Sheila folded her hands together and leaned forward in her seat. "Those editorials were based on solid facts, Larry. But I'd have no problem doing the interview in front of your whole campaign team, if you wanted. Shall we proceed?"

Larry flashed a photogenic smile. "Please."

The opening questions were standard ones Larry and Mark had expected. In responding, Larry articulately laid out his platform provisions, his personal qualifications, and his vision of how Highland could progress under his administration. When Sheila raised some of the typical questions that claimed to point out holes in his dormitory revitalization plan and his alumni donation drive, he quickly refuted her points, increasing his confidence in his ability to handle those issues in the speakouts. He and Mark were feeling their oats when Sheila asked her next question.

"What can you tell me about Ellis Community Center?"

His eyes meeting Mark's momentarily, Larry searched his mind for a guess as to her motive. He had yet to make the center much of an issue in the campaign, with the exception of his pledge to make community service mandatory when he took office. What did she want to know about that for? "Uh, well, you probably know as much about it as I do, Sheila. If you're referring to my involvement there, I am an honorary board member, along with three other Highland students—"

"All of whom are your housemates, is that correct?"

"Well, yes, a couple of us have worked at the center over the years, and when the crisis regarding Ellis's funding became public, we agreed to pool our resources and work to bring in some private funding to hold off their creditors. The Ellis administration was so grateful to have some Highland support they invited us to serve on the board."

"And does your board-member status confer any special privileges?"

Now Mark was squirming in his seat, a small bead of sweat worming its way down his forehead. Larry could tell he was itching to jump in, but was grateful for his restraint. "Sheila, the center is broke. The only privilege we receive from our status is the satisfaction of contributing to a community treasure."

Sheila continued scribbling on her notepad, an engaged look on her cinnamon-brown face. "You mentioned that some of your housemates had actually volunteered at the center. Is that to say that you personally have a history of community service through Ellis?"

Larry pursed his lips, his annoyance bubbling just underneath his copper complexion. "If you're asking if I have ever volunteered directly at Ellis, the answer is no. I have faithfully contributed to their fund-raising drives every year, but their volunteer activities did not fit my schedule."

Sheila aimed a comforting smile his way, leaning back in her chair. "I understand perfectly, we all have to work around classes, extracurricular activities, et cetera. So what volunteer activities *have* you fit into your schedule over the years?"

Larry clamped his right hand on Mark's left shoulder before responding. "Sheila, I don't know that that's any of your business, and if I see this answer in print, you may have a lawsuit on your hands. Since my first year on this campus, I have been a very busy man. But I always give to the less fortunate, be it time, money, or financial expertise. Maybe, unlike certain friends of yours, I don't get involved in the easily pubbed activities like Big Brothers/Big Sisters, but, sister, I do my share." His tone was a dagger.

Springing forward from her semireclined position, Sheila met Larry's cold stare eye to eye. "Larry, I am going to take off my journalist hat right now and tell you why I'm asking these questions. You like to disparage your opponents David and Winston, and don't tell me you don't, because everybody's heard the crude jokes Mark and his cronies have made about them. But you know what they have going for them over you? They're viewed as being real, being in touch. Let's face it. You and David have a lot of friends in common, and probably a few enemies as well. But when I talk to some of these people about who they think will make the best HSA president, the name that continually comes up is not yours. The fact is, there's a view out there that you're too much of a silver spoon, with your luxury sedan, trust fund, and super-model girlfriend, to relate to the average Highland student."

"Oh no, you didn't. Why you gotta bring his woman into this?" Mark was rising out of his chair, a look of genuine betrayal on his face. "You makin' this personal now."

"You don't *really* want to make me go there, do you?" Sheila's eyes were cold steel. "Everyone knows the only way a dark-skinned girl on this campus would ever catch you *or* Larry's eye would be to get a boob job, a weave, and a visit from Michael Jackson's plastic surgeon. People *do* notice things like that, Larry."

Mark was officially through. "You unprofessional, unprincipled, bi—"

"Sit down, Mark." Larry was tiring of serving as his friend's baby-sitter. He tried to tell himself Sheila was off base. "Sheila, you're not telling me anything I don't already know. I do *not* apologize for coming from a privileged background. My personal balance sheet, as long as it is clean, is irrelevant to this campaign. And for you to bring the biases of others into this unbiased interview is complete bullshit. I'd like to see you print that!"

Wheeling forward in her seat, Sheila jumped to her feet, knocking her knees against the crowded desk. Attempting to play it off, she launched into her response. "I have enough information to prepare the interview for publication," she whispered in a taut voice, obviously struggling to maintain her composure. "I apologize for any perceived impropriety regarding my comments. They were just intended to help you understand what you're up against. As an impartial journalist, I wish you the best in your campaign."

Deciding to close things on a classy note, Larry took her extended hand, his adrenaline pumping wildly. As the two held their grip, their eyes locked defiantly. Before Larry realized it, he was staring into Sheila's dark brown pupils. What motivated this clearly intelligent woman to attack him so personally? And more disturbingly, why was he starting to wonder now more than ever what made her tick? He'd never admit it to her, but her earlier crack had been right. Sheila Evans was *not* his type.

Suddenly conscious again of where he was, thanks in part to a sudden shove from Mark, Larry averted his gaze and released Sheila's silken hand. "Good-bye, Sheila."

As he followed Mark's blazing path through the cramped quarters, Larry rubbed his neck in exhaustion.

What was that about?

∞ ∞ ∞

In the undergraduate library a few steps west of the *Highland Sentinel* building, Terence slung his backpack off and slumped into the first plastic chair at the table before him. He saw Matthew X's black briefcase in the chair across from him, so at least he knew Matthew was here in the library somewhere. They had agreed to meet tonight, to finalize some of the details of the Nation's manhood course for the upcoming year, which was based out of Ellis Center. Based on the tenets of the Fruit of Islam training utilized for the Nation's own children, the course, entering its fourth year, taught boys aged ten through eighteen the principles of manhood, using an intense physical and mental conditioning regimen. Although Sheryl Gibson was quick to concede that the course often attracted its students to membership in the Nation, she always noted that the majority of students in the class did not join the Nation or any similar organization. More important, none of the recent graduates of the program had fallen into dealing or gangbanging.

Turning toward the window of the study room, Terence saw

Sam Baker sitting out on one of the red brick benches that lined the covered walkway. His pants hanging low on his sturdy, six-foot frame, Baker was shaking his closely shaved head in animated fashion, reducing his cronies to hysterical laughter with some crack or another. Surprised to feel himself glued to the window, Terence balled his fists as the familiar memories came to him.

Sam had been the first brother at Highland that Lisa had "sampled" when she first decided she and Terence should give each other space.

"Terence," she had said, "I think I love you, but how can I be sure, when you're really the only guy I've ever been with?" Her question had knocked him off balance with force of a gale wind. They hadn't been halfway through their freshman year, but the sights of men with prettier faces, flashy wardrobes, and even flashier cars had turned Lisa's head.

Terence had initially blamed her wanderlust on her parents. Both postal workers, the Pattons had always made Terence feel self-conscious about his home environment. When he and Lisa had first decided they would attend Highland, Mrs. Patton had been improperly intrigued. "And just how are you going to put yourself through school, Terence? If you don't get a scholarship, wouldn't Highland be a little out of your grandmother's price range?"

It had been a stupid-ass question, but Mrs. Patton had known that. It was her way of sending the message that she knew her little girl could do better—marry up, so to speak. Until Terence was out of Highland and earning six figures as an engineer, he would not be good enough for their angel.

Brandon had put forth a different opinion at the time. "Man, one thing I've already realized in six months on this campus—a brother is at a disadvantage when he comes to a historically black school. All of these women here came planning to pull an Al B. Sure or a Blair Underwood who drives a Mercedes or a BMW. And if that's not what they want when they come here, it's what they want when they see that's what everyone else is after. Regular brothers like us don't have a chance."

Terence had told Brandon he was being overly pessimistic, but today he wasn't so sure. Of course there were some wonderful, genuine women at Highland, who were more interested in a man's character than his wallet, automobile, or jock size. And unlike Brandon, Terence had not been hampered by a commitment to limit himself to Christian sisters. During the monthlong stretches through the years when Lisa had broken things off to date other people, Terence had never been at a shortage for good female friends who had provided conversation, humor, and in some cases "no-strings" lovemaking. Unfortunately those friendships never blossomed beyond the platonic, at least not mutually. He always wound up back with Lisa.

Forgiving her had become an involuntary habit, but erasing the anger that welled up whenever he thought of a brother like Sam Baker helping himself to Lisa's body was an almost impossible task. Even now Terence was beset by the memory of Baker's tales freshman year of what he had done to Lisa and where, which Terence had overheard in the cafeteria. That incident had ended with him on top of Baker just outside of the cafeteria, his hands gripped tightly about the braggart's throat, after he had buffeted him with a relentless barrage of blows. By the time Terence was pulled off of Sam, word had spread. Anyone who got busy with Terence Davidson's woman had better damn well keep it to themselves.

Terence knew that was the reason the only details he had of Lisa's subsequent exploits were those she supplied herself. She never talked about the intimate details of her dates or the couple of actual relationships she'd had. She would just come slinking back, slyly inferring that no man could match what they had. And even though both his street and his book smarts told him she was not back for good, he would give in to the childlike connection he had to her and let her back in. His mother had left and never returned for him; how could he reject the one person who always came back, regardless of how much it hurt?

"T-Dog, what's up, man?" Matthew's voice snapped Terence back into reality. A fellow product of D.C.'s meaner streets,

Matthew had played basketball against Terence in both junior and senior high school, laying the groundwork for a friendship that had survived Matthew's conversion to Islam.

Terence rose from his seat and shook hands vigorously with the short, squat brother. "What up, Matt? Let's knock this business out. I'm sure we both got places we need to be."

"Can do, my brother, can do," Matthew said as he took a seat across from Terence. "I've got a summary of the funds that the Nation has designated for the manhood course next year, as per our previous conversations."

Terence took the packet of spreadsheets, skimming until he arrived at the bottom-line figures. "Twelve thousand five hundred dollars for the whole year? Matt, the total expenditures last year were almost twenty thousand. How do you think Ellis is going to make up that shortfall?"

"T, I told you that the Nation was planning to reduce funding on several projects this year in order to free up cash for our new restaurants and bookstores. Businesses can't be capitalized on a hope and a prayer."

Terence tapped his right temple with his pencil. "I understand, man, but Ellis is really under the gun. If you're going to leave 'em out there like this, what are you doing to raise some private funds for the shortfall?"

"Well, that's the good news. Our fund-raising committee is devoting some time to raising money for the manhood program at local temples, rallies, and even on some of the local college campuses."

"Well, show me the money, Matt. Sheryl Gibson and Rolly Orange are trying to determine each program's level of funding as we speak."

"Patience, man. I'll have a check for a few hundred this week, and we're hoping to raise another one to two thousand."

Terence ran a hand over the back of his smooth head. "Well, that's gonna still leave the center up a creek, but your efforts are appreciated. You'll understand if we have to scale back on the number of students next year."

"I know the realities of budget constraints, my brother. You folks do what you gotta do, we'll supply the instructors as long as you provide the location and willing students. Any other questions before I jet?"

Terence took one last flip through the papers in front of him. "Naw, we straight. Can we expect to see you and some other Nation representatives at the rededication ceremony?"

Gathering his materials, Matthew paused. "Isn't that a little premature? I thought you all still have a ways to go to meet your private-contribution goals?"

Terence beamed a broad smile. "Maybe so, but the center has until next fall for that, and nobody's lettin' up. But in the meantime, while the students are still here this spring and the debate over the center is hot, the board voted to hold this ceremony and garner some more attention. It's kind of like a rally. Positive thinking, man."

Matthew returned Terence's smile. "Well, trust the Nation will represent. We'll see you there, T. *As-salaamalaikum*, my brother."

"Hot salami bacon to you, too, Big X," Terence said. "You stay out of trouble now. I don't wanna see you walkin' around with rib juice on your lips or a loose woman under your arm." He chuckled as his friend pretended to ignore him on his way out.

Terence checked his watch, remembering he needed to meet a study group for his electrodynamics final in the engineering building. As he prepared to leave, Rory Perez appeared in the doorway.

"Terence, hey, how are you doin', man?"

"Aw, damn," Terence whispered under his breath as Perez made a beeline toward him.

"This is a great coincidence, man. You're just in time for our Young Republicans meeting. You got time to stick around for a minute?"

Licking his lips, Terence regretted the earnest conversations he had had with Perez during their early years at Highland. Living on the same dormitory floor, they had spent many slow weekend evenings arguing, and often agreeing on, issues both political

and spiritual. Like Terence, Perez was not a believer in any one religion but believed that a man's life was what he himself made it
and nothing else. In addition, they agreed that the federal government served little constructive purpose to the lives of most
Americans, other than to overtax the wealthy and kill the ambition of teenage mothers with welfare. Where they parted ways
was their beliefs about government's role in the lives of black
Americans specifically, and Terence saw no room to maneuver
in such a crucial area. "I really have to go, Rory. I got a study
group."

"Well, let me give you one of our brochures. We're kicking up
an aggressive recruitment drive right now, Terence. We're going
to show that Young Republicans can be real activists on this campus, too. In fact, we're starting out by trumpeting welfare reform
and the end of affirmative action. Heck, we've got the best example of the ills of affirmative action on this campus—all the scholarships the administration is giving out to the Caucasian students.
Now we know how all the white students at the mainstream uni-
versities feel. Discrimination based on race, regardless of whether
you're white or black, is wrong. We'd love to have you join the battle, Terence."

Leaving his backpack on the table for a moment, Terence
folded his arms and met Perez's eyes. "Rory, let me be sure I understand this. You wanna end affirmative action, right? Does that
mean you think we've arrived at a color-blind society, in which I
can go and get any job that Average White Boy can?"

Disappointed, Perez hunched his shoulders without breaking
eye contact. "Well, sure, Terence, this is America, greatest country
on the face of this earth. Look at Colin Powell, Tiger Woods, Michael Jordan, or even John H. Johnson. Black men can do anything
in this country they want!"

"So why are ninety percent of the top jobs in this country held
by white men, when they don't make up anywhere near that percentage of the total population?"

Perez twisted his mouth into an annoyed frown. "You can't
legislate who succeeds based on numbers, Terence. Have you ever

considered that white males are disproportionately at the top because they work the hardest and *are* the smartest?"

"Oh Rory! Don't go and confirm my view of Black Republicans like that! Deep down, you must believe that whites are where they are because they're superior. How else could you take up for them the way you do?"

"Terence, I'm not taking up for them, I'm just pointing out the reality—"

"Black man, I think it's time we end this conversation before I say or do something I'll regret later." Terence slung his backpack over his shoulder, patting the smaller man on the back as he made his way out. "When you get a strong enough swig of racism, you'll come around, man. Black folk have no business being Republican or Democrat. Give me a call when you ready to start up the Ebony party, then we can talk."

As Rory shook his hand, a confused look on his face, Terence let out a husky laugh and strode outside. Pulling a bag of Skittles out of his backpack, he popped a few into his mouth and tried to think good thoughts. The moody weather notwithstanding, Terence decided to enjoy himself. His ribbing of Matthew X and Perez had lifted his spirits so much that he barely registered the glowering stares of Sam Baker and crew as he passed by. He decided to enjoy their attention. They could look, but they knew better than to touch.

Unfortunately the same couldn't be said for the woman who blocked Terence's path as he neared the top of the walkway. Ms. Annabelle Simmons almost ran him over.

"Mr. Davidson." A tall woman, Ms. Simmons barely had to look up to make eye contact with Terence. Locking on to his eyes, she quickly smoothed her navy blue pantsuit. "A pleasure as always. It's good I ran into you." Her smile was radiant.

Oh God, Terence thought. He wondered if Allah, Jesus, or whoever he was got annoyed that he called on him only in desperate times.

Sidling up to him, Ms. Simmons breathed hard enough for her minty breath to fill Terence's nostrils. "We need to talk about this tuition bill of yours, Terence. I don't have the numbers in front of me, but we can't let you complete the year with such a large balance."

Terence could feel his brain bubbling. Not again. She couldn't be pulling this mess. He'd served her "the high hard one" four times in as many years at Highland. He'd never told anyone about the escapades, not that he really thought of them as an escape from anything other than poverty.

Just north of forty, Ms. Simmons kept herself in good shape with a regular aerobics and weight-training regimen. She wasn't exactly pretty, but she had a certain magnetism that was outweighed only by her sour personality. But in the heat of their trysts, she had ravaged his body with the enthusiasm of a teenage girl. Terence wasn't proud of what they'd done those times in the privacy of her Hyattsville home, but it had been those sessions and nothing else that had kept him from having classes dropped and being put out of Highland.

He had always feared what might happen if he sat out of school, even for one semester. He'd known too many others from his hood who had taken a semester off and never set foot on a college campus again. He knew sitting out was an invitation to sink back into the world of drugs and poverty he was working so hard to escape. And he was not going to fail his granny; both his mother and Biggie had already done that. That was the only thing that had kept him going every time he'd walked through Ms. Simmons's front door, spurring himself on with his personal mantra: *Can't nobody hold me down.* His desire to complete school had outweighed his discomfort with the trysts. But he'd thought he was through paying for school with his body.

"Ms. Simmons, you promised me." He paused, hearing the angry tension in his own voice.

Looking to her left and right, Ms. Simmons smiled and placed a hand on Terence's chest. "Don't stress yourself out, Terence. This is not a threat. You just go ahead and complete the school year. We'll discuss your bills . . ." She traced the outline of the buttons on his shirt. "We'll discuss your bills at the start of next year. I have a feeling one last meeting will pay you up for good. You take care, honey. Tell your granny I said hi." The inappropriate smile still plastered on her face, Ms. Simmons sashayed down the steps toward the lobby, leaving Terence rooted where he stood.

Damn! His heart beating like an insistent drum, he yanked his backpack tightly against his shoulder and propelled himself to the top of the walkway. Later for this. If that woman thought she was gonna play him like a violin, ever again, she was due for a rude awakening. He'd sooner drop out. He didn't need this.

16

HANKY-PANKY

The sun had set, and outside O.J.'s bedroom window the Tuesday-evening sky faded to black. He fingered the smooth business-sized envelope in his hand as if it were a precious ounce of gold. His heartbeat slammed against his chest. He was not one who experienced many nervous emotions, but right now he was holding in his hand a letter from the admissions office of Walker Seminary. Walker was his last real hope: the Dallas Theological rejection letter had arrived yesterday, and United was a long shot. Walker had to come through for him. He was O. J. Peters, and he was going to be a rich, famous pastor someday. He needed to have that doctor title in front of his name, if he was ever going to reach the heights of ministry. As he tore the envelope's seal with his right index finger, his desperate thoughts were interrupted by Carla Grier.

Pastor Grier's only daughter had arrived at the house just as he was checking the mailbox, and his excitement at seeing the letter had made him all but ignore her. She removed her Paul Harris blazer and sat daintily on the edge of his bed, her eyes filled with concern. "O.J., what is it?"

With this letter in his hand, he felt like a dehydrated traveler holding a full canteen. He ripped the sole sheet of paper from the envelope, and his heart thudded at the sight of the short paragraph before him. Knowing the answer already, he willed himself to read the impersonal prose:

Dear Mr. Peters, Thank you for your sincere interest in our institution. Walker Seminary is proud of its tradition of educating some of the top theological minds in the country.

"Ha! Top minds my butt," he muttered angrily. Walker had been the lowest-ranked of the schools to which he'd applied. Like a sadomasochist, he pushed through the rest of the letter.

Unfortunately, we are unable to select you for admission at this time. Please accept our best wishes in furthering your career in the ministry. God bless.

Completely unaware of Carla's presence now, he dropped the letter onto the carpet. His head was spinning. If a comparatively rinky-dink school like Walker wouldn't admit him, who would? What was the Lord up to?

"Though he slay me, I will serve him," he whispered. What Scripture reference was that? He knew it was out of Job; he had used it for a recent sermon. It sounded good, but O.J. knew he didn't believe it, not for a minute. Against his will, his head filled with memories of the day his budding faith in God died a sudden death.

He had been two weeks past his thirteenth birthday. Puberty had arrived and left its mark, spurring him to pass his first "Will you be my girlfriend" note to Maria James in English class. She had tittered loudly when she read it, and rolled her eyes as he watched her with a hopeful heart. That had been her only response; the message was clear.

He had trudged home, only to find his driveway packed with the Pintos, Buicks, Cadillacs, and Lincolns of members of his church. What are they doing here so early? he had wondered. His mother had been in the hospital again for the past few days, but his father had assured him God was going to heal her cancer. "Your mother has walked hand in hand with God, son, as have we, and God will honor that. He already told me. Anything we ask in his name, we know that we have it. Your Momma will be fine."

Back then, O.J. had taken his father's word as the gospel itself, so despite occasional sleepless nights, he'd convinced himself everything would be fine. But that day, as he saw the drive filled with cars and members going to and fro with foil-covered plates and casserole dishes, he knew something had gone terribly wrong. He had thrown his books and lunch pail to the floor and run toward that house like it was on fire. *Momma!*

Carla's voice pulled O.J. out of the stinging past. "O.J., are you okay? You're not making much sense." She had stopped by to see him on her way home from work at Coopers & Lybrand. O.J. knew that his moody reaction was probably making her feel unappreciated.

He turned to make eye contact with Carla for the first time since he'd ripped the letter open. "Nothing, Carla, nothing. I was just asking the Lord what this means, is all. These dang seminaries are playing me like Boo-Boo the fool. I guess God never said the road would be easy, did he?"

"O.J., baby, I don't understand why you would let that rattle you," Carla soothed. "Maybe it's not the Lord's will for you to attend seminary. Look at my daddy—he has a degree from a Bible college, but no highfalutin seminary degrees. Think about the people who really value those things."

O.J. leaned against his oak dresser and ran a hand over his wavy mane of tightly pressed hair. "I hear ya."

She stood and walked over to him. "Sure, other pastors and maybe some people in the professional community are impressed by letters after your name, but the *real* church folk, the ones working blue-collar jobs and paying your salary with their tithes, all they want is a good leader who can whip up some good preaching. You know I'm right, and you've got those qualities hands down."

Meeting Carla's luminous, trusting eyes, O.J. almost forgot she was three years his senior. She had been a senior at Highland when he first started attending Light of Tabernacle. As Pastor Grier slowly took O.J. under his wing, O.J. logged many hours at the Grier household. This had given him the chance to work his platonic charms on Mrs. Grier and his wordly wiles on the preacher's daughter. For once O.J. had fallen into a relationship with very little planning or scheming. A natural chemistry between him and Carla had quickly turned into something requiring physical expression. That expression first took place one late night in O.J.'s freshman dorm room, shortly after he preached his first sermon at Light.

Because Pastor Grier had been aware of O.J.'s doggish reputation, O.J. and Carla had agreed they could not carry on a formal relationship. They had to be "secret lovers," as Atlantic Starr would say. Pastor Grier may not have believed his daughter to be pure as driven snow, but he certainly would not have appreciated O.J.'s role in her defilement. Even today they were more likely to rendezvous at local hotels, fearing that her neighbors in Northeast D.C. might put out the word, or that Highland students who noticed Carla's frequent presence at O.J.'s might start wagging their tongues. That was why O.J. had been surprised to see Carla today.

Putting the letter aside, he drank in her beauty: the conservative cut of her dark brown curls, her rosy acorn complexion, her full, pouty lips. This woman was special. Most of the sisters in his life glazed over with boredom when he brought up his interest in seminary. Most just wanted to screw; it was like they could care less about his goals and ambitions. Granted, he never took the time to ask them about theirs, but that wasn't his job. The guys who wanted steady girlfriends could do all the right things and ask all the right questions; that wasn't part of O.J.'s game. O. J. Peters was about getting his first. But Carla was different. Unlike most, she wasn't just turned on by his charisma and charm; she wanted to nurture it, make him a better man.

"Carla, you don't have to play cheerleader with me. I'll be okay. This is just another sign that my career will be what I make it. It may not be God's will for me to go to seminary, or even be a preacher, but I'm a performer before I'm anything else. And ain't no better place for a performer than the black church! So that means I *will* preach, because *I* say so. Besides, it ain't like I can do much else."

Carla touched a hand to her chest. "Step away from me before the lightning strikes you, brother!" She shot him an inviting look and slid onto the plaid comforter covering his queen-sized bed.

Grinning, O.J. slid across the room and deposited himself on the bed next to her. "Sister, I've been believin' that for years, and aside from the color of my skin, do I look singed to you?" He turned toward her and cupped her smiling face in his right hand. "Carla, your father was the first to tell me—preaching is a business, just like any other. We manage people's emotions about God. Now, I believe in a higher power, always have. But I learned a long time ago there's no rhyme or reason to how he works, no clear method of living that satisfies him. My job as a preacher ain't to live a Puritan's lifestyle. I just live my life and do what comes natural. Church is showtime. The rest is real life."

Carla leaned within an inch of O.J.'s warm face. "So exactly what is your job? To just tell people what they want to hear?"

Brushing her face with his free hand, O.J. smiled. "Carla, how many pastors have been run out when they tried to break the mold, reinvent the wheel? The key to a secure ministry is keepin' your people happy. You're right about the seminary. There'll always be churches that'll take me as long as I can move 'em to jumping and shouting. And with a fine sister such as you by my side someday, there's no tellin' what I can accomplish."

A look of pleasant surprise on her face, Carla slid back from O.J., observing him as if for the first time. "What exactly are you saying, Rev. Peters?"

"Just that once I get out of Highland and get established at my daddy's church, I think we should talk about making this thing official. Maybe even take a walk down the aisle."

"Oscar Peters! Do you hear yourself?"

"Hey, I'm not talkin' about throwing out my little black book just yet, Carla, but once you and I can be free of your father's restrictions, I think we should see where this thing might lead."

Carla leaned in again and whispered into his ear. "You may not realize it, but you're not as crazy as I might have thought. Once you deal with Ms. Keesa Bishop, we can have that conversation."

The warmth that had filled O.J.'s body seeped from him like water through a hose. "What are you talkin' about?"

A knowing look in her eyes, Carla placed a finger on his lips. "You don't owe me any explanations, baby. We were never exclusive, and even my father knows of your reputation about town. Just don't play me for a fool."

"But Carla—"

"O.J., you know when it comes to you my motto is Just Be Good to Me. I don't care about your other girls, long as you treat me right when I come around. I'm just telling you not to talk about taking things to another level before you clean house. I don't even want to know the dirty details. I'll know you've reformed when the tongues stop wagging. In the meantime, though, you have my support, in every way possible."

The sensation of her tongue against his cheek silenced O.J.'s response. He swept her up and firmly set her medium-sized, hippy frame close to the headboard of the bed. A creature of habit, he instinctively groped the overhead shelf for SWV's *It's About Time* CD, which he put on with fevered speed. He knew none of the guys were home now; he had heard Brandon revving up his Altima a few minutes ago. Coko, Taj, and Lelee began to serenade them with the harmonies of "Weak," and O.J. decided to take Carla's assurances at face value and seize the moment. As they began their heated dance, he looked on the overhead shelf to check the framed picture he'd taken of his father and Pastor Grier last year. He sighed with additional pleasure as he noted that it still lay facedown; he'd knocked it over before his encounter last night with that Michelle girl.

"O.J., what are you doing? I need you ..." Carla's breathless gasp sounded like air being let out of a balloon.

Grinning as endorphins flooded his brain, O.J. hiked up Carla's skirt and positioned himself atop her. It was time to put the holy hammer down, like only he could.

17

BEAUTY AND THE SAINT

Friday night, and the jammed maze that was the streets of Georgetown was as obnoxious as ever. Weaving and bobbing through the sea of diverse students, young professionals, and hapless tourists that thronged the sidewalk leading to Gino's Pizzeria, Brandon loosely shifted his swaggering frame to and fro. The restaurant was just a few steps away, and he wanted to be a gentleman and reach the front door before Monica and Tara. Pausing to let a tight-lipped white couple in matching preppy gear make their exit, he swung around and held open the oak door. "Ladies, after you, please."

Monica was dressed in a snug knee-length denim skirt, appropriate for the spring weather that had descended on D.C., and a long-sleeved silk top that teased with the promise of her bosom. The sly smile she slipped him as she whispered a "Thanks" made him hope it was all for him.

Tara, dressed in a flattering sky blue jean outfit, followed closely behind. Her mouth was wide open as she cracked up at one of Bobby's outrageous jokes. Brandon had to admire his cousin; regardless of the results, Bobby knew how to turn on the charm.

"After you, man, you need to catch up to your date." The curl of Bobby's mouth was offset slightly by a glint of concern in his eyes. Brandon sensed Bobby was still trying to pin down what was going through his head.

When Bobby had picked him up, he'd eyed Brandon like a store owner glaring at a potential shoplifter. "Brandon, you sure you're straight? You look kinda funny. And what in God's name is that in your ear?"

Brandon had tugged at the shiny new diamond stud in his left lobe before responding with a slight drawl. He'd gotten the piercing at Crystal City Mall the day before, with some playful urging from Larry and Terence. "An impulse buy, my brother. Don't worry about me, I'm all right. Everything's cool." He'd stretched the word out like a man dreading the bartender's last call.

Bobby clearly hadn't been convinced, but he didn't push it. By the time they arrived at Monica and Tara's apartment, Brandon had steered his cousin onto a new subject. He didn't feel like telling Bobby why he was tipsy.

Now that they'd arrived at the restaurant, Brandon shot through the door and around the ladies, barreling his way through the thick crowd in the dimly lit lobby. As he made his way, he could feel edgy glances from several college-age and young-adult patrons as he went—all Anglo-Saxons of stature equal to or smaller than his. He reached the wooden lectern manned by a reed-thin blond hostess. "Ma'am, table for four please. Bailey."

Noting the shortness of her tone as she grudgingly added his name to the list, Brandon shook his head. Here he was again, giving his hard-earned dollars, or at least his parents' hard-earned dollars, to people who didn't really want to serve him in the first place.

As he wound back to join his party near the front door, he paused to consider the overwhelming calm that lay over him like a warm blanket. He hadn't expected to get so anxious about this date, had figured he'd take it in stride and not worry about the outcome. Unfortunately that had been easier said than done. Around five-thirty, two hours before Bobby was supposed to pick him up, his head had filled with the same old worries. Would he be witty enough to hold Monica's interest? Would he come off as too stiff amid the hubbub of Georgetown? Would the subject of past loves come up, revealing that he had none worth discussing—Brandy, as always, was off the table—and would that turn Monica off as quickly as he feared?

Then there had been the ultimate nightmare that kept him up the night before. He wasn't sure how many Highland guys or brothers in D.C. Monica had dated, but he knew they were lurking out there somewhere, and he didn't want to run into any of them tonight. That could only lead to trouble—verbal penis wars, perhaps, or even worse, discussions with Monica about her past lovers. Brandon really didn't think he wanted to hear about which brothers had done what in bed, who had been the best, or any other particulars. Considering his commitment to a life of celibacy until he walked the aisle, how could he compete with Don Juans who treated sex like a toy, instead of part of a lifelong commitment? No, if Monica insisted on a Mandingo who would serve her every lusty longing, they would be sorely mismatched, at least until he'd put a ring on her finger. What was the point of going out with her, then?

That puzzle had driven him to the corner store for a six-pack of Seagram's peach-wine coolers. He'd never drunk before, but his rowdy partners in high school had always mocked coolers as the drink of choice for alcoholic virgins, so he'd figured them to be a safe bet. But was it was wise to drink five of them in one hour? He wasn't so sure.

Tipsy or not, Brandon felt ready to do battle tonight. Sure, he'd been thrown off guard when he first glimpsed the earring this morning, but now he didn't really care. He viewed it as a badge of his new attitude. And he knew he was looking and smelling good; he'd bought his snappy leather vest, Colours cologne, and baggy Bachrach's slacks with Larry's help, and he liked the effect. He realized this was the first time he'd been on a date wearing anything other than Dockers and baby powder.

Back at the bar, the two couples lingered over soft drinks. A half hour later Bobby noted that several parties who had come in after them were already being seated. As was his normal custom in such situations, Bobby decided to clown.

From the bar, Brandon could hear Bobby's verbal assault on

the little white hostess. "Ma'am, we have sat by patiently and watched you seat couple after couple who came in after we did. Is this how you treat *all* your black customers? Let me see the manager!"

Five seconds later the little blonde was scrambling to gather their four menus. As she whipped her trembling, squared shoulders up the central staircase, Brandon and Monica struggled to maintain their composure. Brandon could just imagine the racial epithets the hostess was storing up for her friends that night. *Those darn niggers . . .*

"That is such a damn shame," Tara said breathlessly as she took a seat across from Bobby. "And everyone swears racism is dead. Treatment like that just makes no sense in the nineties."

"Happens every day in every part of this great nation," Bobby quipped in a disinterested tone. "Just part of the informal tax that comes with bein' black in America. All you can do is laugh and have fun with it; otherwise you lose your mind."

Enchanting Brandon with her accent, a mixture of the Bronx and Park Avenue, Monica wasn't ready to let the subject die. "Did you all hear about that lawsuit filed against the Burger Outlet over on Wisconsin Avenue?"

Brandon had heard about the incident. A Highland student had slapped a hostess there after the lady allegedly used the N-word in response to the sister's complaints about being passed over for seating. The *Sentinel* staff was covering the case closely, but most students had not found it to be shocking, given similar incidents in their own hometowns and other areas of D.C.

"Ridiculous, ain't it," Brandon said, chuckling. "I think that sister will be gettin' paid if she holds out."

"She should, if there's any truth to what she's saying," Tara replied. "Who do these *hostesses* think they are, anyway? If they were superior to anybody, they wouldn't need to be working as a name-taker in the first place, now, would they?"

As Bobby and Monica cracked up, Brandon shook his head, a lazy smile flowing across his face. "You know what, though, as my friend Rush Limbaugh would say, we all face discrimination in one setting or another, regardless of our race or sex. Old Rush could say he gets pushed back in line at some restaurants by hostesses who don't think he needs to be stuffin' his fat face. He'd probably say he deals with it without whining, which is conservatives' code word for standing up for yourself. But you know, he might have a point."

"Exactly how do you mean he might have a point?" The taunting look in Monica's eyes and the tilt of her head told Brandon he was on controversial ground. From the protection of his mildly drunken stupor, he decided this was just fine with him.

"Ah, Monica, I'm just saying that we need to spend more time changing those things we can change instead of fretting over culturally embedded racism that may never be overcome. For example, the Ellis Center that I'm working to help save." Brandon hoped he wasn't sounding too self-congratulatory. Especially after that incident with his car outside Sarah's Soul Food. He'd convinced himself the whole thing had been a prank, probably perpetrated by one of Pooh Riley's older brothers. Those little punks, all of them gangbangers, resented his attempts to help Pooh break free of their influence.

"Ellis Center makes a direct contribution to the community's welfare," he continued. "Keeping Ellis afloat means there will be more college-educated youth like us who can face racism and succeed anyway. I think that's more important than complaining about the fact that the racism is there, 'cause it sure doesn't seem to be going anywhere."

"My cousin, the wise sage." Bobby clasped his hands together in front of him, closed his eyes, and bowed his head in Brandon's direction. Tara and Monica chuckled as their waiter, a surfer-dude type, approached and took their drink and appetizer orders.

Once the appetizers came and they dug into the cheese sticks, toasted ravioli, and potato skins, Monica flashed an intrigued look at Brandon. "So, Brandon, what other suggestions have you got to save the black community from itself?"

Brandon leaned forward, taking a liberal view of the woman in front of him. Monica was every bit as beautiful as he had always idealized her to be, and there was a heat generating between them that he'd never felt with a first date. On the drive to Georgetown and during the wait at the bar, he and Monica had dispensed with a lot of the small talk that characterized most first dates. This was going all too well.

Twenty minutes later, as their pizza arrived, they were comparing their favorite music artists. "I don't care what anybody says," Brandon slurred through his wine-cooler haze, "the De-Barge family is the Jackson family with more talent and less business savvy. It's a shame, I tell you. El, Bobby, and Chico should all be major stars, not to mention Bunny, who was a hot little babe back in the day. That family's living proof that success in the music biz ain't about talent. It's about who you know, who can market you the best. It's all just one big game. And the DeBarges have always had inept management."

Monica was enjoying Brandon's embarrassing candor. "*De-Barge* is your favorite musical act of the eighties? Are you for real? All the choices you have from that era? Michael J.—who *is* whack now—Guy, New Edition, Anita Baker, Whitney Houston, Lionel Richie, Jeffrey Osborne, even James Ingram. All those choices, and the best in your book is a family of men who looked and sang like women? Nigga, please!"

The raucous laughter of his table mates would have normally embarrassed Brandon, but he was surprised to feel himself press on with a total lack of self-consciousness. "Hey, hey, I liked some of those artists, too, they were all good," he said as he slid a serving knife under a slice of deep-dish veggie for Monica, "but I'm telling you who stood out from the crowd. See, y'all laugh at a brother now, but if El had come to his senses and cut his hair and worked with Babyface in the mid-eighties, instead of recording that silly 'Who's Johnny' song, the boy would be *large* today, mark my words. He'd be Prince, without the pumps and the buttless pants. Instead he's the most underappreciated artist out there, after Howard Hewett. All it takes is one bad marketing move to tank a perfectly good career."

Enjoying Brandon's thread, Tara threw some kindling on his

fire. "You know what it was, I'll bet that nutty Jackson family shut all the DeBarges out of the business, after Janet canceled James's crazy ass!"

Appreciating her knowledge of the Jackson-DeBarge connection, Brandon howled along with the rest of the table before turning to Monica. "All right, Monica, you're last. Who shows up on your CD player most often?" Brandon wasn't sure he wanted to hear the answer. He whispered a silent prayer that there would be no mention of 2 Live Crew, H-Town, or Adina Howard.

"On the whole, I like my stuff mellow. Unless I'm out at a club hittin' the floor, give me jazz, like Jonathan Butler or Alex Bugnon, classic R&B like Luther, or some gospel like BeBe and CeCe Winans."

"G-g-gospel." Bobby chuckled the words out, a mischievious grin on his mug. "You consider BeBe and CeCe Winans gospel, huh?"

Involuntarily flaring her nostrils, Monica met Bobby's gaze. "Yeah, why wouldn't I?"

"Ohhh, nothin'." Bobby flashed another devilish grin and lifted another slice of the supreme pizza onto his plate, his eyes sending Brandon an unspoken message.

Feeling the effects of the Seagrams starting to lessen, Brandon attempted to volley a distraction. "Uh, what *other* gospel artists does everybody like?"

Her eyes flashing at Bobby's implied criticism, Monica ignored Brandon's attempted diversion. "I wanna know why I shouldn't consider BeBe and CeCe gospel artists."

Bobby, please, Brandon thought to himself, his heart beating just a tad faster. *Don't make an ass out of you and me both tonight.*

"Well, Monica," Bobby replied, putting down his pizza, "let's just say that when I can turn on a soap opera and hear an artist's songs being played while a couple makes love, that ain't gospel, baby."

Tara and Monica appeared to synchronize the crinkling of their foreheads as they considered Bobby's remark. Tara was first to speak. "How do they have any control over what show their music gets played on? Isn't the point that they're making gospel more accessible to the masses?"

Bobby leaned forward and shook his head wearily. "If gospel were any more acceptable to the masses, it would be singin' about freakin' and doin' it all night. Look, we all know that the line between gospel and secular music is in danger of being eroded. Don't get me wrong, I love me some Luther. But I love Luther because he knows what he is. Unlike a lot of jokers who want to sing 'Bump 'n' Grind' one minute and then turn around and sing with BeBe and CeCe of the Winans about 'God is Love,' give me somebody who's consistent in their message. Either you're gospel, singing for God, or you just plain secular."

"Bobby, who appointed you the judge and jury over what gospel or secular artists should be singing about?" The smile in Monica's eyes told Brandon she wasn't about to bolt from the restaurant, but it was clear she was bothered by the turn the conversation had taken.

They were in too deep now. Brandon decided he may as well jump in before he became a permanent bump on the log of this conversation. "I-I think my cousin is making the point that as serious Christians, we're a little tired of the black community's liberal mixing of secular and gospel issues. Let me give you ladies an example: when's the last time you heard of a white Christian singer like Sandy Patti performing with somebody from Bon Jovi or Van Halen? It doesn't happen. White Christian artists seem to recognize the hypocrisy inherent in performing with secular singers whose songs directly contradict a Christian message. But you can't listen to a black radio station these days without coming across a song with R. Kelly and the Winans, BeBe and CeCe and Whitney Houston, or Kirk Franklin and Salt-N-Pepa. This collaboration between those who sing about fulfilling empty desires and those who are supposed to be singin' about God infects our community, in my humble opinion." Brandon could see he was losing the ladies. Both of them had some church exposure, he knew, but they spent more time in the clubs than in God's house.

Monica confirmed his impression. "So you have a problem,

for instance, with Kirk Franklin working with Salt-N-Pepa because they sing about sex?" Brandon wondered if he was imagining the amused tone that seemed to be creeping into her voice.

Bobby nearly leaped out of his seat, intercepting the question. "Monica, it comes down to a question of deciding what Christian values are. If I base those values on the Bible, I gotta be true to what it says about sex outside of marriage. If I'm a gospel singer, taking the Word to my audience, maybe I should be *witnessing* to an artist who does nothing but sing about sex outside of marriage, but it don't seem to me I should be working with them, holding them up as a good example."

Finishing her second slice of pizza, Tara seemed fascinated. "Wait, Bobby, are you making the assumption that most single Christians aren't havin' sex? That's news to me. From what I know, those secular singers are probably no different from the man on the street who whoops it up in church on Sunday after gettin' himself some on Saturday."

It was clear Monica couldn't resist any longer. "You guys talk like any Christian who's gettin' any is the scourge of the earth. How do you justify your own sex lives?"

Clearing his throat with indignation, Bobby leveled his gaze at Monica. "I have no justification to make, at least on that point. Neither does Brandon."

"Bobby!" Brandon's desperate plea escaped before he could stop it. Damn him. Why did Bobby have to run his mouth so much? Tonight was no time to broach the subject of his virginity with the woman of his dreams. Brandon wasn't ashamed of his purity, but he knew no "active" woman would be able to deal with such a touchy issue on a first date. Now was not the time.

Seemingly oblivious to Brandon's throaty protest, Bobby continued, undeterred. "Now, I'll admit, I've tasted the fruits of passion before, back in high school. But to be honest, it caused me nothin' but heartbreak. I knew what I was doing was wrong, but for a while, I'd be lyin' not to admit it felt *good*. Only problem was, I was messin' with a girl who thought it felt even better with several other guys at school, some of them my own football teammates. By the time I'd figured out how many other guys she was seein', let's just say I was glad I used my jimmy hat!" Bobby's down-to-earth account broke the ice that had begun to form over the conversation. Brandon gladly joined in, enjoying the good laugh.

"How do you, either of you, keep from goin' back to it? I don't think I could imagine stopping, even if I tried." Tara was eager for a response from one of the rare specimens before her.

Brandon opted to sit back and let Bobby continue doing damage. He was weary from the combined effect of the coolers, his chemistry with Monica, and the careful planning he was now undertaking to end Bobby's life at the conclusion of this date. He watched Monica pay rapt attention as Bobby described his detailed methods of lust avoidance, even though she would break eye contact at times to send tempting glances Brandon's way. And while Tara was freely spilling over with examples of her own sexual history, in an effort to pick Bobby's brain for a method to his madness, Monica wasn't giving anything up about her own sex life. Brandon hoped her discretion was for his benefit. Bobby had put both of them in an uncomfortable situation.

Yes, Brandon decided, his boy had done it tonight. It was time for Bobby to meet a quick, painless end. At least the boy had already tasted the pleasures of the flesh, and Brandon imagined that a benefit of heaven would be unlimited quantities of the good stuff anyway. In the meantime, he was planning to stay around long enough to sample the delicacies on earth beforehand, preferably within the bonds of matrimony.

As Bobby and Tara continued with their verbal volleyball, Brandon brought Monica into a new conversation about some mutual friends. There would be time to cover the details of their likely opposite romantic backgrounds later.

After he murdered his cousin.

18

TELL ME HOW YOU *REALLY* FEEL

T he morning sun painted the sky above with bright hues of orange, bringing out the richness of the blue background on this April Saturday. From his Mercedes, Nico Lane spied the large white Gothic house at the opposite end of the block. Compared with the congested row houses on most of the surrounding streets, the large detached homes on Moore Street were some of the final reminders of the glory days of this besieged neighborhood. Nico realized his admiration of the house was distracting him from his purpose. He had planned to give one of his water boys the responsibility of staking out the living patterns of the Highland brats, but his curiosity had gotten the best of him.

He would be applying the pressure to Biggie's brother in the very near future— he just had to decide where. The wisest move would be to attack out of the eyesight of the other students. The fewer people who had any idea that Nico even knew Terence, the better.

In the faint light of the dawn, he saw a light come on in the large bay window of the front living room. Revving up his German machine and hurtling past the tall sycamore trees that framed the front yard of 122 Moore, Nico decided to resume his surveillance later. No need to draw unnecessary attention.

≈≈≈

Still wiping sleep out of his eyes, Larry ambled over to the black leather couch in the corner of the room. He stretched out his long legs and rested his Gucci house sandals on the Oriental rug.

"Mr. President, what's up." Brandon bounded into the room fully dressed in a Bugle Boy ensemble, his new earring sparkling in his left ear.

"Getting ready to fight the good fight, my man," Larry replied as Brandon plopped into a beanbag chair to the right of the bay window. "We finally have the first speakout Monday night, so Mark and Janis are taking me through the paces of a practice run this afternoon. Not to mention I've got to finish up my banking and insurance papers for class."

"Ashley's not helping you practice for the speakout?"

Larry turned a weary gaze toward his friend. "Brother, please, don't ask. I'm hoping that situation will take care of itself."

Raising his eyebrows at Larry's cryptic statement, Brandon greeted Terence as he entered the room sporting a Technotronics rugby shirt and a pair of cotton khakis. "Somebody's lookin' clean this morning. What's up, Holmes?"

Terence slapped his housemates two high fives. "Ready for us to take care of business with this Ellis update. I've got to meet Jerry Wallace at work to finish up this project, and then he's taking some of us interns out to an Orioles game at Camden Yards."

"Well, brother, we'll try to dispense with business efficiently so as not to keep you from your Caucasian friends," Larry taunted. "You know they gon' expect *you* to be late anyway."

As the men enjoyed their first laughs of the morning, O.J. slid across the hallway from his ground-level bedroom. "Okay, my brothers, the reverend is here. You may now begin."

Once the men completed their morning salutes, Brandon took the conversation to more somber territory. "Well, brothers, I spoke with Sheryl Gibson yesterday and got an update on Ellis Center. The next board meeting is in two weeks, April 17. By then she and Rolly Orange should be ready to discuss the investment vehicles to use for all contributions raised in the past several months. She also mentioned that she'd like us to release the funds in the separate accounts so she and Orange can place them into

the appropriate investment following the meeting. They'll be sign-
ing off on next year's budget at that time as well."

"That budget's gonna be mighty lean, won't it?" Terence
hunched forward in the loveseat adjacent to the window.

"You got that right. They'll be reducing the number of course
offerings in the after-school programs for this year, and they'll
have to accept fewer students into the manhood and entrepreneurship courses. But, as Sheryl says, it's a case of sacrificing in
the short term for the sake of the long term. If we can keep this
campaign active through fiscal year '97, they'll eventually be able
to put most of the subsequent contributions into actual programs
and course offerings."

Slowly approaching a fully awakened state, Larry frowned.
"Has anyone heard anything else regarding our suspicions of our
friend Mr. Orange?"

"I did have a talk with Pastor Grier about some of our concerns," O.J. confided. "I was as generic as I could be, you know,
fishing to see if Orange has ever been accused of financial mismanagement or extortion before. I guess I shouldn't disclose what
Grier did hint at, but let's just say it had nothing to do with money
matters."

"Oh, Lord, you can stop right now." Larry let out a frustrated
laugh. "We need some cold, hard facts. I could care less who the
brother's sleepin' with."

"I am a little concerned about Sheryl," Brandon said, rubbing
his chin. "When we met yesterday, she didn't really seem like she
was all there. I know she's got her hands full with her daughter's
pregnancy and the ton of responsibilities she's carrying, but it
seemed like there was more to it. I noticed she had a packet on her
desk from some financial adviser, guy named Tracy Spears. The
letter was saying something about his expertise in investments,
including derivatives like futures and forward contracts. What's
that sound like to you, Larry?"

"What the hell? Futures? Why would anybody at that center
be looking at speculative instruments like that? Those are for rich
folk! Did you ask her what was up with that, Brandon?"

Brandon slumped into the beanbag, a defensive look on his face. "Excuse me, brother, but she wasn't exactly offering details. I didn't see how it was my place to ask her about something among the personal items on her desk."

O.J. sided with Larry. "Well, I'm no finance expert like my boy here, but I'm concerned, too. Grier is into some futures contracts, but he keeps his investments *very* small because o' the risk. I don't know why Sheryl would be looking at that stuff. If they're even thinking of placing the donations into something like that, they're outta they minds."

Brandon sighed in frustration. "Well, I don't know what we can do when we have no proof they're looking at the futures investments. At least the separately recorded contributions, which now total sixty-two thousand, are safe."

Terence clicked his teeth together several times. "We need to make sure to get a detailed accounting of the funds administered by the center at that next board meeting. I think we should demand assurances about the investments they're considering."

"These issues are all duly noted, brothers," Brandon said. "I'll follow up with Sheryl informally this week to see what types of investments they're considering. By the way, we should commend Terence for completing the negotiations with the Nation regarding the manhood course, and O.J. has secured the commitment of four new clergy to teach Bible classes next year. These same ministers, including Pastor Grier himself, are also going to help underwrite the cost of the rededication ceremony in May. And of course, the center is staying afloat right now thanks to the generosity of the deep-pocketed family and friends of old Larry junior here."

"Not to mention the Highland alums you and your folks have been rounding up," Larry said, completing the round of back-patting. "Brandon, should we all agree to reconvene at the same time next week, to check up on the status of things? Once I get this first debate out of the way, I think I'll be better able to devote some attention to Orange's shenanigans."

The group adjourned the meeting with one united grunt. As

Brandon lunged forward from the beanbag, O.J. smiled wickedly. "So I hear the Choirboy had a big date last night?"

His eyes burning at the use of the nickname reserved for Larry and Terence's use, Brandon straightened himself up and crossed his arms. "What's this about?"

O.J. smiled. "I hit Club Ritz with my boy Preston last night. He said he saw you and Bobby with Monica Simone and Tara Lee at Gino's in Georgetown. You steppin' up in the world now, huh, boy?"

Brandon tried to hide his irritation. "I don't know what that's suppposed to mean, *Ho-J.* Bobby and I were just out with a couple female friends." Brandon felt his emotional force field go up. He was not going to let a hypocrite like O.J. get to him.

"You brothers don't really think you could hook up with those sisters, do you? Don't get me wrong, they're classy ladies and all, but everybody knows they believe in getting busy with the right guy. What would they want with you boys?" O.J.'s catty grin showed off all his yellowing teeth.

"O.J.!" Larry was wide awake now. He sensed that his friends were going to a bad place.

Brandon made direct eye contact with O.J. "O.J., we've just had a positive, productive business meeting. I got no intention of trampling on that by discussing my personal business with *you*, of all people."

"*Me?* Of all people? Boy, who died and made you Jesus? I've about had it with your self-righteous ass, Brandon. You think you slick, never really comin' out and sayin' anything to me about it, but I got your number, brother. I know some of your old cronies from that corny Disciples group, and I see how they all look at me like I'm Satan himself. Who else would they be gettin' that impression from?"

Brandon turned toward the doorway. He didn't have time for this. "O.J., most folk in the Disciples probably judge a brother by his fruits. If your fruit is funky, don't blame me."

O.J. felt his heart surge at the accusation. He was a minister; nobody had the right to come at him like that. "You know what,

Bailey, you nothin' but a nerd in saint's clothing. Let's just lay what this is about on the table. Just 'cause you've never had the balls to go out and get a taste of the good life that *most* saints experience *before* they come into the church, you think you can look down your nose at anybody who don't meet your definition of a good Christian. Why don't you just go out and get yourself some, boy? Maybe Monica will be merciful and break you off a little beginner's piece."

Before Larry or Terence could restrain him, Brandon charged toward O.J., and O.J. was suddenly reminded that Brandon had four inches and ten pounds of fat-free muscle on him. Brandon grabbed him by the collar and shoved his husky frame down onto the hardwood floor. Pinning him with his forearms and powerful thighs, Brandon was intent on making the reverend repent for his little jibe. "For once in your life, apologize for disrespecting a black woman, O.J.! Now! Maybe all the other women in your life let you treat them like trash, but you've crossed the line with me! Apologize now, you hypocrite!"

Then Brandon felt the crack of O.J.'s knee against his groin. Emitting a soprano squeak, he fell back into Terence's arms.

"Where the hell did all this come from?" Larry's face was full of confusion as he wrapped his arms around O.J.'s struggling torso.

"I was just havin' some fun with the brother, dang." O.J. was starting to calm down, playing the innocent role. He stood, straightening his shirt and trying to catch his breath.

His voice slowly returning to its normal tenor and his knees strengthening under him, Brandon wiped beads of sweat from his forehead and collapsed into the couch. "I'm sorry, brothers. Who am I kidding? O.J. knows I've never cared much for him. His presence in this house is a daily reminder of the failure of the black church."

"What?" O.J. attempted to lunge forward, but Larry still had a grip on him. "*I'm* the problem? I'm devoting my life to ministering to God's people, and *I'm* the problem with the black church?"

Remaining seated but looking ready to rumble, Brandon

wiped at his forehead. "O.J., you know the number-one reason I hear from people who don't want to have anything to do with Jesus, or any religion, for that matter? Hypocrisy! Can you think of a better example than a preacher who crows about walking like Christ, and then goes off and sleeps with half the congregation? I know there are hundreds of opinions on what Jesus was like, but I've yet to hear a claim that he was a player!"

"Damn, this is too deep for me," Larry said, releasing O.J. as the preacher stopped struggling.

Placing his hands on his hips, O.J. fixed his stare on the floor, his chest heaving. "Brandon, what business of yours is it who I see, and what I do, on my own time?"

"I don't know, O.J., I suppose it's none of my business at all. But that's easier said than done when I look at our community. You think there would be a need for a place like Ellis Center if there weren't so many kids and young adults screwin' around outside of wedlock, that we have almost a whole generation of kids now who don't even *know* their fathers? And the church is no better. You can't look down a pew at a church these days without seeing a woman who's had a child or is pregnant outside of wedlock."

"That is true, it's almost commonplace at my grandmother's church." Terence's involuntary comment surprised him almost as much as it did Brandon.

Crossing his arms, Brandon continued. "I'm not saying all teens and singles can abstain from sex, nor am I sayin' we'd be problem-free if they did. But you can't tell me it wouldn't make a hell of a difference. A child born out of wedlock, into poverty, black or white, has a much higher likelihood of winding up as a burden or danger to society. Now, we all know of plenty of exceptions, many of 'em at Highland. But the success rate isn't staggering."

"Brother, I'm not gonna argue the big picture with you." O.J. stood, his back against a wall near the entrance to the living room. The picture of Keesa loomed in his mind like a dark cloud. "But I do my best to be responsible with sex. In some ways, I was like you before women started throwing it at me left and right. Join the ministry someday, and see the way sisters parade themselves before brothers of the cloth. We're like the black community's rock stars. And you'd also find, my innocent friend, that once you taste the pleasures of the flesh, it ain't so easy to give up. When I feel I've reached a point to settle down with one woman, I will, but in the meantime I try to make sure I don't bring any children into a situation like the one you describe. Your argument falls flat with me."

"O.J.," Brandon replied, "that might be fine if you kept your business quiet and didn't hold yourself up as a paragon of virtue. How do you explain away the effect on kids and students in your congregation who look up to you, who admire your sermons and songs, and then hear that Rev. Peters gets his business on when and with whomever he wants? If even one of them decides to play around with sex as a result, you think they'll be as responsible as you? All it takes is one slipup to have an unplanned pregnancy, you know. You wouldn't at all feel guilty about that?"

O.J.'s stomach churned. "Brandon, I have ugly needs. Besides, I ain't convinced everything the Bible stipulates in that area is cast in stone. Times change, brother. Let's not forget, in Bible days they could pray for a sick loved one, and boom, Christ might raise them from the dead. When my mom had cancer back in the day, I prayed my little behind off, and she just got sicker. When she passed away, that was a big lesson for me. The Bible is a history lesson, bro, not a manual of how God expects us to live today. Why don't you judge me when you've walked a mile in my shoes?"

Wiping his eyes, Larry jumped from his seat on the floor and headed for the staircase. "I know one thing, you brothers will never solve these religious questions. Yeah, Brandon, it would be a nice world if everybody could be as good and pure as you are, and I mean that sincerely. But that's just not how it is. You ask me, I respect what both of you do as an expression of your spiritual beliefs, the people you help, the examples you set. How you live your private lives is your business. Can we all agree to squash these morality arguments, knock out our course work, and help save Ellis Center?"

As O.J. blew past Larry to return to his room, Brandon sighed. "I didn't start this little episode, but I have no right judging anyone. Jesus can help me forgive and forget. O.J., are we straight?"

"Don't sweat it!" O.J.'s halfhearted shout barely beat the sound of his door slamming shut behind him.

"Black men, I gotta go." Terence grabbed his keys and briefcase. "I have to be on the eight-fifteen bus if I'm gonna be at the office on time."

"I'll give you a ride, man, I'm heading out anyway." Brandon gathered his own items and straightened the mess he'd made.

Watching his boys leave, Larry popped a Bic pen into his mouth and began to chew it like a chicken bone as he headed down to his basement-level room. In less than seventy-two hours he would be in the midst of his biggest political battle at Highland. He had to stay focused, but the blowup he'd just witnessed was going to stick with him for a while. Couldn't four brothers unite for the good, for once, without letting their differences separate them? Somehow, he told himself, they were going to have to lay that mess aside. For Ellis and for each of them personally, the stakes were too high to do otherwise.

19

HOPE

That night, Brandon held his phone to his right ear and leaned wearily against the Fred Hammond poster near his desk, shaking his head in mock defeat. He was on the line with his folks, spilling the news about his hopeful date with Monica. He knew he should have held out longer before telling them, but even if she never went out with him again, last night had convinced him his interest was not completely one-sided. He had to share the news with somebody, but aside from his brothers and Bobby, there were only so many people who knew just how starved Brandon's love life had been in recent years. To shoot off at the mouth over one date—which hadn't even ended with a real kiss, for fear he'd have planted one on her nose by mistake—would have exposed him for the romantic novice he was. But he had to tell the folks, and the news had even overshadowed that of his admission to Duke Medical School.

The Baileys took Brandon round and round, thrilled to hear about Monica, ecstatic with pride and eager to analyze his success. "Brandon, honey," Mrs. Bailey said, "I just want to say I sure am glad you got out of that Disciples of Christ group. From what you've said, you'd never have asked this girl out when you were under its spell. I'm happy for you. Nothing's more important than thinking for yourself, even where God's concerned."

"Well, I gotta admit," Brandon said, "if my membership in the Disciples hasn't been officially revoked yet, it will be now. Oh, well!"

Dr. Bailey sniffed in what sounded like confusion. "I just don't understand how those kids got you thinking that dating is a sin, son. I mean, I believe God played a role in my meeting your mother, but he doesn't drop mates for us out of the clear blue sky. If I believed that, I'd never have gotten your mother to date me. She wouldn't give me the time of day, no matter what, but I—"

"I know, Dad," Brandon said, chuckling. "You kept trying and trying, calling and calling, until she said yes. I could tell *you* the story after all the times I've heard it."

Sounding slightly offended, Brandon's father defended himself. "Now, look, you may have heard that story and others a zillion times, but there's a reason I repeat myself, son, and it's not because I'm a couple years shy of fifty. I tell you and your brothers these things so you don't forget them, so they become so deep in your memory that you act on them without thinking. Forgive an old man if he prattles on now and then."

Brandon smiled. "I know you mean well." He leaned against his desk and waited patiently as his parents made rosy pronouncements about his potential with Monica. Don't let life pass you by, they encouraged. You are what every single black woman wants: handsome, well-educated, spiritual. Sounds like the main traits those *Ebony* bachelorettes list every year.

"The girls out there, they don't relate to a brother like me," Brandon said. "It's not the fifties anymore, folks. Girls don't respect guys who talk about God and wanna save sex for marriage. Ask Brian or Gregory," he said, reminding them of his brothers. "We ain't sittin' around being single for the heck of it."

As his parents continued their assessment of his dating life, he heard his other line and depressed the flash button. "Hello?"

The voice on the other end made his heart gallop like an overeager stud. "Hi, is Brandon in?"

"M-Monica?" He slid over to his stereo and turned down Eric Benet's *True to Myself* CD. Why was he sweating? Mopping his brow with the sleeve of his rugby, he began to pace the creaky floorboards of his room. Whoa, he thought to himself. *Chill.*

Monica's voice sounded cool and calm, the way Brandon wanted to sound around her. "Mmmm-hmmm. Thought I'd see if you really stayed home to study for that microbiology final. I thought you might just be trying to get out of a second date. You've only got a few weeks left in town, right?"

"Yeah, can you hold on a second?" Brandon clicked over and let his parents go, after giving them a few seconds to rib him about Monica's flouting of tradition. A young woman calling a man after a first date, indeed. What did she think this was, the nineties?

Brandon clicked back over. "So, Monica, what's up?"

"You tell me. You been takin' care of business with your studies?"

"You know it. I spent most of the day at the library with two study groups, histology and microbio. My brain is good and wracked, but I'll be recharged after talking with someone as stimulating as you."

"Oh, is that your version of a mack-attack line? Brandon Bailey, I didn't know you were such a sweet talker. Aren't you just full of surprises."

Brandon smiled to himself. "Ah, girl, I thought ya knew."

"Well, I'm learning. Look, would you be mad if I asked you for a quick favor?"

Brandon checked his watch. It was 11:06 on a Saturday night, and a beautiful woman was asking for a favor. Was this one of those "booty calls" Larry and Terence always joked about? "Now how could I get mad at a fine black queen such as yourself? What's up?"

Monica paused before she replied, almost sounding unsure of herself. "Well, I know it's late, but Tara and I were just sitting up saying we've got a hankering for one of Chappy's cheese steaks. We wanna go, but we know we shouldn't be out this late by ourselves. Could you meet us over there? We'd feel so honored and protected."

Something in the sound of her voice told Brandon he wasn't getting the full story. That only made him more curious. "Now, this isn't some ambush, is it? I mean, if you didn't enjoy our date last night, just tell me so. You don't have to lure me out into the hood and have me jacked up, understand. I'll just leave you alone."

Monica chuckled. "I will be there, Brandon. Come on, it'll be a chance to build on our conversation last night. Maybe even make up for the fact that you haven't called me yet."

"I said I'd call you before the weekend was over. Have you heard of Sunday?" Brandon paused as he realized he should be flattered by her impatience. "Well, anyway, never mind, I can meet you guys at Chappy's. You sure you don't want me to pick you up?"

"No, it's fine to meet us there. We're all studying over here, too, so the apartment is *not* in a shape that I would allow any guy to see it in. Are you gonna grab Bobby or one of your house-mates to come with?"

"Can't. Bobby's out of town and the housemates are busy. Larry's staying at the Hotel Ashley tonight, Terence is locked away in his room with Lisa, and Reverend Ho-J is out doing his normal thing. It's just little lonesome me here."

"Well, be safe. See you in half an hour?"

"Deal." *As soon as I down that last Seagram's cooler,* Brandon thought. A brother had to keep his cool somehow.

At quarter till midnight, Brandon cruised into the 1200 block of Alabama Avenue and whipped his Altima into a space across the street from Chappy's. The aging storefront restaurant, with its peeling exterior, was an eight-block walk from Highland's cam-pus, deep in the heart of Shaw. Like most blocks in the area, this one had seen better days. All that remained was a smattering of liquor stores, Asian-owned convenience marts, and a crowded Hardee's swarming with folks up to no good. As he turned his wheels toward the curb and reached for his Club, Brandon pre-tended to ignore the group of three older men sitting in front of the abandoned building where he had parked. He could hear their coarse language and hoarse laughs through his window as they yukked it up with passing juvenile street dealers, broke-down prostitutes, and idle observers. As Brandon climbed out of his car, his nostrils burned with the combined odors of incense, Colt 45, Red Bull, and the weed the older brothers were helping them-selves to.

As he braced against the crisp night air and waited for the stream of whizzing cars on the road to die down so he could cross over, one of the men yelled to him. "Hey, Highland man, you want some real brew? Or a toke? It's on us, young bro!"

Thankful for the safety provided by the crowded street, Brandon looked over his shoulder quickly. "Oh, no thanks, brothers." He had walked through this neighborhood plenty of times as a freshman and sophomore, when he lived on campus. He, Bobby, and assorted friends had made late-night runs to Chappy's when they'd needed a study break and some greasy food to salve their weary souls. The place had been a legendary Highland hangout since it opened its doors during Brandon's parents' sophomore year. But this was his first time journeying over here on his own. He hoped the elder brothers would leave his ride alone.

As he leaned against his car and prayed for its safety, a small boy in an L.A. Lakers jacket and ratty Wrangler jeans darted up to him. "Hey, mister, can I get a dollar? My momma is sick. She needs money to buy some medicine."

Shielding his eyes under the glare of the street lamp overhead, Brandon stepped back just far enough to get a clear look at the child. His head shaved bald and his right earlobe sporting a gold hoop earring, the boy looked to be ten or eleven years old. His pudgy face was trapped between unblemished childhood toddler and hardening adolescence. Slowly, the face became familiar to him.

"Pooh Riley, is that you, boy?" Forgetting his surroundings, Brandon dropped his guard as he recognized the child he had tutored for the past two years. "What are you doing out here at this time of night?"

Pooh sniffed and locked his eyes on Brandon's chest. He spoke in a halting but hard tone. "Uh, Mr. Brandon, I didn't know that was you. Please don't be tellin' Ms. Sheryl that I'm out here in the streets. She done told my momma to keep me inside after dark. I don't want her to get in trouble."

Glancing at the men near his car, Brandon knelt down to meet Pooh's eyes. "Pooh, what do you really need the money for?"

Pooh's eyes filled even though his mouth remained in a

straight line. "My momma tryin' to buy some booze, you know, take the edge off her pain from that surgery on her knee. If she can get to sleep, then I can sleep. I'm sorry, Mr. Brandon, but I got to get this money somehow."

Knowing there were plenty of others who would give Pooh the money for a much higher price, Brandon knelt low enough so he was out of sight of the men near his car. He placed a hand on the boy's shoulder. "Where's your house, Pooh?"

It turned out Pooh's house was three blocks away. Brandon followed the boy past several more liquor stores and a Church's Chicken. At a small grocery store he walked up to the glass-encased counter and paid for a couple of painkillers, which the elderly clerk slid through a circular opening.

When they reached the porch of Pooh's rented home, Brandon removed a twenty-dollar bill from his wallet and handed it to Pooh. "Stick this in your socks, for the next time your mother really needs you to get something. You should never go out in the streets looking for money."

Pooh wrinkled his nose. "Mr. Brandon, don't worry about me. I ain't no punk."

"I don't care if you look like a punk, I want you to be safe, little man. Now go inside and tell your mother Mr. Brandon said she should use those to relieve her pain and get some rest. Don't buy her any alcohol. She doesn't need that. Just make sure she gets that stuff and stays in the rest of the night."

Pooh put a hand on the metal doorknob. "Thanks, Mr. Brandon. I'll see you next week at Ellis, man."

"I better." As Brandon watched the door swing shut behind Pooh, he realized he had forgotten about Monica and his car. There was so much need in the life of someone like Pooh, and he wasn't equipped to deal with all of it.

Stuffing his carefully lotioned hands into the deep pockets of his Union Bay jean jacket, Brandon briskly walked the three blocks and darted back across the street. He parked himself beneath Chappy's neon sign. Half of the bulbs in the neon had burned out, meaning the sign actually read PPY'S, but any real Highland student could find Chappy's blindfolded. Carefully eyeing the snaggletoothed bag lady who stood just outside the entrance, carrying on a conversation with herself, Brandon scanned the street for a sign of Monica. He feared he had missed her when the restaurant door creaked open behind him.

"Uh, hello, Mr. Bailey. You are officially late. How you gonna leave a couple of sisters hanging like that?" Brandon turned to see Monica standing in the entryway, the door propped open. His eyes flitted over her white Nike sweatshirt and the respectably snug fit of her Levi's 501s. She had her hair pulled back into a ponytail, and her face was well scrubbed but free of makeup. On top of everything else, the woman had the nerve to be a natural beauty.

As he stepped inside, Brandon glued his eyes to hers. "You'll have to excuse me, I'm on CP time tonight. *Je suis tard.*"

Smiling at his use of French, Monica led him past the crowded tables of rowdy high school and Highland students to the short line of people waiting to place their orders. The smells of burning grease, melting cheese, and fried meat hung heavily in the air. As they took their place in line, Monica waved at Tara, who stood at the head of the line with a male friend of her own. "Think you're gonna throw me off with the use of French? Don't you know I've had four semesters of it at Highland, not to mention three years in high school?"

Brandon grinned. He wasn't going to tell her, but he still recalled those exact facts from a rare conversation they'd had on the Yard last year, back when he did well to squeak out a hello as he crossed her path. "Well, I thought I'd heard you were fluent *en français.* Now, tell me, did you and Tara really come here without any men? Who's *l'homme* in line with her?"

"Don't worry about it, just be flattered I invited you out. *Peut-être je t'aime.* Ever thought of that?"

Reaching back to his last French class, freshman year, Brandon translated the line in his mind. *Maybe I like you.* A prickly, happy sensation climbed his leg, heading straight for his most sensitive region. "Ah, flattery will get you nowhere with me, lady."

"What ya want!" The boom of Chappy's hoarse voice told Brandon it was time for them to order. Chappy was slumped behind the greasy glass counter, his matted Afro protruding from beneath a soiled white chef's hat. Chappy was hard at work preparing his trademark sandwiches and making small talk with his patrons, his crinkled brow awash in sweat, some of which had dried on the bottle-thick lenses of his maple-colored bifocals. He looked at Brandon with sudden recognition. "Hey, partner, how ya doin'? You know this pretty lady here, huh?" He pointed a mangled spatula at Monica.

"She's the one who got me out here tonight. Chappy, how you been?" Brandon never ceased to be amazed at Chappy's ability to recognize him, even though he'd only stopped in a handful of times since sophomore year. "The lady and I will each have a cheese steak. Pile 'em up with everything!"

"I got your back, son, you know that." Chappy went to work feverishly, barking orders to his teenage assistants like a military general while continuing to build cheese steaks piled high with beef, American and cheddar cheeses, green peppers, tomatoes, lettuce, mayonnaise, mustard, salt and pepper, and a dash of his special sauce.

Five minutes later Brandon took a seat across from Monica in a cramped wooden booth near the front door. After dusting off his seat and again refusing a complimentary edition of *The Final Call* from one of the Fruit of Islam standing watch near the entrance, he eyed his cheese steak skeptically while Monica finished her first bite.

She waited for him to tear into his sandwich. "Aren't you hungry?"

"I don't know. I guess something other than my stomach motivated me to come here tonight."

"Oh, ha-ha, Mr. Choirboy. I'm gonna tell those Disciples on you if you keep talking like that. Now give me some scoop. I wanna know about the real Brandon Bailey." Her eyes burned with a playfulness that made Brandon's heart flip with joy.

"Meaning?" He batted his eyes like a confused child.

"Meaning I don't know much about who you've dated at Highland. Who have you been sneaking off with?"

"You mean you haven't asked around?" Brandon hoped she

hadn't. There was nothing for her to find out where he and Highland women were concerned. "I've spent years now using Bobby
to get your four-one-one from Tara." Brandon knew he must be
getting high on himself. He should *not* have shared that fact just
yet.

"And what exactly did you find out?" A smile pulled at the corners of Monica's moist mouth.

"Just that you don't date many Highland men. Don't worry,
Tara always had your back. The most she ever gave Bobby was
vague stories about you havin' a man back in New York."

"Well, if things go well, maybe you can get the story from the
horse's mouth. When are you gonna answer my question?" Her
patience obviously running short, Monica laid her cheese steak
back into its pool of grease and locked eyes with Brandon.

Brandon chuckled to himself. He'd tortured himself before
last night's outing over how to respond to this question. Now,
having survived their first date and remembering that he'd be
out of D.C. and Monica's world in a matter of weeks anyway,
he decided to shoot from the hip. "You wanna know who I've
dated at Highland? Let's do a laundry list, shall we?" Pretending to
be pensive, Brandon pinched his lips together and and let his
cheeks balloon like a feasting chipmunk. "Well, there was Kelly
Grant."

"I know Kelly. I used to see you hang out with her all the time,
both freshman and sophomore year, right?"

Brandon flushed. So she did notice, even back then. Why
hadn't he encouraged that interest? "Yeah, for all the good it did
me. Kelly and I were bosom buddies. We witnessed to folk on
campus and on the Disciples' mission trips, studied together for
English, black lit, and econ, and had the type of long talks I
thought would lead somewhere. Then I went and ruined it."

"How's that?"

"Told her I liked her, was interested in more. How do you like
this response? I'll never forget that night. She looks at me like I'm
a little boy who just offered her a bite of his sucker. She pats me on
the head and says, 'Thank you for sharing that with me.' She for-

got to tell me how nice I was. Looked at me like a teacher looks at a prize student but never addressed my interest."

"Maybe she wasn't ready for a relationship at the time."

"Yeah, you're right, I'm sure. I'm sure that's why she's dating that basketball jock Scott McKnight now. Just 'cause he stepped to her at the right time. I bet he's a real gem."

Monica slid a handful of slender fingers under her chin. "You sound bitter."

"Oh, why would I be bitter? Because despite the fact that I'm cute—if nothing else, I *know* that—I can't get the women I show interest in to give me the time of the day? Let me complete my list of rejections. Melba Miller said she had no time for a man, she just needed Jesus; Donna Williams said she might be able to like me, if I didn't mind waiting until she made up her mind between me, her ex-boyfriend, and another 'friend' of hers; and Alicia Holland never even bothered to return my phone calls. With experiences like that, in this day of the black-male shortage, why would I be bitter, baby?"

Monica smiled slyly. "Uh, Brandon, maybe you gave up too quickly."

"Oh, no, trust me. If anything, I spent too much time—"

"I don't mean those other girls. You ever think that if you'd kept going, you might have hit on someone who was already curious about you?" The curve of her lower lip told Brandon exactly what Monica meant. "You just ruined the one excuse I always gave you. I had always assumed—"

"Assumed what?" Brandon could feel his freshly scrubbed armpits growing clammy.

"Oh, I don't know. That you never asked me out because you were seein' other people. Your interest was obvious."

"I-It was?" Brandon realized he didn't even need to ask how. Monica had probably smelled the lust emanating from him the first time they met. "This is embarrassing. Look, Monica, I was all set to ask you out a couple of times, right, but when I got into the Disciples, well, let's just say I was socialized to be very particular about who I dated. Or tried to date."

She eyed him with insincere confusion. "You *do* know I'm a Christian, don't you?"

"Yeah, but I'm guessing you've never considered joining up with a ministry like the Disciples."

"I believe in expressing my spirituality in my own way, Brandon. We've talked about that. I don't understand why you would let almost four years go by without asking me out, just because I wasn't *religious* enough for you."

Sucking down a piping-hot bite of the steak, Brandon held up a hand. "Monica, I can't explain it. There's no excuse. I know it was lame to ask you out so late in my last year here. But I couldn't have forgiven myself if I didn't find out what you'd say." Feeling like he was approaching an emotional slippery slope, Brandon reined himself in. "I guess all I'm saying, Monica, is I'm into you. I just want to spend time with you. You set the terms, I'll follow for these last five weeks. We can do what you want, where you want. Like Levert said, I ain't no Casanova, but I'm also no dog. Where's the harm in giving me some pleasant memories, on your grounds? You might even find me enchanting before all's said and done." He wiggled his eyes playfully, trying to lighten the mood.

Setting her sandwich aside, Monica reached forward and tapped his hand, sending a wave of heat through his body. "I just wanted to hear you say it, Brandon. I'm not blind, you know. I just needed to know where you were coming from. Look, let's just get to know each other and enjoy each other's company. Why don't you tell me why I should go out with you again?"

Wondering if he was really sitting in Chappy's with Monica or just in the middle of a good dream, Brandon pitched his sandwich aside and jumped into a bout of verbal gymnastics with Monica. They delved into dreams and goals. She shared her plans to attend a top MBA program and start her own advertising agency. Her mother was a partner at a major agency in New York, and her father was an author of corporate-communications textbooks. She preferred the East Coast but wasn't ruling out some grad programs in the South and Midwest. Brandon talked freely about his plan to eventually start an inner-city clinic once he had worked in private practice a few years. He wasn't sure what specialty he would choose yet, though the way that managed care looked to be driving down the compensation levels for specialists, his father's suggestion that he follow him into family practice was starting to look pretty good.

Another half an hour, and they finally swerved into what Brandon had once considered forbidden territory. Monica's curiosity about his views on sex had predictably been stirred by their double date with Bobby and Tara. Brandon talked openly about how his interpretation of the Bible forbade fornication, and Monica respectfully shook her head in disbelief.

"I guess you can't miss what you've never had, but . . . never?" Pushing his history with Brandy from his mind, Brandon wowed Monica as he explained his parents' success in waiting for marriage, as well as the shared commitment he and his brothers had to maintaining their purity.

"Three celibate men in the same family?" She asked to see pictures. "They're as cute as you are," she said. "You sure you're all straight?"

Brandon vigorously set the record straight on that issue. He and his brothers were not bigots. What folk did in their bedrooms was their own business, but the day he or his brothers went that route would be the day Louis Farrakhan and Rush Limbaugh became golfing buddies. Hoping to open Monica up to a new perspective, Brandon tried to challenge her thinking. "What type of world—no, what type of black community would we have, if just fifty percent of the single folk were committed to abstinence? Think there'd be a drop in the number of illegitimate babies, fatherless children, drug use, murders, and poverty? Think that a woman with four kids, on welfare, couldn't be earning a degree from Highland if she had kept her legs closed and kept herself unburdened?"

Monica wasn't going to be won over in a night. "Brandon, if that many people were celibate, you'd have more murders and crime, because all you brothers would be out your damn minds. Testosterone buildup would make your brains bubble over."

Brandon had no choice but to laugh. By the time he walked her and Tara to Monica's Saturn an hour and a half later, they had become fast friends. As he opened the driver's side door of her car, he tugged gently at the arms of her sweatshirt. "You know this conversation isn't finished, ma'am. We've still got to settle up on this matter of diggity. Someone's going to have to compromise here."

Monica placed a warm finger on Brandon's lips, her Certs-fresh breath teasing his aching nostrils. "Now, you know I'm no nun, Brandon. But let's say we squash the argument after we've been out a few times. I don't sack-hop with just anyone, you know." With that, she smiled, slid into the car, and was gone.

When he got back to the house, Brandon felt as if he had entered an alternate reality. He was so high on the night he walked right past O.J.'s door, ignoring the ungodly blasting of his Daryl Coley CD. He might have to block out the bass of O.J.'s boom box, but he was going to sleep good tonight.

20

SNEAK ATTACK

From his position across the street from Ellis Community Center, Jay Turner, David Winburn's campaign manager, impatiently smouldered in the driver's seat of his Ford Probe. Waiting in this bucket of bolts was adding to his frustration. It had broken down on him three times in as many months, and he was tired of pumping his hard-earned summer savings into this lemon. Of course, that headache was secondary now. The informant he was to meet was ten minutes late, and the main speakout of the HSA campaign was to begin in Carlton Auditorium in twenty minutes. Where was this fool?

Turner froze in his seat as he realized that a small boy dressed in an L.A. Lakers starter jersey and blue jeans was moving rapidly toward his car. With a determined look on his cherubic face, the boy stopped within an inch of Turner's window. Hoping he wasn't about to be carjacked by the five-foot preteen, Turner cracked the window and mumbled a greeting. "Were you sent to meet Turner?"

Without opening his mouth or altering his blank expression, the boy reached into the Lakers backpack on his shoulder and produced a large manila envelope. Turner whisked the package through the crack in the window, feverishly checking its contents as the messenger stared him down.

"Mr. Orange said you was s'posed to pay me fifteen dollars." Apparently the child was not mute.

Turner grinned and slipped two crisp ten-dollar bills through the crack. He decided to play dumb; he was sure the kid shouldn't have mentioned Rolly Orange's name directly. "There's a tip for you, Pooh," Turner said, reading the name engraved on the kid's jacket. He told himself the tip would salve his guilt over accepting help from anyone using a child as a go-between. "You have a good night now." As the boy turned and retreated back into the darkness from which he had emerged, Turner punched the accelerator on his ailing auto. There wasn't much time to get up to campus, but when he got there, he would hold David Winburn's political salvation in his hands.

⁂

Monday night, and the first debate for the Highland Student Association presidential election was about to begin. Even though they hadn't been talking much lately, Ashley was by Larry's side minutes before the curtain was to rise on the main stage of Carlton Auditorium. Watching the election-committee volunteers do some last-minute tweaking of the head table at which the candidates would be seated, Larry allowed her to play with his tie while Mark ran down his list of final reminders.

"All right, remember, we gotta come out looking like the picture of cleanliness. You need every poll point you can win tonight! Don't let David bring you down into the mud unless absolutely necessary, least not at first. Pound home the security plan, alumni donations, and dormitory finance. When it's time for the pissin' contest, lampoon his security ideas, reliance on Congress for funding, and the results of his past administrations. Then, however you have to do it, get him between the eyes with those memos to Dr. Johns just before the closing statements. He'll never recover!"

Larry frowned as Ashley took one final tug on his designer tie. "Mark, I told you the memos are an absolute last resort, brother. We don't need any more negativity up in this place than we've already got. I can beat Winburn on the merits." Larry knew his attempt at morality would disappoint Larry senior, but he was feeling his oats tonight. Debates were the perfect forum for someone with his looks and charm; if nothing else, he'd lock up the female vote tonight.

Higher on adrenaline than the candidate himself, Mark flashed a bright smile and leaned in toward Larry. "That's a nice sentiment, Larry, showboating in case Sheila Evans or one of her *Sentinel* cronies is listening in on us. You just do what you know you need to to win! Spank Winburn's ass!"

"Candidates, please report to your marked seats at the table so we can ensure that your microphones are working." Courtney Jackson, the head of the election committee, was ready to raise the curtain.

Larry exhaled. "I'm out. Wish a brother luck." He gave Mark a back-slapping hug and planted a brief kiss on Ashley's lips before entering into the fray that awaited him onstage.

Within minutes the black stage curtains opened and revealed an auditorium full of eager students and faculty. From his seat between the beleaguered Winston Hughes and his true rival, David Winburn, Larry could feel himself swelling. Whether he liked to admit it or not, he was definitely Larry senior's son. It was showtime.

"Ladies and gentlemen, thank you for taking the time to attend this evening, to hear our candidates for Highland Student Association president put forth their qualifications for office. This speakout is sponsored by the election committee, of which I, Courtney Jackson, am director, with Ann Benson serving as my assistant director. The format this evening will consist of a two-minute opening statement for each candidate, followed by one half hour of questions, which I will read, as they were submitted to the election board by the general student body. From there we will allow open-mike questions from the front of the auditorium for forty-five minutes. We will conclude by allowing another two-minute statement from each candidate. We ask that you observe some speakout etiquette this evening, as we always request. Please refrain from acknowledging any candidate's statements with applause until they have yielded the floor. Anyone who boos or otherwise openly derides a candidate will be subject to removal from the auditorium. And when asking questions from the front, we ask that you read or state your question within thirty seconds' time and immediately return to your seat. With that we will begin the evening's program."

His legs crossed in front of him, Larry pretended to pick at the right arm of his gray single-breasted Bill Blass jacket. He knew that Winston had won the coin toss earlier in the evening to see who would speak first. He hoped the brother would not hurt himself too badly.

Noisily sliding his chair back from the table, Hughes clodded his way to the lectern, which stood to the left of the candidates' seats. Larry noticed that his tie was crooked. Didn't the dude have handlers to catch that sort of thing? The brother was already beginning to show his discomfort with public arenas, as evidenced by a trickle of sticky sweat that was making its way from his right temple to the collar of his overstarched white shirt. Audibly clearing his throat, Hughes leaned a little too closely to the microphone, spurring a loud squawk that caused several students in the front rows to jump in their seats. "Excuse me, my brothers and my sisters. I'll get the hang of these mikes sooner or later!" Hughes's chuckling attempt at humor earned only a smattering of faint laughter.

As Hughes painstakingly stated his qualifications for office, along with what he viewed as his most significant policy initiatives, Larry bit his lip every few seconds to keep from laughing. Everywhere he looked, he saw women stifling smirks and men sliding into their seats in naked amusement. Hughes just didn't have the way about him required to succeed in Highland politics. You had to either be fluid or fiery, or both. Hughes was stiff and awkward, his huge intellect serving no purpose in a forum such as this. That limiting fact aside, his actual policies were sound but were nothing to write home about, and his scholarly method of putting them across did nothing but shoot them over the heads of most of the audience.

Old Winston was quite amusing. As he attempted to play up his credentials, Larry chuckled and slapped his knee good-naturedly. He had nothing to fear from Hughes's misguided arrows.

As the crowd erupted in laughter at Hughes's closing sentence, which came out in a sudden nervous squeak, Winburn placed an ebony hand on Larry's shoulder. "Is this dude serious?" Flashing a knowing smile at his rival, Larry turned back to face Hughes, patting him on the back as he returned to his seat. Regardless of what he and Winburn thought of each other, each greatly respected the other's political abilities. In that context, it would have been criminal for them not to take mutual delight at Hughes's ineptitude.

Hughes's bottom had not hit his plastic seat before Winburn rose from the table. Striding to the lectern with an ethnic bounce that both relaxed the audience and announced his confidence, Winburn attacked the microphone like a lion ripping into raw meat. "Highland, this is your first opportunity to observe the men on this stage and begin to make a judgment about who you want to lead this student body into the next century. Tonight I expect you will want to hear our opinions and policies regarding the critical issues we must address. I am up to the task. But I feel that, tonight, as you consider the type of character you'd like to see in your leader, you should carefully consider what each man up here"—Winburn paused and turned to make a grand gesture to his right, drawing the audience's attention to Larry and Hughes—"has done up until this point to better this university. And I'm not talkin' about what they've done to bolster their résumé, or line their pockets, either. No, my brothers and sisters, I was always taught that democracy is founded on leaders who represent the *people*. That means you need a leader who has shown himself to be concerned with the life of the average student here. John and Jane Doe Highland, if ya know what I mean."

Larry sat back in his seat and enjoyed watching his opponent drape himself in populist garb, painting Larry as an elite, out of touch blue-blood. Once he had revved up the crowd with a summary of his policies and his campaign theme, Winburn brought the house down with a concluding shot. "You want this university to take steps toward a safer campus, a more solid financial foundation, equitable distribution of financial aid, and a return to the glorious reputation it so richly deserves. I am the only man on this stage who has already taken steps to make these goals a reality! As liberal arts president, I brought the first job fair for that college to this campus! As your undergraduate trustee, I brought an ATM to the Student Center, lobbied the board to get the students' choice for trustee, General John Chaney, elected, and oversaw the approval of the King Chapel renovation. People, no one on this stage brings my leadership experience or my knowledge of what you, the heart and soul of this community, want from your university.

"Let me continue my record of service. Superior intellect won't save us! Lord knows, corporate America won't save us! Cast your vote for proven leadership. Martin Delany, who cofounded the *North Star* with Frederick Douglass, once said that 'our elevation is the work of our own hands.' Join with me! Let us unite our own hands and elevate Highland to the next level! We can do it, and with your votes on April 21, *we will!*"

Shaking his head as Winburn high-stepped his way back to the table, Larry took in the roar of the crowd as it rewarded Winburn's dynamic delivery. He took note of the diverse members of the audience who appeared to have been won over. Some were friends of Larry's from his business-school classes; others were folk he had become well acquainted with at the many clubs and bars that lined the streets of D.C. Surely these people couldn't be naïve enough to believe Winburn was his superior in this race?

Undeterred by the frenzied reaction, Larry sprang from his seat and paused a few feet from the lectern. Feeling the inquisitive eyes of the audience on him, he calmly and coolly buttoned the top button on his suit jacket, lingering just long enough to incite a few breathless sighs and exclamations from the more attentive females in the auditorium. Stepping to the lectern, he surveyed his trio of advisers in the front row. Mark, Ashley, and Janis all looked more nervous than he felt. Several rows back, he saw Brandon and Terence, flanked by Monica and Lisa. To the far left, he knew, O.J. was commiserating with a couple of his fellow student preachers. Time to give these folks what they came for.

"Ladies and gentlemen, you will hear a lot this evening that is designed to distract your attention from one central fact: I am the most qualified candidate before you, and I come with the most concrete plans to aid in the revitalization of this beloved university of ours. Let's talk facts, shall we?" Taking an opportunity to connect with his peers, Larry grabbed the microphone and stepped out in front of the lectern. "Highland University, when all is said and done, is a business. Now, I don't believe acknowledging that fact diminishes the worth of this institution. I simply believe that effective management demands that we analyze this university on the basis of what it produces. This university produces the top African-American college graduates in the world. My mission, therefore, as HSA president, will be to enact policies that further the university in producing top students.

"From what I see, we have three major obstacles to that process. First, we have a far-flung student body, the majority of whom live off campus. Second, we have a campus that is not safe enough for any student to walk across after dark. Third, and most crucial, we have a crumbling financial base. Too long we have relied on the goodwill and support of Congress, and now Newt Gingrich and his boys are ready to pull our financial rug out from under us." Maintaining his sharp focus on the issues, Larry masterfully cupped the audience in the palm of his hand as he forcefully stated his policies. By the time he delivered his closing sentiments, the audience had almost forgotten that Winburn had stood before them moments earlier. "I believe that Highland today echoes the words of our dear departed U.S. congresswoman, Ms. Barbara Jordan. Highland students simply want a university that is as good as its promise. I would like to work with you to fulfill that promise. Vote for Larry Whitaker, the Promise!"

As the crowd swelled with applause, Larry exchanged grudging glances with Hughes and Winburn. Returning to the table, he took his seat and met Mark's eyes. Both he and Ashley could hardly contain themselves. Clearly they were confident, as evidenced by the audience's reaction, that Larry had just hit a home run.

Thirty minutes later the polish on each candidate's image was starting to wear thin, to varying degrees. Hughes was clearly beginning to feel ignored, considering that only one of the evening's questions so far had been directed his way. His answers were beginning to sound increasingly terse, adding to his wooden image. Winburn's showy exuberance was tempered as several questions forced him to explain his ability to purchase a new car, his first ever, after being elected undergraduate trustee. In addition, he clearly lost out to Larry when responding to questions comparing their approaches to campus security and financial aid. Larry was impressed by how many of the questions he and Mark had designed had made it onto Courtney's list. Mark's idea of having several people submit questions had paid off.

Now Courtney was instructing those with questions from the floor to form a line at the front of the center aisle. Larry found he was able to place a name with almost every face in line, identifying most by their political camp just as quickly. There were some exceptions, of course. He was most curious about the presence of Kwame Wilson, the current HSA community relations officer. A tireless activist and member of the Highland Muslims student chapter, Kwame had a reputation and recognizable timbre that were legendary throughout the Highland community. As the most influential member of the HSA cabinet after the president and vice president, he was a painstaking guardian of his political turf. He and Larry had worked together in the cabinet and had fought a few turf battles—as financial adviser, Larry had cut the budget for one of Kwame's programs last year—but they had agreed to leave their political differences at the door of the HSA office.

The first student stepped to the microphone. Toni Wyatt, who personally knew all three candidates, wore a deceptively sweet smile on her pudgy face. "David, you mentioned the value of your experiences as a student leader. I believe that experience includes learning from our failures. What did you personally learn from the ten-thousand-dollar budget deficit you caused when you set up the liberal arts job fair two years ago?"

As the crowd oohed and ahhed in amused shock, Larry eyed Winburn. The first punch of the night had landed.

Shaken but not stirred, Winburn motioned to Courtney impatiently. "Do I have to respond from here, or can I speak from the lectern?"

Stepping back from the lectern, Courtney extended her arms in his direction. "You can speak from either location, as long as you keep it under two minutes."

Bolting to the lectern, Winburn was obviously working to maintain his composure. He plastered a sly grin onto his face and gripped the podium. "What I learned, Ms. Wyatt, from my experience as president of the liberal arts student council, is that leadership is not always comfortable. I was committed from Day One to the vision of providing liberal arts majors a ready vehicle through which they could find out about and obtain *viable employment*. We've all heard the jokes that business, engineering, and communications majors like to throw at us, that we don't know what we want to do with our lives and won't have anyone willing to hire us. Well, I wanted to put an end to that stereotype. I worked with my council to build a program that was the first of its kind, so, yes, it was bound to have some kinks in it. We did overrun our budget, but I wonder if any of the liberal arts graduates who found jobs through the fair care about that. I'm going to guess not. Part of leadership means doing the right thing, even when it opens you up for attack. Sister, your question has reminded me of that all the more tonight. But that is my honest answer." Satisfied with Winburn's passion but unimpressed by the substance of his remarks, the crowd gave him a mixed reception. Winburn suddenly looked to be on edge for the first time since the curtain had parted.

Five questions later, Larry knew he was out in front of Winburn and probably in a different galaxy altogether from poor Hughes. He had defended himself against some silly questions about his handling of payments to this year's homecoming entertainers, whom he had hired on behalf of the HSA, and had easily deflected a planted question about how someone whose parents were paying his way through school could sympathize with students' frustrations over financial aid. The way this was going, he would prove Mark wrong; there should be no need for those memos of Winburn's, at least not tonight. The lead he'd carry out of here would probably hold, as long as nothing disastrous happened in the next few days. Once again, he was going to prove Larry senior's mantra: Whitakers Don't Lose.

"My question is for Mr. Whitaker." Kwame Wilson's firm baritone shook the auditorium. His back erect and his broad shoulders set in a straight line, the brother was all business.

Wondering why Kwame had singled him out, Larry searched the brother's face for a clue as to his motivation, an impossible task due to Kwame's untamed dreadlocks and tinted maple-colored glasses. All Larry could make out was the upward tilt of his head as he began speaking.

"Mr. Whitaker, I believe you have some explaining to do regarding your involvement with Ellis Community Center. You stated previously that you receive no financial return for your services and involvement as a board member." Before Larry could respond, Kwame's right hand shot up, clutching a large manila envelope. "I have in my possession copies of canceled checks, for a total of seven hundred and fifty dollars, made out in your name, from the Ellis Center's bank account." Ignoring the panicked reaction breaking out around him, Kwame continued. "In addition, I have evidence that the very donations you and the other Highland student board members have been raising for the center are not in fact under the center's control. They are being held separately in an account that you alone have access to. Sir, if you would be our president, you will have to address these questionable acts."

The phony revelation seemed to have split the audience down the middle. Mark, Janis, Chuck Dawkins, and all of Larry's housemates led those who immediately dismissed the allegations.

"Kwame, you oughtta be ashamed!"

"Damn that! Larry wouldn't do that shit!"

"Next question: what kinda joke is this?"

"Get the hell away from the microphone and sit down!"

On the other side of the divide, Winburn's supporters, including a beaming Jay Turner, gathered around the mike in defense of Larry's attacker. As Kwame turned from the mike to take Chuck Dawkins up on an offer to rumble, Courtney moved quickly to restore order.

"Anyone who touches *anyone* is out of here and will be subject to suspension, immediately!" The sudden shriek in her normally placid voice shocked even the most rabid onlookers. "Everyone will take their seats now, or be escorted out by campus security, who *are* actually in attendence tonight." The crowd laughed, rewarding Courtney's attempt to lighten the mood. "As is standard, Mr. Whitaker is now afforded two minutes to respond to the question."

"Larry?" Larry snapped to as he felt Hughes's fishy breath on his right cheek. He had been running for, and winning, political offices since junior high, and he'd never been blindsided like this. He imagined that if he'd been ambushed with real facts, he might better defend himself. But this? He had never even considered being charged with the outrageous crap Kwame had just spun. Instinctively, his eyes searched the sea of faces for Mark. As their eyes locked, Mark took his right hand and quickly flicked it across his neck. Get out, he was saying. There was no point in dignifying this crap with a long response. If he could come up with a wiseass deflection, maybe something borrowed from a Teflon don like Ronald Reagan, he could walk out with at least an even score and pound Winburn with the memos at the next debate, when the effect would be fresher come election day.

Larry knew Mark was right. Unfortunately, that wasn't enough to keep his father's genes from taking over. Larry senior had raised him to take no prisoners in life. Who the hell did Kwame think he was? Those rumors he'd heard about Kwame's hopes of being selected as Winburn's vice president must have had some truth in them. Damn! Bounding to the lectern, Larry could feel his sense of restraint and calculation shed like a snake skin.

"Kwame, whoever put you up to that diatribe should be disqualified from this race." His eyes flashing with fire, he shot an ugly glare at Winburn, letting the accusation sink in. Winburn leaned forward in his seat and blinked back innocently.

"Anyone who knows *anything* knows that Larry Whitaker is not motivated by money. For God's sake, people, you know my background. If I was in this for the money, I'd have dropped out a long time ago. I can get thousands of dollars whenever I need them; why would I take seven hundred bucks from a nonprofit, broke community center? This is a joke. I don't owe one damn explanation to anybody!" A collective gasp rose from the floor in response to the first four-letter word of the evening.

His eyes still smouldering, Larry stepped back from the lectern. His mind an angry blaze, he stormed to the table and grabbed up Mark's manila envelope. "Ladies and gentlemen, I didn't want to have to do this, but I fear the dirt that is being thrown now leaves me no choice. I have in my hand copies of correspondence between Mr. Winburn and a member of the Highland board of trustees, in which he promises"—Larry paused, shocked to hear himself floundering after the appropriate words to finish his accusations. He realized for the first time that he had failed to review the memos, and the exact way to frame the issue, since going over it with Mark Saturday. He'd hoped he'd never need to use the memos, and now he remembered why. What did a memo really prove? How the hell could he make this argument? "—Well, in short, your undergraduate trustee agreed to limit his activism on the board, in return for favorable treatment by the board . . ."

Continuing to grasp for words to authenticate his accusations, Larry felt himself losing the balance he had maintained so well all night. After rambling on for what felt like five minutes, he pushed himself to close on a strong note. "In short, don't think you can question my integrity without looking at all of my opponents in the same light. I will refute—"

"Mr. Whitaker." From the wings of the stage, Courtney's mellow voice startled him. "Your time has expired."

As Winburn's supporters cackled shamelessly at Larry's inept defense, he trudged to his seat, refusing to meet either of his opponents' eyes.

The speakout was over before Larry regained full awareness of his surroundings. As the auditorium began to empty, he pretended to review his debate notes. His mind was heavy with thoughts of revenge. Kwame would get his, but Larry knew he was just a pawn. He would have to tie this to Winburn, and nail him for it. No one so crooked deserved to hold office at his beloved Highland.

"Nothing to be gained by rehashing the evening." Mark stood in front of Larry's microphone, flanked by Janis and several other campaign workers, including Brandon and Terence.

Larry looked up at his friends wearily. "You're right, Mark. Listen, everybody, you all did a great job gettin' us this far. I know we hit a rough patch tonight, but we can come through it. Hope to see you all at our next meeting. We'll lick this yet!" Larry told himself he really believed that.

As his entourage began to disperse, Terence jumped onto the stage and leaned over the table. "Something real foul is up, man. We gon' have to get to the bottom of it. Anyone who would use the center for political gain deserves to be strung up."

"We'll get 'em, brother. You guys get out of here. I'll be all right for tonight. I'm gonna have a war room session with Mark and Janis, so we can undo this damage. We'll rap tomorrow."

"All right, I'll let Brandon and O.J. know. Hang tough, big dog."

Larry flashed a smile he did not feel. "You know I always do."

Mark placed a supportive hand on his partner's shoulder as he removed his car keys from his pants pocket. "Larry, I'm gonna go walk Janis to her car, then we'll pull around front and meet you, all right? We'll all get some pizzas and hole up at my place for the night. Ashley comin'?"

The simple fact that Mark had to ask told Larry all he needed to know. "I'll talk to her. If she's coming, she'll be with me when you pull around." The men slapped high fives, and Mark leaped off the stage and began to shepherd Janis toward the front entrance.

"Well, congratulations." Now that the stage had cleared and the overhead lights were being flipped off one by one, Ashley emerged from the shadows behind him, her arms crossed ominously. The cold stare that met Larry's eyes was exactly the opposite of what he needed at that moment. "A stellar performance, Mr. Whitaker. You sure as hell got my vote."

"You know, Ash, I don't need this right now. If I want somebody to trample on me, I can always call up Winburn, Kwame, maybe even your uppity father. I don't need the woman who claims to love me piling on."

"Oh, the woman who *claims* to love you, that's all I am now, is it?" The hand was on the hip once again, a routine sight for Larry in recent days.

"Dammit, Ashley, why don't you just come out and say verbally what your body is already tellin' me? I know you don't expect me of all people to sit here and take your mess like some whipping boy. You send me a message like you're sendin' now, you're gonna get a smart-ass comment, know that."

Crossing her arms, Ashley inched closer to the table. "Larry, chill out, okay? I just don't believe in condoning failure. There was no reason for you to lose your cool like that tonight. Do you know how much that frightens me, how ghetto you sounded when you lost it like that? I need a man who can guarantee me success in life, Larry. Not just another black man who comes undone, or puts himself into an early grave, because he can't control his temper. I don't have time for that."

Larry felt his teeth grind, and his eyes open wide in shock. "You're kidding me, right? My personal crisis doesn't even register to you, does it? This is just another criteria on which to judge me, isn't it? I don't believe this! I got news for you, Ashley. Not everybody can live life as coldly as you do. Some of us believe in concepts like unconditional love. I guess your parents forgot to include that lesson when they were buying your Porsche and setting up your trust fund! Do me a favor, and high-step out of here right now, before this evening ends on an even more dramatic note."

Her eyes burning a hole through him, Ashley turned and began to descend the steps leading to the main floor. "Larry, you like to make me the villain. Fine. Maybe it's time you see how you like it when I allow men with more to offer to step to me. There's plenty of them, you know. You know how to reach me when you're ready to come at me with some respect."

Angrily watching his lady whip her statuesque frame up the

center aisle, Larry couldn't keep himself from replaying their most recent romantic interlude in the shower, just last night. Even when they were on the outs like this, they could do things to each other no one else seemed able to. But in spite of that and the many other perks that came with having Ashley Blasingame as your woman, it was time to admit this relationship was in need of major repairs.

For a moment he departed the reality of his surroundings and saw himself standing on Highland's main yard with his father, on the day his parents had dropped him off to begin his freshman year. Larry senior had pulled him aside and instructed him on the type of woman he should date.

"See, son, that's what you need," he had said at the sight of every redbone who walked past. "You want a woman who will make your competitors, be they in business or politics, envy you. Understand me? *Envy.* Your woman's appearance says more about you than anything else in your life. If your wife's tore up, people assume you're a settler, and nobody who plays to win likes a settler. They want a winner!" He had paused to put Larry through a quick test run as a short, hippy honey with finger waves and a hickory complexion sashayed past. "Would you sport that in public? Don't disappoint me now."

Larry, of course, had already known the drill, even back then. "Well, Pop, she's cute, and her color's right—you know, she could pass the brown-bag test. But there's two problems. Her hair's too short to make any white man jealous, and her figure's a bit too sisterly. Big butts don't make the best display at those corporate gatherings."

"Damn straight." Larry senior had patted Larry on the back like a pleased professor. "Done taught my boy well."

Wiping his eyes and clearing his mind, Larry shook his head violently. What had following his father's advice gotten him? A gorgeous girlfriend who didn't care about anything but herself. Why couldn't Ashley be like other women on campus, those who were passionate about causes and looked out for the little guy? Girls like Sheila Evans, for instance. Sheila Evans? Why was she in his thoughts again? Once more Larry reminded himself: she didn't fit the Whitaker profile. And she'd never make a white man green with envy.

Squaring his jaw, Larry reminded himself of the more immediate crises he now faced. He decided not to worry about Ashley's little threat; she'd be there after the election, if he decided to fight for the relationship. Right now he was more obsessed with David Winburn and Kwame Wilson than anyone else. Throwing his suit jacket over his shoulder, he stood and headed out to meet Mark and Janis.

Who needed a freakin' love life anyway?

21

Mind Games

It had been two long months since Keesa Bishop had moved into the one-room efficiency apartment near UDC's campus. Located on the top floor of a three-story house split into six miniature living units for financially strapped boarders, the room didn't make for much of a home. The beige paint on the walls, probably first applied in the early seventies, had peeled off in several large patches, revealing the gummy white surface beneath.

Keesa was hunched over the humming white toilet in the far left corner of the room, the result of morning sickness.

"Oh, God!" Nearing the third month of her pregnancy, she was starting to experience all the symptoms that her mother and her friends had warned her about. Every day she could feel a new layer of flesh attach itself to her body, and hurling chunks of her stomach into the toilet had become a frequent ritual. She wondered how some of her friends continued to have baby after baby, as if each new one was just an afterthought. This pregnancy thing was more than a notion. As she steadied herself against the toilet bowl cover, she rose on shaky legs and wondered why she hadn't stayed home in the first place. Momma had fought her when she insisted on moving out, but she'd had no idea then that pregnancy and living alone would be so tough.

Momma, on the other hand, had seen it coming. "Chil', how in hell are you going to live on ya own, when you know you can't take care of yo'self?" Her mother had seemed more amused than hurt at Keesa's plans to leave. "What's so bad about ya momma that you can't stay up in my house?"

"Momma, I've told you, I can't get any studying done when you partying all night with your friends."

"Oh, you think you slick. This ain't about my friends, it's about yo momma gettin' busy up in here, ain't it? Baby, just cause men still find me attractive, what, I got to 'pologize and become a nun for your benefit?"

Keesa had known that the argument, which they replayed on almost a monthly basis, was going nowhere. "Momma, in a place this small, I can hear everything that goes on in your room. With the hours I work and my course schedule, I need to be able to study at night, and I can't do that when you entertainin' men over there all the time!"

Her mother had blown a fresh puff of menthol smoke into her face before responding in her typically deadpan manner. "Girl, you act like you out your mind. You ain't exactly some Pollyanna yo'self. I done heard enough rumors about you myself, don't try to play innocent with me. You and me is birds of a feather."

"Momma, anything I do where men are concerned, I learned from you. Maybe that's why I need to get out of this environment anyway."

That had been it. "Well, get out then, ho! I don't know who you think you is, tellin' me how to live my life, then claiming I'm some environment that you need to escape! Ain't that some shit! I didn't have to keep your little illegitimate ass in the first place. I coulda had an abortion if I wanted, your daddy did offer that when I refused to marry him. Go on, get outta here now!"

Leaning back on the creaky twin bed she had moved out of her mother's house, Keesa wondered again if she should have told Momma that, through the years, several of her mother's boy-friends had taken to crawling into her bed in the quiet of night. Granted, some of the sex had been voluntary on her part, but most had not. Not that it mattered; Keesa knew Momma would never believe her anyway. If anything, she would blame the whole mess on Keesa, who honestly believed that her mother could kill her over a man. Her desire to stay at home had not been great enough to risk any more of Momma's wrath.

Trying to decide if she should muster the energy to go to campus for classes in a couple of hours, Keesa was surprised to feel her thoughts turn to O.J. By now it had been three weeks since he had delivered his little ultimatum regarding his involvement in her pregnancy, and he had yet to initiate contact with her. Her heart burned with a hatred she had not known existed. She had been duped and dumped by more than a few hustlers, roughnecks, and wannabe players, but none had been as crass as O. J. Peters.

She recalled, almost fondly, the striking impression he made when she had first seen him officiate at Light of Tabernacle's morning worship service. She had started to attend Light after graduating high school, in her hope of making a meaningful life for herself and escaping the traps that bogged Momma down in a swamp of self-hate and callous disregard. When the short, dark-skinned young brother with a head full of wave pomade ascended to the pulpit, she had been instantly smitten. He was not handsome in the conventional sense, but his dancing eyes, shining skin, and warm smile outweighed the round paunch and the waxy sheen of his hair. Their paths had crossed naturally when she joined the church's college ministry. O.J., who obviously had many of the church women in his pocket, had paid her immediate attention. She had been surprised at how forward he had been sexually, even though she knew better than to expect men of God to have clean hands in that area.

At first he had impressed her as a patient and sensitive lover, sometimes even taking time to bask with her in the afterglow, reading Scriptures to help her get through the coming week. She never expected or asked for an exclusive relationship, but she'd started believing their arrangement would last indefinitely. When he'd ended things suddenly after a Friday night embrace, her heart had shattered with an intensity that astonished her.

"O.J., how can you do this? Nigga, you ain't even gonna give

202 ≈ C. Kelly Robinson

me a reason? At least tell me that you're cuttin' ties with all your women now, before you graduate and go back to Atlanta?"

O.J. had allowed a long pause before responding. "If that makes you feel better, Keesa, fine. I'm cuttin' ties before I go back to Hotlanta. Feel better? Good. There's really nothing to explain, baby. I got my hands full with graduation, my seminary decision, classes, and my work with the Ellis Center. There's only so much of me to spread around, baby."

His cavalier attitude had cut her more deeply than their breakup. It had only been a short time later that she'd had to acknowledge the fact that her period was late. Fearing the worst, she'd had her cousin Marcus take her to a doctor friend of his, who confirmed the pregnancy. By the time she admitted to herself the number of times she had let O.J. climb atop her without a condom, whispering assurances that her pills were adequate protection, she couldn't fix her mouth to ask how this happened. She had simply been a fool, and since that time she had determined to be a fool no more.

Feeling her muscles tense at the thought of her baby's father, Keesa tried to calm her nerves. She would give O.J. a few more days to call. He had promised to help her get a scholarship, right? That would contribute directly to their child's welfare, wouldn't it? Sure, he hadn't given her a straight answer about putting his name on the birth certificate, but if she agreed to his bribe, she could probably extract that as her price. Her mother, all of her aunts, and most of her friends had raised or were currently raising babies without their fathers. Surely she could, too. But that nigga O.J. was going to respect both her and this baby.

The sudden ring of the phone startled her. Debating whether or not to answer, Keesa finally lifted a shaking hand and grabbed the receiver. "Hello?"

The deep tenor voice of the caller, obviously a well-mannered brother, warmed Keesa's fragile heart. "Yes, may I speak with Ms. Bishop, please?"

"This is her."

"Ms. Bishop, I am a fellow member of your church, Light of

Tabernacle. How are you doing this morning?" On the other end of the line, Nico Lane hoped he sounded convincing, like a real churchgoing bore.

"I'd be doin' a lot better if you told me your name, stranger." Keesa scrunched her face into an annoyed scowl. This better not be some punk prankster.

"I'm sorry, Keesa, I can't do that, my sister. As a respected member of Light, I can't let it get out that I'm putting the interests of a fellow member over one of the clergy."

Keesa shot forward, her back forming a ninety-degree angle with the wobbly bed. "Clergy? What are you talkin' about?"

"Ms. Bishop, I think you deserve to know how that rascal of a reverend, O. J. Peters, is doing everything in his power to trash your name." Nico bit his lip at his use of the phrase "rascal of a reverend"—it sounded so funny he wanted to laugh. But he'd have to wait until he hung up.

"What are you talkin' about?" Keesa was suddenly livid. She had told no one at the church about her pregnancy, much less who the father was.

"Keesa, you don't have to hide anything from me, sister. I'm an observant brother. It doesn't take a rocket scientist to know the two of you have been intimate. The only reason I know any more than that, my dear, is due to his comments at a meeting of the church leaders last week."

Her jaw clenched tight, Keesa pushed the words out in a breathless huff. "What comments?"

"We were closing our prayer session when Pastor Grier asked O.J. to share a trial he's going through. O.J., whom everyone knows is a ho, excuse my French, stands up with a straight face and asks us to pray for you. Says that you're spreading lies that he got you pregnant, when all he's ever done is treat you kindly, something he says you obviously weren't used to, because you've fallen in love with him. Sister, he did everything but sport a halo. Pastor Grier even followed up by saying we all need to pray for you, that you'd clean up your ways and be able to responsibly raise your child. It was a sad day, in my view."

Keesa was out of her bed now, pacing. "Why the hell should I believe any of this crap? If *any* of this is true, some ass is gonna get kicked! You willin' to reveal yourself and give me some proof, brother? If not, get off my phone!"

Nico took a labored pause. "Keesa, I honestly didn't want to hurt you. I know enough about you to respect the obstacles you've overcome so far. That's why I didn't feel I could sit by and let this pass. But I understand if you don't trust a stranger. How's this? If you need to verify everything I've said, just ask Rev. Archibald, Grier's right-hand man. Between you and me, he's no fan of Peters, so he'd probably tell the truth if you ask him nice. But ask yourself: if I was lying, would I even suggest you talk to him?"

"Damn you!" Keesa slammed the phone down before the smooth talker could stretch her strained nerves further. Tasting the salty flavor of blood in her mouth, she realized she had bitten down on her lower lip with too much force. The call had to have been a stunt by one of the more mischievous church members. But how would anyone have known to antagonize her, unless they had heard about the pregnancy from O.J.? And who would be so sick as to share such painful revelations, if there wasn't at least a shred of truth to them?

Slowly Keesa felt herself lifting from the cloud that had shrouded her mind for weeks. The answer was clearer to her than ever before. O.J. had no intention of acknowledging his paternity of her child, and worse yet, he had no concern for her as a human being. He would sooner see her already soiled reputation completely destroyed than allow so much as a speck of his private dirt to be revealed.

Leaning back against the bed, she slid to floor and grabbed the rotary phone again. She could feel her voice tremble as her cousin answered her call. "Hey, Marcus," she said in a shaky monotone. "Can I borrow your car sometime in the next week? I have to go set something straight."

Meanwhile, seated snugly in the backseat of his Mercedes, Nico Lane erupted into raucous laughter. "This is *too* easy!" he howled. "That pudgy preacher will be out of the picture in no time! I can't stand hypocrites anyway." He slapped Buzz Eldridge on the back before tossing his cell phone onto the seat.

Eldridge grinned, despite himself. The girl had been easier to rile than even he had imagined. Disrupting these kids' lives was proving to be less of a challenge than he, Nico, or Orange had imagined.

22

THE PLOT THICKENS

Maddy Nouri was enjoying her third week as a waitress at the Fourteenth Street Bistro, a casual gourmet hangout for local college students, young political operatives, and the occasional tourist, most of whom were lily-white in complexion. Though a five-minute car ride up Fourteenth Street would land you in primarily African-American territory, the bistro was not a place in which people of color normally chose to spend their time. Maddy supposed that was what piqued her curiosity about the black couple that had just been seated in her serving area. She was guessing that they weren't there on a date, so she felt no shame in finding the man attractive. She had had a few flings with black men over the years, although she knew better than to bring one home to Daddy. But this guy looked like he could be right up her alley. She searched her mind for the name of the actor he reminded her of. Prince? No, the Fresh Prince, the silly guy who kicked alien butt in *Independence Day*. He was okay, but this mystery man was even more enchanting.

As she approached his table, she threw some extra emphasis into the movement of her hips and even ran her hands slowly through her spiked black locks. She hoped he liked nose rings. "How may I help you this evening?" As if it was necessary for taking their order, Maddy leaned in close enough to Larry that her ample bosom rested a couple of inches from his face. From the corner of her eye, Maddy could make out an annoyed smirk on the face of his female companion. She realized she might be endangering her tip.

Pretending to be ignorant of the extra attention he was receiving, Larry shut his menu and met Maddy's eyes innocently. "My friend here will have a house salad, a glass of your peach tea, and an order of your breadsticks. I will have a California Chicken Grille, fries, and a Sam Adams."

Maddy took one last chance at pissing his table mate off. "Anything *else* I can get ya?"

Sheila Evans flashed the coquette a withering glare. "No, you can just fill the order as it's been requested, thank you."

As the waitress whirled off, Sheila shook her head in wonder at Larry. "Hmmph! You get that type of patronizing treatment from women everywhere you go?"

Feeling more relaxed than he had since the night of the debate, Larry flashed a smile. "Ah, trust me, it's not so bad normally. In all honesty, I gotta admit I really used to take advantage. Used to be a time when any fine cutie who paid me some attention could get with me, at least on a short-term basis. Fortunately, I've outgrown that phase. I started to learn, after the first few rushes of excitement, all you get is harassing phone calls, paranoid accusations, and grubby hands in your wallet. Come-ons like that are just embarrassing now. I want to be with a woman who respects herself too much to just toss it at me."

Smiling, Sheila got down to business. "Well, Larry, let me thank you for agreeing to meet me here. You know you didn't have to. I really felt you deserved to know something about what happened the other night."

"Well, I'd like to hear it. Truth be told, I'm just glad to be alive right now. I figured you were luring me off campus to have me assassinated or somethin'."

Laughing at his recognition of their antagonistic relationship, Sheila said, "Larry, let me apologize for the heated interview we had. I admit I let my personal opinions infect the nature of our discussion. Let's just say I called you here because I think the attack on you at the debate goes deeper than you might imagine."

Larry cast a confused expression at Sheila. "What do you mean? Sheila, I was sincere with what I said about clearing my name, as well as Ellis Center's. Mark will be presenting you with evidence tomorrow to disprove all of Kwame's charges."

"Well, the *Sentinel* will publish any credible evidence you have to refute the charges, believe that. What I'm concerned about has to do with where the charges originated."

"That's no secret. I'm sure if you snoop through your boy Winburn's trash long enough, you'll come across evidence he engineered the whole story." Larry felt his right temple tense at the thought of Winburn. The smug S.O.B. had ruined his good name, at least for the moment. Some of his A-hole supporters had even tacked up signs around campus calling him Larry "the Broken Promise" Whitaker. He knew time was short; if he was going to save his reputation, he had to clean things up quickly.

As Maddy set their drinks and Sheila's salad in front of them, Sheila placed a finger over her lips. "You'd be surprised where I think the story actually came from. At best, I think Winburn's campaign just took bait that was dangled in front of them."

Larry frowned. "Dag, Sheila, I knew you were tight with Winburn & Company, but you've really got some inside info there, huh?" He was starting to wonder if she'd had advance knowledge of Winburn's sneak attack.

"Well, I know that David was fed this story because it was offered to me a few days before the debate. I got a mysterious call from an anonymous source one evening, claiming he could get evidence you were receiving money from Ellis and misappropriating the private contributions you've been raising. To be honest, it sounded so ridiculous to me, especially considering the caller's evasiveness, that I passed on the story. After that mess the other night, I decided to use my caller-ID option and get a statement showing all calls received that night. You wanna guess where the call came from?"

Unable to fathom where she was headed, Larry shrugged his shoulders wearily. "Office of the undergraduate trustee?"

"Try the Ellis Community Center."

"Rolly Orange!" Larry saw Sheila's eyes pop. "I knew that fool was up to no good! Who else would be out to trash the rep of one of the board members? I don't know what Orange is trying to do to Ellis, but someone's got to stop him."

Larry summarized to Sheila his suspicions about Orange and the decision to set up segregated investment accounts. The journalist in her rising to the surface, Sheila stopped him before he could complete his diatribe. "Do I have to take off my journalist hat regarding all this?"

"I think it would be best, Sheila. But I would be more than happy to give you full scoop rights once we've uncovered some concrete evidence and get Orange on the path to prison, if that's appropriate."

"I think I can be that patient. Of course, depending on how long you take, I may be employed by another paper by that time. Graduation's only four weeks away."

Larry smiled. "Where you thinkin' about going after graduation?"

"Well, I have an offer from the *Chicago Tribune* right now, working as an editorial assistant. Besides that, I've interviewed with *USA Today* in Alexandria, and *The Washington Post*. I think I'd rather stay here, actually. My parents still can't believe I'm not coming back to Detroit. You think they'd just be grateful that I'm finally taking my little boy off their hands."

Larry had heard through the years that Sheila had given birth to little Andre shortly before beginning her freshman year at Highland. Her parents, a steel-mill foreman and a grade-school teacher, had insisted on raising the baby while she went ahead and got an education. Unlike some who might have taken unfair advantage of such a generous offer, Sheila was clearly anticipating the opportunity to be in her child's life on a regular basis.

"I'm a little on edge about taking him out of his environment when I move him, though. He'll be four by then, and I just don't know how he'll react. Fortunately, my parents have agreed to go with us whenever we move, so by the time he realizes they're leaving without him, he'll already be settled in with me."

Larry set his beer back on the table. "I suppose staying here in the D.C. area would make for an easier time, in terms of commuting and knowing your way around."

"You're right. I already know we could get a small apartment in Alexandria or Arlington on the little bit I'd make at either paper. The squeeze will be paying for day care, but there's always loans, right? That's a price I'll have to pay to bring my child up in a safe environment."

Larry had to pick with his new friend. "Oh, so you're gonna sell out and move out of the hood, huh, sister? Thought you were down with the cause."

The playful bounce in Sheila's eyes warmed Larry's heart as the waitress placed the breadsticks and Larry's sandwich in front of them. "Hey, I'm just like most Highland folks," Sheila said. "We come in ready to save the world, proclaiming we'll always live in or near the hood, to help nurse it back to health. Then, after four years of feeling like nothing's changed, we're ready to become Republicans!"

Laughing heartily, Larry met her eyes intently as he fingered the wheat roll of his chicken sandwich. "No, seriously, sister, you do what you must to make sure you're raising your child in a safe environment. I can't condone that Republican business, but family has to come first." As he took a bite of the sandwich, he brimmed with admiration for the woman across from him.

Sheila paused with a breadstick halfway between the basket and her mouth. "So where will Mr. Whitaker be settling when he leaves Highland land?"

"Most likely Wall Street, Manhattan, New York. It's just a question of which investment bank shows me the most money, as Cuba Gooding would say. But I'm not completely wedded to New York yet. Matter of fact, I'm lookin' at taking an internship with a major bank in Los Angeles this summer. I've gotta respond in a couple of weeks. If I don't do that, I could always work at my pop's company this summer."

Sheila smiled. "Well, that's your calling, isn't it? Your résumé reads like a CEO-in-grooming."

"It's not that simple, Sheila. My old man would like me to succeed him, but I think I wanna focus on building my own fortune first. If I don't run the company, there's always my sisters."

"What, you don't want to go back to lovely Ohio?" Sheila was toying with Larry in return now. "The Buckeye State is such a live place, who wouldn't want to be there?"

Larry took a quick bite of his sandwich. "Ha, very funny, Miss Motor City. You name me one other state besides Texas or Cali that has as many major cities as Ohio—Cincy, Columbus, Cleveland, Toledo, Akron, Dayton, Youngstown—"

"Oh, Larry, stop, you're going to break that limb you've crawled out on. The last four cities you named are nothing but big towns, and who can tell Columbus from any other run-of-the-mill city in the Midwest? Cincinnati is notorious for a place where the Klan can still march freely, and Cleveland is known primarily as the king of the smokestack. That's the best defense you can provide of your state?"

"Ah, we not even gonna get started on Detroit city. You and I both know the *Mo* done been gone from Motown for quite some time. What's left downtown other than the headquarters of GM, that paragon of efficient management techniques? Didn't your momma ever warn you about throwing stones from a glass house?"

When Maddy returned to take their plates, it was obvious that the dynamic between this strikingly handsome man and his plain but pretty companion was taking on a new edge. Maybe they weren't even aware of it yet, but Maddy decided to steer clear of showing any more interest in the Fresh Prince's twin. It would probably only annoy him, and possibly draw the young lady into an unnecessary confrontation. She sighed as she rang up the couple's bill, although she sensed they would not leave the booth anytime soon. If she wanted to meet a cute guy tonight, she would have to hit one of the clubs when she got off work.

⮫⮫⮫

Sheryl Gibson leaned back in her plaid cushioned chair, the door to her office open just a crack. She was yelling into the phone, setting her daughter straight. "Nikki, don't get smart with me, girl. Have you lost your mind? You know I got contacts at hospitals and clinics all across this city. You keep trying to run around town with your friends when you've got an almost full-term baby inside of you, and I will have you committed to Highland Hospital for the duration of your pregnancy. That little one's security comes before your own comfort or pleasure, understand? It was your desire for pleasure that got you in this situation in the first place." Rolling her eyes as she concluded another difficult conversation with her wayward daughter, Sheryl hung up the phone and stared longingly out the window.

She was so tired. Her entire life she had tried to do what she felt was right, and now this seemed to be her reward. A husband who bolted after being laid off from his fifth job, a teenage daughter who had seemingly gotten herself pregnant on purpose, and a place of business that was crumbling before her eyes. It would be enough to make some women in her situation either give up or chuck it all and go for it on their own. But not Sheryl. She loved her daughter, and she believed in the center's mission with a passion that had only grown stronger in the years since she had been appointed director. Regardless of how bleak the odds might appear, she was going nowhere.

Checking her watch, she flipped through another stack of the invoices covering her desktop. Some of these vendors, especially the utilities and food-service companies, were getting downright nasty. Most hadn't cut Ellis off completely yet, thanks to pleading phone calls that she and Rolly Orange were making every morning. Sheryl was still amazed at the depth of contacts Rolly had throughout the D.C. metropolitan area. Having him aboard seemed to be the one bright spot in Ellis's recent past. Brushing a piece of hair out of her eye, she sighed as she read the latest letter from Office Mates, their office-products supplier. It had been written by the company president and stated in no uncertain terms that he would not allow any further sales to Ellis until they had paid off their $6,200 balance. Sheryl hoped Rolly would be able to help free up some of the center's restricted funds or recent contributions to pay off Office Mates and some of the more insistent vendors. Of course, when they paid off one, word would probably spread to the others, increasing the pressure. Sheryl laid the threatening letter aside and whispered a prayer. It was too early in the day to let the weight of her world come crashing down on her now.

"Sheryl, you got a minute now?" Before he had even poked his head through the crack in her door, Sheryl could see Rolly Orange's rotund belly creep through the doorway. As the door swung wide open, he stepped through, flanked by a small, dark-skinned man with an unkempt Afro. The man was dressed in what looked like a seventies-style olive leisure suit, complemented by a wide-collar white dress shirt and a thin polyester tie covered in speckled goldfish. Not sure where to sit, the man hesitated as Orange nonchalantly plopped into one of the two deep leather chairs facing Sheryl's desk. He patted the other chair. "Have a seat here, Tracy. Sheryl, I'd like you to finally meet my friend, Tracy Spears."

As the little man, who reminded Sheryl of Miles Davis without the curl, approached the chair, she rose and extended her hand to him. "Pleasure to finally meet you, Mr. Spears. I've heard some very exciting things about your financial management skills. I'm hoping you can help Rolly and me stabilize our organization's financial base."

From behind his wire-rimmed glasses, Spears's eyes twinkled. "Ms. Gibson, you are even more attractive than Rolly described. I, too, am excited about helping such a valuable treasure of the community take advantage of some good investment opportunities." Flashing a smile at Orange, who seemed a little annoyed at the reference to Sheryl's appearance, Spears pressed ahead with his introductory spiel. "Ms. Gibson, if you've had a chance to review some of my brochures, you already know that I have a well-established track record of helping unconventional investors, such as churches, nonprofit organizations, and educational institutions, solidify their financial security through the use of derivatives and related instruments."

"Before you give me the dog-and-pony show, Mr. Spears, I

need to get clear on a few points." Sheryl's interruption surprised the two men. Spears clearly had not expected Sheryl to question him so actively. "Mr. Spears, do you have all of the necessary credentials to engage in securities transactions? What type of training and certification do you have?"

Spears smacked his lips lightly before answering, an almost hurt look on his face. "Why, my good woman, I am a licensed certified public accountant, a chartered financial analyst, and I have an MBA from UDC. I have laminated copies of all my certificates and degrees, if you must see them."

"That won't be necessary, Mr. Spears. I just have to ask about these things. I need to be sure that you can put our money to work legally so that when our next audit comes up, we don't get slammed. I hope you can understand that after years of having a solid, government-provided financial base, I still get a little queasy at the thought of risking my money in the stock market."

Spears's southern accent emerged as he adopted a patronizing tone. "Ms. Gibson, I understand completely. We as a people have been conditioned to think like my own parents, who kept all of their savings under a bed mattress; we think that risk is a bad thing, when the upper classes prosper every day because they know that to make money you have to risk money. It's the only way to get a real return. I'm here, Sheryl, to help you and Rolly turn the recent private contributions you've received into a sum large enough to pay off all your debts and get your creditors off your back."

Sheryl smiled. The odd little man appeared as if he had stepped out of a time capsule planted in the seventies. He seemed pleasant enough, but this was not how she had expected Orange's financial guru to look.

Shifting his weight in his chair, Orange turned toward Spears. "Tracy, why don't you brief Sheryl on the nature of the investments you would utilize?"

"Well, we would use the contributions you've received so far—I believe Rolly says something in the range of ninety thousand dollars—to purchase a portfolio of stock-index futures and fixed-income security futures. In short, Sheryl, a futures contract is a firm legal commitment between a buyer and a seller, wherein they agree to exchange something at a specified price, at the end of a designated period. So, in our case, we will set up contracts agreeing to buy or sell shares whose values are tied either to one of the major stock indices or to a group of fixed-income securities, such as Treasury bills or corporate bonds. In short, we will be speculating as to what we believe the market will do, and propose our buy or sell prices accordingly. Given Ellis Center's immediate cash needs, we will do short-term contracts so that we can see returns in ninety to one hundred and twenty days." He continued to wax eloquent on the complexities of futures and options investing, thoroughly confusing Orange, himself a Highland MBA, in the process.

Sheryl, who had no business training, hung tough with the little man. She peppered him with questions that simplified his message and helped her get a handle on his schemes. Orange admired the way Sheryl could dig into something so far outside of her expertise, especially when she could have easily let him handle this issue. But that would not have been Sheryl Gibson's style.

Forty minutes later Sheryl rose from her seat and extended a hand to Spears. "Well, Tracy, you've certainly given this old gal a mental workout, but I appreciate your patience. I'd be lying to say I'm not still scared, but when you're in dire straits like we are, I guess there's no way to go but up. I'd like you to speak with our board at our meeting this Saturday, so we can get approval to invest our funds with you."

Spears flashed a wide grin. "That will be my pleasure, ma'am. I see I'm running late for an appointment. If you don't mind, I will see myself out. Rolly, thanks again. We'll be in touch."

As Spears turned and sped out the door, his flimsy suit flapping loudly behind him, Sheryl sighed and crossed her arms. Orange noted that his old friend was not looking her best these days. He wished again that his own survival did not depend on her failure.

They had known each other since high school, when he escorted her older sister to the local debutante ball. He had been more interested in Sheryl than her sister, but being a few years ahead of her, he'd assumed he had no chance. Regardless, their friendship had lasted through the years, and Sheryl had hired him when no one else would. Maybe he should warn her of the coming trouble. The Highland students were being picked apart one by one; it would just be a matter of time before their contributions would cease and they would resign the board. Then all the money could be placed in the reliable hands of Spears, who would eventually funnel them to Nico Lane. From there it would be easy for Spears to weave a web of lies about the downside risk of derivatives, explaining how the market had eaten up all of the contributions. Embarrassed, and unable to refute Spears's complicated claims, Sheryl would have no choice but to resign in disgrace, sealing Ellis's fate.

Who would prop the center up when the last symbol of its vitality walked out the door? Nico Lane would finally have what he wanted, a neighborhood free from the distractions of the Ellis Center; Buzz Eldridge would have land for his Develcorp Living Complex; and Rolly would have his life spared, along with enough money to move out of the country and still send money to his ex-wife and children. But maybe he could warn Sheryl to get out now, while her dignity was still intact. Maybe . . .

They were interrupted suddenly by a violent knock at the door. Accustomed to such savagery, Sheryl yelled, "Hello! I'm in here!" It had to be the latest uncouth parent, trying to start some trouble.

The door swung open to reveal a tall, gaunt young man with an unkempt head of kinky burrs. "You Ms. Gibson?" The sharp stench of fresh alcohol sprang from his person as he approached Sheryl and Orange.

Noting the young man's menacing tone, Orange placed his bulk between the stranger and Sheryl. "How may we help you, sir?"

"You ain't got to block me off like that. I got sent up here by the secretary. My little girl, Misha Starr, is enrolled in your grade-school program. I came to get her out early, 'cause weeknights is the only time I get to see her. The secretary come callin' herself stopping me from takin' my own child out of here, saying I gotta come through you first."

Her irritation level rising, Sheryl forced a calm smile across her face. "Oh, I'm sure she didn't state it that way. You sound like you're threatening me, young man." She eased around her desk and came to stand beside Orange, looking the impatient man in the face. She hadn't forgotten Jerome Johnson from the days when she'd kicked him out of the center's ninth-grade program. "Now you need to understand something. Your little girl Misha does nothing but benefit from her time here. If I recall, she's showing a lot of promise as an artist, doing some beautiful drawings and paintings. That may be her ticket out of this neighborhood some-day. The fact, Jerome, is that you have no custody rights over that child. You apparently chose not to acknowledge paternity when she was born, and all of her mother's legal paperwork indicates that a blood test would have to be documented to prove your pa-ternal rights. Have you visited a hospital lately?"

His face contorted in rage, Jerome spat out his response. "Look, woman, you don't know nothin' about me and my family. Just 'cause I wasn't around at one point don't mean I cain't look after my daughter now. Her mother lets me spend time with her. That should be proof o' somethin'."

Sheryl stepped closer to Jerome, a stern but motherly look in her eyes. "That is very admirable of her, Jerome. Hopefully you can reciprocate by getting a blood test and taking on some of the financial responsibilities of fatherhood. You do that, and get some legal rights, and you can come complain about Misha's participa-tion in the program. In the meantime, she stays here, and if you show up here again, I call the police. Are we clear?"

"Whatevah." A look of angry defeat in his eyes, Jerome turned on his heels and blazed a trail out of the office.

"Sure would be nice to be able to afford some security guards for that front desk again," Sheryl said to Rolly, a laugh offsetting the sincerity of her remark. Chuckling lightly, Orange wondered why he was feeling hungry so early in the morning. Finally, as he turned to leave his friend's office, he admitted to himself what the sensations in his stomach really were: pangs of conscience.

23

THE PRESSURE

D.C. rush-hour traffic was as relentless as always. Brandon, still not able to compete with the thoughtless antics of most D.C. drivers, clamped his teeth tight as a gray minivan cut off his attempt to get into the far left lane of Thirteenth Street. They were nearing the heart of downtown, and he had to get this next left in order to drop Terence at the Technotronics office on time. He had offered T a ride so they could catch up on the events of the past couple of days, but he was starting to regret it. He was in danger of being late for his zoology final, and he had to pick up his graduation cap and gown before lunchtime. He was nearing the finishing line of days like these, at least at Highland, but he still had to get through these final ones.

"Dang, I don't believe these folk ain't trying to let me in." Hearing the blaring horns of the cars behind him, Brandon steeled his nerves, keeping his Altima in its inconvenient position as he waited for one of the speeding cars in the left lane to let him over.

"Bro, you gonna just have to take that," Terence prompted him. "You know these folk ain't worried about anyone but themselves, 'specially at this hour." Seeing that Brandon was in no hurry to put his Altima in harm's way, Terence tried to get a nearby driver's attention. "Yo, bro!" he yelled at the top of his lungs at the conservatively dressed, middle-aged black man in the black Cadillac to Brandon's left. Obviously annoyed at Terence's nerve, the driver made brief eye contact with the two, then began to look away.

Terence was on the case. "Hey, help a brother out, let us in, okay? Didn't you go to the Million Man March, brother?"

A look of irritation on his face, the man reluctantly gestured them over. As Brandon waved in gratitude and hopped into the coveted lane, Terence laughed to himself. "There, that wasn't so painful now, was it?"

Cruising through the intersection, Brandon shook his head wearily. "Hey, look, I'm not like Larry, I haven't had my car here since freshman year. This was my first year adjusting to D.C. driving. I know Chicago's notorious for its drivers, but a brother like me spent more time drivin' through the burbs than the downtown Loop, so dealin' with this stuff's not exactly second nature." Checking his watch, Brandon decided he had exaggerated his risk of being late for the final. "Hey, I'll have a few minutes before I need to leave for campus. You want to get a bite of breakfast at that cafeteria in the lobby of your building?"

As they sat down to devour their food a few minutes later, Terence returned to one of their earlier topics. "So, I hear Larry got some valuable info out of Sheila Evans last night."

"Apparently so. He briefed O.J. and me last night when he got back, then he went out to scheme some more with Mark and Janis. They're going to try to track down proof that Rolly Orange conspired with Winburn and crew to plant those allegations of Kwame's. They've already given Sheila copies of the investment-account statements, as well as a statement from Sheryl that no money has been paid to Larry or any of us. That should neutralize this as a campaign issue, but who knows what it means regarding Ellis's future. If we can't pin down what's going on soon, the center's days could be numbered."

Terence crunched a brittle piece of bacon between his teeth. "I just wish there was something more I could do. Man, I don't know about you, but I feel so out of touch. My time has been so tight lately. It's obvious something's going on, but how do we help clear it up?"

Touching his fingers to his chin, Brandon pondered the question. "Probably the healthiest thing we can do is continue to watch Orange, especially when we discuss the budget and the investment of the contributions at the board meeting Saturday. Other than that, it's probably best to leave the investigative work to Larry and Sheila."

"Larry and Sheila? Who ever would have thought we'd hear those two names together?"

Rising to the bait, Brandon set his fork aside. "Uh, what exactly are you speakin' about, bro?"

Terence let a sheepish smile slip out. "Oh, I don't know. Let's just say I always suspected the strong emotions between those two had a root beneath the waistline."

Brandon frowned. "Oh, Terence. Come on now, I know I'm not exactly in the loop where sexual matters are concerned, but I've never picked up on any chemistry between those two. Shoot, just look at 'em."

Terence shot a self-righteous look at his friend. "What you mean, man? You mean you think your own boy is so shallow he wouldn't be attracted to Sheila, just 'cause she's not a redbone?"

"Look, this is no attack on Larry. I know he judges women by more than their looks, but you can look at his past dates and see a pattern. He's not the only one. I've got certain minimum looks standards myself, even though complexion and hair length aren't included. But I've turned away more than my share of girls who didn't measure up on one attribute or another—"

"See, see, that's your problem." Terence playfully wagged a finger at Brandon. "All that lampooning you do of the black male shortage? Well, there may not be a shortage for the women who look like Ashley, Monica, or Lisa, but for those who have a few too many pounds, not quite enough hair, who are too tall or too short, or who don't look like Whitney Houston or Vanessa Williams, life is rough."

"You ain't tellin' me nothing new, T. But I don't believe in settling. Shoot, why would I of all people settle? You think I've kept Brandon junior under wraps all these years so I can marry a woman I'm not physically attracted to? Guess again, Genius. There's somebody for everyone. Just 'cause I don't find a given girl attractive doesn't mean another guy won't."

Terence leaned back and patted his gut. "Hey, all I'm saying is, those of us having a hard time findin' a good woman might think about lowering some of our less important standards. *Some* black women seem to have figured that much out."

Brandon frowned. "You know what I've figured out? There's no guarantees when it comes to dating. You can have everything women say they want on paper, and get zero play in real life. And I suppose the same goes for some sisters. But it's an individual problem, you know what I'm sayin'?" He used his fork to pick at the pool of runny eggs on his plate. "What about your search for a good woman, T? You think Lisa's gonna act right this time?"

Terence's eyes dropped to his plate. "You wanna know the truth? I don't know. All I know is that I love her, man. I have since the day we first met, and I probably will until the day I die. I decided a while ago I could either try to live in denial of the truth, or accept it, and take the journey with her as it comes."

"So what happens if she winds up marrying someone else?" Brandon knew he was in danger of running late, but he rarely took the opportunity to probe his friend's confusing relationship. "You'd just keep carryin' that torch?"

"I'd cross that bridge when I came to it. My life would go on, don't get me wrong. But, yeah, if she married someone else, that might cut that tie for good. I mean, as it stands now, Lisa is the only person other than my granny who's always been there for me. You can't relate to that, Brandon, and you shouldn't feel guilty about it. But those are the facts. My father didn't raise me and serve as a role model like yours; he never bothered to come around until he was sentenced to life in prison, and what good could he do me then? And my mother, well, you know she didn't teach me life's lessons or live an example for me, like your Moms. She flipped out a few years after Aaron was born, dumped us off on Granny, and split town to work the streets. I've spent my whole life wondering what I did to run them off, Brandon." Brandon sat in uneasy silence across from Terence, watching him play with his fork. "Lisa always comes back. She may need time off from me. Hell, why should she be different from anyone else, right? But she always comes back. That's why I put up with her. Maybe it ain't love, but beggars can't be choosers."

Brandon took his last bite of oatmeal and began to clear his place. "Well, T, being romantically impaired as I am, I respectfully decline to pass judgment on you and Lisa. Hopefully things will work out this time. I just want you to demand the best for yourself, the way you already do in school and on the job. But hey, what do I know, I'm about to go on another date with a sister who can hardly relate to my most deeply held sexual principles. I guess that makes me a hypocrite just like the rest of the Christians you lampoon, huh?"

Standing and grabbing his tray, Terence reached out with his left hand and popped Brandon on the shoulder. "Brother man, you are one of the few righteous folk I can relate to. But you've been dreaming of Monica since you stepped foot on Highland's campus. You'd be crazy not to investigate the possibilities there before you leave this place. You go, boy! But I do expect a call if you find yourself in a sexual situation, young man. If you need 'em, I can bring a box of Trojans over in a flash. Can't have you knockin' Monica up on a second date!"

"You are too funny," Brandon said, an amused scowl crossing his face. "I've faced sexual temptation down before. I'll be all right. Look, you have a good day of work. See you at home tonight."

As Brandon left the cafeteria, Terence emptied his tray into a nearby trash can. Smoothing his tie and checking the look of his rumpled powder blue dress shirt in a window, he strode out of the cafeteria and headed for the escalator at the center of the lobby. He had to meet with Jerry Wallace promptly at eight-thirty, to review the Reveal project's status. Jerry was counting on Terence's summary to serve as his guide when he met with the board of directors later today. He knew he had fifteen minutes before he was due at Jerry's office, but he wanted to be early, so he increased the pace of his long steps.

He was only inches from the escalator when a loud voice shook his insides.

"*Terence! Yo nigga!*"

Gritting his teeth, Terence whirled around and faced the young man who stood a few feet away, not far from the central security desk. He was almost Terence's mirror image, but an inch shorter and several pounds lighter. The only other difference was his attire, a baggy leather Adidas sweat suit. Terence could feel the curious stares of the mostly white crowd that surrounded them. One of Terence's worst nightmares had come true. Aaron "Biggie" Davidson had invaded his place of work.

Moving toward his brother with the speed of lightning, Terence grabbed Biggie's arm and held it tightly. "Biggie, you gonna shut your damn mouth this minute," he whispered hoarsely. "You gonna turn around and walk out of here with me. Whatever the hell brought you here will have to wait until we get out of this lobby." Freezing his brother with a steely stare, Terence led him out the revolving door of the lobby and walked him around to the west side of the building.

"What the *hell* do you think you're doing?" Terence let his brother's arm go and stepped back far enough to get a clear look at him. "What are you, using your own drugs again? I guess seein' the effect crack has on your clients ain't enough to wake your ass up to reality, huh?"

"T, I can explain," Biggie pleaded, sweat beading across his forehead. "I never wanted to have to show up at ya place of bidness, nigga, but I had no choice. I got over to your crib too late to catch you this morning, but I called Granny and got your work address. Hell, I had to catch you before you made it up the escalator!"

Terence's heart leaped as he realized Granny would never willingly give Biggie his work address; she believed in keeping them separated as much as possible. Biggie better not have threatened her again. He brushed aside that wrinkle long enough to get an explanation. "Very thoughtful, Biggie. Why in the world would you bring your triflin' ass into this part of town anyway?"

"I-I had no choice, T. My life is in danger, man, I don't know what else to say." The pleading in Biggie's eyes took Terence back to their days as children.

"Your life has been in danger for as long as I can remember, Biggie, for two reasons. First, you place yourself in jeopardy every time you take drugs from those big dealers and sell them to those suburban clients of yours."

Clearly impatient with his brother's sermon, Biggie flailed his arms wildly. "Look, I ain't got time for this now, T—"

Terence thrust a forefinger into the center of his brother's chest. "Second, you know you take your life in your hands every time you bother Granny. If you ever hurt her again, I'll kill you myself. So don't act like your life being in danger is anything new. Now tell me what the hell's goin' on."

"T, look, uh, I'm really up against it this time. And I ain't figured out why, but my boss wants to hip you to it. They threatened your life if I didn't let 'em talk to you, man! Will you listen—"

"Biggie!" A loud voice from across the street startled both brothers. Turning to face the street, Terence saw a fair-skinned man with narrow eyes and a thick head of hair pulled back into a ponytail. Draped in an aura of impatient arrogance, the man leaned against the side of a gleaming white Mercedes, his arms crossed. Childhood memories came rushing back to Terence as he recognized Nico Lane.

Terence began to dance in place, balling his fists. "What the— Biggie, why is he here, what is this? You're workin' with Nico, *again?*"

"Terence, why don't you prolong both your and Biggie's lives by continuing this conversation in my car?" Nico jerked his head back toward the car, which was parked in front of the Hard Rock Cafe. "Come on, there's plenty of room."

Terence knew a demand when he heard it, and he knew Nico Lane made good on all threats. As Terence climbed into the back-seat of the luxury car with Nico, Biggie slid into the front seat beside the driver.

Nico leaned back against the leather cushions of his seat and lit a fat cigar. "Bobo, get us out of here. Let's tool onto 395 South and roll through some of scenic northern Virginia, shall we?" As the massive, mute driver put the car into gear, Terence listened with confusion to the music playing over the speakers.

"Excuse me, is that classical music?"

Settling back in his seat like a proud lion who had cornered his prey, Nico looked Terence up and down before smiling lazily. "That it is, my man. 'Beethoven's Third Symphony,' one of my favorites. What did you expect, N.W.A. or Too Short?"

Trying to hold his peace as the Mercedes roared through the tunnel leading to the expressway, Terence crossed his arms impatiently. "What you listen to is your business. What you want with me?"

Nico remained in his reclined position, barely making eye contact with Terence. "Terence, I am not a monster, let's get that straight right now. I'm just a product of the hood, like you. I make my own way, understand? I'll never be one of those homeless, out-of-work, welfare-siphoning losers that we all grew up around. Oh, I know you look at me and see a drug dealer, a bad guy. But I'm not a bad guy, Terence. Very little, if any, of my product gets used by the folk in Shaw or LeDroit, for that matter. I make my highest margins on customers who can afford to pay top dollar for the crack and coke. Who do you think that is?"

Terence could do nothing but stare blankly at his captor.

Nico smiled. "Sure ain't none of these poor-ass niggers up in D.C. The suburbs of Virginia and Maryland are my market, man. And you can guess the color of most of my customer base. I service politicians, businessmen, doctors, teachers, and plenty of attorneys. I'm their dirty little secret. Those 'trips to the store' they tell their families about always seem to land them right down in my hood, paying me top dollar for the good stuff. They think of themselves as recreational users, but somehow they keep coming back, right on schedule. As far as I'm concerned, that makes them habitual, which translates to permanent revenue for my business."

Knowing he was out of his turf but unable to stomach Nico's

monologue any longer, Terence let loose. "That's all good and well, now do you wanna tell me why you're makin' me miss a very important business meeting?"

"You have no idea, do you?" Nico suddenly leaned in Terence's direction, menace filling his voice. "Your little business meeting ain't shit compared to what I got you here for! That company ain't trying to put any real money in your pocket, boy! If they were, you wouldn't still be begging Highland to let you stay in school. What a loser. That's another topic altogether. You're here because I am going to kill your brother if he does not pay his debts to me by the end of this month." Nico's face spread in a wide smile as the first look of shock filled Terence's eyes.

"Well, maybe that's too harsh. I won't kill Biggie. Bobo here or one of my other associates will. But I'll order it, so it'd be the same as if I did it. Here's the bottom line, Terence: Biggie has accepted about thirty thousand dollars' worth of product from me, and then either lost it or used it himself. Now, I normally don't stand for that at all, Terence. Normally his ass'd be cold right now. But I think so highly of you, as his former father figure and all, I wanted to give you a chance to save his life, maybe even rehabilitate him someday."

Feeling his underarms grow gummy, Terence put a respectful tone to his voice. "If you know anything about me, Nico, you know I don't have the money to support myself, much less pay a debt like that. What you want me to do, man?"

From the passenger seat, Biggie tried to help his brother out. "Terence, go easy, nigga. You got to show Nico respect."

Nico glanced at the front seat. "Biggie, you just sit still and keep your mouth shut. Terence and I gon' work this out, all right?" He popped Biggie on the back of the head with an open hand before continuing. "Terence, I need your help, man, something real simple. I can't go into detail, but I believe that the Ellis Community Center, which I know you're involved in, is on its last legs. I admit it served the community well in the past, but this is a new day, the day of Nico Lane. My business requires young people in the neighborhood who will push my product. If Ellis keeps clouding kids' heads with the notion that my profession is evil, how am I gonna keep my labor costs down? I can't be going all over town and into the suburbs recruiting dealers. Those spoiled middle-class brats want too much money. Kid from the projects gets psyched over a few hundred a week. I take all profits, see; I'm in this business to live large.

"The center has to go," Nico continued. "It's entirely jacked up anyway. I hear that Rolly Orange character has mismanaged shit to the point where Ellis's banks will be foreclosing on them any day."

Terence's eyes danced desperately over the glittery waters of the Potomac River, his mind racing. Why was Nico making such a big deal out of Ellis? Granted, Ellis's purpose ran counter to the aims of a drug dealer, but was it really that serious? And how did he know details of its finances? "How do you think I could shut down the center? I don't have any power there."

"Ah, Terence, don't give me that. You're a top student, a star engineer. Don't tell me you can't figure out a way to get rid of those contributions the center is hoping will save its ass. Why, I'll bet if you worked on your boys, they'd free those funds up for Rolly Orange to invest them. And you've probably already figured out that his incompetent ass will lose the money, right? Suppose you did that, or planted a few items in Sheryl Gibson's office for me, the type of stuff *The Washington Post* would find real interesting? You know, Terence, I've got a number in my mind, and it corresponds to the amount of money I'd pay someone who could do those things for me. You wanna hear the number?"

His heart burning with rage, Terence shut his eyes. "What's the number?"

"The thirty thou that would save Biggie's life, at least as it relates to me, and another thirty thou that would probably cover the rest of your Highland tuition. You might need that after you lose your job at Technotronics today."

The last sentence turned the blood in Terence's veins to ice. "What the hell are you talkin' about?"

"Don't worry, Terence. We all know black folk in corporate

America are last hired, first fired. I doubt that Jerry Wallace will appreciate the fact that you won't show up at work until after lunch today, by which time you will have thoroughly embarrassed his pasty ass. Gonna be hard for him to give his opinions on the Reveal project when you never briefed him this morning!"

Terence wanted to lunge at the gangster, reach across the seat and strangle him until his irreverent threats were silenced for good. He'd have done it, too, if not for the glimpse he'd had of the handgun lodged in the leather holster under Nico's coat. He answered in a shaking, squeaky baritone. "You can't expect me to give you an answer immediately, Nico. I can't sit by and have my brother jacked up, but you're asking me to betray my friends and an organization I respect a great deal. I'm gonna need some time." Terence hoped his voice didn't betray the rumble of fear and rage contorting his insides.

"Bobo, let's go on out to Potomac Mills and get Terence a gift for his service to us," Nico said as the driver neared Crystal City. "Terence, we'll eat lunch out there and then drop you off at work for your pink slip. You'll have until nine o'clock next Saturday morning to give me an answer. If I get the wrong answer, you'll be reading Biggie's obituary on Sunday." Tired of conversation, Nico slapped Biggie, who had fallen asleep, in the back of the head. "Biggie, put in that Herb Alpert CD, please. We'll ride in silence from here on."

As the Mercedes sped further south into Virginia, Terence began to lose all feeling in his body. The numbing sensation rippled rapidly from his feet, through his legs, and into his heart, where it choked back his ability to breathe. This morning his biggest concerns had been the Reveal project, his future with Lisa, and what was happening at Ellis. Now he'd been plunged back into the very world he had worked so hard to escape. As he did in every time of crisis, he felt an internal stirring, a desperate longing still unfulfilled. More than ever, he needed a compass.

24

ONLY HUMAN

Buzz Eldridge fingered a crystal globe sketched with the shape of the seven continents as he reclined in his leather lounge chair. A feeling of calm seeped through him as he stared out the picture window of his downtown office. It had been almost two weeks since the Whitaker kid had been ambushed at his campaign debate, and Mr. Hollings, the private investigator, reported that the boy was scrambling left and right trying to clear his name. As expected, Whitaker hadn't been on so much as one fund-raising call for Ellis Center since. On top of that good news, the Davidson kid had all but promised to put the Highland kids' money into Rolly Orange's hands. The plan was definitely coming together.

Now Eldridge had to help drive the final nail into the coffin. They weren't worried about the Bailey kid; one lone student was no threat.

O. J. Peters wouldn't be a problem either. Eldridge wheezed in amusement as he held the photographs Mr. Hollings had delivered last night. The first few were almost pornographic; apparently Hollings's surveillance equipment was state-of-the-art. How had he picked up such a clear picture of Peters's romps with his pastor's daughter, from outside the bedroom window? Peters obviously wasn't too careful about closing his drapes all the way. Oh, well. As amusing as Eldridge found the photos, he was most interested in Pastor Grier's reaction. Hollings had placed prints of these same photos in the mail to Grier yesterday. Even though Eldridge had held aside the most revealing photos out of respect, he knew Grier would have no choice but to put Peters out of commission when he saw this handiwork. That would be three down, and one nonthreatening boy to go. Game, set, match. Ellis Center's land would soon be his.

※ ※ ※

Brandon sat on a secluded bench in the Just Quadrangle, down the hill from the main yard of campus. He could tell, from the boom of house music and idle chatter making its way over the hill, that the yard was packed. Everyone was thanking God it was Friday.

His world was going a little crazy lately. First there had been the unexpected attack on Larry at the first speakout. Larry had been so busy clearing his reputation and reviving his campaign since that he hadn't raised money for Ellis in weeks. On top of that, now Terence was shamming on his responsibilities regarding Ellis. It was clear he hadn't been keeping up with the Nation of Islam, or the other donors he was supposed to have called. And the brother wasn't exactly eager to explain himself. Time was growing short to shore up Ellis's base of donations, and the flood of money had slowed to a frightening trickle. Brandon checked his watch, readying himself for his meeting with the Disciples of Christ. They'd promised him an answer about Ellis's support today. He hoped they'd be one of the center's saviors.

Despite these problems, Brandon's mind was really most occupied with another subject: Monica. When they went their separate ways, he'd have to work hard to act like his nose wasn't wide open. But darn it if he wasn't hooked on Monica Simone. They had been out five times in less than two weeks, since their outing to Chappy's, in addition to talking on the phone every day. They'd done movies, jazz clubs, restaurants. All that, and they still hadn't run out of subjects to exhaust or differences to explore.

Brandon knew he was going to have to pray hard to forget Monica when their time together ended. It was all he could do to banish the sensual curve of her lips and the captivating glint of her large brown eyes from his mind, whether he was in the midst of Bible study, fund-raising for Ellis, or studying for his zoology final. He remembered now why he used to steer clear of sisters with Monica's style and sensuality. In the presence of a woman who looked like she should be the love interest in a Babyface video, even a disciplined choirboy could lose his mind.

On top of that, the letter he had just opened was rocking his world.

Tara had edged up to him as they walked out of the zoology final and slipped him the folded sheet of paper as if it was a vial of crack. "Brandon, you need to read this. If you have questions, get them to me through Bobby. I'm looking out for you and Monica both." She had burst up the steps and out onto the quadrangle before Brandon could get any more explanation.

His eyes narrowed, and his heart began to beat like a bass drum as he read Tara's flowery handwriting.

If you ever tell Monica I shared this with you, I will deny it until the day I die. And we both know who she'll believe, so don't even think of confronting her about this. Wait until she decides to bring it up, if ever.

What? Looking around to make sure no one was within peeking distance, Brandon inhaled deeply and forged ahead.

I know you know, from the snooping you did through Bobby all these years, that Monica has gone out with very few Highland men, but you don't know why. There's one reason, and he's her no-good ex-boyfriend from home, Victor. Victor's a record executive back in Manhattan, a little successful, and very full of himself. He and Monica were hot and heavy our first couple years here at Highland, which is why she was back in Manhattan almost every weekend, in case you noticed. Anyway, they broke up when he started hitting her for no apparent reason, about the same time his record company went bankrupt. Say what you want about her being hooked up with the ass in the first place, but I believe she cut out as soon as he started raising that hand. Anyway, she hangs tough most of the time, regardless of the stunts he tries to pull to get her back. She has not forgotten the pain he caused her, Brandon. That's why she steers clear of most of the jokers on this campus, the dogs who want to add another notch to their belts.

That's where you come in. She's always liked you, babe, but you lacked that element of danger, the imbalance that turns more than a few of us girls on. Well, I guess getting knocked around opened her eyes. Maybe someday it'll open mine. Anyway, Brandon, I just want you to know she's dating you because she really likes you. You're not just something to do.

I see the way she talks about you. You're a breath of fresh air, honest and open, and free of all the game playing. I think that's why she's so much quicker to hang up on Victor these days, when he comes calling. You're doing something right, baby boy. But my point is, don't fuck it up (please pardon my French, God is not through with me yet—smile). This is my girl's heart, and if you do anything to drive her back into that fool's arms, you'll never make it to Duke Med, understand?

Brandon assumed he should grin at that line.

I really, really hope I'm not freaking you out with this, Brandon. But I can't see my girl hurt. I think I know you well enough to know you wouldn't do that, but we sisters have to look out for one another these days. Please, prove us wrong; show that there are some good brothers out there, that you're not all dogs. Peace, Tara.

"All righty then." Brandon clamped his hands together tightly and shook his head. His head began swimming with mixed emotions. Monica liked him, apparently quite a bit. Great! On the other hand, he now had proof that she was just like the rest of the sisters he'd pursued: hooked on dogs. What was it that made some women run to the men who treated them worst? He knew there were women who appreciated stable, sane, monogamous brothers, but dang it, why weren't they the ones he wound up liking? Maybe he was no different from women who chased dogs. It wasn't like he couldn't get a perfectly nice, Christian, moderately attractive girlfriend whenever he wanted. Maybe he had no place judging Monica and her kind. Or maybe, just maybe, he was through trying to figure it all out. Apparently Monica was tired of dogs for now; he'd be a fool not to get in while the getting was good.

"Brother Brandon, what up?" Milton "the Bishop" Hobbs materialized at Brandon's side before he could finish digesting Tara's letter. Slightly annoyed at having his privacy cut short, Brandon glanced up at his old friend. Before he stopped taking part in the Disciples' activities, Brandon had worked side by side with Hobbs as a student leader in the movement. He and Hobbs weren't in contact much these days, but Brandon was hoping their friendship would push Hobbs to direct some financial support Ellis's way. Hobbs and Allen Gilliam, the movement director, had held on to his proposal for almost a month now.

Brandon stuffed the letter into the pocket of his olive Dockers. "What's up, Bishop? I'm hoping I'm not late for this meeting with you and Gilliam. Guess I'm doing okay timewise, huh?"

Matching strides, Brandon and Hobbs ascended the hill separating the quadrangle from the main yard and hopped the steps to Morrison Hall. One of the newer structures on campus, the building still had a few extra classrooms, a rare thing on campus that the Disciples were quick to take advantage of.

As they stepped through the oak doors leading into the central hallway, Brandon paused and let Hobbs lead the way to the basement level, where some extra rooms, still smelling of fresh concrete and sawdust, were located.

"Hey, brothers!" Gilliam, a short, bulky man with the build of a champion wrestler, was facing away from them, studying the blank blackboard on the far side of the classroom. "How my fellas doing today? That yard is startin' to jump again already, ain't it? The sun comes out, and the sisters—boy—they just ready to take it all off, ain't they?"

Enjoying Gilliam's poke at the campus heathens, Hobbs cackled mischievously. "I mean, the first thought I have is, have you ladies *heard* of self-respect? How these women think they ever gonna snag a good man, if they show off all the goods before a brother even asks 'em out?"

His eyes searching Brandon for a response, Gilliam took a seat at the wooden desk at the front of the room. "Brandon, have a seat, brother. Why don't you two pull your chairs up to the desk and we'll rap. Brandon, I gotta ask, how do you deal with the temptation to look at those sisters out there as sexual objects?"

Annoyed at the direction of the discussion, Brandon slid into the knee-high desk. "Ah, Allen, there's no magic secret. I just do what I've done all my life—look once, not twice. It's that second look that can get you."

Gilliam frowned. "I only ask about temptation, Brandon, because I respect the discipline that brothers like you and Milton here have shown. A brotha like me was in the world for so long, I fell victim to that sort of thing more times than I can count. You fellas should be proud of yourselves. You're living out the one Christian principle most brothers can't handle."

Brandon leaned back in his chair and clasped his hands behind his head. He decided not to share the thoughts cascading through his mind. He loathed being placed in the same category as Hobbs, who legalistically avoided dating and claimed to see women only as platonic friends. Complete freedom from good ol' red-blooded lust was just not natural, not even to Brandon. To his mind, the Christian man saving himself for marriage was still a simmering, bubbling cauldron of pressing sexual energy; after all, salvation didn't equal castration. Besides, Brandon knew he'd done better than most, but he was far from perfect.

After Gilliam opened their discussion with a short prayer, Brandon plunged into the business at hand. "So, what type of support can Ellis expect from the Disciples of Christ?"

Leaning forward with an intensity in his twinkling eyes, Gilliam looked at Brandon like a disappointed parent. "Brandon, brotha, I'm sorry to say, I don't think we can make any direct financial contribution to the center. Milton and I wanted the chance to fully explain to you in person. We're not tryin' to waste your time. You got time to hear us out?"

Brandon propped up his chin with his right hand and grunted softly. "Go ahead."

Making fleeting eye contact with Gilliam, Hobbs took over the conversation. "Brandon, we're concerned about the integrity of Ellis Center and its management. The revelations about Larry Whitaker's involvement in Ellis's finances were pretty disturbing." Seeing Brandon's mouth fly open, Hobbs held up his hand. "It's not just that, even. We'd already had concerns about the involvement of the Nation of Islam and other non-Christian religious groups. The Word says we should only be aligned with like-minded individuals, founded in Christ. That's the real issue."

Brandon flew forward in his seat, an edgy calm in his tone. "The real issue? I'm sorry, I thought the real issue was the lives of the children in this neighborhood, who are being given an alternative to the call of the pimps, dealers, and prostitutes around here! I thought the real issue was how the Disciples could help bring the Word to some children who need to hear it. You don't think you could win a battle with the Nation in a religion contest?"

Gilliam shook his head, meeting Brandon's eyes again. "Brandon, our national charter forbids us from being involved with any secular organizations without approval from the national office in California. I want you to know that we did send an application in regarding Ellis, but it was rejected."

"Why? What possible valid reason could they have? They can evangelize to a group of mostly middle-class college students, but not to low-income children and teenagers?"

Gilliam folded his hands dutifully, shifting into his formal role as a staff member of the Disciples. "The decision of the national office is final, Brandon. Our other concern is for your own well-being."

"What?" He'd feared this was coming. *Gotta be kidding me . . .*

"Brandon, don't take this personally," Hobbs said, "but I always warned you and Bobby about hanging with non-Christian folk. When you two decided we Disciples were too restricting, I wished you the best in finding new friends. But you've gotta be connecting the dots with your housemates and this Ellis Center, man. That speakout was an out-and-out embarrassment, the way Larry handled himself, even throwing curse words around? What is the boy, crazy? Then let's not even touch your boy O.J."

Glancing at Gilliam for support, Brandon squinted in confusion. "*What* are you talkin' about, Milton?"

Hobbs leaned forward and lowered his voice. "Word is his house of cards is coming down around him, too. I'm hearing from reliable sources that he knocked up one girl at his church and is seeing Pastor Grier's daughter on the side. *At your house.* Do you endorse that type of activity in your home, brother?"

Standing up so quickly that his desk toppled to the floor, Brandon leaned over Hobbs. He measured his words with care. "Bishop, I am not my brother's keeper. What each of my housemates does in that house, as long it does not infringe on my lifestyle, is none of my business. Since when were you so bold as to spread your little gossip in front of Allen here, anyway?"

"Brandon, I'm sorry, brotha, but I think he's right in this case." Gilliam's bald dome glistened with a thin glaze of sweat. "I'm no expert on campus happenin's, but these brothas sound like bad news. I think you need to back out of your involvement with them and with Ellis Center."

Brandon frowned. "I'm graduating and leaving D.C. in a couple weeks, that's a given, Allen. But I'm doing what I can to help solidify the center before I leave. I'm not backing out now."

Gilliam met his eyes with an almost judgmental stare. "Maybe you need to focus on solidifying your spiritual status first."

"What's that supposed to mean? Come on, let's cut the bull. Just come out with it." Brandon felt his forehead bead with sweat.

Hobbs was indignant now. "Come on, Brandon, it's that girl you're running around with! Whether you want it as your legacy or not, brother, you are the talk of campus! No one can believe you and Monica Simone have anything in common!"

Brandon glared into Hobbs's eyes. "Milton, that's none of your—"

"You got people placin' bets on whether or not you're getting busy, Brandon! Did you ever think about what type of witness you'd be providing by dating her?"

Placing his hands on his hips, Brandon inhaled deeply. "I should have known it would come to this, judging my dating life, now that I have a little bit of one. Let me tell you both something. When you have an abstinence record that can compete with mine, you can lecture me about who to date."

Gathering his satchel and slinging it over a shoulder, Brandon strode toward the door, pausing to turn and face his old friends. "You brothers disappoint me. You don't surprise me, but you definitely disappoint me. Don't expect an invitation to the rededication ceremony. God bless."

Stung by his own sarcasm, Brandon propelled himself through the doorway and up the steps. Another plank of the Ellis Center's support had fallen. He had been counting on the deep pockets of Gilliam's contacts to pad the private contributions, not to mention the spiritual good that could have been done by an army of Disciple volunteers. He realized now that there was no point analyzing it further. The same old politics that always arose when black folk tried to work within a white framework had snuffed out Gilliam's will to aid Ellis. That was life. He'd have to break the news about the Disciples at the board meeting tomorrow, but that would not be the biggest issue; the challenge would be to make sure Rolly Orange didn't get his hands on their private contributions.

As Brandon descended the front steps of Morrison Hall, the weight of Hobbs's accusation about O.J.'s affair with Carla Grier hit home. Where in the world had he picked that up? Granted, Brandon figured he'd be the last to know if the rumors were true, but he hoped O.J. was aware they were floating around. Even though he was no fan of the preacher, he'd already seen one housemate laid low in the past week, and that was plenty. He decided to head to the Student Center and leave a voice mail for his unsuspecting housemate. He hoped O.J. checked his messages regularly.

❧❧❧

Pastor Grier's eyes were milky balls of hatred. "You little Judas, you can't run from me!"

O.J. had shown up at Light of Tabernacle for Friday-evening service and sauntered into an ambush. He had barely crossed the threshold of Pastor Grier's study before the large man had bolted from his leather chair. He darted at O.J., throwing aside the two chairs opposite the desk that separated them and tossing off taunts that made O.J.'s skin crawl. The man before him had completely lost his spiritual veneer, and there was little question why. Somehow, the inevitable had occurred; Carla was no longer O.J.'s dirty little secret.

"What kind of fool do you take me for, boy? Paradin' my little girl around town, bringin' her up in a house teeming with young men? Are you out your mind?"

Ducking to his left to avoid the glass paperweight Grier tossed at his head, O.J. pivoted and slammed the door to Grier's office, the deafening smack nearly cracking his eardrums. Regardless of the price he was about to pay for his sins, he didn't want Grier's image before the church harmed; the man was in the throes of paternal rage.

The next thing he knew, O.J. felt the veins in his neck tighten as Grier's scabby hands gripped his throat. "Turn a nd and face me, Reverend. You got a few seconds to explain yo'sen, be I see to it Light has one less associate minister."

His neck locked in Grier's vise grip, O.J. turned and faced the taller man. Grier's face was swimming in a pool of perspiration, some of the droplets resting in the small crevices that marked his complexion. O.J. felt he should apologize twice, first for Carla, and second for putting Grier into such a state. Judging by the labored movement of his chest and bulging belly, the man seemed worked up, to the point of endangering his health.

"P-Pastor, there's nothing I can say to undo what I've done.

You know my ways with women, sir. I've never lied about how I am."

Grier released one hand from O.J.'s neck and silenced him with a wag of his large index finger. "Oh no, son. I knew of your ways with the hot little numbers, the bad girls, the Keesa Bishops. Every church has them. We pastors learn to accept them as they are, pray for their growth, and maybe provide them some physical comfort when things are tight. That is *not*, however, how we treat women of substance, like my Carla."

Feeling the grip on his neck tighten again, O.J. respectfully grasped at Grier's hands. "Sir, please?"

"Oh, you think I'm tryin' to send you home to the Lord ahead of schedule, Peters? Never. A piece of work like you needs even more grace than I needed in my day. I think my point is clear." Releasing his grip, Grier stumbled back, a crazed look flickering in his eyes. Slowly, he began to walk back toward his desk. By the time he returned to his deep leather chair, O.J. was almost breathing normally again.

For several moments the wood-paneled study was quiet as Grier sat with his head in his hands and O.J. remained planted against the door. Grier was emitting a sound not unlike short sobs. His shoulders were heaving, and he appeared to be wiping tears from his eyes. As he tugged at the rips in his dress shirt, O.J. took in the sight of his grieving pastor with more humility than he could ever recall feeling. He had reduced plenty of women to tears over the years, so many that plaintive wails and wounded looks bounced off him like Nerf balls now. Seeing Grier overcome with emotion, however, threw him off completely. His deception had hurt one of the few people, aside from his parents, that he had ever admired or respected. He had never wanted Grier to find out this way. His hope had been that he could wait until he and Carla had taken a step to make the relationship concrete, whether that meant getting engaged or simply agreeing to an exclusive relationship. Someone had stolen that chance from him.

At a loss for words for one of the first times in his life, O.J. just stood there, groping for a way to express his regret. Grier began to lift his head from the desk, returning his gaze to meet O.J.'s. The tears were still in his eyes, but as the pastor reached to grab a fistful of tissues from a desk drawer, his lips spread open, allowing a high-pitched cackle to escape. What O.J. had mistaken for tears of sorrow had actually been waterfalls of amusement.

"Whoo-hoo, boy, I really had you goin', didn't I? What'd you think I was gonna do, Peters, do you harm up in God's house? I may be angry, but I ain't crazy."

"Pastor, I don't understand."

"Oh, yes you do, son. I had no choice but to punish you somehow. I figure the moment a man most regrets his sin is that instant in which he's found out. So, even though I have no cause to do anything else, the least I could do was put a scare into you. And what a job I did! Come have a seat here, Peters." Grier motioned toward the leather chairs facing his desk.

Tentatively, O.J. dragged himself to the desk and sank into a chair without removing his eyes from Grier. With their vast differences in height, he couldn't afford to be taken by surprise again.

Grier smiled. "You wanna know how many different women thought they were engaged to me, back in the day, before I settled down with First Lady Grier?"

Confused by the question, O.J. decided to give a straightforward guess. "Oh, we all have that one that got away, sir."

Grier's grin was so wide it looked like it would split his face. "Eight, Peters. Eight women I had wrapped around my admittedly conniving little fingers, before the Lord brought me to my senses. You see, son, you ain't doing nothin' I ain't already done, and more. And for that matter, I always knew Carla was no Snow White herself. The issue here, son, is respect. Next time you wanna take up with my daughter, just give me some warning, will ya? If she's gonna be tomcatting around, I'd prefer it be with a fella I know somethin' about. I got no problem with that. I just don't wanna find out about it from someone else. You know how foolish that makes me look?"

His curiosity piqued, O.J. shifted in his seat, crossing his legs to compose himself. "Just how did you hear about all this?"

"Well, let's see." Grier was now reclining comfortably in the leather chair. "Rev. Archibald had been tellin' me for months that you were involved in some lascivious activities with members of the church, but he could never give me any names. I imagine now that was out of respect for Carla. Anyway, I'd been blowin' him off, you know, saying that maybe you had some of that in your past, but certainly the Holy Spirit had helped you overcome it by now." Grier snuck a sheepish smile O.J.'s way before continuing.

"You see, Peters, I could never be too straight with someone like Archibald when it comes to young brothers and women. Archibald is one of those men who 'saved' himself for marriage because he had no choice. Nobody wanted his scrawny behind until he met his plump little wife. So he finds it easier to be judgmental about someone like you. I could never tell him about your escapades, or mine for that matter."

O.J. respectfully leaned in toward the desk. "So you found out about Carla and me from someone else?"

"Oh, yeah, that. Well, O.J., you may not wanna know how I found out. Someone has it in for you, son. I walk into my office this morning, and what do I have on my desk, but a *big* ol' manila envelope, ominously addressed to 'Pastor Grier, from a concerned citizen.' Thought I was receiving a package from the FBI, CIA, KGB, or somebody." Turning momentarily toward the oak credenza that lined the wall behind him, Grier turned back to face O.J. and plopped an open, legal-sized envelope in front of him. "See what you think."

Pulling out the contents and rifling through them, O.J. was amazed at what he saw. There were six photographs. The first showed Carla parking her car outside his house. In the far right corner of the photo was stamped "9:32 P.M." The next photo showed him walking her to her Saturn, which was parked in the same space. She still wore the same outfit, but now the time stamp showed the hour to be 8:12 A.M. The remaining photos bore additional evidence of his time spent with Carla: a rendezvous at the Holiday Inn in Hyattsville; a dinner date at the Prime Rib restaurant on M Street; even a midnight cruise on the Potomac. Examining the plethora of evidence, O.J. was reminded that he had become very sloppy in the last month. When his fellow dogs in the ministry heard about this, they'd be sure to let him have it.

"Whoever it was had me dead to rights, that's for sure." He was starting to feel like he could take Grier's assurances at face value now. "Don't worry, sir, I'll find out who engineered this trickery. I hope you understand, Pastor, that I've always treated Carla respectfully, and I always will."

"Son, you not tellin' me anything my little girl hasn't already told me. She was not embarrassed in the least when I called her about this evidence. Her only concern was for you. That alone told me I had no cause to assault you. Now, if my baby had any complaints . . . well, no need to go there, is there? Peters, I'm gonna tell you this one time. Your time at Light of Tabernacle is winding down. Soon you'll be training to take over your daddy's church when he retires. As you embark on that journey, I want you to remember one thing that makes the difference between a successful ministry and a failed one."

His eyes affixed to Grier's, O.J. couldn't hide his anticipation. "What would that be, Pastor?"

"You're only human. Never forget that, son. You're only human. Some of these folk out here will try to tell you that you're less of a preacher because you have faults. Never fall under their spell, Peters. The minute you do is when you start behavin' in ways that get you caught with your hand in the cookie jar, like today. Stop the secret-agent shenanigans and live your life, boy. You may always love the ladies a bit too much, but you better believe some of your other colleagues in ministry will be tempted to dip their hand into the money till a few times more than they should, or skimp on outreach and other vital activities of the church. We all got shortcomings, but in God's eyes all sins are equal. That's why he came up with grace in the first place! Tell other ministers about your temptations. They'll pray for you to overcome them, but they'll also have your back when you slip up. That's the only way to build a successful ministry, son. Don't ever forget it. Now, clear out of here before I decide to pick up where we left off a minute ago!"

Returning Pastor Grier's bright grin, O.J. hopped from his seat and clamped hands with his beloved mentor. The mingled scents of his Dax wave pomade and Grier's Old Spice cologne intoxicated him with pride and utter relief. They had weathered this storm with their friendship intact.

After Grier closed their session with a short prayer, O.J. released his grip and headed for the door. "God bless you, Pastor. I better get downstairs and review my message for tonight's service."

"You do that. If Sister Parker asks where I am, tell her I'll be downstairs shortly."

"Yes, sir." As he clicked the office door closed, O.J. headed toward the main sanctuary with a new zest in his step. When he got home, he would have to touch base with Larry about the mysterious manila envelope; odds were whoever had supplied Grier with that gift was also responsible for the speakout fiasco. After they put their heads together and devised a response, he could hit the town with his boy Preston to celebrate. He had just survived what he had always expected would be his personal Judgment Day. He couldn't believe the amount of grace Grier had shown him; surely his father, if crossed in any comparable way by an associate minister, would have had the perpetrator removed from the ministry without a moment's hesitation. Why had Grier been so lighthearted? Slowing his step, O.J. began to realize the lining of this cloud might not be silver.

"You're only human." That was exactly what Grier said. As if he was speaking to a run-of-the-mill, degenerate kid off the street, one with no self-discipline or self-control. Was that all that should be expected of a young minister of God? Didn't most of Paul's letters preach that those who claimed to bring the word of a Holy God to the people, regardless of age, were to be held to a higher standard of conduct? Although O.J. didn't think he'd ever truly bought into that line of thinking, something inside him wouldn't let him brush the thought aside. Suddenly Brandon's words from their earlier argument came rushing at him. What had the Choirboy said? He'd called O.J. living proof of "the failure of the black church." What did Pastor Grier *really* think of him? It was one thing to refrain from judging a young minister's occasional indiscretions, but the pastor's words had endorsed everything about O.J.'s lifestyle, maybe because it was no different from his own.

What would Momma think? The thought made O.J. consider his life in a new light. His mother hadn't lived long enough to see him accept "the call," and he knew she would have been thrilled to see him preach. But what would she think of how he treated women, how he lived his life outside the pulpit? Somehow he knew neither she nor his father would be too happy if they knew the real O.J. As he knelt at the secretary's desk outside of Grier's office, O.J. made a decision. In a few years, once he had finished showing off in the pulpit and playing the field, he was going to make his parents, especially Momma, proud. She deserved that much. He was not going to be like Otis Grier thirty years from now, an old freak who cloaked his nature in a phony spiritual image. He would be the real thing, the genuine article. Someday.

In the meantime, he still had some livin' to do.

❧❧❧

In her room a few blocks east of the church, Keesa Bishop pulled her hair back into a tight ponytail, fastening it with a greasy metal clip she'd been using every day for the last two weeks. She looked at her pallid skin, her slightly protruding belly, and the circles forming under her weary eyes. The glow of pregnancy was proving elusive so far. But that was okay. She'd stewed long enough over what to do about the man who'd put her in this situation, and she was finally going to make a move tonight. She knew how the nigga operated. He'd probably preach at tonight's service, go out drinking with Preston and his girlfriend, and then pick up some girl to bone for the night.

As Keesa pulled on a black sweatshirt to match her wool pants, she whispered to herself, "Stay cool." There was no more sense rehashing what he'd done to her, or what he was planning to do to the next sister who shared his bed. After tonight, O. J. Peters would never disrespect a black woman again.

25

WILD NIGHT

Stirring the gooey shrimp-and-chicken mixture that sat amid the clumps of rice in his Hunan Garden takeout container, Larry tried not to look too closely at Sheila Evans. They had been poring over their research into the Ellis crisis for the last hour, but he was just beginning to appreciate the fact that Sheila suddenly had a new look. When he picked her up from Bethune Hall, she had emerged without the trademark baseball cap and sweat suit. Her hair was swept up into a curly oval of waves, her face was adorned with light touches of makeup, and her outfit looked like it had been freshly purchased from The Limited. Larry was sure he was just imagining that she might have made a special effort for his benefit. He and Sheila were strictly about business; he in order to salvage his good name and Ellis Center's fortunes, she to grab one last big scoop before leaving the *Sentinel*. Sure, they'd talked on the phone every day this week, but the conversation always eventually turned to Ellis.

Sheila punctured Larry's introspection. "Larry, are you listening to me? Hello-o?"

Snapping to attention, Larry got up from the living room couch, where he had been perched since they returned to his house. "Sorry, Sheila, you know I've got a lot on my mind these days. Could you repeat that one last time?"

"Larry, how could you miss what I just said? It's the first real lead as to who might have it in for the center! All those other arti-

cles from the *Post, Times,* and the *Defender* just laid out the fact that
the Center was going to be high and dry without the government
funds it lost."

Larry crossed his arms and grinned. "Well, duh!"

" 'Duh' is right. But what I was trying to tell you before, Mr.
Whitaker, is that the last couple of *Post* articles I found detail a dispute between Ellis and a local businessman. Have you ever heard
of William 'Buzz' Eldridge?"

"Can't say I have. Come on, Sheila, I can't know *everybody.*"

"Well, you should know *this* somebody." From her position
on the floor, leaned against the couch, she held a copy of the article out to him. "This story, dated two months ago, details a dispute
between the Ellis board and Eldridge. Eldridge is some type of real
estate developer, owns a few buildings downtown and in northern
Virginia. Apparently he was so hot for Ellis's land that he stormed
into a city council meeting and asked for support in buying Ellis
out."

"Is this guy a brother? Why's he feenin' to invest in the hood?"

Sheila smiled playfully. "Stop and look at his picture. It's there
in the article, Larry. He's an older white gentleman who wants to
buy up land in Shaw."

"What for? Gentrification? There is some of that going on
round these parts now. Just over on the other block from us, as a
matter of fact."

Sheila shook her head. "No, in the article he's quoted promot-
ing some Develcorp Living Complex. Apparently it's a modern
high-rise apartment and shopping complex Eldridge wants to
construct on Ellis's land. He goes on and on about how it would
be clean, affordable housing for underprivileged residents. He's
interested in that area of town for some reason, and I guess he
thought he had an opportunity when Ellis lost its funding."

Larry scanned the article attentively. Providing contrast to the
picture of a crusty, pasty-faced Eldridge was a smaller photo of
Sheryl Gibson, from the same city council meeting. According to
the article, she attended personally in order to rebut Eldridge's
claims. Larry read a quote attributed to her in a postcouncil meet-

ing interview: "Ellis Center will never be for sale. Mr. Eldridge seems to be under the mistaken impression that we will accept a fat price for the land, without any commitment to help see that the center actually survives." When further pressed by the reporter concerning her resistance to Eldridge's offer, Sheryl was quoted as saying, "Even if we took the money, we'd have no place to go. We are committed to staying in the Shaw neighborhood, and there is simply nowhere else in the community with land and space available. Ellis will never be for sale."

"You've got to give it to the sister, she has guts." Finishing the article, Larry returned to his perch on the couch, just above Sheila. "How many of our community leaders, here or anywhere else in the country, would resist a fat-cat offer like that?"

"Those who are more committed to their mission than to being comfortable." Sheila eyed him impatiently. "Do you wanna hear why Eldridge wants that land so bad, or not?"

Larry leaned back into the couch, preparing himself. "But of course. Please, do go on."

"I did some more digging through the archives of the *Post* and came across a story from December. Apparently Eldridge's company is among several developers bidding for a piece of that riverfront development project."

"The one right outside Southwest D.C.? That's supposed to be the envy of every businessman in town, everybody wants a piece. It's gonna compete with Georgetown. Full of shops, restaurants, theaters, you name it. My Pops has a couple of buddies here in D.C. tryin' to get in on it. They say a little pinch of a project like that could make or break a small bidness."

Sheila turned her head enough to make eye contact. "Well, Eldridge would probably agree. After some diligent searching using the old LEXIS-NEXIS at the *Sentinel*, I found an article on Eldridge's company, Develcorp, from a local real estate magazine. Apparently he has an impressive history restoring properties and reselling them at a profit, but he's up to his armpits in debt. This article made it pretty clear his company's hurting to get in on some major projects. And they even mentioned they have high hopes for the riverfront project, to the tune of one hundred and fifty million in potential business."

"Doesn't sound like he'd let anything stand in the way of getting in on that, huh?" Larry reclined, his lacing and unlacing his fingers in nervous energy. "Don't suppose there's any tie between the riverfront and Ellis?"

Sheila grinned playfully. "Why am I doing all the work here? Eldridge talked in the article about his desire to do the Develcorp complex. But he brought it up only when he was asked how he planned to comply with the city's desire to give the riverfront project business to contractors who employ or somehow contribute to the welfare of minorities and women."

"Well, Lord knows putting up a property in Shaw would make ol' Buzz seem like he was down with the people," Larry said with a laugh. Even in the late nineties, affirmative action continued to rise up and bite the Man on the butt when he least expected it. Larry had his own doubts about the pros and cons of quotas and racial preferences, but as long as white racial preference was the unwritten rule in America, he figured affirmative action was a necessary evil. Still, it seemed ridiculous when government entities made demands on contractors that they themselves couldn't live up to. Eldridge's record on minority hiring and charitable giving must have really sucked, Larry thought, if he had to build a freakin' apartment complex to prove his commitment to the black community.

"Well, we have our motive now, don't we?" Larry sat up and rested a hand on Sheila's shoulder. "Time for me to take over, sista girl. I really appreciate all your help. I hope I've made that clear."

Turning to face him, Sheila locked eyes with Larry. "But this doesn't prove anything. How are you going to make something out of this?"

Reluctantly withdrawing his hand from her shoulder, Larry leaped to his feet. "Bottom line, Rolly Orange is playing funny with the center's finances. Now, understand, if I had the time and opportunity, I'd take this cat out myself. There's no financial mismanagement he could spin that I couldn't pick apart. Unfortunately I've still got an election to win, a couple of finals, and some, uh, personal business to handle in the next few weeks. Not to mention deciding what job to take for the summer."

The hesitation before Sheila responded told Larry he had caught her interest with the reference to his personal life. Why was he flirting with her?

Sheila wasn't smiling but her eyes were. "Well, exactly how will you attack Orange with this info about Eldridge?"

"There's the work. I've gotta tie Eldridge to Orange, somehow. Come on! A millionaire developer who's worked closely with city government in the past wants Ellis out of the picture. Now a former councilman with a shady past is playing with Ellis's books. Coincidence? I think not. We just have to prove it."

"Prove it to whom?"

"Sheryl Gibson. I know Sheryl is legit. If we bring her credible evidence, it's on."

The sound of a key in the front door startled them both. Relaxing as he saw Brandon step into the foyer, Larry laughed at himself. What was he expecting, some goons sent by Eldridge?

Dressed in a navy blue Claiborne sport coat, matching slacks, and white rayon shirt, Brandon fit the image of a dashing Highland brother coming in from a night on the town. Stepping into the foyer behind him, Monica Simone made for a flashy but striking counterpart. Larry was aware of the differences that separated these two, but he could see they made a cute couple.

"Evening, folks. Somebody's been grubbing on Chinese up in here! Smells good." Brandon beamed a smile so bright Larry almost blushed with happiness for his friend. Things must be going well. Larry decided to keep the info on Ellis on the down low for tonight. No need to interrupt what looked to be a promising date.

"If only it tasted as good." Larry helped Sheila to her feet. "Have you guys met?"

"Everybody knows Sheila Evans. What's up, girl?" Monica gave Sheila a familiar wave. There would be no games played between these sisters tonight.

Smiling, Sheila returned her greeting. "You guys didn't know Monica and I lived on the same floor in Tubman Hall freshman year? Girl, the stories we could tell!"

Placing his hand playfully over Sheila's mouth, Larry winked at Brandon. "Uh, sisters, we men may not wanna hear them stories. Some things are best kept between sisters."

After they all sat and shared a few laughs and small talk, Monica stood up and said, "Brandon, when are you going to deliver on your promise to give me a tour of this lovely house?"

"Give me a second, would you please?" Brandon said, rising. "I got you, I got you. If you'll excuse us, people, I have a promise to fulfill."

Standing against the wall near the couch, Larry eyed Brandon suspiciously. "And where will you two kids be once the tour is finished? Don't forget, Choirboy, we got that Ellis board meeting in the morning. Don't be doing anything I wouldn't do."

Catching the jibe, Brandon shook his head as he led Monica out toward the kitchen. "You silly, man. We'll see y'all later."

"All righty then." Larry decided not to push the joke any further, but this was the first time he had seen his boy take a date up to his bedroom. Larry liked to give Brandon a hard time about his rules regarding women in his room, but he had to respect the fact that it helped the Choirboy stay sexless, something Larry would never consider. After all the effort Brandon had put into being a monk, Larry was almost disappointed to see his boy playing with the sexual equivalent of fire. According to Brandon's rules, if there was anyone who should never set foot in his room, it was Monica Simone.

Sheila's voice snapped Larry out of his thoughts. "Larry, is there a phone I can use? I need to check my voice mail."

Pointing Sheila toward the wall unit in the kitchen, Larry sank into the sofa, wishing for a moment of rest before continuing on the Ellis trail. The pace of the past week was starting to take its toll, but he couldn't afford to let up now. He was closer than ever to clearing his name and uncovering something at Ellis. He hadn't spoken to Ashley since the night of the speakout, even though

Mark claimed she was acting like everything was still hunky-dory between them. Apparently she'd even had her father set him up with an interview at Goldman Sachs in Manhattan, which would mean they could spend the summer together. So why wasn't she calling him? More important, why hadn't he called her, and why didn't he care that she hadn't called?

His musings were interrupted by the frantic sound of another key turning in the lock. Checking his watch, Larry figured it was still too early for O.J. to be home. Friday nights were usually his time to run the streets. He was proven right as Terence burst through the doorway like a hound from hell. "T! What's goin' on, man?"

Terence froze midstride, his eyes cold and distant. It was as if Larry had interrupted him in the midst of some crucial task. "What's up, Dog."

Larry flashed a smile. "What you been doin' all night, boy? Out with Ms. Lisa again?"

Terence looked at Larry as if he had insulted his momma. "You got a problem with that?"

Still reclined on the sofa, Larry scrunched his brow in confusion. "Uh, okay, brother. I have no problem with that whatsoever. It was an innocent question."

"Hey look, we can't all pull the Supermodel of the Week whenever we feel like it, Larry. It's only so many good women out there in the first place."

Larry met Terence's steely glare. "My man, you must be under the mistaken impression I was tryin' to hold some symposium on male-female relations. Who you date is your business."

The tense air bottled up within Terence slowly oozed from him as he leaned against the living room entryway. "I didn't mean to trip, man. Damn. You got to cut me some slack, I got a lot of shit on my mind."

Larry arched his eyebrows in concern. "Anything you wanna share?"

Biting his lip, Terence focused his eyes on the refurbished wood floorboards. "Um, naw, it's nothing you need to worry 'bout."

Hoping to lighten the conversation, he nodded in the direction of the kitchen. "That Sheila Evans's voice I hear?"

Larry grinned. "See, now I get to act ignorant with you. Hell yeah, it's Sheila. You got a problem wit' that?"

"Now, Larry, does Ashley know that another woman is visiting you at ten o' clock on a Friday night? Remember, in this day of AIDS, monogamy is the only way. The day of havin' a little thang on the side is over!"

"You're freakin' hilarious, Davidson, you know that? For your info, Sheila and I are going to solve the riddle of what's going on at Ellis."

Terence pursed his lips. He never wanted to think about Ellis Center again. "You all, uh, find anything of interest?"

As Sheila returned to the living room, Larry updated Terence on their discoveries and disclosed their plans to uncover the suspected link between Eldridge and Orange. Larry noticed Terence fidgeting uncomfortably.

"T, you sure you're okay?" He eyed his friend like a mother hen.

Waving his hand in front of him, Terence frowned. "Just nervous energy, man. I was workin' late tonight on a project for Jerry Wallace, think I had one too many cups of coffee. Look, if there's anything I can do to help with this Ellis business, let me know."

"Brother, right now I would just say make sure you show up at the board meeting tomorrow. They'll be having the vote regarding the investment of the contributions and completing plans for the rededication ceremony. We've gotta be represented up in there. I'll do my best to go, but if I get a hot lead, I may not make it. So you brothers have got to be in the house. Are you sure you straight, man?"

Terence's knees felt ready to buckle. "I-I'm fine, yaw, really. I just need some rest. Have a good night, hope things go well with the investigation. Hopefully we'll see each other at the meetin'. Peace out."

As his friend skulked up the central staircase, Larry turned to Sheila. "I worry about him sometimes. He's already overcome odds I've never even had to imagine, but sometimes I wonder how much he can take, you know?"

Sheila laid a warm hand on top of Larry's. "You can't be everyone's savior, Larry, and I don't think Terence needs saving. He didn't get this far without being stronger than most."

"You're right, but I still worry about the brother. Once we get through the school year and this Ellis fiasco, we'll have to take him out and blow off some steam. We've all earned it."

Now Sheila was rubbing her eyes. "Well, I agree. How about we continue this conversation while you drive me back to Bethune?"

Larry rose from the couch and wiped his brow. "Aw, my hospitality ain't enough for you, sister? That's all right, though. Let's jet."

As he retrieved his car keys from his leather satchel, Larry watched Sheila gather her things. Would she invite him up for coffee when he dropped her off? Sure, the forty-year-old dormitory had long outlawed the use of electrical appliances like coffeemakers, but then, coffee wasn't really the issue, was it? Once again, he reminded himself: she don't fit the profile. For the first time, as he opened the front door and watched Sheila walk through the doorway, Larry wondered if he really believed that.

❧❧❧

Upstairs in his room, Terence gripped his phone and cradled his head against his right shoulder. His grandmother was pleading like he'd never heard before.

"Terence, you and I both know you got no choice, son. This man already got you fired from your job. You don't think he'd take Aaron's life?" Granny's words rang in Terence's aching head like an obnoxious bell. He appreciated where she was coming from, knew that she was just being a realist where the life of her youngest grandson was concerned. He, on the other hand, was burdened with a broader view of his dilemma.

"Granny, if I help sabotage the Ellis Center, do you know how many young kids' lives would be affected? Some of those same kids you taught in Sunday school could end up standin' on street corners slangin' rocks, instead of being educated within Ellis's walls. You want me to have that on my conscience?"

"Boy, since when did you develop this conscience? I been tryin' to git you to accept Jesus since your momma birthed you, and you never paid me no mind. For once, Terence, let your worldliness motivate you to do something for your brother and no one else."

"What do you think, I wanna see him die?"

"I know you don't, that's why you gonna do whatever this Mr. Lane say."

"For God's sake, don't give that fool a title—"

"Boy, where did you get that mouth. You want me to come through that phone right now?"

"I'm sorry, Granny. All I'm sayin' is, how do I know if I save Aaron this time that he won't go out and get himself killed anyway? Then I'd be hurting all those kids for nothing!"

"Terence," Granny weeped, "*Please* don't let this man kill your brother, your only sibling! What kind of man would let anyone hurt his family?"

Nearly losing the strength to maintain his grip on the phone, Terence leaned forward to rest his head in his hands. He was flooded with memories of the Biggie he once knew and loved, the cherubic, goofy little brother who followed him around like a loyal puppy dog. The sniveling, whimpering six-year-old whom Terence had personally shielded from the fists of their mother's boyfriends. The nine-year-old who had written a class essay for Father's Day identifying Terence as his father figure and role model. The eleven-year-old who walked to the front of Granny's church, to her eternal delight and Terence's admiration, to accept Jesus into his heart.

At some point that precious child had died and been replaced by a coldhearted clone. By the time he turned fourteen, Biggie had joined up with Nico Lane's gang, dropped out of school, and started on a quest to sleep with every teenage girl in Northwest D.C. Terence admitted to himself that he had been so busy with school when it all first started, he'd never gotten a handle on what changed his little brother. He'd done everything possible to mend the relationship and show Biggie the way back to a better road, but from the day he was infected by Nico Lane, his brother had been beyond his reach.

Their last attempt at a heart-to-heart had ended with a savage tirade from Biggie. "Forget you, nigga! I ain't the pudgy little kid who does nothin' but look up to your ass no more. I'm about gettin' *mine*! I may not have your book smarts, but I sho' 'nuff got the smarts enough to slang some crack!"

"Biggie, I'm just sayin', you can do better—"

"Hell naw, that's what this is about, Terence. I'm already doin' better than your broke ass. You runnin' around workin' for the Man, tryin' to pay your way through school, all your bills are over-due, and you can't even keep your woman. I'm clockin' more dollars than I can spend, gettin' the honey I want, and living free of white America. Hell, the only time I gotta bother with a cracker is when I sell my shit to those lame-ass suburban fools. And *I'm* the one with the power! Naw, nigga, face it, you need to be *me*, not the other way around."

Terence had stormed out of that argument before Biggie's attitude pushed him over the edge. Even though he could beat his brother in a fair fight with no effort, he never knew when Biggie might be packing heat. He reflected on these moments through a haze of enraged tears, his heart thumping loudly in his ears over the searing rhythms of Marvin Gaye's "Inner City Blues."

"Terence, are you still there?" His grandmother's voice, still soggy with tears, was weighted with concern. "Please talk to me, boy. Say anything."

"I'm here," he said, sniffing. "You right, Granny. I can't let any-body take my flesh 'n' blood out. I'll work something out with Nico. Biggie's life will be spared, okay?"

Once he had assured Granny, he hung up the phone and hurled his Nerf basketball at the window over his desk. As he watched it bounce lamely off the glass, scattering the small flock of olive pigeons nesting outside, he wished it had been a fully pumped leather version. He needed to break something tonight.

It was time to face facts. Nico was promising money and the

protection of Biggie's life, and right now both were crucial to Terence. The day Nico had taken him for that ominous ride in the Mercedes, he'd returned to work at Technotronics so late that Jerry Wallace already had his desk cleaned out. A gavel pounded in Terence's brain as he recalled his confrontation with Jerry.

"Jerry, I can explain why I was so late this morning! Please, you've got to hear me out. I would never leave you hanging on the day of a big board meeting, if I had any control over what happened."

Jerry had barely looked up from his computer before cutting Terence off. "Terence, I just had my ass handed to me by the CEO himself *and* the entire board! You know how foolish I looked, not being able to provide the latest specification data on the Reveal project, all the shit you were supposed to update me on this morning? It's a wonder they didn't burn my fat ass at the stake. Terence, I'm sorry, but I can't survive any more fuckups like that."

Knowing he could never give a truthful explanation for his absence, Terence had considered lying for a minute. He'd actually started down that road. "Look, my grandmother was ill this morning—"

"Terence, I can't hear you. There is no acceptable excuse. You wanna know the truth? My fellow managers have had me on the hot seat since the day I took a liking to you. Of course no one ever mentions your color, but I know they watch you closely. That reflects on me. Today's episode played right into their hands. I'm sorry, son, but I can't have my career capsized on your account." Jerry had waved his hand menacingly at the door of his office. "See Marlene on your way out. I had her type up a strong letter of recommendation for you. I'm sure you'll do well in life if you get away from the influence of your peers, Terence. Take care."

Fighting back angry tears, Terence had blotted out his surroundings and fled the office before pure rage overtook him. Four years of diligent work and study, and one absence beyond his control had derailed his corporate career. What was the point? Now he was broke, and he'd eventually have to tell Ms. Simmons he would need more time to pay off his tuition. And he knew what that meant: more payments made in the privacy of the trifling woman's bedroom. No way! Rising from the bed now and wiping away the remnants of tears on his cheeks, Terence repeated his promise to himself: *Can't nobody hold me down.*

It was time to look out for number one.

❧❧❧

In the near-pitch black of his room, the face of Brandon's alarm clock burned a faint glow, the only light except for the thin beam of moonlight that escaped through a crack in the drapes of the window above his desk. The clock read 1:12 A.M. He shifted his head toward the right side of his bed, wondering, momentarily, if Monica was still awake. She was clinging to him still, obviously desiring to be held. As he turned back to her, cradling her Dark & Lovely–scented head of wavy locks against his still-thumping chest, he replayed the previous hour's events.

The trip up to his room had started innocently enough. Some lighthearted conversation about the jazz show at Takoma Station. Her playful criticism of his room—the tattered plaid comforter on his bed, the exhaustive collection of DeBarge CDs, the outdated clothes in the back of his closet. He responded by tickling her firm abdomen, which wound up with them lying on his bed, their eyes locked together like magnets. Before he knew it, he was clumsily following her lead, feeling her soft palms on his inflamed face, the realities of life falling away as Monica stretched out beneath him like a warm, inviting river, taking him on a rolling ride that convulsed into a wild tide, rising and sinking with the ebb and flow of the percolating charge that connected them. Knowing mentally, if only in minute flashes, that he was outside of his moral zone, he had clung close to her fountain, letting her warm waters cleanse and clear his senses, elevating them to new heights, making him strong and keen, until she finally lifted him to dry on a cooling, sunlit bluff under a deep blue sky, his hands raised in confused adoration for her warm, pliant hospitality.

Her voice woke Brandon from his mental replay. "Hey."

In the waning light, he could see her eyes slowly open, looking innocent as a doe's. "You're not about to kick me out, are you?" The laughter in her voice said there was no shame in her game over what had happened.

Unsure of himself, he tried to make his voice sound confident. "Of course not." The answer felt like a lie. He asked himself when he had lost control. Had that really been him, in this same bed, minutes ago? Staring through the murky darkness at Monica's frantically folded Donna Karan ensemble, Brandon faced up to the situation for what it was. He'd heard it said time and again, always dismissed it as the excuse of the weak, but now it fit him like a glove: one thing had sure enough led to another.

As Maxwell's "Suitelady" serenaded them from the CD player to the right of the bed, he felt Monica's fingers tugging at his cheek. "Brandon, are you okay? Don't go quiet on me."

Hearing her voice without processing her words, he tried to make sense of what had happened. It wasn't like he hadn't fled direct temptation before. He remembered the time in the ninth grade when he had stupidly agreed to go home with Sharon Riley after school. Her parents both worked second shift, and Sharon had a reputation for abusing her latchkey status by having frequent male company. He had walked into that situation thinking he could play with fire and not get burned, and actually succeeded. Even now he stifled a laugh at the sight of Sharon, half-naked, braids flying, chasing him out her doorway, tossing books and shoes at him. "Who you think you are, not wanting to go all the way with me? I tell my brother you did this to me, your butt gonna get kicked!" Now, almost seven years later, the joke was on him.

His silence was disturbing Monica. "Brandon, I need you to talk to me." She rubbed her naked body against his and touched her lips to his left ear. Her breath was still minty, but it had a slight tang to it now. Her full lips brushed his cheek as she spoke. "I know it happened sooner than we planned, but we can't change the past now. Why don't you lay back and relax?"

Biting his lip, Brandon turned and cupped Monica's face in his hands. "I'm gonna go get something to drink. You want anything?"

Her eyes full of confusion, Monica sank back into the pillow beneath her, her mound of ebony locks covering it almost completely. "No thanks. Hurry back."

He slipped into a pair of plaid boxers, house slippers, and his pale blue cotton robe before stepping into the hallway and shutting the bedroom door behind him. He stumbled downstairs, his head swimming with the pleasant aftershocks of the last hour, his stomach curdling with conflict.

The kitchen and living room were still fully lit, though it was obvious neither Larry nor O.J. were home. Opening the cabinet over the sink, he yanked out a Chicago Bears glass and thrust it under the spigot. Draining the twelve-ounce glass in seconds, he spat out the last few drops of metallic H_2O and reached for his cordless phone, which he had quietly slipped into the pocket of his robe.

Bobby's line rang four times before his machine picked up. "Homies, you know what to do. Jesus loves you. Peace!" As the machine beeped obnoxiously, Brandon chuckled despite himself at the goofy message, one Bobby could afford now that he had locked up his admission to Emory's med school.

"Bobby, I hate to call you at this hour, man, but if you're there, I need you to pick up—"

Bobby's voice was drenched in sleep. "Brandon! Wh-what's up? Everything okay?"

A new sense of shame flooding his body, Brandon was too choked up to respond. He rested his head against his right palm.

"Brandon? Am I dreamin' here?"

Brandon pushed the words out. "Bobby, I had to talk to somebody. I did it again, man."

Bobby hacked out a round of coughs. "Brandon, at one-thirty in the morning, I can't be playing guessin' games. What happened?"

"Bobby, Monica is up in my room right now, and she's not exactly dressed."

"Brandon! You didn't . . ."

Brandon allowed the silence to supply the answer.

Bobby grasped at words like they were wisps of smoke. "Aw,

hey, man . . . I'm not gon' say I told you so. Dang, did you, uh, use protection?"

Brandon sighed. "You remember that safety stash of condoms my folks insist on replenishing every year, just in case my *jones* overtakes me?"

"Yeah."

"Well, I gave Terence half the pack a few weeks ago. After tonight, there's only two left."

"Praise God," Bobby said, "at least you wore a hat. How many condoms you use anyway? I'm sorry, don't answer that. You say she's still there?"

"Yeah."

"You need to take her home, man, before you do anything else. No sense sorting through your emotions while she's there."

"I got you. I guess I should go get her up, then. How did I let this happen, man?" Remembering that Terence's room was just above the kitchen, he lowered his voice a notch. "How do I square this with all my moralizing all these years? I feel it in my gut, man—it's gonna be Brandy all over again!"

Bobby sighed. "Brandon, all sins are equal in God's eyes. Don't go making a martyr out of yourself over this. This doesn't have to end like Brandy's story did."

"I'm afraid, Bobby. This was just like with Brandy—every minute! I'm never gonna get over this. Monica's gonna break my heart. It's what I deserve."

Bobby grunted. "Cut this crap now, Brandon! Monica has her act together. She won't do you like Brandy. Until you figure out how to handle this sex thing, you may have to steer clear of her for a while. But don't worry about that now. Just get her out of there safely, and we'll talk more when you get back. I'll be up."

Brandon inhaled sharply and headed toward the stairwell. "I can't thank you enough for picking up the phone, bro. I'll call you when I get back. Later."

He slid the phone back into the pocket of his robe and stared blankly up the stairway. His insides felt as uneasy as the wobbly maple banister that lined the staircase. His groin tingled still, fresh from the white-hot sensations Monica had shared, but his mind turned again to that last night at Brandy's.

He'd broken his vow of virginity for Brandy Tower, a statuesque cheerleader for his high school football team. Her complexion was a rich molasses, her exotic braids smelled like honey, and her kisses and warm embraces were smooth as butter. Six long weeks it had been, but the thrill had ended for Brandy by that last night at her house. She hadn't returned his calls in a week, and she'd been seen out with two different jocks from competing schools.

"Why won't you just talk to me," he'd said that night on her lawn, tugging at her arm with an intensity that frightened him. "Why are you ignoring me?"

"It's over, Brandon, damn." Brandy had jerked herself from his grasp and stepped closer to her black jeep. "You need to go home before Dante finds out you were here. He won't stand for this."

"B-Brandy, I don't understand." Brandon had blocked her way one last time, hoping his desperation would win her over. "You said you loved me. You held me. What we have is real."

"Brandon, get a life. I swear, I'll never mess with a virgin again! Now leave me the hell alone!" She had turned from him then, leaving him sulking in place as she adjusted her halter top and hopped into the jeep, blasting a Keith Sweat CD and tearing off into the night. Brandon had stayed there in her front yard, in plain view of Brandy's parents, his eyes full of tears and his heart completely rent.

As he loitered in the stairwell now, Brandon relived the aftermath of that scene. Brandy had died that night in a head-on collision. The officers had found both her and Dante's bodies in the jeep, along with three drained forty-ounce bottles. The whole thing had nearly taken Brandon out. He'd never lost a friend to death, least of all one who had been his only lover.

Was that the real reason he'd forsaken all romantic activity since? Sure, he'd had help from his parents as well as other Christians, all of whom agreed a lesson of his heartbreak was the dangers of fornication. He still believed that. At least, he had until tonight. How could sex, an act that had been so wonderful each time for him, truly be wrong? What kind of God would make people long for one another at young ages, then limit the expression of that longing to the confines of marriage? Was his abstinence really an attempt to flee the pain Brandy had caused him, the pain he now feared Monica might expose him to? For so long, Brandon had walked the straight and narrow and pitied hypocrites like O.J. Maybe he was really the one who had been deceived all these years.

His head pounding, he steadied himself against the rickety banister and realized he had covered only the first two steps. He took a longing glance up the stairway to the door of his room. She was still in there, waiting, and she didn't deserve to be dragged into his inner battle. Willing himself to finish his climb, he whispered a near-silent prayer.

"Please, let her be fully dressed, Lord. I can't lie about what'll happen if she wants some more."

⋖⋖⋖

At that moment, Preston turned the corner onto Moore Street. His backseat passenger, realizing where he was, shouted in glee.

"Brotha, it has been one heck of a day!" O.J. said, his chest still heaving with enthusiastic laughter. He was riding in Preston's pitch-black Ford Mustang. It was almost one-thirty in the morning, and never had he been so happy to see his house just one block away. It had been a draining day, mostly due to his encounter with Grier. On top of that, he had just spent the last four hours partying with Preston and his girlfriend, Tammy, who was in the passenger's seat. He'd never made it home to discuss Ellis Center with Larry first, but he'd deal with that after a few hours of sleep.

"O.J., I didn't think we'd be bringing you home alone," Tammy said, her arms draped over Preston's shoulders as he navigated the Mustang to the front curb. "You didn't want any company tonight?"

"Sister Tammy, I'm just glad to have my health and wealth tonight, you know what I'm sayin'? Don't forget, I just got caught creepin' with my pastor's daughter today! I'm blessed to still have control over my bodily functions!"

"Ain't that the truth!" Preston stepped on the brakes and met O.J.'s eyes in the rearview mirror, the gold in his front teeth gleaming in the dark. "Most fathers would have been ready to put a cap in your rear, boy! You *must* have God watching your back!"

"What can I say, the Lord takes care of his own! Let me out of this bucket of bolts, P! I got an important meeting at Ellis Center in the morning. A brother needs his beauty rest."

Easing off the brake as O.J. stumbled out of the backseat, Preston turned his head toward the curb. "Awright, playa, take it easy. We'll rap to you Sunday."

O.J. turned back toward the Mustang. "I keep telling y'all to come hear me preach again! I'll let you know when I'll be ascendin' to the pulpit next. Stay up!"

Waving at his friends as they zoomed away, O.J. shifted the weight of his sport jacket to his right arm and sauntered through the freshly mown grass toward the cement walkway that led up to the front porch. He was going to enjoy some real rest tonight. After the meeting tomorrow, he would have to do some major cramming for his last black-lit final, for which he was woefully unprepared. Hopefully the Lord would be merciful.

When he first heard the rustle from the bushes that lined the driveway, O.J. figured it was a harmless squirrel fleeing at the thud of his heavy footsteps. So what was that rush of hot breath on his neck? Pausing to turn, O.J. yelped as the crush of solid wood smacked him in the back. The impact sent him hurtling forward, simultaneously blotting out his vision. As he lay on the ground twitching uncontrollably, he pleaded for mercy.

"Please, no, take whatever you want, d-don't kill me! I-I got money in my wallet! You can have the whole thing, p-please, take it!" The words gurgled out through splotches of blood that began to collect in his mouth and throat.

An insane smile of satisfaction across her face, Keesa Bishop leaned over O.J. and whispered into his ear. "This ain't about money, Reverend. This is about respect!" Before he had time to process her voice, she rammed a sparkling, footlong stiletto deep into his abdomen, producing a spouting spray of red that covered his white oxford and began to form a small pool on the grass.

"Uhhh!" Kicking and screaming like a stuck pig, O.J. yelled at the top of his lungs, praying, as earnestly as he ever had, that one of the brothers would hear him. As Keesa twisted the sharp instrument into the billowy roll of his abdomen, he was unable to defend himself; his paralysis and blindness that were setting in, combined with a stinging guilt over the depths to which Keesa had sunk, robbed him of the will to resist her.

"K-Keesa, please! Y-You don't wanna do this—"

She dropped to her knees and held the knife to his neck. "Don't ever, ever think you can treat any woman like this again, fool, you hear? You think women were made just for your enjoyment? You don't know *what* we're capable of! I oughtta cut you open—"

Her tirade was cut short by a sudden beam from the powerful lights atop the patio. As Keesa gripped his greasy head, O.J. could feel her hesitate suddenly. "Damn!" she slammed his head into the moist grass, bound to her feet, and returned to the rusty Escort parked across the street.

By the time Brandon descended the steps and made out O.J.'s bulk on the front lawn, the only evidence of her presence was the roar of the wiggly Escort halfway down the street.

"O.J.!" Falling to his knees, which were immediately soaked in blood, Brandon cradled the minister's head and surveyed his body for damage. "What happened, man, where were you attacked?"

"They . . . hit me in the head . . . with . . . bat." Coughing up blood, O.J. attempted to heave forward, hoping to gain energy to complete his account. "Then . . . stuck me . . . over here . . . knife . . ."

"Sweet Jesus. We gotta get you inside and get this wound covered up, get you to a hospital. Can you hear me, O.J.?"

The young preacher's eyes flickered open and shut, evidence

that he was in danger of losing consciousness. Brandon gripped his face forcefully.

"O.J., listen, you *cannot* fall asleep on me!"

Glancing around, Brandon hesitated at the thought of moving him in this state. He didn't see how he had a choice, though. The commotion outside hadn't been loud enough to get Terence or Monica's attention. He had only heard it because he had been halfway up the stairs when O.J. screamed. If he took time to go get one of them, O.J. would probably black out. Pulling the minister to his feet, he locked his arms around O.J.'s shoulders and dragged him as quickly as his slippered feet would allow, before stopping at the foot of the steps.

"O.J., adrenaline can only do so much. You gotta help me get you up these steps."

When they reached the foyer, Brandon dropped him as gently as possible before running upstairs to the bathroom that separated his and Terence's room. Once he had wrapped O.J.'s wounds and called 911, he would wake Monica and Terence. Terence could take Monica home in his car, and he could ride to the hospital with O.J. in the ambulance. Brandon prayed this would not be an instance in which 911 was a joke.

Bounding back downstairs, he gasped out directions to the dispatcher on his cordless as he dressed the wounds and elevated O.J.'s head. When he hung up, O.J. looked up at him, his glassy eyes haunting Brandon with their intensity. Grunting like a whipped horse, O.J. whispered, "If I didn't know better, Choirboy, I'd actually think you like me." His energy spent, O.J. let his eyes shut. His head thudded to the floor.

Hoping God would still hear him, Brandon knelt over his friend and lifted his voice in prayer. "Please, don't let it end like this."

26

DEALING WITH THE DEVIL

Terence barked into the hospital phone like a drill sergeant. "Damn, Big Dog, where you been, man? Armageddon went down at the crib last night. You were nowhere to be found!"

From his room at the house, Larry sighed impatiently. He needed to know what was going on, not be lectured about the fact that he'd stayed out all night. "T, I called as soon as I got home."

"But I left a note taped to both the front door and the garage, in case you came in that way."

"It's a long story, man. I didn't get in until almost seven this morning, all right? Sheila and I stayed up talking—let me stress, just talkin'—until around one, then I went by Mark's to bend his ear about my women problems. Anyway, what the hell's goin' on? Who's in the hospital?"

For several minutes Larry sat in shock as Terence recounted the early morning's events. Nine months they had lived in this house without incident, if you discounted a few taunts from local thugs. Now this. "Does O.J. have any clue who attacked him?"

"To be honest, he bein' kind of coy, man. He told Brandon something about a group of folk attackin' him, but Brandon only saw one person in the car that pulled off. It was too dark to get a good description, though."

"Did they take his wallet and things?"

"Didn't take anything of value, just tried to gut him like a fish. Brandon won't say it, but I wonder if it wasn't a personal attack."

"I don't suppose guessin' at the culprit would serve any purpose right now." As much as Larry liked O.J., he knew the list of women who would like to see the preacher pay an earthly penalty for his sins was pretty damn lengthy. No point trying to lay blame right now. "How's he doin'?"

"It was touch-and-go last night, but the doctor told us this morning that he'll be okay. He may be on crutches for a couple of weeks, while the nerves in his spine and neck heal, but his knife wound has already been stitched, so they should release him in the next couple of days."

"I need to stop over there, but we've got the Ellis board meeting in a couple of hours, and I've got to work with Sheila on tying out this trail of evidence between Rolly Orange and Buzz Eldridge."

Gritting his teeth, Terence decided to go ahead and break the news. Hopefully Larry wouldn't make the meeting anyway. "Well, uh, Brandon says he's not goin' to the meeting. I agreed he should be the one to stay here with O.J. He's actin' kinda funny anyway. That's another story altogether. Anyway, Pastor Peters won't be gettin' into town until tonight, and none of O.J.'s other friends sounded ready to rush down here when I called 'em."

A slight sense of foreboding sweeping over him, Larry began scratching at his five o'clock shadow. "Uh, Terence, you know that means you'll be the only Highland rep at the meeting? Not to pressure you, man, but you'll be our last line of defense. Whatever you do, *don't* let Orange get permission to remove our contributions from the segregated account! That happens, and he's liable to run off with every red cent! You got me?"

Shifting his weight as he stood at the hospital pay phone, Terence could feel his temper boil to overflowing. Who did Larry think he was, talking to him like some untrustworthy child? He had enough stress on him without this attitude. Besides, he couldn't let his little brother be murdered when he could do something, anything, to stop it.

"Larry, don't go and forget that I'm a grown man, just like you. I will be at the meeting, okay? Chill out."

"Sorry if I was a bit overbearing, T. We're all doing well to keep our heads on straight right now. You comin' home to change clothes and shower?"

"Yeah, I gotta call Lisa and cancel our breakfast date first. See ya later."

"All right." Turning to his closet, Larry yanked out a navy blue suit and white oxford before heading to the bathroom for a quick shower. Something about Terence's attitude didn't sit right with him. He hoped he could run his mission with Sheila and still make the board meeting. Time was going to be of the essence.

✵ ✵ ✵

Five minutes later, Nico Lane received a collect call from the halls of Highland Hospital. "Terence, my good man. How nice of you to grace me with the pleasant sound of your voice." Nico's voice dripped with ridicule.

Grimacing, Terence tried to keep his cool. "Nico, you've had your fun. I got a way to aid your scheme regarding Ellis Center, but it's all I can do to save Biggie. You gonna have to take it or leave it."

"Big talk from a man whose granny will skin his hide if anything happens to her precious grandbaby. What's your offering, brother man?"

Checking his surroundings on the hall, Terence lowered his voice a notch. "I can see to it that all of the contributions raised by the Highland contingent are placed under Rolly Orange's control. He'll have to handle it from there. But that's it, Nico. No planting shit in Sheryl Gibson's office, no fabricating evidence, nothing more. So what's up?"

Nico paused in thought on the other end. "Hmm."

Terence gripped the phone tightly, sweat gathering on his brow in the uncomfortable silence.

"Hmm." More silence. "Hmm. Terence, Terence. Hmm . . . Okay, sir, you have a deal. If I hear through my sources that Orange has control of the funds following the meeting today, I consider Biggie's debts paid and spare his life."

Terence exhaled like he never had before.

"But, because you chose to select your own method of payoff, disregarding my preferences, I can't give you any money, Terence. You'll have to handle your school bills yourself."

"Wouldn't want your blood money anyway. I gotta go. A friend of mine damn near lost his life last night."

"Let me guess, the good Rev. Peters? I tell you, that is a damn shame. I can't imagine who would want to harm such a pure, up-standing servant of God. What *is* this world coming to?"

The line filled with Nico's mocking laughter. Terence slammed the receiver into place and stormed back down the hall. One thought silenced the guilt.

Can't nobody hold me down.

27

ROCK OR A HARD PLACE

Sheryl Gibson checked her watch. It was 10:00 A.M. sharp, but none of the young Highland board members had arrived yet. Seated at the head of the round oak table in the middle of the conference room, she rubbed her eyes patiently. She had been up late last night, schmoozing some local bankers at a charity ball. Rolly Orange had been pestering her to get out with him and press the flesh for months now, and the latest round of nasty calls and terse legal letters had finally pushed her to lay aside Ellis business long enough to comply. Things were nearing the breaking point. Ellis was barely able to purchase operating supplies, and they were dipping into loan repayment funds for that. No local business would sell them anything unless it was C.O.D. Work on uniforms for the children in the manhood courses and the sports programs had been canceled when the manufacturer insisted on a down payment before filling the order. And now Pepco and the phone company were promising to shut off all utilities if their balances were not paid up by the end of June. She had brought this evidence along today, to convince the Highland men to release a portion of their segregated contributions.

Sheryl had to admit, she was feeling desperate. She believed too strongly in Ellis's mission to let it go down without a fight. She knew that was the only reason she had invited the ridiculous-looking Tracy Spears to this meeting. She believed, out of sheer thirst and hunger, that Spears was going to help save Ellis. He would have to take control of all the contributions and bring a significant, no, a miraculous, return before September rolled around. That's when the banks were promising to foreclose. Spurred by clutching hope, Sheryl was anxious to push ahead and get the Highland students to sign over access to their contributions. She appreciated all their efforts, and she knew she could never thank them enough for all they had done. But right now she was ready for them to get out of the way of what she saw as Ellis's only hope.

"Sheryl, I believe we should call this meeting to order, don't you?" Seated at her right side, Rolly Orange met her eyes sympathetically and lightly placed a hand on her right shoulder. Sweeping his large pupils around the table, he said, "We have very important business to cover today."

Smiling faintly, Sheryl arched her back and reached for her eyeglasses. "You're correct, Rolly. If it be so approved, I would like to call this meeting to order, the official time being—"

She was interrupted by the sudden whoosh of the large oak door of the conference room as it swung open. She raised her eyes to see Terence Davidson's tall, rugged physique bolt across the threshold.

"Sorry to be late, ladies and gentleman." Removing his windbreaker in a heartbeat, Terence studiously avoided eye contact as he yanked out a chair and plopped himself down across from Spears. As soon as he opened the door, he felt as if he were chipping his way into a frozen tundra, the tension was so thick. But after the past few days, he knew why. Terence refused to believe Sheryl was mixed up in it, but the attacks on Larry and O.J. had clearly been no freak occurrences. Combined with the coincidental events that had sidelined Brandon, circumstances had been orchestrated exactly to Nico Lane's advantage. And now he had no choice but to play along.

"Quite all right, Terence. We appreciate your presence. We were worried that we weren't going to be able to cover our most important issue. But we'll come to that in a few minutes." Sheryl looked at Terence with a mix of calm and confusion. She was relieved that he was here; now they could bring the matter of the Highland contributions to a vote. She was wondering, though, why he was alone. Where were the others?

Sensing her curiosity, Terence coughed before offering an explanation. "Um, so you all know, I'll be the only Highland student in attendance today. O.J. was mugged last night, and Larry and Brandon are with him at the hospital. He'd probably appreciate your prayers."

Sheryl's eyes grew wide with concern. "Oh, my Lord! Terence, is there anything we do? Will he be all right?"

"Yes, ma'am, he'll be fine, just out of commission for a few days. Look, I don't wanna tie up this crucial meeting with distractions we can't do anything about." Terence was ready to move on to the business at hand for two reasons. First, he wanted to sell his boys out and save Biggie's life before his conscience got the better of him. Second, he was afraid letting on too much about the guys' absence might stir suspicions and foul up Larry's little mission. Already he was sickened by the grin tugging at the edges of Orange's greasy mouth. Terence knew the fat man had to be in this with Nico somehow. *Damn!*

Orange patted Terence on the shoulder and shook his head. "Well, we will be praying for him, Lord, Lord! What kind of community do we live in, where our finest young men can be attacked for no good reason."

The meeting began with a reading of the minutes, and then Tracy Spears gave his presentation to the board.

Thirty minutes later Spears returned to his seat, Terence's head swimming from the little man's baffling jargon and arcane mathematical examples. None of the concepts he spoke of were any more challenging than his course work in the school of engineering, of course, but you didn't pick up an understanding of financial derivatives overnight. Terence was glad his vote regarding the funds had been predetermined. If not, he'd have felt clueless as to how to make a decision. Looking around the table, he could sense that the rest of the board members were even deeper in the woods than he was.

"Any questions?" Sheryl's voice rang with an urgency that was both insistent and wary. After a few moments of silence and a couple of clarifying questions from Rev. Banks, who was clearly asking questions only in order to hear his own voice, she stood before the table.

"My brothers and sisters on the board, we will now undertake two votes in response to Mr. Spears's presentation. The first concern will be the disposition of the eighty-seven thousand dollars of Highland contributions that have thus far been segregated in a freestanding investment account. The second will concern whether or not we the board will authorize Mr. Orange to work with Mr. Spears and invest all the contributions we have received to date.

"For the first vote, there is only one person here other than myself who can decide the course of action." Terence felt the hairs on his body bristle as Sheryl turned to him, her glowing eyes projecting hardened desperation.

"It is now time to decide how to invest the contributions, so that we can earn a maximum return on them in the few months we have remaining to relieve our indebtedness. Terence, you are the only one here who can give me authorization to unlock the segregated funds and place them under our business manager's control. I am making the motion now that a vote be held to authorize the desegregation of the Highland contributions. That is to say that Terence and I would sign the bank forms that I have in hand today, which will effectively close out the account, and have the funds transferred into the unrestricted fund account that Ellis maintains at U.S. Bank. Is there a second?"

"Second the motion." Rev. Banks stirred from a catnap to move the process forward.

Without breaking eye contact with Terence, Sheryl continued. "I call for a vote that these transfer-authorization forms be signed today, so that the contributions may be placed under the Ellis board's direct control, effective this Monday. I vote yea."

Terence leaned forward in his chair as he felt the eyes around the table rest on him like a glaring spotlight. Wishing he could spot-weld his eyes to the table, he willed himself to avoid looking at Orange. He knew one glimpse of the big man's obnoxious mug would keep him from accomplishing the life-saving task before him. Feeling ponds of sweat condense across his forehead, he parted his lips, full of both shame and resolution.

"I vote . . ." He did not want to do this. Suddenly, an image of Granny, her spirit broken and her face twisted into a howl as she leaned over Biggie's casket, ripped through him. He had no damn choice.

"I vote, um . . . I vote yea, in f-favor of the motion."

The words fell from his lips in slow motion, echoing in his ears as he saw the jubilant reactions on the faces of Orange, Spears, and the other board members. With the possible exception of Orange, they had no idea he had just sealed Sheryl's fate, as well as that of the hundreds of children who stood to benefit from Ellis's continued existence. As he blindly grabbed a pen and began to fill out his section of the bank transfer authorization, Terence blotted out the action around him. Trying to push the images of the local children from his mind, he forced himself to think of Biggie and insisted on his affirmation.

Can't nobody hold me down.

≈≈≈

Larry tooled his Lexus down Sixteenth Street, heading toward Pennsylvania Avenue. As was always the case at ten on a spring Saturday morning, the streets were teeming with tourists headed for the house of the Man Himself, which sat just a few blocks from where he and Sheila were ensnarled in traffic. He never enjoyed these jams, but today it actually served their purpose. They were a few blocks from Buzz Eldridge's office, but Sheila needed more time to wrap up her conversation with William Beam, Esq.

Beam's voice boomed over the speaker attached to Larry's cell phone. "Sheila, you know I can't legally disclose any of my clients' business."

"William, trust me, I understand. But I've explained to you what's at stake here. There's no way that the ex–Mrs. Orange could be held liable for the sources from which her husband is obtaining his alimony payments, right?"

"Legally, no, as long as she has reason to believe he's earning the money legally. But if word ever got out that I divulged any information regarding their divorce settlement—"

Working to put her friend at ease, Sheila thumped her chest playfully. "Come on, William, man, this is Sheila. The sister who published that glowing profile on you in our alumni issue last year. You know I wouldn't do anything to endanger your gilded rep, brother."

The speaker crackled as Beam mulled over the request. "All right, I won't mention no figures, though. All I can give up is yes and nos."

Hearing the conciliatory tone, Larry pounced eagerly. "Attorney Beam, this is Larry Whitaker speaking. Why don't we treat this like a bad game of cards? I'll read you my hand, you just nod to indicate the gist of what you've got."

"I read you."

"The Ellis Center's annual report lists the salaries of its officers. The records show an annual salary of fifty-one thousand dollars for the business manager, Mr. Rolly V. Orange. Is that consistent with the amount of alimony he's currently paying his lovely ex-wife?"

Beam chuckled. "Let's just say if that's his only source of income, he must be living out of a cardboard box after he remits his alimony each month."

Unable to hide her excitement at the revelation, Sheila flashed a pleased grin at Larry. "Well, William, that must mean that Mr. Orange has filed notice with you of additional income he earns, right?"

"Please!" Beam caught himself. "Uh, I mean, I cannot positively agree with that statement."

Larry tried to keep his tone serious. "So you're saying he has told you that Ellis is his only source of income?"

Beam was starting to enjoy himself. "I cannot answer the question on the grounds that it might incriminate my client's ex-husband. Sheila, it's been fun, but I really have to sign off now before I cross a line."

Leaning into the speaker, Sheila smiled and thanked her friend. "William, you are so precious. Thank you very much. We'll be using this four-one-one to bluff some information out of the councilman, if we can't find proof of it ourselves."

"Don't mention it. No, I mean *really* don't mention it. Look, drop me a line when you decide about that offer from the *Post*, hear? I'm out."

As the dial tone reverberated through the Lexus, Larry reached over to click the phone off, a wry smile spreading across his face. "So you got that offer from the *Post*, huh? You weren't gonna share that with ol' Larry?"

As he revved up the concrete driveway of the parking garage adjacent to Eldridge's building, Sheila waved him off. "Larry, we don't have time to deal with that now, do we? Don't worry, I will tell *all* of my friends what the deal is once I make up my mind. Who knows, it may just take one little thing to tip me one way or the other." She stifled a laugh as Larry fought to keep from blushing.

Develcorp occupied the fifth and sixth floors of the Waterston Towers building. As Larry and Sheila rode the elevator to the fifth floor, they noted a sign forbidding visitors from entering the sixth floor, due to extensive renovations in process. A minute later they stepped off the elevator into Develcorp's spacious lobby. As they crossed the plush carpet toward the reception desk, Larry caught a glimpse of himself and Sheila in the mirror that covered the wall behind the receptionist. Dressed conservatively in business attire, they each looked to be a couple years out of college, an effect he was counting on to get them where they needed to go.

The receptionist, a thin, elderly white woman with glasses that rested in the crook of her long nose, was obviously startled to see persons of color in this office. "May I help you?" Larry imagined she was less interested in helping them than she was in redirecting them to wherever she figured they really should be.

"Yes, ma'am, my name is Calvin Barnes, and this is Marilyn Richards. We are representatives of HealthNotes. Our office courier was sick yesterday and couldn't pick up our check. Wally Ricker said we could get it today before noon." They had read about HealthNotes, a health claims processor that Develcorp used to track its health insurance, in a recent issue of *Real Estate Advisor*. That was also where they'd read that Eldridge insisted on keeping his office open a half day on Saturdays. Larry had cribbed the names of the HealthNotes employees from an annual report. He'd gotten the name of Wally Ricker, Eldridge's chief accountant, from the magazine article. He'd learned through research that Healthnotes had an office in the same tower and figured they routinely sent someone to pick up their checks.

The secretary adjusted her glasses and glared at Larry. "Oh, well, Mr. Ricker isn't in today. Why don't I have him call you on Monday—"

"Well, ma'am, HealthNotes is frankly a little crunched for cash. We'd really like to pick up that check today, if at all possible. Can you help us out?"

Fixing her eyes on her computer screen, the receptionist barked into her headpiece. "Susan, who is in the accounting office today? I've got two individuals here with HealthNotes, looking to pick up their check." After nodding for what seemed like hours, she looked up at Larry and Sheila.

"Betty Brock, our accounting manager, is doing time in there today. If you walk back to your right and take the first left, you'll see the accounting office. Betty should be there to let you in."

They were one step closer. Larry nodded respectfully toward the woman as Sheila eagerly leaped past him. "Thank you. By the way, is Mr. Eldridge in today? I was supposed to drop a note to him."

"Yes, he is in. You'll pass him as you head to the accounting office. I'll let him know you'll be stopping by."

Larry wasn't sure he liked that. They'd have to work quickly. "Uh, thanks again." He followed Sheila down the hall.

Betty Brock clearly had a lot on her mind. The woman looked to be several months pregnant, a fact that her tight sky blue pantsuit was trying hard to deny. Her frumpy head of curls and lop-sided wire-rimmed glasses added to the image of a woman who had no time to be concerned with appearances.

"Come in, Mr. Barnes and Ms. Richards. Can you wait here while I go and look up your files? You guys never send the same person for checks, but I'll look at the authorized checklist to verify you're on there. I'll just be one minute."

Larry's mind whirred into action. "Uh." There was no way they'd complete their mission if Betty checked that list. How to keep this train from going off track?

"I feel faint." Sheila touched her hand to her forehead, affecting the believable aura of someone growing green around the gills. "Where is your nearest rest—"

Larry was overcome with admiration as Sheila spewed what had to be her entire breakfast across Betty's pantsuit, the goo and spittle running down to join the puddle that lay at her own feet. She slumped quickly to the floor. "Oh, I knew something looked funny about that bagel I bought this morning . . ."

Revolted but concerned, Betty blinked rapidly before coming to. "Oh, dear, let, let me help you up and show you to the ladies' room. We've both got some cleaning to do! Oh, dear . . ." She stopped in the midst of pulling Sheila to her feet, seemingly realizing that a trip to the rest room would leave the office exposed to the strange black man. "Um, Mr. Barnes, would you stay here and watch the office while I take your associate to get cleaned up quick? There's no cash or anything in here, so there's no real danger."

Larry stifled a smirk at her candor. "Um, no problem, ma'am. I'm really sorry. Ms. Richards just found out she was pregnant a few days ago. You know how it is." He flashed a wink at Sheila as she scowled at him from behind Betty's trusting face.

As soon as the door shut behind him, Larry moved into warp speed. He had glimpsed three tall shelves full of large plastic binders as soon as they stepped into the central lobby. Surrounding the lobby were five cubicles that separated the bean counters from one another. He burst past the first cubicle to the row of shelves and quickly scanned the titles printed on the side of each binder. Not until he had come to the third shelf did he see the magic words: *Check Register*. He grabbed hungrily at the most recent register and placed it on the shelf at eye level. He didn't really think Eldridge would have been arrogant enough to cut Orange's checks out of Develcorp's account, but he figured anything was possible; he had a feeling Eldridge was no Einstein.

By the time Betty knocked at the office door several minutes later, Larry was standing calmly against the wall just inside the main entrance, in plain view. He imagined he was the perfect picture of innocence. "Uh, is everyone okay now?"

Whisking her rotund form into the office, Betty smiled innocently. "Well, I don't reek anymore, and Ms. Richards is past the worst of it, aren't you, dear?"

Proffering a weak smile, Sheila reached for Betty's hand. "Thank you so much, Betty. I really have to go home and rest. I'll go lie down in the lobby while I let Calvin get the check." She shot Larry a smile that dared him to get out of that one.

Moving suddenly to help prop Sheila up, Larry smiled sheepishly at Betty, glad he'd done his homework. "Actually, Betty, I'm embarrassed to admit something. While you were in the rest room, I opened up my wallet to get you something to reimburse you for the cost of that lovely suit. I don't imagine those types of stains come out easily."

Betty's eyes brightened as Larry handed her two hundred-dollar bills. He had guessed right; she probably knew the market value of that pantsuit wasn't half of what she was getting. "Oh, oh, Calvin, this isn't necessary—"

"But it is. You didn't have to be so gracious to us. Besides which, looking into my wallet revealed the embarrassing fact that I don't have my driver's license on me today. Unfortunately, company policy forbids me from taking any property of the company to my house, so I'd have to deposit the check today. I can't very well do that without my license and account information now, can I?" Larry threw out a goofy chuckle.

Betty bought it. "Oh, dear, well, what can you do? Sorry you had to go through this trouble. We'll have the check when you come back Monday." She fingered Larry's C-notes. "You two have a good weekend now."

As they made their way toward Eldridge's office, Sheila elbowed Larry. "You're just a born liar, aren't you? If this wasn't for such a good cause, I'd report you to the Highland student body!"

"Who are you to talk, Miss Hurl-on-Request! How in the hell did you do that?"

"Let's just say years of growing up around my ignorant male cousins finally paid off. But I'm still not in your league!"

Larry pulled her back into the dark corner opposite Eldridge's office. "Nobody does it better, baby. Signed, sealed, and delivered, I have pages from Develcorp's check registers from the last four months, showing disbursements to one Rolly V. Orange! We're in there!"

Sheila lowered her voice to match his. "Should we get out of here while we can, then? Would it be best to give this info to Sheryl Gibson, and let her handle it from here?"

Larry's blood was reaching a pleasant boil now, adrenaline from the mounting discoveries bolstering his already bold nature. "Why make Sheryl do unnecessary work, girl? Watch and learn."

"Larry!" Sheila hesitated as Larry strode toward the dark corner office, strutting like a peacock at a county fair. She whispered aloud to herself, "This fool's out of his mind!"

Resolute, Larry faced the cherry-wood door and knocked authoritatively. "Mr. Eldridge?"

As Sheila materialized at his side, the massive door swung open, powered by an automatic button. A quick look around revealed an office that would have made Larry senior jealous. It was the size of a small apartment, bordered on two sides by full-length windows that afforded sweeping views of the White House, the Washington Monument, and the flight of airplanes heading in and out of National Airport. To the far left was a large aquarium, teeming with fluorescent rocks, large goldfish, and an odd assortment of other swimming creatures. The mahogany-paneled wall above the aquarium was the only one that held any fixtures, namely, pictures of Eldridge with a heavyset woman and four young adults who looked like Eldridge had spit them out himself.

Eldridge sat to the far left, at his desk; it was obvious he had been tunneling through piles of paperwork before pausing to admit his unexpected visitors. Surveying his gaunt face and knitted brow, Larry was tempted to feel sorry for the crook.

"Who the hell are you?" Eldridge was confused by the sight of two black kids invading his space. The receptionist had said an official from HealthNotes was here. He had never worked with either of the children before him. He bolted from his chair defensively. "I'll have security come up here right now, I don't know you—"

"Buzz, take a good look." Larry sauntered up to the entrepreneur's desk, fingering the buttons on his Hugo Boss jacket. "You *know* me, hell, you've probably studied every aspect of my life these past few weeks. Don't play shy now."

Balling his fists, Eldridge was unable to stop his face from turning an even paler shade than normal. "Whitaker!"

Sheila watched in amazement. "This guy actually knows who you are?"

Larry stood in front of the large desk, arching his back and smiling calmly. "Of course he does, Sheila. He knows me, Brandon, Terence, and O.J., too. Don't you?"

"I don't know what you're talking about." Eldridge was fuming. He wanted them out, but he was afraid to push this Whitaker kid too far. How much did he know?

Larry began to pace Eldridge's office as if they were business associates. "Buzz, let's not play games. Not only am I hip to what you've done to throw me and my housemates off the track of your schemes, I have proof of your little games. Rolly Orange confessed to everything."

Eldridge folded his arms tightly. He was walking a tightrope, but no kid was going to intimidate him. "I don't know who you're talking about, son. And if you ever claim this conversation took place, I will deny it until the day I die. Take a guess as to whose word will stand up in court between the two of us."

Unable to conceal the smoking gun, Larry snatched the check-register copies from his jacket pocket. "What'll the court think of these, Buzz?"

Feeling his breath grow acrid, Eldridge asserted brave face. "Would you like me to pull one of those check copies for you, Silver Spoon? Let me assure you, each of those checks is made out to Rolly Orange, officer of Ellis Community Center. The center's account number is even specified on every copy."

Holding to his best poker face, Larry smacked his lips. "What?"

"That's right, Einstein. Those checks are made out to support the center in its mission. I've been a faithful supporter for several months."

"For the several months since Orange came aboard, to help reduce any suspicion of your culpability. Buzz, you sly dog, you! That's a nice cover, but you've got one problem. Rolly's already told me about the way he set up a separate account in the Ellis Center's name. He puts these checks in and then makes withdrawals for his personal use. I ain't no fool, now." Larry grinned as widely as he could, knowing every word was bull. He was bluffing worse than a poker player with a hand full of twos.

Eldridge placed a hand over the speaker button of his phone. "You two can leave now, on your own, or you can leave with the aid of security. Take your pick."

Defying the lack of evidence before him, Larry fired his last shot. "Buzz, I suggest you enjoy taking the liberty to call security. This time tomorrow, Rolly Orange will be hidden away by the police, and they'll be comin' to shut you down. You always knew Orange would be the weak link, didn't you? For the record, don't think he caved in for the hell of it. Apparently one of his kids found out about his extra income, and one thing led to another."

Eldridge stood firm against the desk, trying to compose himself. This jerk kid handled himself extremely well. He was either handing him a well-spun load of bull or telling him the painful truth. "I don't understand! How did you find all this out?"

Larry turned and headed for the door with Sheila in tow.

"Two things, Buzz. First, you and Orange's little pack of lies endangered my campaign. Nobody screws up the Whitaker Master Plan without paying a price. We Whitakers believe in winning at any cost."

Scratching at his crew cut, Eldridge frowned. "What's your second point, young man? I don't have time for your little games."

Undaunted, Larry threw in a final bluff. "Well, Buzz, Rolly Orange discovered a conscience. He talked to me this morning, before going to the cops. Said he couldn't let a group of young brothers, fellow Highland men, be caught up in this mess. Guess race still matters, huh?"

Before he could undo the damage he hoped he'd done, Larry turned and disappeared out the door, with Sheila close behind. As they hightailed their way to the elevators, the crash of shattering glass—Eldridge's aquarium?—ripped through the hallway. Larry pumped his fist enthusiastically. Mission accomplished!

28

REDEMPTION

Pitch black was all that met him when he opened his eyes. As panic filled his soul, O.J. shook his aching head gently, praying for a ray of light to break through. Slowly, his prayer was answered as the circles of ebony gave way to shimmering, blurred waves of yellow, white, and blue. In seconds his vision was focused on the beige plaid wallpaper opposite his bed. His nostrils confirmed that he was in a hospital; the smells of antiseptic, liniments, and Pine-Sol bombarded him. He had been awake off and on several times today, but he had no clue how long he had been asleep this time. He could actually feel his spine pulsating, which was an improvement from the first time he had awakened. The doctor had told him that he was probably out of the woods, that his knife wound had been fully stitched and they expected him to regain full nerve sensitivity within two to three days. He hoped the doc was right. Graduation was coming up and he was scheduled to deliver his farewell sermon at Light in two weeks.

"O.J.?"

He knew immediately that the voice was his father's, heavy with anxiety and exhaustion from a long day of travel. Wincing at the pain, O.J. pivoted his head carefully so he could meet his father's smiling, weary eyes. "He-hey, Dad."

His father's leathery face beamed as he leaned over the bed. "Oh, boy, I'm praisin' God for your health! All through the morning and afternoon, while I was travelin', I told the Lord! I told him, you promised me in your Word that anything I ask for within your will, I can *know* that I already have it! I knew you were gonna pull through this, boy! Doctor says it may take you a while to heal fully, but the most important thing is you got your life and all your faculties! I need to cut a Holy Ghost rug up in here right now!"

A familiar feeling of comforting warmth overtook O.J. In his father's presence it was impossible to keep from viewing life through spiritual eyeglasses. It wasn't as if his father was a stranger to adversity. Knowing all that Pastor Peters had come through made his father's faith one of the most inspiring elements of O.J.'s life, although he had never personally shared in that faith.

Taking a seat beside the bed, Pastor Peters adopted a more somber tone. "So, how are you really feeling?"

O.J. tugged at his IV and shook his head. "Better, I think. Last time I woke up, Brandon was still here. I couldn't even hold a real conversation with the brother. I was still woozy, I guess, from when they knocked me out and stitched up my wounds. He still around?"

"No, he left a few minutes after I got here. It's almost eight o'clock now, son. That boy stayed here the better part of the day with you, O.J. I thought you weren't very close with any of your housemates."

"I-I really haven't been. I got in on the house deal through Larry, we used to hit some of the same clubs freshman year. But Brandon's saved, Dad, a real Goody Two-shoes, and I guess he proved it by looking out for me tonight."

"Well, praise the Lord! You never know where God has his people planted."

"Yeah, I suppose I'll always owe the brother one now." A wave of guilt swept over O.J. when he thought of how he'd taunted the Choirboy recently. And the brother had still watched his back.

After a couple of minutes of relaxed silence passed, Peters rubbed his head of receding gray curls and said, "Now look, O.J., I'm not talkin' about getting revenge here, but do you know who did this to you?"

O.J. leaned back and shut his eyes tight. He'd had twelve

hours of consciousness to accept reality. Keesa, a sister who adored him only months ago, had attempted to take his life. His initial reaction had been complete indignation. Who on God's green earth did she think she was to threaten his life, his very existence, over a baby who most likely was not even his? His immediate thirst for justice had been followed by horror at the thought of what the attack would mean to his image, and his future, as a clergyman. Just about everyone had skeletons in the closet, but how many had been personally attacked by a member of their own flock? The tongues had no doubt been wagging even as he had lain there fighting for his life. He panicked at the thought of Pastor Grier's reaction. Would he be too embarrassed to even allow O.J. back into the pulpit one last time? Would word even spread back to Atlanta, infecting his image in the minds of his home church and the other heavy-hitting clergy throughout the city? That thought alone had filled him with the desire to see Keesa Bishop pay the ultimate price for her sin against him.

How had she even dared to go there, trying to take him out? He'd done nothing to her that he hadn't done to tens of other women, in D.C. and back home. Granted, the only other time he'd been accused of fathering a child had been high school. Myrna Hillman had been his first, so it had been a unique sense of obligation that made him submit to a test in that case, only to find that her ex-boyfriend was the father. After that, he'd sworn he would never again let a woman yank his chain.

How dare Keesa act like rejection was an excuse for violence! He'd never attacked any of the triflin' little hos in his junior high classes, the skinny, pretty girls who had laughed at his pokey stomach and acne-ridden complexion. After a couple of years, their nos had turned to yeses, when he called himself to the ministry and quickly became the most sought-after teen preacher in Atlanta.

By the time he'd graduated high school, O.J. had exacted his revenge. He'd had his way with one woman after another, before humiliating each one with sudden, vague rejection. That was how you got revenge—bringing someone to their knees emotionally, not knocking 'em upside the head with a blunt object.

His father's voice beckoned him from his reverie. "O.J.? Are you all right, son?"

Returning to the present, O.J. opened his eyes slowly. "Dad, I-I can't lie to you. I was attacked by a girl."

"Someone from the neighborhood? What did she want, money for drugs or something?"

"No, no. She was after me."

His father's face twisted into a confused frown. "After you? What do you mean, son?"

"I mean she . . . she . . . uh, she was out to hurt me personally, maybe kill me." Attempting to look his father in the eye, he returned his gaze to the end of his bed as he saw the look of horror on his face. "She's been claimin' that I got her pregnant, and I've been denying it."

His father's eyes filled with hopeful desperation. "Oh, son, I could tell you some stories about crazy women in the church who think they can trap a preacher with wild allegations—"

"Dad, these weren't allegations." O.J. choked the words out, feeling himself tear up. "I had my way with her, plenty of times. Sometimes without any protection."

Pastor Peters stepped back from the bed and ran his hand through the remains of his silvery Afro. "What . . . you . . . what are you saying, O.J.?"

"I'm sayin' she was some ghetto girl I had an empty fling with! I thought she was just trying to land me, you know, using me to get out of the ghetto by accusing me of being the father and—"

"And you told her that?"

"Yeah!" He regretted how defensive that sounded. But he knew there was no point soft-pedaling it now. He had to get this out into the open and get his father's reaction over with.

"Did you offer to help her out at all, O.J.? A paternity test after the birth? Money for an abortion? Not that you should consider that an option."

"I tried to pay her off to go away and leave me alone, Dad. Clearly, she's convinced herself that I'm really the father. She's crazy as a road lizard!"

His father began speaking at a creeping pace, as if he couldn't fully accept the words. "Let me . . . get this straight. This was her way of getting revenge because you denied getting her pregnant, even though you knew it was entirely possible?"

"Um, yeah."

"So what are you gonna do, O.J.? Turn the police on the potential mother of your child?"

Through the tears starting to frame his eyelids, he glared back at his father. "What choice do I have?"

"O.J., I want you to tell me right now, is this how you always treat God's most precious creatures? I am your father, son. I'm not here to judge you, but I know how your momma and I raised you, and weren't nothing we taught you that should have landed you in this state. Talk to me, boy." The pulsating veins in the pastor's right temple told O.J. this was no time to be coy.

He lost his composure as he removed the invisible mask he had worn for his father through the years. He could've kept him there all night with exhaustive details of his exploits, but he knew the simple examples he confessed were more than enough to paint the picture. He recounted how it had all started, as a ploy to prove he wasn't the fat sissy that the kids at school and church accused him of being. He'd started out just doing what it took to convince them that he was normal, that he wasn't some Goody Two-shoes preacher's kid. But that didn't stop the womanizing, the liquor, and the games from turning into daily habits. He let it all out.

"Oh, dear Lord," Pastor Peters whispered, to himself as much as to God. "Please forgive my son for stepping far outside the direction of your Holy Spirit. You know I've done all I could with the boy, Lord, as did his mother, may she rest in peace with you. We was never perfect, Lord, but he can never say he wasn't taught right. But Lord, you can do all things, and I pray you will reignite the fire of the Holy Spirit in my son's heart. Help him to walk as you walked when you trod this earth, with dignity and honor toward all. Please . . ."

"Dad," O.J. whispered reverently. He couldn't take any more of his father's anguished prayers right now. Every word was a knife piercing his softening heart. "I understand you praying over me, but I got to finish my confession. I-I know I need to do something to help Keesa out. She can't go free, not when she'd pull somethin' this wacked, but she is in a family way. Brandon mentioned earlier that the police plan to talk to me tonight or tomorrow morning. I need you to sit in when I speak to them, okay?"

Exhaling deeply, Pastor Peters placed a hand over one of O.J.'s. "We'll work somethin' out, son. So you will take responsibility for this child, if it's yours?"

"I don't see how I have a choice, huh? Wouldn't that be something, me a dad?"

Rising from his chair, Pastor Peters backed away from the bed, his eyes dim and dark as he motioned over his shoulder. "I-I need to go and call Deacon Smith and Sister Parker, they got a phone chain set up to spread word about how you doin'. When I come back, we'll figure out how to get this girl picked up in the most peaceful way possible, okay?"

Shaken at the veiled look of disgust on his father's face, O.J. slurped up new tears and sighed in response. "All right. And Dad, thanks."

He had barely finished the sentence before his father burst out into the hallway. O.J. knew why he had left so suddenly, and it had nothing to do with the urgent need to call Deacon Smith. Oscar Peters, Sr., was no Otis Grier. He would never abandon his son, but O.J. had seen the disappointment on his father's face. His heart was rent. Yesterday he'd thought betraying Grier had been rock bottom; he'd had no clue. Hoping that the nurse wouldn't emerge for another few minutes, he bent his head into his chest, soaking it in seconds with salty drops of guilt. There had to be a special place in hell for him now.

29

TO THE WIRE

Brandon lay stretched out on his recently defiled bed. It still reeked of Monica's peachy, rapturous scent, and he didn't plan on changing the sheets anytime soon. Propping his phone against his ear with his shoulder, he checked his watch. It was almost nine o'clock. Where was Terence? He'd come home expecting to see Larry and Terence discussing the Ellis meeting. He knew Larry had been hot on Rolly Orange's tail, and that Terence had served as their lone representative at this morning's board meeting. He regretted the fact that he'd let his and O.J.'s problems distract him all day, but now he was ready to find out what was going on. Where were these brothers?

"Brandon, you're not listening to me, are you?" Floating through the phone receiver, Monica Simone's voice had an edge he'd not heard before.

Jumping to his feet to keep his mind alert, he paced the floor. "I'm sorry, there's just been a lot going down today."

"Well, I'm glad that O.J.'s okay. What I wanna know now is, how are you?"

"What do you mean?"

"You know what I mean. Why didn't you call me this morning after O.J. had his surgery? I told you to let me know what was up."

"Monica, look—"

"Don't give me excuses, Brandon. I want the truth. You blame me for what happened last night, don't you? Do you think I planned for things to go that far?"

One night together, and she was reading him like a book. "Monica, i-it's not about blame. Last night wouldn't have happened if I didn't want it to."

"That's what bothers you, isn't it? The fact that you *enjoyed* it?"

Brandon was so frustrated. By most people's morals, he should be strutting like a prize pig right now. Not only had he just lain with the woman of his dreams, but now she sounded like she was interested in more. And here he was, pushing her away like she was some depraved criminal. "Monica, I don't know what bothers me anymore. I don't know what I should believe. Yes, I enjoyed last night immensely. But it's not that simple."

"Why not? It's simple enough for anyone else who's ever tried it. Brandon, come on, how many of those ex-friends of yours in the Disciples do you really think are celibate? Even my grandmother's known for saying everybody has a little freak in them. Why should you be any different? Don't you think you deserve some pleasure in your life?"

"What the Disciples, or any other Christians, do or don't do is none of my business, Monica. That's between them and their God. You don't understand, this is about me and nobody else. To just toss away what I've viewed, correctly or incorrectly, as part of my spiritual integrity? I can't do that. I can't accept that last night was okay."

Monica sighed. "Brandon . . ."

He could tell his self-torture was alienating her. Maybe that was for the best. It was either that or try to explain about Brandy.

"Brandon, I've never dealt with this before. Usually I'm fightin' brothers off. I'm used to being the one who questions myself when I give it up to a guy. This is freaking me out!"

Brandon bit his lower lip and shook his head. He was convinced he and Monica had a connection deeper than one night of fevered passion. The emotional chemistry he'd felt with her since that first double date had proven that four years of carrying a torch for her had not been in vain. God must have had some hand in all that, right? They were enjoying each other's company, and, illicit though it was, the sex had shown promise. But none of that mattered to him now. He could see they were separated by a deep chasm that neither was willing or able to cross, at least not now. He would be leaving town in a matter of weeks. Why prolong the inevitable?

"Monica, I can't handle you. You need a man who can serve you hot-buttered lovin', guilt-free. I need a woman who respects my wishes enough to keep her body off limits. We're wasting our time."

"Wasting our *time*?" Her tone immediately made him wish he could snatch back the last sentence. "That's what last night was to you, a waste of your time? I think that qualifies as the most insulting thing a man has ever said to me."

"Monica— "

"You know, Brandon Bailey, for such a choirboy, you sure can be an ass when you want to. I don't need this."

"Monica—"

The phone line went dead before he could clean anything up. He wasn't proud of his behavior, but at least the drama was behind him.

As he dropped the phone back onto his bed, he heard the front door open and slam shut. Time to get some Ellis news. A couple weeks and graduation would almost be here. Brandon told himself the time would fly; he'd help solidify the Ellis crisis, bust his last final, and hang out with Bobby and a few friends before skipping town. He prayed that would be enough to keep Monica hidden away, locked in the deepest dungeons of his subconscious. He tightened the belt around his Dockers and stepped into a pair of Dexter loafers. Terence had some explaining to do.

≈≈≈≈

Lisa clutched wildly at Terence's windbreaker. He'd failed to hide his self-hatred from her all afternoon. He'd left the board meeting and ridden the bus across town, out to Virginia, back through town, and out into Maryland before finally landing at her doorstep. He'd hoped that an hour of frantic pleasure in Lisa's arms would reduce the sting of what he had done, but the throttling power of his orgasms had been no more than a temporary diversion. By the time he and Lisa had dressed and gone out for a bite to eat near campus, the events of the past week had cascaded from his tongue like prisoners fleeing a jailhouse. Now that he'd fully vented, Lisa was full of ideas about how to resolve the situation. As they returned to the house, she continued to pound home her opinion.

"You've got to tell the guys about this, Terence! You are going to tell them, aren't you?"

Pausing at the front door, he searched his jeans pockets for his keys. "Lisa, I'm not gonna tell you again! I can't! I do that, Nico's likely to kill us all, Biggie included! I had no choice. The only hope is that Larry figures out what's goin' on and cracks things open. Hopefully Nico wouldn't blame me for that."

"Oh, so he can blame, maybe even *kill*, Larry instead?" Her eyes searched his face for a sign of sanity. "Terence, have you lost your mind?"

"Maybe so, Lisa. All I know is I just saved my brother's life. It's too late to go back now."

"I don't believe that. Between us, we can figure out something! What good are our Highland educations, if we just let a vital institution of this community go under?"

Ready to end the discussion, Terence swung the front door open, lowering his voice. "Lisa, do you know what would happen to my grandmother if Biggie or I were to be murdered? Her life would end. I don't want that weight on me. I've got us out of harm's way, and I'm not goin' back in."

As he ushered her into the kitchen, Lisa glared at him. "I don't believe you. The Terence Davidson I know is about more than looking out for himself. You make me wonder why I'm even thinking about taking a job here in D.C."

Terence stifled the smile that wanted to spring to his face. "I-I thought you were Jersey-bound for sure."

"So did I, and maybe I should be. But I can't help but think we need one more year, Terence, one last chance to—but that doesn't even matter right now, does it? If you let your friends stumble in the dark over this Ellis fiasco, you will not be the man I love. Do you understand?"

Reaching into the refrigerator for the glass water pitcher, he filled two plastic cups. Hoisting one before him, he rolled his eyes before meeting Lisa's. "To my new momma, thank you for showing me the way." He knew he was sounding like a pompous ass, but who was she to judge him? She could tell him what to do when it was her family's life on the line.

⚜

Larry was seething. As he pulled the Lexus into the driveway, he continued to spray the car with profanities, even pounding the steering wheel at several points. He was still in shock over his discussion with Sheryl Gibson. He had called her from the Highland library, where he and Sheila had conducted some additional research before changing clothes and regrouping.

"How the *hell* did Terence sign over access to the Highland contributions? What is he, a retard now? I may not be able to design computer software, but I damn well know how to follow instructions: do not give over access to the contributions! What the freak is his problem?"

Giving his hand a few light pats, Sheila sighed anxiously. "I'm sure he'll have some sort of explanation, Larry. Take it easy. We've had a pretty hair-raising day as it is."

Looking into his rearview mirror, Larry was struck with the realization that the day was not going to get any easier. The automobile lights bouncing off his mirror were unmistakable. A 1995 candy red Jaguar XJS. Property of one Ashley Blasingame. "Oh, *shiiit.*"

Turning in her seat, Sheila surveyed the luxury sedan as it hemmed them into the driveway. "Larry, is that who I think it is?"

"It's cool, Sheila. Why don't you go on in the house and find Terence. I'll deal with this."

As Larry and Sheila emerged from the Lexus, Ashley shot out of the Jaguar, staring them both down with a look tailor-made to kill. "You two make such a lovely couple, you know that?"

Larry's heart leaped as Sheila moved to separate them. He was struck again by their contrasts. Although the women were roughly the same height, Sheila's Detroit Pistons cap and Champs sweat suit were the polar opposite of Ashley's glistening mane and dazzling Anne Klein ensemble. Substance versus style.

Sheila held her hands up innocently. "Ashley, there's no need to start a soap opera here. Larry and I are just friends, working on an investigative assignment—"

Ashley stepped to within an inch of Sheila's personal space, her voice rising several decibels. "Look, Aunt Jemima, you can step off me right now, bitch. I got your number! The whole campus is laughing at me, seeing you run around with my man!"

Sheila began rolling up the sleeves of her jacket. "Aunt What? You prissy-ass little prig! I oughtta give you a Motown-style beatdown—"

Larry gently grabbed Sheila around the waist, depositing her on the other side of him and Ashley. "Sheila, please go in the house. I got this one."

"Handle your business, then." Shooting a final glare at Ashley, she turned and huffed up the sidewalk.

Larry knew he had to move quickly to defuse this thing before it turned truly ugly. Another second and he'd have had a catfight on his front lawn. Filled with regret and determination, he stood toe-to-toe with Ashley, locking hands with her and meeting her moistening eyes.

"It's over, isn't it?" The whisper in her voice sounded like a small child's.

Refusing to let his gaze waver, he touched her lips lightly. "I think we both figured that out a while ago, Ash. I really do think I loved you. You've got everything I ever thought I wanted. But it's not working."

"But Larry, weren't we good together?"

"We *looked* good together. We *were* good in bed, good at stylin' and profilin'. Could have had a family out of Central Casting and the family wealth to match. But would we be happy?"

Ashley's words sounded like a whimper. "What is happiness, anyway?"

Larry locked eyes with Ashley. "Ash, be honest with yourself. Could you really get behind things like the Ellis Center, or stick with me through a down time, like what happened with my campaign?"

Wiping the pearl-shaped tears that rolled down her golden cheeks, she reached for him and pulled him close, planting a soft, vulnerable kiss on his lips before responding. "Larry, I don't understand what I did wrong. No man has ever asked anything more of me than my beauty, my body, and my money. Now all of a sudden you want to come along and invent rules I've never played by. Go ahead and live like the other half, if you want to. One day you'll miss this."

Larry frowned but kept his eyes on hers. "I guess we'll never know, Ash. I guess we'll never know. I'll call you later, okay? Before I leave for the summer. I got my hands full right now."

"Fine." She wiped her eyes, which slowly turned into cold, hard blocks of ice. As she climbed back into the Jaguar and revved up the engine, Larry waved slowly and watched her back out of the driveway. Later tonight, or sometime after the madness ended, he knew he would have to shed some tears. There was no time for that now.

When he stepped into the living room seconds later, Sheila and Lisa were perched on the couch, shaking their heads at each other. Brandon was pacing the hardwood floor as Terence stood in front of the couch with hands on hips.

"Terence, this is a joke, right, brother? How could you just hand over the contributions lock, stock, and barrel?" Brandon was as edgy as Larry had ever seen him.

Larry and Terence met each other in a deadlocked stare. Terence seemed defensive, determined to keep everyone out of his family business. Larry was still reeling from his confrontations with Eldridge and Ashley. Brandon was wrung-out emotionally and physically, and Sheila and Lisa felt as if they were trapped in the middle of a train wreck.

"Whitaker, what you lookin' at?" Terence said. "You better not come at me crazy. You got somethin' to say, say it. Quit tryin' to show out."

As Brandon huffed and puffed, perching himself on the edge

of the loveseat, Larry stayed rooted to his position just inside the entryway. "Terence, I don't know about anyone else, but I'm confused, brother. You knew Sheila and I were closing in on a link between Orange and some seedy elements, especially Eldridge. You also knew that to release the contributions to Orange and his crony Spears could spell financial disaster for Ellis. Why would you betray us like this?"

Stepping over to where Larry stood, Terence pointed a thick finger in his face. "You need to watch the use of that word *betray*, Larry. I did what I had to do today. Who are you to judge me? Maybe I'm tired of all this pussyfootin' around with the damn contributions." He turned to face the entire room. "You've all been acting like some punks, thinkin' you could second guess Rolly Orange and Sheryl! Come on, brothers! I know we like to think we can save the world, but be real! Who are we to tell an established community leader and an accomplished politician how to run thangs? The whole segregated-account thing was silly!"

"So you went over our heads and vetoed it, without so much as a peep to your own boys?" Brandon's brow grew sweaty as his nerves tensed and pulsated. Nothing was worse than having a knock-down-drag-out with one of your best friends.

As he shook a hand at the room, Terence's face filled with bile. "Hey, look, nobody told you all to back out of the damn meeting. It's a free country. You could have come and offset my vote."

Larry crossed his arms tightly, trying to choose his words calmly. "T, you knew why we couldn't make it, and I specifically asked you to keep in mind—"

"Back up, Big Dog. You *told* me to make sure Orange didn't get access to the contributions. No questions *ever* about my damn opinion! Who am I but a poor egghead engineer, right? Nah, you gon' just *tell* me how I should vote. Stop and think how you sound, company man."

Larry had had enough. "Naw, Terence. Hell, no! I will *not* let you turn a discussion about the future of a center that can save kids' *lives* into some petty bickering over whether or not I respected your *feelings*. Damn your feelings! Who was getting hurt when the segregated account was in place? Nobody! What if we're actually right about Orange, who gets hurt? Everybody! Damn, man! I never figured you of all people to be such a fuckup!"

"I'll show you a fuckup!" Unable to defend his actions, Terence gave in to raw emotion and surged forward to take Larry on. Brandon leaped from the loveseat to restrain him.

"Terence, don't!" Pleading for peace, Brandon breezed alongside his friend, placing an outstretched arm in front of Terence. "We're gettin' way off track here. Just go upstairs and cool off, please! This house has seen enough violence, man!" His brow moist with sweat, Brandon paced between Terence and Larry. "Have we all lost our God-given minds? O.J.'s layin' up in the hospital, Ellis Center's future is in doubt, and what are we doing? Threatening one other with more black-on-black violence!"

Looking past the back of Brandon's round head and outstretched arms, Larry met Terence's eyes again. They were hardboiled, full of indignant shame. Something was wrong. Larry knew his friend would not behave like this under normal circumstances. Someone, or something, was behind this wacked behavior. Frantically, his eyes danced over to meet Lisa's.

"Terence, look at yourself, what you've come to." She rose from the couch and went to his side, placing a hand on his heaving shoulder. Her voice took on the quality of a concerned mother. "Are you really gonna throw your friendships away over this? Was that the plan when you all started working at Ellis? To kill a friendship? Tell them, baby, just tell them now."

"Damn!" The expletive exploded from Terence like a cannon, shaking the house. The room filled with anxious silence as he bent forward and doubled over. "I don't . . . I don't know what to say . . ."

Brandon could tell Larry was as embarrassed as he was by Terence's tears. "Well, why don't you walk us through whatever led to your decision, man. Take your time."

Terence took a deep breath, then painstakingly laid out the dilemma regarding Biggie and Nico Lane. When Terence completed his account, he looked up into the faces of his friends, all of whom were seated again. Brandon and Sheila looked shell-shocked at his tales of Nico's gangland threats; Larry already looked like he was already cooking up a response. Too exhausted to solicit any more reaction, Terence stayed in his upright position, swaying to and fro like a venerable oak.

"Got a suggestion." Larry's fingers were woven tight, a bundle of nervous energy. "Brandon, why don't you take Lisa out to pick up some coffee and Cokes. We all need to put in a long night of strategy to bust this hump. I'll give you the money. Sheila, T, and I will get started in the meantime."

Brandon pulled his car keys from his pants pocket. "I'm with that. Lisa, you ready?"

"I'm coming." As she headed out to the foyer with Brandon, Lisa squeezed Terence's arm. "You can thank me later."

Only after she had left the room did Terence raise his head and meet Larry's eyes.

"That is one hell of a woman there, T. Now let's get busy."

❧❧❧

The next morning, William "Buzz" Eldridge strolled coolly across the marble floor of the Waterston Towers lobby. He spotted the security guard, Wardell Burton, at his station. An amiable middle-aged man, Burton had worked the desk on weekends for some five years running. He could have been mistaken for Eldridge's younger twin, so similar were they in height, weight, and hair color. Eldridge almost found the man's presence embarrassing. He could hardly look at Burton without feeling that there but for God's grace went he himself.

"Mr. Eldridge, fancy seeing you here, sir." Burton looked at him with glassy eyes. "Five years, and I've never seen you here on a Sunday morning. Shouldn't you be in church?"

Eldridge smiled wryly as he signed in at the desk. "Wardell, church is a nice institution to partake in when it's convenient. But when a big deal requires my time, well . . . you do the math, my friend."

Burton beamed broadly. "Well, gee, you do have a point.

You're probably doing better than most poor saps who are in church right now, huh? You have a good one, sir."

Eldridge flashed a condescending smile as he headed toward the elevator bank. "You, too, Wardell, you too." He wanted to make sure not to say anything memorable, nothing that would tip off the authorities if they ever interviewed the security officer.

As the elevator climbed to the sixth floor, Eldridge denied the urge to stop at the fifth and take one last look around. There was no point. Savoring the beauty of his offices and possessions would only reduce his will to do what he must for the sake of his family, especially his children. Orange had done his best to play dumb when confronted with Whitaker's allegations yesterday. He could hear the fat man's stumbling, bumbling claims even now.

"Buzz, wh-what are you talking about? I ain't sold nobody out! We just got Terence Davidson to sign over access to the money! Don't you see? We're on the ten-yard line now. Spears will be back in town Monday, I'll sign everything over to him, and he'll have the money wiped out by week's end! Game, set, match, Buzz! What are you babblin' about?"

Eldridge had been unable to contain himself. "You stupid, stupid fool! There's no way that Whitaker kid could have figured out all the things he did without hearing something from you! He told me everything!"

"Buzz, what—"

Buzz had hung up on the buffoon before his rage got the best of him. By the time he'd accepted what was happening, he'd realized it was time to make peace with Plan B. The most important thing from the start had been the survival of Develcorp, so that his children could run the business and make a good living long after he was gone. Now, whether Orange was telling the truth or not, this Whitaker kid, as bright and charismatic as he was, was sure to make enough of a stink about his links to Orange to draw media attention. That would mean the immediate end to his hopes of getting in on the riverfront project. And no riverfront project meant no Develcorp. It was time to utilize the only other source of capital to which he had access.

He laughed to himself as he stepped off the elevator onto the sixth floor. A large printed sign sat just outside the elevators:

THIS FLOOR IS OFF LIMITS TO ALL PERSONNEL
EXCEPT FOR DEVELCORP OFFICERS AND CONSTRUCTION WORKERS.
FLOOR IS CLOSED FOR BUSINESS UNTIL
RENOVATIONS ARE COMPLETE.

Eldridge swept his eyes across the area, which had been stripped almost bare. To his immediate right was a large room framed in gray concrete. The floor was full of rooms just like this one. This one would be the main conference room when it was complete, chosen as such because of the panoramic view it offered of the Mall skyline, almost identical to the one from his office. The workers were in the process of enlarging the window so that it would cover almost the entire length of the wall—one of the reasons the floor was so dangerous now. Stapled across the large gaping hole in the wall was a thick latex sheet; a few strong winds had already loosened one corner, exposing an opening large enough for a person to slip through.

Eldridge checked his watch. The construction supervisor, Joe Klein, would be here soon. He had called Joe this morning and told him of some concerns he had about how the work was coming along. He'd agreed to meet Joe this morning to go over the floor, claiming that he would be out of town the rest of the week. He'd chuckled when Joe suggested he wait for him in the lobby for safety's sake. Surely he knew Buzz Eldridge would be too naïve and arrogant to wait for him like some dependent child. When Joe arrived to find that a horrific accident had occurred, he would be sure to report to the authorities that he had told the foolish old man not to venture up there on his own. The claims adjuster for his life insurer would have no choice but to fork the dough over to the Eldridge family. No one would suspect him of suicide.

As Eldridge gingerly lifted the plastic flap, feeling the harsh rush of wind and the cold smatter of raindrops whip his sport coat, he wondered what Nico Lane would think. He'd not even bothered to call the boy. What did he have to fear from him now? He regretted ever getting entangled with the thug, but what did it matter now? The way things had turned out, he'd have bought it one way or the other. As he ripped the flap loose and began to remove his jacket, he stifled a sigh at the thought of his Katie, whom he had kissed good-bye an hour ago, before driving in from Alexandria. He would miss her, but whether she admitted it or not, she would be happier as a lonely but wealthy widow than she would have been as a loyal but impoverished wife. Her constant questions about his success in getting the riverfront project always sounded genuine, but the message there was obvious: no romance without finance. He'd have lost her love along with the business, if he'd ever allowed it go under. And there was no question that this was best for the children.

His heart broken but his spirit resolute, Buzz stepped to the ledge of the building. He reached underneath his sweater and removed the small kitten that had meowed softly from beneath his coat for the last hour. He set the purring feline onto the ledge, a few inches to his left. The kitten was frightened out of his wits, evidenced by the high pitch of his purr and the wooden quality of his little legs. *He'll be all right*, Buzz told himself. *He'll be perched here innocently when the police arrive, a living testament to my attempt at a heroic act.*

Teetering on the cement ledge, Buzz retrieved his cell phone from his pants pocket and held it limply in his right hand. "Wardell," he shouted into the phone above the roar of traffic and the heavy roll of thunder, "when Joe Klein gets here, please have him come right up. I just saw a kitten out on the ledge." He sighed for dramatic effect. "It looks like one of the cats that fat secretary on the fourth floor is always sneaking in. I'm going to bring it back in. I'll be out on the ledge if Joe arrives in the next couple of minutes."

Burton's voice was full of foreboding. "Sir, you should not be out on any ledge. Especially as windy as it is! Trust me, sir, we got workmen who can handle the situation. I'll just call—"

"Not to worry, Wardell. I can handle myself. Just send Joe up as soon as he's here." He clicked the phone off before Burton could object further. Everything was set now. It should never have come to this, but the welfare of his family demanded it. Before he could change his mind, William "Buzz" Eldridge lifted his right foot and stepped forward into thin air, implementing his final business decision.

❦❦❦

Biggie Davidson was sound asleep, a crooked smile across his crusty face. His was a peaceful rest, aided by the knowledge that his brother had delivered on Nico Lane's demands and saved his life. Nico had called personally last night, ensuring him that he was officially off the hook. In celebration, Biggie had painted the town red, one reason he continued to sleep soundly on a Sunday afternoon. He didn't know how he was going to support himself, now that Nico had kicked him to the curb, but he was planning to get up later this afternoon and troll through Northeast D.C., see if he could break into some markets there. As his bony chest, covered only by the thin cotton comforter stretched over him, rose and dove in rhythmic fashion, he was oblivious to the slow turn of his doorknob.

The silent intruder tiptoed across the threshold and looked across the stuffy, musty room at the boy's wiry frame. Before moving to his target, he sniffed in amusement as he surveyed the one-room apartment. The neon blue walls were plastered with posters featuring Lil' Kim, Foxy Brown, Smooth, Wu-Tang Clan, and a few old heads like Run-D.M.C. The kitchen sink, off in the right corner, was stacked high with generic plastic dishes, many of them still sticky with uneaten food and buzzing with curious flies and ants. In front of the boy's bed, in the far left corner, sat the most obvious testament to Biggie's Big Willie lifestyle: an eighty-four-inch wide-screen TV equipped with Sega, Nintendo, two VCRs, and a gigantic Sony system, flanked by an arrangement of powerful-looking Bose speakers. How the wealthy lived. The intruder slipped on leather gloves and headed toward the bed. He would be doing good, removing the boy from this life of wasteful misery.

Seconds later, Biggie was awakened by the whump of a

cheesecloth bag as it enveloped his unkempt head, Afro puffs and all. Shooting forward in the bed, he instinctively clasped his hands to his throat, hoping to release the bag before it was too late. The intruder's strong grip immediately told him resistance would be futile. This was no ordinary man sent to take him out.

"Bobo, p-please, how you gon' do a brother, man?" The words came out muffled through the speckled holes in the bag's skin. "Nico," he pleaded. "Nico promised!"

With an unforgiving grunt, the intruder pulled the drawstrings of the bag tight around his neck before grabbing him around the middle. As best as he could, Biggie kicked, screamed, flailed his arms and legs like a fish wriggling on a line. Left with no choice, the intruder dropped Biggie and stood over the boy's quivering body. Biggie was covered only by a skimpy pair of silk boxing shorts, which he had bought just last week to impress his latest skeezer. Now his panicked reaction had ruined them.

"Oh, Lord . . ." The intruder had not expected to have to deal with urine. "Geez, where are your clothes, kid?"

Still unable to see, Biggie choked out the answer, meekly extending an arm behind his head. "In . . . the . . . closet, over there."

"Thanks." The intruder ceased Biggie's movements with a smacking uppercut across the lower portion of the bag. "Now be still."

Five minutes later Chuck Dawkins emerged into the back alley of Biggie's apartment building, the boy's body slung over his shoulder like a sack of potatoes. The car that Larry had rented for him was idling faithfully just outside the door. Right on time. He went to the back of the white Taurus station wagon, set Biggie against the wall, and opened the back hatch.

As Biggie felt his body being tossed into the backseat, he came to. "Please, Bobo, I ain't never hurt you, man. I—" He tensed as he felt rough hands move to rip the bag off his head.

"Biggie, this ain't Bobo."

"T-Terence?"

"Damn skippy. What up, lil' bro?"

"What . . . how?"

"Biggie, I got good news, and I got bad news. The good news is, Larry, Chuck, and I are gonna make sure Nico doesn't get his paws on you. The bad news is, you're goin' away."

"A-Away where?"

"See this big lug in the driver's seat?"

"What up, Biggie?" Climbing into position, Chuck turned his head and shot a cheesy grin at his prey.

"That's Chuck Dawkins, one of Larry's boys. He's gonna see to it that you get safely to your new digs down in South Carolina."

"What? Nigga, is you—is you crazy?"

"Crazy or not, brother, I'm the only hope you got of survivin' this mess. Now listen to me. Chuck's uncle runs a home for wayward boys down in Charleston. He don't take no shit. When Chuck drops you there, I suggest you make nice and do as he says. I mean it."

"Wayward boys! What is you sayin', man? I ain't no boy!"

"Technicalities, Biggie. You just turned eighteen, you barely over the threshold. Besides, Uncle Dawkins could care less about that, right, Chuck?"

"You know that, T. Biggie, my uncle takes in strays like you all the time, former gangbangers who realize they need to learn a trade and make something of themselves. Granted, he normally takes dudes your age when they come to him voluntarily, but I've already cleared the way for you. He's got a mop, broom, and lawn mower waiting for you, all with your name on 'em. That'll help you earn your keep, you know. Oh, and Biggie." Dawkins grinned, turning around to face the backseat. "My uncle makes me look like Spud Webb. You'd do well to heed his every word."

Terence bore his eyes into his brother's. "Besides, after he kicks yo' tail, he'd just report you to the authorities, after he calls me, of course. By the time the police hear from him, they'll have a hand-delivered package tying you to all your most recent crack deals. I know you got mad evidence sittin' up in that rathole apartment right now."

Biggie's eyes bulged like a chipmunk's cheeks. "This, this, naw, nigga, this—"

"Biggie, I love you, man." Leaning over into the backseat, Terence embraced his brother's trembling shoulders. "I'll explain everything to Granny, don't worry. Once Nico's taken care of, I'll fill yo' babies' mommas in, too."

A loud honk from behind momentarily startled the men. Larry and Brandon pulled alongside the station wagon in Brandon's Altima. Through his open window, Larry yelled, "Dawkins, you ready for your road trip? You straight on cash?"

"Your check set me straight, boy. I'm rett'."

Terence opened the passenger's side door. "Biggie, you stay cool now. Those handcuffs of Chuck's can chafe the skin pretty bad, if what his girlfriends say is true. Don't fidget. Just lay back and enjoy the ride. Chuck, can't thank you enough."

As Terence climbed into the Altima, he paused to watch Dawkins zoom the Taurus down the alley and up onto Euclid Street, heading for 395 South. The last glimpse he had was of Biggie's panicked, tortured face, pressed tightly against the glass of the back window. Terence stifled a weary laugh. The boy would thank him for this someday.

30

BOYS TO MEN

"Mr. Peters, wake up. It's dinnertime, and you have a visitor. Are you up for some company?"

O.J. opened his eyes and exhaled softly at the sight of the shapely, toffee-colored nurse laying his dinner platter on the tray before him. This was the second evening she had served him, and her presence was starting to stir up the canine rumblings that had been all too familiar since he first entered adolescence. Before he could be tempted to take a second look at the knit of her snug white uniform, he fixed his eyes on the steaming plate of veal Parmesan and succotash. "Thank you, ma'am. Who's the visitor? I'd like some company."

"Do you know a Larry Whitaker?" His smile gave her the answer. "I'll send him right in."

After a warm greeting, Larry sat beside the bed and talked while O.J. ate his meal. Then he lifted the tray off the bed and set it on a nearby chair. "So, playa, anything else you wanna get up to speed on?" He had already briefed O.J. on the guys' progress regarding Ellis.

"Well, for starters, when are you gonna be crowned HSA president?"

Larry strolled over to the window in the corner and began to loosen his tie. "Well, that's kind of a long story. I just left the last debate; the election is tomorrow. I pulled out of the race tonight."

Shocked, O.J. shot forward, wincing in pain as he straightened his back. "You did what? Larry Whitaker passed up a spot in Power Hall? What's *really* goin' on?"

"I don't even think I know, man. These past few weeks have had a funny effect on a brother. You think I'm trippin', you shoulda seen the look on David Winburn's face when I threw my support to Winston Hughes!" Larry erupted into laughter at the memory. Ever since he had started to clear his name last week, Winburn's position in the polls had dropped steadily, as the Highland body came to the realization that he had been behind the unfounded attack on Larry. On top of that, Hughes had actually gained some ground since the first speakout, on the strength of his well-informed proposals to restructure some of the university's debt and address the financial aid crisis. With the benefit of Larry's supporters behind him, Hughes was set to give Winburn an exhausting run for his money.

Smiling at Larry's glee, O.J. pressed him for more gossip. "You ain't sayin' nothing but a word, these weeks have changed you. When Preston stopped by yesterday, he was goin' on and on about you kickin' Ashley to the curb. None of my bidness, but—"

Larry shook his head, staring at the floor and smiling gently. "Your boy's right, man. I don't know, working to try to salvage Ellis Center, it's made me look at life in a different light. I ain't met your God or Jesus yet, understand, but something's changed. Choosing between the politics of a campaign and doing something to help some young brothers and sisters, well, it was no choice at all. And who was by my side when the crap hit the fan? Not Ashley. She didn't want to deal with anything that varied from her narrow expectations."

O.J. smiled. "So man cannot thrive on pumps and a bump alone. You think Sheila Evans is the answer?" O.J. had suspected the chemistry lurking between the two long before Larry had been hip to it.

"Well, I . . . look, man, how I'ma sound stepping to Sheila two days after breaking up with my woman? I'm trying not to make a decision about her for a while. She's gonna take a job at the *Post,* so she'll be around."

Still waking himself, O.J. stretched his hands heavenward. "Well, playa, one thing I can say for sure. Don't leave her waitin' too long, if you're interested. It's only so many good women out there."

"What you mean, O.J.?" Larry inspected his friend's face carefully. He had never known O.J. to worry about how good a woman was, except where the bedroom was concerned.

"Look, man, let's just say my trial by fire has made me appreciate the principled, straight-up sisters that are out there. I know I brought a lot of this mess on myself, but you wanna know what? Black women made me what I am, Larry. You have any idea how many of the women I've been with at Highland would turn their back on a nice brother like the Choirboy? These the same women who come to my church, wave their hands all during the service, complain about brothers being dogs, and then go home with me! I'm just saying, there's a lot of women out there like that. When you find one who knows what's good for her, you better grab her while you can."

Chuckling, Larry slumped against the wall next to the bed. "I wouldn't worry about Brandon's progress with women, O.J., but you are right on. Guess it takes a playa to know one, hey? You wanna know what's tight, though? I'm gonna have to squash the last remnant of my old playa self before I get into any relationship with Sheila and her little boy."

"What's that?"

"How do I explain it? When I go out in public, on campus, or anywhere, I still find myself judging sisters on that same old shallow-ass criteria my pop trained me to use: hair length, complexion, height, and figure. And let's face it, based on the most stringent and shallow measures—"

O.J. nodded. "Which used to be your forte—"

"Sheila doesn't quite measure up. But you know what, when I'm with her, *I don't care!* The personal connection, the chemistry, the shared ambitions—they blot out the superficial mess."

"Look, Larry, Sheila is an attractive sister in her own right. She's no Ashley, but Lord, other than Lela Rochon or Halle Berry, who is? Wanna know the truth? Up until a few days ago, I'd have taken Sheila into my room—"

Larry let loose with a hoarse laugh. "Hold up now, Chumpy. Point taken, you ain't got to go there. All I'm sayin' is, I can see myself with Sheila, but I know it's gonna take a while to completely let go of my old concepts of beauty. That's why I want to take it slow."

Sighing in admiration of his friend's determination, O.J. turned his head to face the window. "Well, just make sure you're not *too* slow. I've already lost out on the one good woman I had. Carla and Pastor Grier stopped by yesterday before church, and, bro, it weren't pretty." Putting on a strong face, O.J. proceeded to explain to Larry how upset Carla had been. She and Pastor Grier had come bearing cards, gifts, and homemade goodies from the church members. After Grier prayed with him and offered some general words of support, he had left O.J. and Carla alone. Carla had wanted to take the attack as a sign that it was time for O.J. to settle down, namely, with her. By the time she'd arrived, though, he had already agreed with his father as to his next steps, and it had hurt him to tell her that she was not a part of them.

"You fired her, just like that?" Larry was surprised, considering that Carla had always been O.J.'s favorite.

"Man, I'm leavin' town the day after graduation, and long-distance relationships have never been my thing. Besides, I did it for Carla's good. I got no business being in anybody's relationship these days. I got to get my life together."

"Well, you're gonna go home and preach at your pop's church, right?"

"I may never step into the pulpit again, brother. My father reminded me of the Scripture that says, 'Man looketh at the outward appearance, but God looketh at the heart.' Larry, I gotta tell you, when God looks at my heart right now, I know what he sees is pretty frightening. I can fool man any day. I'll tell you now I can outpreach my daddy, Rev. Grier, Jesse Jackson, anybody you put in my path. I'm a performer. But God ain't fooled by those outward charms. It's time for me to stop gettin' over on God, blaming and hating him for taking my mother, making me short, making me dark, whatever. I got to get to know him one-on-one. Who knows what I'll find, but once I know him, then I can tell others about him. Until then, I'm chillin'."

Larry leaned against the windowsill and eyed O.J. dubiously. "O. J. Peters, doing something other than preaching? How you gonna pay the bills, man?"

"Gonna get my teaching certificate. I figure my charm can be put to less destructive use on impressionable elementary school kids. I may not teach forever, but it's as good a place as any while I straighten myself out."

The conversation was interrupted by a rap at the door. The attractive nurse inched open the door, smiling shyly as she made eye contact with Larry. "Sorry, but visiting hours are over. Please sign out at the front desk as you leave."

"No problem, ma'am. Thanks again." Larry leaned over the bed, his hand stretched out toward O.J. "Be strong, kid. You'll be out by Wednesday, right?"

O.J. gripped Larry's hand in a firm handshake. "Yup. You guys'll have to get me up to speed on the rededication ceremony for Ellis. Take care, bro."

As Larry followed the nurse out into the hallway, O.J. lay back and rested his head against his stiff pillow. Larry had already told him that he suspected Keesa's attack had been prompted by the enemies of Ellis. There was no point trying to prove that, but he was hoping that his remarks to the police yesterday would encourage some leniency, maybe get her some mental health treatment instead of a lengthy prison stay. He checked the clock on the opposite wall. His father should be returning shortly from the police station, with news about Keesa's arrest. Willing himself to stay awake, O.J. punched the TV remote and settled back for an episode of *Melrose Place*. He was looking forward to helping out Ellis in whatever way possible, once he got out. Already, the experience had gained him more than he could ever give back.

࿇ ࿇ ࿇

Brandon stepped into the glass-enclosed lobby of Crystal's, a five-star restaurant on the waterfront of Southwest D.C. He crossed the cobblestone floor and approached the middle-aged host, who stood before a maple-colored lectern, dressed in a traditional black tuxedo. "Good evening. I have a reservation for three at eight, in the name of Bailey."

The host smiled crisply before locating Brandon's name in his book. "Ah, yes, sir. Is the rest of your party with you?"

Brandon turned around and greeted his parents as they strolled into the atrium arm in arm. His father cut an imposing figure, his six-foot-three frame cloaked in a chalky gray pinstriped Pierre Cardin business suit. His mother looked deceptively younger than her husband, her magenta-tinted hair cut close and curled. "They're here now, sir." To his parents he said, "I don't know why you guys insisted on searching for parking down the street. They have a valet."

As the host led them to a table overlooking the glittery boardwalk below, Dr. Bailey berated his son. "Son, why would I waste good money on some punk kid to park my car, when I can do a perfectly fine job of that myself? Besides, you know your mother already set the budget for our trip this week, to the penny. Valets weren't included."

Brandon grinned as his mother tugged at his father's sleeve. "Now, Brent, you know better than to try to pull that, blaming me. Without that budget, you wouldn't be able to buy yourself some more new suits at outlandish prices this week."

"Oh, please, wife, I always shop for deals, now, come on. What's the harm in a hardworking man treating himself to some harmless spoils?"

"They're only harmless as long as you can afford them." Mrs. Bailey fixed her husband with a playful glare. "Boy, Visa and Master-Card must love you."

Enjoying his parents' familiar banter, Brandon leaned back and took a swig of his ice water. Solidly upper middle class, with just one more child to get through college, his parents seemed to enjoy bickering over money, pretending they were members of a lower tax bracket. He had been looking forward to graduation week for a while, in part because he knew his parents were going to spend the entire week in D.C. as a vacation, before his brothers and extended family arrived. They had promised to stay out of his way until Friday, but he had asked them out to dinner tonight so he could get things about Monica off his chest. Bobby and his brother Gregory had helped him think things through some, but Brandon felt like he needed to unload to someone with a little more life experience.

Once the waiter had taken their orders, Brandon tiptoed toward his revelation. "Well, you asked why I didn't want Bobby or any of my other friends to accompany us here tonight. I think it's time I told you the real reason." His father hunched his eyebrows and chewed on a hot roll. His mother's eyes filled with concern. "So you know, everything's fine with me, at least surface-wise. I'm happy about attending Duke, and everything's going smoothly there. I already mentioned that we're close to securing the Ellis Center's future, God willing, and everything's gone great with school this year. But something happened last weekend that's made me question things deeper than school or work."

Clearly growing impatient at Brandon's awkward buildup, his parents shifted in their seats. His father took the lead. "Uh, son, what exactly are you trying to say? You're not about to pull an Ellen DeGeneres on us, are you? As your little brother says, I'm not tryin' to hear that."

"What? No! Dad, come on. Look, you guys remember when I had to get tested for HIV, after Brandy died?"

The Baileys inhaled in unison and peered at Brandon.

"You all told me," he said, "that it was a wake-up call, the way things ended with Brandy, the fact that her boyfriend had tested positive for HIV."

Dr. Bailey sniffed impatiently. "Well, that sounds about right, son. You were blessed, being able to walk away from that girl with your health intact. We always reared you and your brothers to save that stuff for marriage. It's in the Bible, and God's Word doesn't lie. And for the record, I've always taken a bit of pride in the fact that my boys have managed to be the exception, keeping yourselves set apart from worldly immoralities—for the most part. I mean, I look at my sister's kids, how some of the ones who were just born yesterday are already pregnant with their own kids, and it's just—"

Brandon raised a hand. "Dad, maybe you should hold off and let me finish. I've always agreed with your view about sexual temptation. The problem is, I've been using that as an excuse for my lack of a social life. This girl I've been seeing, Monica . . . I know I did the right thing finally asking her out, but it's already gotten more serious than I'd planned."

Pausing to let the waiter set down their salads, Brandon shifted his gaze between his parents and watched his words sink in.

"Oh." His mother's voice had an "Ah ha!" tone to it. "Well . . ."

"Wait, wait," Dr. Bailey pleaded. "Am I missing something here? What exactly do you mean, son?" Dr. Bailey had a brilliant medical mind, but his affinity for implied knowledge, by comparison, was limited.

The admission rushed from Brandon like a bubbling spring. "Dad, I slept with her! I lost my virginity, again!" Brandon stared down at the tablecloth as he felt the eyes of other diners on him. "Um, well, you know what I mean."

Dr. Bailey rolled his eyes and clicked his tongue against his teeth, looking deep in thought. "Well . . . sounds like you had yourself quite a time, son. Does this explain that sissy earring, too?"

"Brent, this is not about his earring—"

"It's okay, Mom. Dad, let's not get sidetracked. The earring's a long, separate story. After the other night with Monica, I feel like I can't win. Not only did I break my promise to God, but in order to keep from doing the same thing again, I'm holding off a woman I used to dream of being with."

"It's difficult, isn't it?" Brandon's mother's voice was full of sympathy.

Brandon ran his fingers over his brow. "Tell me about it. I'm gonna be straight up with you guys—I'm ready to say that celibacy is an unrealistic ideal in this day and age. If I hadn't run from passion, I might have pulled Monica a long time ago. You know how many lonely, painful nights I could have saved myself?"

Dr. Bailey leveled a skeptically paternal gaze at his son. "Is this you talking, Brandon, or your johnson?"

"Truth be told, it's probably both. I just wish my romantic life could make sense for once. I was supposed to wind up with a good girl, like a Kim Fields. Instead, I'm under the spell of a Toni Braxton."

Mrs. Bailey placed a hand on Brandon's wrist. "Brandon, what exactly is bothering you? Do you want to continue seeing this girl? Are you just disappointed in yourself? What are you feeling?"

Meeting his mother's concerned eyes, Brandon groped to express his frustration. "I . . . just . . . I don't know what the point is anymore. First, I was disillusioned with the Disciples of Christ. Now I'm questioning something I thought symbolized my commitment to God. Have I been kidding myself?"

Pausing first to look at her husband, Mrs. Bailey patted Brandon's hand again. "Brandon, listen to me. You should be *proud* of the way you've lived your life. Regardless of what the Bible or anyone else says, your behavior has ensured that you never shattered a young girl's heart, fathered an illegitimate child, or caught or passed on any sexual diseases. That's an accomplishment for any young man these days. And I do believe that abstinence before marriage is God's will. It makes too much sense when you look at the pain caused by loose living.

"But as a human being, you'll never be perfect. No one is. Try to keep what we taught you in perspective. I know we've instilled in you and your brothers the importance of abstinence before marriage. But no one's perfect. And unfortunately, in the area of sex, more people have failed than succeeded."

Dr. Bailey lowered his voice and leaned in toward the center of the table. "Brandon, if you ask me, the issue is not that you screwed, I mean screwed up with this girl. Look, most people I know, Christian or not, got some diggity, as you kids say, before they got married. Premarital sex is nothing to play with, but if it happens, it's no different from lying, stealing, cheating. We all fall short! The question is, what are you going to do about it? Is this girl a Christian?"

Brandon shrugged. "Well, yeah, but—"

"Then you need to decide if you're willing to throw away what the two of you have over one issue. Unless she's stated some ultimatum about sex, I don't see why that would be necessary. Just my opinion."

"Brandon," his mother said, "this decision is between you and God alone. I think your split with those Disciples, and your aggravation at these confused black women of the nineties, has made you lose sight of what your faith is about. You need to decide for yourself how to handle sex and dating, in a way you can live with. We've never acted like sex was an unthinkable thing for you guys to take part in. Who provided you with those safety stashes of condoms, which I'm trusting you used with Monica?" She paused as Brandon's sheepish grin confirmed her hope. "We just equipped you with what we felt was best, based on our experiences and our faith. Now you need to carve your own path. We'll love you wherever that path leads you, never forget that."

His eyes lighting up as the waiter approached with a tray of piping hot entrées, Dr. Bailey flashed a smile at Brandon. "Your mom said it best, son. Anything we can do for you, we will. But it's on you from here, okay? Can we continue this vein once we've gotten into our grub?"

Turning his attention to the meal, Brandon silenced his rumbling stomach and looked appreciatively at his parents. "I guess it's moments like this that make Terence call us the Cleavers. Thanks for hearing me out." He grasped his dinner fork. "I'm ready to eat." As the conversation slowly turned to lighter fare, Brandon decided to enjoy the moment and the company. He could start the hard work of defining himself and his feelings for Monica tomorrow. Until then, he'd leave it in God's hands—even if he was unsure of exactly what that meant.

❧❧❧

Sitting in the high-backed desk chair in his office at Technotronics, Jerry Wallace wiped his damp brow and ran his fingers over his eyelids. He tapped the flash button on his speakerphone. "Send them in, Marlene."

As the oak door swung open, he frowned unconsciously at the two black police officers who filled the doorway. Behind them he could see Terence Davidson's imposing frame. What were they, teaming up on him? Four years Jerry had invested in Terence, and now that he'd fired the kid for screwing up the board meeting, the boys in blue were invading his office. What were they going to do, charge him with violating some racial-preferences law? You couldn't fire black people for *any* reason now? Jerry knew he was no racist, but he was through being told to treat minorities with kid gloves. He stood as the men stepped toward the three chairs opposite his desk. "Look, Officers, I don't want any trouble. My firing of Terence was based completely on fact—"

The shorter officer, a lean man with a salt-and-pepper mustache and a thinning head of kinky curls, interrupted Jerry. "Mr. Wallace, we're not here to charge you with anything. May we have a seat?"

Meeting Terence's eyes briefly, Jerry waved toward the seats and returned to his. "Help yourself."

"I'm Officer Perkins," the salt-and-pepper officer continued. "Officer Benson and I met with Terence a couple of days back about some criminal activities that have endangered his life and that of his family, not to mention a treasured community institution in Shaw, the Ellis Center. We're not really allowed to go into too much detail, as these matters are still under investigation, but when Terence mentioned how his job was affected by all this, we felt an obligation to back up his story."

As Jerry's mouth dropped open in relief, he decided to do the obligatory thing and keep asking questions. He made a point of directing all questions at Terence, who proudly and directly answered every one. The negative stereotypes of black men that had begun to reinvade Jerry's subconscious began to beat a hasty retreat. Terence *wasn't* like all those kids he saw in the news and on TV every night. It was time for Jerry to prepare his own explanations. People were sure to ask why he was rehiring an intern he'd just fired.

❧❧❧

Later that evening Annabelle Simmons answered the shrill ring of her phone as she lay prostrate on the couch in her finished basement. "This is Annabelle."

"Ms. Simmons, this is Terence Davidson."

Twirling a piece of her weave in her right hand, Ms. Simmons smiled to herself. "Terence, I wasn't expecting to hear from you just yet."

Pacing the floor of his bedroom like a man possessed, Terence spat out his response. "I'm puttin' you on notice, Ms. Simmons. The Terence Davidson Love Train has left your station. I've been through enough the last few weeks. I could care less if you have me declared financially ineligible. You see, I'm Terence Davidson. I've already overcome obstacles that would make most spoiled Highland brats roll over and play dead. If I could come this far, I can survive a semester off, if need be. Hell, that'll give me time to work full-time at Technotronics and pay off my tuition."

Annabelle sat forward, perched nervously on the edge of her plaid couch. "Now, Terence, you're not making sense, dear. I've done a lot for you. Don't think you can just throw me away—"

"We're not even gon' talk about what you've *done* to me, Ms. Simmons. My guess is Highland's officers know damn well about your arrangements with students, and I don't have time to try to get you fired anyway. I got my own concerns. Let's just go our separate ways."

"Terence, what do you expect me to do about your unpaid bills?"

Terence bopped his head up and down to the slamming beat of L.L. Cool J's "Mama Said Knock You Out." "Ms. Simmons, I'd expect you to do whatever you would have done if I'd visited you one last time. I'll pay my bill off as early as possible next year—all of my summer earnings will go straight to Highland. But that's it! No more deals, no nothin'. I'm out!" With that, Terence was gone.

Smiling to herself, Annabelle dropped her phone and lay back on the couch. He'd finally stood up for himself. She hoped this wouldn't prove to be a pattern among her "visitors." Sighing, she reminded herself to check her list of students with overdue accounts tomorrow. There was always someone else willing to pay any price to stay in school.

31

Crime Don't Pay

🙥🙥🙥🙥🙥🙥🙥🙥🙥🙥

It was an unusually humid May morning this Tuesday, and as the sun illuminated the sky overhead, Rolly Orange was swimming in a sea of his own perspiration, his dashiki almost soaked through. It was nine o'clock, and the rededication ceremony was just two days away. He wanted desperately to believe that things weren't falling apart, despite clues telling him otherwise.

He had spent the better part of last night begging Nico Lane for his life. When the news of Buzz Eldridge's death hit the papers, Rolly had been confused; Nico had been livid. It had completely eclipsed Rolly's positive news about the contributions, which had been fully delivered to Tracy Spears yesterday afternoon. Spears was planning to hold the money for a few days, while Rolly and Nico agreed on how to split it. With Eldridge out of the picture, there was one less person to share with, but now the battle was directly between Orange and Nico, odds that Rolly didn't particulary like. He was not afraid of the Kid, but he wasn't stupid either. What Nico Lane wanted, Nico Lane got.

They had argued over whether Eldridge's death has been self-inflicted. "He was a pussy," Nico had steamed, "an over-the-hill dinosaur. I don't know why I ever agreed to work with him. He wasn't committed to seeing Ellis go under. He was just trying to hedge his bets. Damn!"

Rolly had given Eldridge a bit of credit by comparison, not wanting to mention the vengeful call he'd received from Buzz hours before his death. "The newspaper accounts said he was up on that floor inspecting some work. He had apparently gone up without the construction supervisor. He wasn't in the best of health, Nico. It may have been a genuine accident."

Nico had glared at Rolly like a disgusted parent. "Believe what you want. We've got work to do."

By the time Orange emerged from Nico's condo earlier this morning, they had made arrangements, using Nico's hired hands, to ransack Eldridge's office for potential evidence and destroy any trail that could lead back their way. They were fortunate that the media had treated the incident as an accident, pending further investigations. They were counting on that to keep police from digging too deeply into any of Buzz's involvements with Ellis or the Develcorp project. The one loss they had to concede was the pressure they had counted on from the banks. Eldridge had been responsible for using his contacts with local bankers to convince them to call Ellis's loans this week. Now that he was gone, to go behind him and mess with the moneymen would only stir unnecessary suspicion. They decided it was best to count on the theft of the contributions; that blow would embarrass Sheryl out of office and close the center in a matter of days.

Wiping his moist brow, Orange turned the key in the lock of his flimsy office door, a wooden rectangle with a small glass pane. The house of cards he and his conspirators had built was off balance, but there was no reason that they couldn't keep it standing a few more days. Nico had already given him the money to buy his one-way ticket to the Cayman Islands, and he had several suitcases packed, just waiting for Friday to come. Sure, he was still having occasional nightmares about how all of this would affect Sheryl, not to mention some of the cherubic children and at-risk teens he passed in the halls each day. But he had come too far to turn back now. He couldn't afford to end up like Buzz Eldridge; his only hope of enjoying life would be to start fresh, equipped with enough cash to finance some new ventures.

As he shoved open the door and cleared a path to his peeling wooden desk, his phone rang. At this hour he knew who it was.

He lumbered toward the phone and grabbed the receiver, opening his dusty window blinds as he answered. "Rolly Orange."

"Rolly, good morning." Sheryl's voice was full of optimism. She clearly had no clue. "How are you today?"

"Oh, I've been better. Just a little tired, is all. What's up?"

"Well, I was just wondering if you could let me know when our friend Mr. Spears starts investing the cash contributions. I'm very excited to follow the investments myself, even started picking up *The Wall Street Journal*. Have you talked to him yet today?"

Orange placed a hand on his right hip. What did she think, Spears was going to double the money in twenty-four hours? "Uh, no, Sheryl, the exchange is just now opening. He's probably sizing up initial vehicles still. Investment analysis can be a painstaking process. But I'm sure he should have some investments made by Friday. I'll definitely call him today, but I doubt if I'll have anything to report until tomorrow."

"Oh, well, okay. I've got plenty to keep me busy in the meantime. I'm getting letters out to all of our vendors and suppliers, assuring them that we'll be able to pay off balances within the next three months. I'm also renegotiating some of the bills for this fall's programs, promising to get some checks out as soon as possible. Now that the Highland contributions have been invested, we can put future monies directly toward operating expenses. I've got a feeling things are going to turn around, Rolly."

You're too smart to be that naïve, he thought. "Hopefully so, Sheryl, hopefully so. Look, I better get with the accounting clerks and review April's numbers. Let's do lunch, okay?"

Before he had said good-bye, he was interrupted by the smack of a booted foot against his door. As the door hurtled open, glass shattering against the wall, Nico Lane burst across the threshold, dressed in a black Fila sweat suit that rippled from the bulging and twitching of his muscles. "Orange, have you lost your damn mind?"

His eyes frozen with horror, Orange was unable to free his gaze from Lane's steely stare. "Uh, Sh-Sheryl, let me call you back, okay? I got a visitor. I think he's a vendor upset about a financial matter."

Sheryl's voice sounded like she was frowning. "Well, do you want me to stop by?"

"No, no, no. That won't be necessary. Let me get back to you." Slamming the phone down, Orange looked at Nico, his eyes darting between the enraged dealer and the shattered office door. "We can't talk here, Nico." His voice was a whisper. "What, what the hell are you doing?"

Bounding forward, Nico backed Orange up against the wall behind the desk, pinning his large frame. "You think I'm that stupid, Rolly? Do you really? Do you know who I am? I want you to tell me why I got a call, not one hour ago, from a reporter with the *Times*, claiming he has a copy of a suicide note from Eldridge!"

"A what? A suicide note? Buzz?"

"Don't act like you don't know. Why does this reporter claim Eldridge lost it when he heard you ratted us out to those Highland students? Supposedly he had proof that you were cooperating with D.C.'s finest, Rolly! Buzz flipped out, couldn't take it. But Rolly, I'm not Buzz Eldridge. If you've given me up, your time is real short. Do you understand me?"

The rage pent up within him after so many weeks of torture from this playground bully exploded, and before Orange realized what he was doing he had grabbed Nico by his jacket collar and sent him hurtling back to the wall opposite his desk, where the dealer stumbled and fell to his knees. "I've had *enough* of you," he spat out. "Do you understand me, you little asshole? I told you before, if you wanna make good on your threats, do it now! I ain't afraid of you! I have *never, ever* sold you or Eldridge out! Do you realize how ridiculous you sound?" Nico jumped to his feet, shaking off the impact of the attack. The murderous glint still wavered in his eyes, but he seemed too shaken by Orange's show of spine to continue the fight. "Why would I still be here if I was cooperating with the authorities, huh? Stop and think before you go charging off like a bull in heat! Now get out of here before you ruin everything!"

The look of calm on Nico's face chilled Orange to the bone. "Oh, I'm getting out of here, Rolly, that's for sure. I'm committed to this plan, so I'll wait you out. But I don't need to threaten you anymore. Regardless of what you have or haven't done, you just signed your death warrant. You know it and so do I. We'll settle up Friday. In the meantime, I'm watching you." Lane formed the fingers of his right hand into a make-believe gun, pointing it at Orange. "I'm watching you," he said again before mimicking the firing of a shot and speeding out of the office, the trail of his deep laughter permeating the hallway.

As Orange collapsed into his chair, the buzz of his phone jolted him again. "Rolly, uh, Orange."

Sheryl was clearly concerned. "Rolly, is everything okay?"

"Um, yeah, don't worry about it. It was a personal matter, Sheryl. I'll handle it." He hoped he sounded convincing.

"All right," Sheryl said. "Look, let's still do lunch. I'll call you around noon." As she hung up her phone, she went to her window and looked over the stone staircase that led up to the main entrance of Ellis Center. Within seconds the main door swung open violently, and the hot-tempered intruder emerged. As Sheryl took in the fleeting sight of the striking young mulatto who had just threatened her business manager, her heart began to burn with recognition. She had told Nico never to show his face around Ellis again. She didn't like it, not one bit.

❧ ❧ ❧

An hour later Brandon bounded down the stairs from his bedroom and slid into the living room, his cordless phone in his right hand. "Yo, does anybody want to guess who just rang me up?" Larry, Terence, and O.J., who had just arrived home from the hospital, looked up from their positions on the floor, where they were reviewing strategy. "Sheryl's concerned, brothers," Brandon said. "She asked my opinion, actually *our* opinion, on Rolly Orange and the whole concept of stock market and futures investing. She sounds suspicious of him. Nico must have really gone off."

Larry slapped the knee of his Guess jeans. "So you gave Nico a taste of his own medicine! He impersonated a church member to poor Keesa, you convinced him you were a reporter with the *Times*. Brilliant!"

Crossing his arms in joy, Brandon grinned. "Well, all I had to do was stick a match over the flame of distrust between those two. I think Nico's been looking for an excuse to take Orange out and keep the money for himself. Anyway, Sheryl didn't elaborate, but she's clearly out of sorts about Nico's appearance at the center."

"Well all right!" Terence jumped to his feet. "What's she gonna do?"

"Well, I gave her the lowdown. I reminded her of the risky nature of investing and suggested the contributions be placed into conservative investments, now that they're approaching a more significant level. I also mentioned some of Larry's suggestions about refinancing options, so they can pay some or all their bills now and go on a payment plan to pay off their balances. I think she's gonna pull the money back from Spears."

O.J. knew enough now to appreciate the significance of this fact. "Praise God! What's she gonna do about Orange's association with that dealer?"

"She's playing her cards close to the vest on that one. I don't think she's tryin' to take Nico on—she's a little too smart for that. She sounded like she's going to spend the next couple of days digging through Orange's office. I did share our opinions about Mr. Orange, and I told her I'd drop off the little packet of info Larry picked up at Buzz Eldridge's office, along with those articles on Eldridge's lust for the Develcorp and riverfront projects. That should connect the rest of the dots for her."

Larry clapped his hands loudly. "Man, we are in there! Sheryl can handle Orange now, and get the contributions back. You know that only leaves one roadblock. Are we ready to take him on?" He searched his friends' faces, looking to gauge their resolve to complete the mission.

Folding his arms across his chest, Brandon leaned up against the wall near the entryway. "I think the man who has to answer that is Terence."

Still pacing the floor excitedly, Terence hesitated before answering. He wasn't feeling indecisive; in fact, he was giddy with anticipation. They had already accomplished more than he suspected was possible when Nico first leveled his threat on Biggie's life. These recent successes had increased his confidence. Knowing that his housemates had his back was all the assurance he needed; the days of questioning his Highland brothers, in the way he had as a freshman fleeing that angry mob near Johnson Hall, were behind him. Minutes earlier, Brandon and O.J. had led the group in a prayer for the survival of Ellis Center, including specific requests for Terence's safety with the final step in their plan. Now Terence was ready to stand with these brothers and make a mark on the community, one that would hopefully outlive them all. He clasped his hands together and met his friends' eyes, one by one. "You betta believe I'm down. Let's do this!"

જીજીજી

That evening Terence stepped from Larry's Lexus and eyed the twenty-six-floor apartment tower across the street, wiping his sweaty palms on his pants legs. As Larry pulled away from the curb, Terence noted that the weather had taken a turn for the worse, the setting sun eclipsed by gray clouds and cold, insistent rain. Terence's baggy Redskins jersey hung loosely from his frame, its curved edges drooping over the waist of his jeans. Shielding his near-bald head from the rain, he bolted across the sidewalk and leaped onto the carpeted, awning-covered walkway that led to the front entrance of Fairfield Towers, the luxury condominium building that Nico Lane called home. Acknowledging the elderly doorman, Terence stepped into the lobby. He was involuntarily impressed by everything he saw. At the center of the high-ceilinged room was a large stone fountain, spewing three jets of blue water that met in a central arc before returning to the pool below. The floor was pure marble, the ceilings were lit by ornate golden chandeliers, and the vanilla-colored walls were lined with contemporary paintings.

After giving Nico's alias—"Antoine Mervin," the birth name known only to people like Terence who grew up in his hood—to the receptionist at the front desk, he was buzzed up. Terence slumped against the velvety wall of the elevator as it sped up to the twenty-fifth floor. He was starting to feel his nerves now. His bravado from this morning was beginning to ebb. Maybe he was pushing his luck. Who was he to try to take out Nico Lane? Blotting out rational thought, he slammed his fists together and gritted his teeth, recalling the way he steeled himself when running big basketball plays in high school. He had learned the art of positive visualization, thinking only of the sensation he got when he broke through a line of defenders and slam-dunked a basket, before hitting the floor like a rock. It was time to apply the same technique in this instance. The good accomplished by removing the threat Nico posed to Ellis Center, Biggie, and the community at large outweighed his concern about the consequences if things backfired. Besides, if Nico were to catch on and send him to an early grave, at least he would finally know who was right about this whole religion and afterlife thing. Once he got out of this bind, he was determined to sample all the major faiths, starting with Christianity and Islam. It was time to at least start down the road toward a decision.

As the ten-foot door to Nico's condo swung open, Terence's heart beat a high-stepping rhythm in his chest. Standing in the doorway was a tall, shapely, coffee-bean-colored woman dressed only in an expensive-looking silk bathrobe. Looking him up and down, she scratched lightly at her gold-tinted braids and smiled warmly. "Are you Terence?" The Carribbean rhythm of her accent danced into Terence's head like a saucy reggae tune.

He averted his gaze from the cleavage rising from the opening of her robe and blinked before responding. "Uh, yeah, I'm Terence Davidson. Is Nico in?"

"He's been expecting you. Hi, I'm Tangy. Come on in." Tangy turned and shimmied her way down the expansive foyer; he followed her to a sunken living room surrounded on two sides by massive windows that flooded the room with cloudy light from the darkening sky. "Have a seat here. Nico will be with you shortly." Turning to smile at him again before she headed down the hall opposite the living room, Tangy made it clear she appreciated the effect she was having on Terence. He hoped Nico would be out soon, he didn't need to get caught up in any freaky games tonight. There was business to tend to.

Fidgety, Terence sat down on the sectional sofa, picked up a copy of *War and Peace* from the coffee table, and began to peruse it. In the center of the table sat a foot-high brass statue in the crude shape of a man's testicles. Surrounding it was an assortment of literature, including copies of *Native Son*, *The Autobiography of Malcolm X*, Dennis Kimbro's *Think and Grow Rich*, and magazines including *Emerge* and *Business Week*. Nico was many things, but the brother was no fool.

"Terence, my boy, make yourself at home." Terence dropped the book as Nico emerged from the hallway, dressed to the nines in a tailored blue plaid suit and matching power tie. He took a seat on an adjacent section of the sofa. "Now, I agreed to meet with you on such short notice, T—you don't mind if I call you T, do you?—only because I'm in your debt. If you hadn't provided access to those contributions, well, let's just say recent events would have rendered my plans virtually impossible. What do you need? You'll have to make it quick, I've got a social function to attend in an hour."

Terence leaned forward in his seat, meeting Nico's eyes head-on. He hoped he sounded as confident as he needed to. "Nico, I think you got a problem. I couldn't decide for a while if I should hip you to it, but I've always believed there should be honor among thieves. And Rolly Orange is not a man of honor."

Squinting his already narrow eyes, Nico unbuttoned his jacket and sat back against the pillowy suede cushions of the sofa. His eyes sparkled, a sign of the rumblings of his wary temper. "Why in the world would a man I blackmailed into helping me out give a damn about my business with Rolly Orange?"

"Nico, look. I ain't no fool. There ain't one bit of love lost between you and me. You know I was never your biggest fan, from the day you first tried to recruit me into the Rocks, over on U Street. I always figured your hard-core act was a way of makin' up for your embarrassment over who your daddy was. I know kids can be pretty cruel about other races. Shoot, I imagine after hearing enough jokes about fortune cookies, chopsticks, and buckteeth, you did what you had to do to prove your credibility on the street, damn what it meant to anybody else."

Annoyed by Terence's crude psychoanalysis, Nico waved a beige hand across his face. "Terence, I could care less what you thought or think of me. Stop rambling."

"I'm just sayin', I'm not tryin' to make nice with you, Nico. But I know how you operate, and if anything happens to spoil your plans for Ellis Center, I won't have you blamin' me, and tryin' to take out me and Biggie both. I don't want to let Rolly Orange's antics put my family's life on the line again."

Skeptical, Nico rose from his seat slowly, like a distinguished politician approaching a foreign diplomat. "Talk to me." He strode over to the one of the windows, savoring the evening view of the nearby Georgetown University campus.

"Well, it's like this. At that meeting Saturday, where I signed over the contributions, Orange asked Sheryl Gibson to approve the release of the Highland money into an investment account run by that Tracy Spears guy." Terence flirted with the thought of walking over to Nico so his response would be audible for the tape. He sighed in temporary relief as Nico turned and walked back toward the couch, stroking his chin thoughtfully.

"Which is precisely what I told him to do. The Highland money, the only funds to which he didn't have access, was to be put into Spears's hands."

Praying he sounded nonchalant, Terence continued. "What's the deal with Spears anyway? He's an odd-looking brother if I ever saw one."

Nico chuckled. "Oh, he's a former CPA who ran into some ethical and criminal charges a few years ago. He's laundered some money for me in the past, so he was a natural for this assignment."

"Does he have any investment knowledge? Was he just supposed to take the money and run?"

Nico smirked. "Uh, yes, T, basically. The idea was to get your money out of the picture, so Sheryl would freak out and resign.

That alone will scare off any more potential donors. No donors, no Ellis Center. And I reclaim my hood, all for the good."

Nico's unconscious admission of guilt sparked a rush of adrenaline in Terence—not entirely a good thing, because it increased the amount of sweat filling his brow.

Nico crossed his arms and eyed him suspiciously. "You okay, Terence? You're sweating like a hog."

"I-I'm all right, Nico. Look, I don't mean to be gettin' in your business, so let me cut to the chase. How much money did Orange tell you was in the Highland accounts?"

"Accountssss? What are you talking about? There was only one account." Nico reached into his jacket pocket and pulled out a fat cigar, which he swiftly lit.

Terence tried to sound flippant. "Uh, no, there were two accounts, Nico. You see, Larry and Brandon had mad success raising money from their parents' friends, so they set up a separate account for individual donations over five thousand. They said that made the record keeping cleaner, for tax records and stuff."

Nico took a long puff on his cigar. "Exactly how much was in this second account, Terence?"

"Well, as of Saturday's meeting, there was eighty-eight thousand in the general account, and"— Terence pulled a fabricated statement from his pants pocket—"one hundred and seventy thousand dollars in the individual donor account. We signed both of 'em over to Orange and Spears's control. Funny thing, though, Rolly had us write two separate checks, even though we could have done one combined check since the accounts were linked. He said it was easier to track them separately, which sounded okay to me. Weird thing was, Spears said he would put the eighty-eight thousand to work on Monday but hold off on the hundred and seventy thousand until some tax issues had been dealt with. He never touched that second check. Has Rolly mentioned that, or given the second check to you?"

Nico flung his suit jacket onto the couch. He looked ready to bite the smoking cigar in half. "Oh, this is rich. Rich. I'm trying to figure why you'd be here lying to me, Terence, stirring up trouble for no reason, when you know I hold your brother's life in my hands. But dammit, you're not the first person to make me question Rolly Orange's loyalty." Nico placed his hands on his hips anxiously, his mind obviously whirring with indignation. "I'm not worried about it, T. I'm convinced that fool has leaked information to someone—Buzz Eldridge didn't flip out for no reason—but I already got Rolly back for whatever he's done. I stormed in on him at Ellis's offices yesterday, how ya like that! I'm sure Sheryl Gibson will have his ass hauled off in short order. But I'm intrigued about this money."

"He never told you about the second account?" Terence tried to look surprised.

Nico slammed his fists together. "Hell no. Look, I hate to do this, T, but you have a natural in. I need you to go over to Ellis tomorrow morning and bring me some hard proof of this second account. Your little statement there raises some questions, but I need a more concrete trail. I don't believe Orange held out on me like this! The brother obviously doesn't value his life." Nico focused his dancing eyes on Terence's sweaty face. It was clear he was not going to take no for an answer.

Sensing his moment of truth had arrived, Terence stood up and rounded the couch, nearing the hallway. "Uh, Nico, look, this is gettin' too deep for me. I'm trying to graduate college. I can't get caught up in this business anymore! I already got fired from my company, man—that's gonna take a toll on my résumé as it is. Look, I hooked you up by warning you about Orange. Ain't that enough?"

With the speed of a gazelle, Nico hopped the couch between them and stood toe-to-toe with Terence, pulling a snub-nosed handgun with a silencer from the leather holster at his hip. He held the weapon to Terence's shiny nose, his eyes exuding an edgy calm. "Now look here, kid, I own you, do you understand? I can take Biggie out whenever I want! It's time for you to officially recognize. You don't make a deal with the devil and then announce when it expires. That's my job. You got me, Davidson?"

As the cold steel pressed against his flesh, Terence thought fleetingly of Granny. Pushing the panic from his mind, he gave a defiant response. "N-Nico, you *don't* own me. What I did to aid your plan to close Ellis, I did under duress. I would never have done that if you hadn't threatened to kill Aaron."

Stepping back and training the gun toward Terence's chest, Nico paced without taking his eyes off Terence. "You have no idea who you're dealing with, do you? I will kill you right now, and then go hunt Biggie and your precious Highland friends down like the dogs they are! Don't ever doubt that! Do you know how many fools I've taken out over the years? You knew the Perry twins, remember the pretty boy little assholes that lived up the block from you when you were in grade school? *I* took 'em out, just a couple years back. They thought they could muscle in on my turf, just 'cause they were a little older, and I trained in the business under some of *their* boys. Well, I showed they ass, now, didn't I?" Nico was slipping back into the crude slang of his street dealers. "Pumped 'em full of lead myself! That's been a while; these days I have Bobo or another one of my boys handle my business, but don't think I've lost my nerve! I'll take *you* out right now if I have to!"

Standing on the balls of his feet, ready to jump, Terence shuddered as the faint sound of sirens crept into the apartment. Sirens in D.C., even in as swanky a neighborhood as this, were almost an hourly occurrence and normally would not cause any pause. But something was different right here, right now. Scampering over to the window in front of the couch, Nico looked down quickly before returning a rabid face toward Terence. "I just realized, you've been using Biggie's formal name this whole time," he said, reaching into his suit pocket. "Where I come from, there's only one time folk use formal names—when the pigs are listening."

Moving before fear could overtake him, Terence dove to the floor as Nico fired a silenced shot directly at his head. Landing on his chest, Terence arched out his right arm and snatched the brass ball statue from the coffee table, taking cover again behind the couch, which Nico pummeled with bullets. As he heard Nico curse and reload the gun, Terence felt a cool breeze behind him. Tangy had decided she wanted no part of this gunfight.

"Tangy, get back in the bedroom," he heard Nico say with chilly calm.

Tangy wasn't having it. "You're crazy, Nico, crazy! You told me you were going legit! You're nutting but a two-bit hoodlum! I'm leaving!"

"Dammit, Tangy!"

Terence's heart caved in as he heard the squeak of a shot whiz overhead. Expecting to hear Tangy's luscious body thud to the floor, he was heartened slightly by the strong screech of her voice.

"You son of a beetch! I don't believe you took a shot at me!"

"I told you to get back in the bedroom! Do it now or I won't miss next time!"

As the bedroom door slammed with a deafening thud, Terence rolled over, gaining momentum he hoped would be adequate to build up a head of steam. As he tumbled to the wall, he catapulted to his feet, hurling the brass statue directly at Nico's head, the stifled report of Nico's handgun clipping his eardrums. His momentum propelled him to the right of the couch, causing the bullet to graze his shoulder as the statue smashed squarely into Nico's forehead. For several heartbeats both men lay on the floor, motionless.

His adrenaline pumping violently, Terence scrambled to his feet and turned to the front door, which burst open as a team of D.C.'s finest swarmed across the threshold. The six officers, dressed in navy blue, streamed into the living room, where Terence sent two of them back to the bedroom to check on Tangy. His head bubbling, Terence stumbled along with the other four officers over to Nico, who lay in front of the window. His eyes were closed like a sleeping baby's, save for the large blotch of red seeping from his welted forehead. The brass statue, splattered in blood, lay a few feet away.

"Is he, is he . . ." Gulping in air like an exposed fish, Terence felt ready to faint.

The senior officer, a brother in his fifties, looked up at Terence from his perch over Nico's body. "For better or worse, this piece of trash is still alive, kid. Don't worry, you didn't take a life today."

Somewhat relieved, Terence felt a firm hand on his shoulder. Officer Perkins, who had been his main contact since he and Larry first contacted the police Sunday, began to guide him toward the door. "Terence, you've done a great, I mean, a *great* service today. We've gotta get you back out to the surveillance van and get you unhooked, but there's a chance the murders and conspiracy you got Lane to admit to on tape will be the beginning of some charges that will finally stick. And I gotta say, you were the easiest immunity case I've had in my years on the force. Now let's get out of here before any of Lane's goons show up."

As he crossed the threshold of Nico's condo, the full weight of what he had just done, and what the outcome could have been, hit Terence with the force of a gale wind. As he filled with pride at the thought of sharing the news with Granny, his boys, and Lisa, his body insisted on some rest. Allowing his knees to buckle, he collapsed into Officer Perkins's arms. He had survived a great deal, but he was no Superman.

❧ ❧ ❧

Rolly Orange had decided it was time to get the hell out of Dodge. It was almost five o'clock Wednesday afternoon, and the rededication ceremony would kick into full gear the next morning. Ellis's halls were swimming with volunteers from throughout the District and Maryland, people donating their time and talents to help fill balloons, stitch costumes, assemble the outdoor platform stage, and do the many other last-minute preparations required to pull the ceremony off in respectable fashion. In a couple of hours Sheryl was expecting him to give the board a last-minute update on the expenses incurred for the ceremony, as well as his success in raising additional private monies to offset the cost. That was what she thought he was doing now, preparing a summary report. What he was actually doing was packing. Not everything, of course. If anyone happened to peek through the plastic-covered space in his door where the glass pane had been and seen packing boxes, his jig would be up. He wasn't that much of a fool. He knew precisely what he needed to take from the office, and it could all fit in the leather satchel he carried with him every day.

He removed his family pictures, checkbook, and Rolodex and neatly deposited them into the satchel, before looking longingly around his dingy office. His flight was leaving National Airport in two hours; it was time to go, before his conscience took him in a stranglehold and forced him to reverse the considerable damage he'd already done. Smoothing his dark suit, the most conservative outfit he'd worn in months, he looped the leather bag over his right shoulder and headed toward the door. He was halfway there when he saw something he knew he couldn't leave behind.

Just to the left of the door hung a laminated, framed copy of the last major profile the *Post* had run on him. "The Comeback Kid," the article headline read. The story, printed ten years earlier, outlined how Orange had reclaimed his seat on the city council after resigning a year earlier to help care for his gravely ill daughter. Reading of Angela's bout with lupus again, even years later, caused a stirring pain in his stomach as he again thanked a now distant God for her complete recovery. His daughter wasn't returning his calls these days, but he believed she would always understand the special place she held in his heart. His eyes filled with proud tears as he read the article again. The reporter wrote admiringly of the younger Orange's reputation as a "man of the people; one who represented the best of what they could be without leaving them behind. One who never forgot from whence he came." Sighing as he reread his own bold quotes, many of which promised to bring a sense of honor and dignity back to public service, Orange reached up with a quivering hand to remove the article and place it in his satchel. A reminder that, with his new cash and newfound freedom, he might recapture that glory in another time, another place.

He was stopped short by the sound of Sheryl's voice. "Rolly." Her tone was fraught with accusations.

Leaving the article in its place, Orange leveled his eyes to meet Sheryl's. She stood just inside the doorway, her arms crossed grimly. Orange felt a surge of crippling cold shoot through his entire body. "Uh, yeah, Sheryl, what do you need?"

"I have some friends I'd like you to speak with." The words had barely escaped Sheryl's mouth when Brandon, Larry, and O.J., his neck still in a brace, stepped into the office behind her. Languishing behind them was a young boy dressed in a familiar L.A. Lakers windbreaker.

"Pooh? Not you, too?" Orange knew he had no right to feel betrayed by the youngster. Pooh Riley, like all of the at-risk children served by Ellis, was the real victim.

Feeling triumphant but slightly embarrassed, all three men were strangely mute, almost avoiding eye contact with Orange. They were glad they'd agreed beforehand to let Sheryl do all the talking.

Sheryl stepped in front of Pooh and crossed her arms, maternal rage burning in her eyes. "Rolly, my Highland friends and little Pooh here have provided me with a string of very disturbing information, all of which calls into question your stewardship as business manager."

Orange's eyes rolled into the back of his head as he stumbled forward and reared back suddenly, like a wounded horse. Instinctively, Brandon stepped forward, helping to steady the large man and navigate him to a nearby chair. "Easy, Mr. Orange."

As his judges stood over him, Rolly Orange swept his eyes over each face before breaking into a heaving, wracking sob. At last, for better or worse, it was all over. He had tried to tell himself that this was his last jig, his last game, his final thrill, one that would get him off to a new start. But he had known all along he was lying to himself; he had done nothing to address the addictions and other demons that had ended his marriage and his political career, not to mention his relationships with his children. He didn't know how to identify or attack them, but now he would have no choice but to face them head on. "Sheryl, please, you must understand. Oh, God!"

He collected himself, sniffing up the tears and reminding himself to restrict his admissions as much as possible. There was no point making the cops' job easier for them. "Sheryl, I have more respect for you and what you've done here at Ellis than just about anyone I've ever worked with. You've got to believe that I never would have gotten involved in this if not for the money. I needed money, Sheryl, to support my family, to try to build a new life for myself. It was nothing personal—"

Sheryl turned her back on Orange's pleas. "Rolly, maybe you should save your comments for the police. I've already called them, and they'll be here shortly. Besides, I'd be lying if I said I can even hear you at this point. There is no justification for what you've done. I have nothing to say to you."

Unable to suppress his emotions, Larry stepped over to Orange's droopy frame. "You know, Rolly, I hope I never lose sight of my goals the way you have. You were a great man in your own right, once. You must have really hit rock bottom to try to pimp a center dedicated to the people, somethin' positive. Was that really the best you could do, brother?"

Rising with determined speed, Orange fixed his eyes on Larry. "Son, you can judge me all you want. I know I found that easy to do when I had a full head of hair, a washboard stomach, all the women I wanted, and my whole life in front of me. But you talk to me twenty, thirty years from now. When everyone speaks of you in past tense or as a 'Where is he now?' When your seventeen-year-old daughter pins her hopes to attending your alma mater but you can't afford to send her anywhere other than the local community college. When men who used to depend on you to get business done in this city won't return your phone calls. Then you can come and preach to me about who to pimp. Get out of my face."

"Mr. Orange." Officer Perkins stepped into the room, trailed by two younger men in blue. "We have just completed our interrogation of one Nico Lane, who provided us with some interesting information." Perkins paused to grin at Brandon, Larry, and O.J. "Ms. Gibson, why don't you escort these young men outside? We'll handle business with Mr. Orange from here, before we go pick up his friend Mr. Spears."

As Sheryl led them out of the room, Orange called to her. "Sheryl, please," he said, "you may never forgive me, but I'm asking for your understanding. J-Just remember that this was never about you."

Sheryl paused in the doorway, her icy stare repelling his earnest pleas. "I know, Rolly. It was all about *you*."

32

HARAMBEE

The weather had taken a sharp positive turn on the morning of Ellis Center's rededication ceremony. The sun shone brightly, bathing everything and everyone in a hazy golden halo. The skies were ocean blue, and the air was free of the humidity that would likely weigh it down in the summer. The courtyard that separated Ellis's main structure from its football field and swimming pool was packed with a crowd three hundred strong, cheering on Sheryl Gibson, the board members, and assorted VIPs lining the platform stage. The program had kicked off promptly at 11:30 A.M., with a rousing performance by the St. Albans teen choir, who had brought the house down with their own version of Kirk Franklin's "Stomp." That had been followed by welcoming addresses from the mayor and the honorable D.C. delegate Eleanor Holmes Norton. When the Rev. Banks completed his invocation, Sheryl rose and shook his hand before assuming her position at the lectern. Even from where they sat several feet behind her on the platform, it was obvious to Brandon, Larry, Terence, and O.J. that Sheryl was on the verge of being overcome with emotion.

"I love this community!" She seemed to be shouting with someone else's lungs, her voice carried so effectively. "Ellis Center exists because of this community, and you have made it what it is!" The crowd, full of children, teens, and adults who had received knowledge, home training, and sustenance within Ellis's walls, rose to its feet, showering Ellis's embattled matriarch with loving praise. "My brothers and sisters, this beloved institution has come a mighty long way! Some of you agonized with us and for us when our key sources of funding were withdrawn. Many of you have personally dedicated your time, your financial resources, and your prayers to help us make up the financial shortfall. And I am here to announce that we have almost arrived at the other side of the mountain! I have faith that we will raise the remaining twenty-five thousand we need to repay the bank loans that come due this fall. We are also actively investing the tens of thousands of dollars that you and many other good-hearted citizens have provided. We are doing it!" She paused to allow the throng to express its joy and adulation. "Before we complete this program, I cannot sit by without recognizing the dedicated efforts of the Ellis Center's board of directors. It has been their leadership and dedication that has seen us through these trying times. Please show them your appreciation, as they stand so they can be acknowledged!" As Rev. Banks, who had to be nudged from a catnap, and the ten other board members stood before the row of chairs they shared on the stage, the crowd clapped and whooped as if they were at a Highland football rally. As the board members began to take their seats, Sheryl's voice froze them in mid-motion.

"I would like to ask four of these great board members to remain standing one minute longer. Mr. Brandon Bailey, Mr. Larry Whitaker, Mr. Terence Davidson, and Mr. Oscar Peters, Jr.! These young men went far beyond the call of duty in ensuring the fiscal safety and salvation of this institution. I cannot thank you enough!" Sheryl's voice cracked audibly as she stepped back from the lectern and clapped in unison with the crowd.

The men had barely begun to take their seats when Sheryl and Rev. Banks held them up again, this time so that they could present them with tokens of appreciation. Each gift had been carefully selected to fit the individual. Little Pooh Riley, sporting a new L.A. Lakers jersey, presented Brandon with a photography portfolio, featuring the work of the preteen students he had mentored at Ellis. O.J. was given a leather-bound, pocket-sized Bible with the words ELLIS—A PLACE FOR ALL GOD'S CHILDREN imprinted on the front. It took all of O.J.'s manly pride to keep from bursting with tears when he found the dedication page was filled with signatures of the nine-year-olds he had tutored in English. Larry guffawed in appreciation when he was handed a leather checkbook case with the words CHIEF FINANCIAL OFFICER, ELLIS COMMUNITY CENTER inscribed across the front. Most impressive was the presentation to Terence of a gold-plated plaque recognizing him as the first annual recipient of the Spirit of Ellis Award, to be presented, in Sheryl's words, "to an individual whose ability to overcome economic adversity mirrors the spirit Ellis encourages in all of its youth." Terence's surprise was increased by the announcement that Technotronics, Inc., would be assuming responsibility for all of his remaining Highland tuition costs.

When the men took their seats, the program continued with personal testimonials from Ellis alumni. The board members themselves as well as many onlookers sat in awe as elderly, middle-aged, and young adults took the stage, tying their time at Ellis into the productive lives they had come to lead. Most touching was the testimony of Jenae Watkins, a tall wisp of a woman with a girlish face. Her story of how she had first arrived at Ellis's door fifteen years earlier, as a pregnant teen with a heroin addiction, held the audience rapt. She told how the staff had helped her beat the drug addiction, study to earn her GED, attend college for an associate's degree in nursing, and make a stable home for herself and her child. "And a few weeks ago I was accepted to attend medical school, right here at Highland!" Her face streaming with tears, she urged the audience to withhold applause. "I-I'm nobody special, really. The special people are the ones who keep this place runnin'. Sheryl, Rev. Banks, and now these young men from Highland, their work makes it possible. If Sheryl Gibson and her predecessors hadn't believed in me, I might have died in the streets fifteen years ago. Instead I'm going to take a shot at becoming a physician. Brothers and sisters, I mean this: the next time a place like Ellis, or any worthwhile institution in our community, asks for your money or your time, please remember me, if you don't remember anything else! Me, the person who might still be walking up to you and asking for money for my habit instead of preparing to treat your infirmities. Giving back can make a difference!"

More than an hour later the proceedings were finally winding down. As he bopped to the Highland Gospel Choir's rendition of Fred Hammond's "Glory to God," Terence leaned over to whisper in to Sheryl's ear. "Sheryl, are you going to make any announcement about the status of the monies needed to pay off the banks?" He and the other fellows had been expecting a little more information about how close the center was to satisfying all the banks. They knew that their contributions, which were now safely out of Spears's hands and in Ellis's bank account, were going to help reduce the debt, but Sheryl had given no indication of how they were going to close the remaining gap.

Sheryl let a sly grin slip and winked at him. "You'll hear how it goes, soon enough. Just enjoy yourself." With that, she rose and returned to the podium, giving the crowd a few seconds to collect itself before making her concluding comments. She removed a printed document from the pocket of her slacks and beamed brightly. "Before I dismiss this great celebration, I must confess I chose to save the best news for last. I mentioned earlier that we had a twenty-five-thousand-dollar shortfall that we needed to cover in order to completely satisfy our creditors and avoid closure. Well, I was a little coy with you all. We received, just yesterday, the final dollars needed to make that goal." Pandemonium took over as the weight of Sheryl's words settled in.

Terence and his friends and fellow board members could barely restrain themselves; they crisscrossed the stage trading hugs, backslaps, high fives, and proud, thankful shouts of glee. When Sheryl had finished cavorting with the others, she returned to the microphone.

"To show my special gratitude for these last-minute donors, our black knights, if you will, I'd like to recognize a representative of each group. As I call your name and your organization, please come join us on the stage so this assembly can express its appreciation!" She slipped on a trendy pair of eyeglasses and began to make her way down the list. "Mr. Matthew X, representing the Highland chapter of the Nation of Islam, donating twenty-two hundred dollars! Mr. Allen Gilliam, representing the Highland chapter of the Disciples of Christ, donating fifty-one hundred dollars! Mr. Jerry Wallace, representing Technotronics, Inc., donating six thousand this year, with a five thousand annual endowment! Pastor Otis Grier, representing Light of Tabernacle Church, donating fifteen hundred dollars!"

Terence, Brandon, Larry and O.J. looked on in astonishment, wondering how many donors there had been. There was still a little ways to go to hit that twenty-five-thousand figure. The rest must have been due to someone with major duckets, or a large group of folk making small donations. Sheryl paused dramatically, then resumed. "Lisa Patton, representing the Women of Highland Society, donating twelve thousand, five hundred dollars!"

As Lisa, dressed in a tasteful spring suit, climbed the steps to join the throng of donors lining the stage, Terence was unable to hide his amazement as he went to join her. "Lisa, where in the world did you get that type of money?"

Taking his hand, she leaned in, kissing him gently on the cheek before responding. "Let's just say the Women of Highland is a front for we sisters who consider ourselves to be important in the lives of you and your housemates."

His eyes searching the crowd, Terence looked furtively at his friends on the stage before continuing. "Is you saying—are you saying that Monica, Sheila—"

"Monica, Sheila, Carla, and, believe it or not, Ashley are all in on this. You got it, babe. Did you all think we've been blind these past weeks, while your work for Ellis almost ate you all alive? We've been using our pull, all over the campus, combined with Ashley's pocketbook, to make our own impact. How ya like us now?"

Unable to be heard over the roar of the crowd, Terence made do by drawing his woman close and planting a warm display of his affection on to her lips. They were surrounded by Brandon, Larry, and O.J. The time to celebrate, as one unit, one household, had finally come.

Larry senior was unable to hide his naked glee at his son's news. "Hot damn, I knew my boy would come to his senses! How many times I gotta tell you, ain't nothing those snobby Wall Street worker bees can teach you about business that I can't! It's about time you gave me another chance to show you the ropes, son!"

His shoulders trembling in silent laughter, Larry rested the phone in the crook of his neck. His hands freed up, he shushed Sheila before responding. "Well, Pop, what can I say? I got a nasty call from the boys at Goldman Sachs Monday, and I didn't have any time to talk. Basically, they wanted me to accept their offer to work there this summer. Dad, a brother's been busy, so I had to tell them to check me out next year. After the last couple of weeks I've had, I think I need to be in familiar surroundings this summer. I got the rest of my life to bow to the Wall Street power structure. I figure I may as well enjoy this last summer and give the family business a chance before I graduate next year. Besides, I've got a lot to fill you and Mom in on regarding these last few weeks. Amy, too."

"Well, you know we'll have bells on in anticipation of your arrival. This is gonna be too sweet, Larry, you'll see. Everyone at the corporate headquarters has been asking about you, ever since your days working here when you were in high school. And every year I've had to hide my embarrassment when they ask if you'll be returning to us. Every summer, it's been 'No, he's interning at

Merrill Lynch, Bankers Trust, General Electric.' Anyplace but your old man's company."

"Pop, you always said you wanted me to expand my horizons first."

"And I did, but that doesn't mean it didn't hurt to see you put off Whitaker Holdings like some stepchild. But hey, no hard feelings, son. I'm excited about your summer. You can live it up! The renovations of the guest house were completed last month, so you can have that all to yourself, or stay in the room we designed for you when the house was built. Your sister can take the leftovers when she gets back from behind that godforsaken Iron Curtain."

"All right, Pop, sounds good. Look, I gotta go. We can talk about my work assignments when I get home. I'm gonna stick around to see Brandon and O.J. graduate tomorrow, then I'm gonna help the guy who's subleasing my room get settled. I'll plan to drive home Monday, after I meet with Winston Hughes about forming the HSA cabinet for next year."

"My son, the vice president of the Highland Student Association! Didn't have the juice to follow your old man's legacy and make president, huh?"

Larry chuckled. His father was so predictable. "Pop, when I explain everything that went down here lately, you'll understand why I withdrew from the race. I was hoping that Winston would pull out a victory like he did, but I never expected him to select me as his vice president! I almost said no, but when I thought it through, I realized I had made time to be president next year, so why couldn't I be vice? Besides, a socially impaired brother like Winston needs a smooth operator as his right hand. Who better to fill that role than *moi*?" Larry's eyes locked with Sheila's again. "Hey, look, Pop, I really gotta be out this time."

Larry senior wasn't too happy to let Larry escape that quickly. "Okay, Okay, look. I'm really proud of you, son. The fact that you and your boys were able to help get Ellis Center stabilized speaks volumes about your abilities. I know Brent is just as proud of Brandon as I am of you. Now it's time for you to bring those skills to the family business. I've got some of everything lined up for you—acquisition analysis, troubleshooting in our PR and operations departments, and some financial projections for the new branches. When you're done, those snobby bankers won't be able to so much as turn your head."

"Well, we'll see, Pop, we'll see. I gotta go."

"Hey, son, by the way, will that fine thang Ashley be coming to see you this summer?"

Pretending not to hear the question, Larry clicked off his phone and let it rest gently at his side. Across his partially packed room, amid growing piles of cardboard boxes and packing tape, Sheila sat atop the silvery black comforter of his bed. It was early Friday evening, and they had agreed to go out and have a private celebration of the end of the Ellis affair, despite the fact that they had gone drinking and grubbing with the guys after the rededication ceremony. Sheila was once again more spruced-up than usual, her business casual attire almost matching Larry's. They had reservations at Houston's in an hour, so they needed to leave shortly. Romancing a target of his affections with an expensive evening on the town was old hat to a man of his experience, but tonight he had decided to let the pomp and circumstance follow the substance. He had both craved and feared this moment, this facing up to the powerful emotions this sister induced in him. But the time for games had passed. Her parents and Andre were already in town for graduation; her parents were going to stay an extra week to give Sheila time to get accustomed to full-time motherhood before starting her position at the *Post*. This woman now had too many responsibilities on her to deal with some flaky player. Larry playfully kicked aside a couple of boxes and took a seat on the bed, which he slapped loudly. "So, Sheila Evans, what exactly are we?"

Her dark brown eyes drinking him in like some divine milk shake, she put a hand to her chin in mock thought. "Now, Mr. Whitaker, what ever are you talking about?"

He repressed the urge to scoot closer, an urge intensified by the magnetic pull between their bodies. "Geez, now I know how nice guys like Choirboy feel." He wiped his brow of the moisture that had sprung up without warning. "Sheila, you gotta understand. I've never had to do this before."

"Do what?"

"I don't know, tell a girl how I feel about her before anything else has taken place. See, normally, I take a girl out, show her a good time, get physical, *then* we worry over the semantics of how we feel about each other."

"And what does this have to do with me?" Sheila was enjoying this a little more than Larry preferred.

"Sheila, the old way got me nothing but one-night stands and empty relationships, like Ashley. I'll be straight up with you. I have no clue as to how to build a real, solid relationship. That's never been a concern for me. Until you."

"Larry, what are you saying?" No longer looking coy, Sheila rose from the bed, one hand to her chest.

Fastening his eyes to hers without leaving his bedside perch, he spoke slowly, hoping his words made sense. "I think I could fall in love with you, Sheila, that's what I'm trying, ineptly, to say. I'll admit, this is just based on a few weeks of close friendship, and maybe things will be different now that we no longer have the Ellis drama to juice things up. But ... I don't know what I'm saying, okay? I look at you, and I see a woman with intelligence, beauty, heart, and selflessness, someone who I could wake up every day excited to be with, today and fifty years from now. I want us to have a chance to see if that feeling is mutual, if we could actually be a couple. This ain't no marriage proposal, understand. This is just an honest declaration of feelings. Am I making any sense?"

The room seemed to be void of sound for several seconds as Sheila leaned against Larry's closed door, chewing her lower lip softly and crossing her arms deliberately. "It all sounds good, Larry. And I'd be lying if I told you that my feelings don't mirror yours. There's not a sister at Highland who hasn't considered what it would be like to be your lady. But I never gave you much thought before these past few weeks, when I came to see your wit, perseverance, and loyalty to others up close. God, that sounds corny. My girlfriends would kill me if they heard me right now. But I may as well be real. I'd like nothing better than to give us a chance. But I have to tell you a story first."

Intrigued, Larry rose and dragged a chair over to where she stood. "Have a seat and tell me about it."

"You may want to sit down for this one."

"I'm straight. What's the story, Sheila?"

Her back erect as she took a seat in the desk chair, Sheila gazed into Larry's eyes, the look on her face more distant than he was accustomed to. "Larry, on the surface, and I stress the surface, you have always reminded me of someone. When I was in high school in Detroit, there was a guy who was Big Man on Campus, a senior when I was a sophomore. His name was Byron Wiggs and he was Mr. It. Tall, dark, handsome, and hung like a bull moose if the girls' locker-room talk was to be believed. Yes, girls can talk just as foul as you boys, and unlike you guys, most of girls' high school sex talk is based on fact. Well, from sophomore year on, I heard how hot Byron was. Every girl wanted to be on his arm, in his pants, you name it. Personally, I always claimed to have no interest in him. I never cared for the jock type. I had always been a track star myself, but I wasn't drawn to the big, brawny buffoons who populated men's sports. I would normally date the more gentlemanly of the guys who asked me out, who were usually the plainer, nerdy guys. I didn't really have the type of assets that horny teenagers ran after, so I made do and told myself I was content.

"Then the summer before my senior year, I'm out at a party when who do I run into but Byron Wiggs, along with a crew of his underachieving partners from his high school class. He kept bad company, but he was still doing okay for himself. Top running back in University of Detroit's history, and he was on the cover of every local sports mag and paper. Personally, I had started to blossom a little bit, but I was still no Jayne Kennedy. Regardless, I guess I still had enough to draw Byron's interest. To make a long story short, he coaxed me onto the dance floor at that party and before I knew it, I had given him my virginity, my car keys, and my self-respect. He never pretended to be faithful to me, but I rationalized that I could deal with that in return for the excitement, pleasure, and attention being with him brought. Girls who used to think they could ignore me started paying me props, and brothers who had treated me like I was invisible suddenly wanted to mack me so they could say they stole Byron's woman. Well, I just knew I was Miss It.

"In fall of my senior year I was editor of the school paper, vice president of my class, and the number-three student in academic rank. Highland sought me out for a full ride early on, and I was on cloud nine. Life couldn't be any better. Then my luck train ran out of steam. I had been too embarrassed to tell my parents I was gettin' busy, so I'd relied on Byron's Trojans to keep me from getting knocked up. I'm sure you've been around enough to know that was just courting disaster, and it was early October when I found out I was pregnant."

"Oh, Sheila." Larry was not so surprised to find that this Wiggs was Andre's father, but the simple fact that Sheila was sharing such personal info threw him off balance.

Although it had been four years ago, Sheila's voice still sounded ready to crack as she continued her story. "So I figured, it's not the absolute end of the world, right? Pregnant teens weren't exactly an anomaly at the time, so I figured if I had to be one, at least my baby had the most famous father in the Detroit area. I never even questioned whether or not Byron would take responsibility, Larry. Never. The men in my family, they've always taken care of their responsibilities. I knew Byron was no saint, but I expected him to take care of his child and respect me in the process.

One thing is sure, he was smooth. I called him the day after I got the news, and he treated me the way he probably treated the other girls he'd knocked up. Talked a big game about how 'we' would get through this, how he was there for me, loved me. He said he would call me the next day so we could figure out how to tell my parents. He also said he'd look into getting a part-time job to kick in child support. I decided to believe him. I had to. Two weeks later, after he still hadn't called, I called his house. His mother answered and *read me out*, saying I was like all the other whores who tried to land her son with pregnancy stories. Larry, I was too shocked to respond. I hung up the phone and cried harder than I ever have. I haven't talked to Byron since. Larry, I never want to feel pain like that again."

Moving to her, Larry buried Sheila's head in his shoulder, feeling her warm tears bleed into his rugby shirt. "As long as I have anything to say about it, Sheila, you never will." Wiping the tears from her eyes, he took her trembling face into his hands. "I want to take this slow, as slow as you need it. And I'll do whatever you want regarding Andre, whether you want me to be his best buddy right away or keep my distance until we decide we have a viable relationship. But I want to be there for you, starting today." Hugging her tightly, Larry wiped any concerns about smoothness or style from his mind and planted an earnest kiss on Sheila's quivering lips. As he tasted the warmth of her welcoming mouth, he made a promise: no more "profiles," no more choosing a woman to satisfy anyone other than himself. It was time to step up to the plate and learn how to love like a real man.

Terence had been too dog-tired to let Lisa drag him out into the streets tonight. She'd tried to get him to go out with Larry and Sheila to Houston's, but he had killed that notion instantly. He'd been running on empty for the last month, and this past week's events would have drained Arnold Schwarzenegger of his strength. He was determined to do nothing but sit on his butt tonight. That hadn't stopped Lisa from coming over, though. She was in the kitchen, preparing him a late supper of spaghetti and meatballs while he sprawled across the couch, tripping off some episodes of *Martin* and *Living Single* he had taped. This was always one of his favorite ways to unwind on weekends, but he'd had no time for this guilty pleasure for weeks. He would chill tonight, check out his boys and Lisa at their graduation tomorrow, and then get down to business for the summer. A brother had things to do.

"Dinner is served, Boo." Lisa emerged from the kitchen, a steaming plate of spaghetti balanced in her right hand. Her hair was pulled back into a slick ponytail. Seeing the simplicity of her appearance, Terence was transported back to their days in high school at Cardozo. Life had seemed so simple then; she had made his senses soar like no other girl had, and he had believed the feeling was mutual. Now, four years later, his heart still ached and longed for those days. Sure, she was here for him now, and had proven herself in ways he never expected throughout this Ellis crisis. His heart told him that should be enough, that he could consider their "here today, gone tomorrow" days a thing of the past. They were now ready to be a fully committed, stable couple, right?

As he reached for the plate of spaghetti and placed it on the coffee table, he examined Lisa's sparkling eyes. He knew the answer to one half of the question plaguing his mind, but he needed Lisa's help for the complete answer. "Lisa, when you're with me, do you still think of other guys?"

Pursing her lips and knitting her forehead into a frown, Lisa loosely placed a hand on her hip. "Okay, so where is this coming from? I cook you a meal, and the only comment you have is a question like that?"

Flicking the TV off with a punch of the remote control, Terence leaned back into the couch and patted the seat beside him. "Sit down. This ain't some inquisition, I don't want you getting defensive. Just answer my question, babe. The first time you stepped out on me, freshman year, you said it was best we split up for a while, because you found yourself thinkin' about what it would be like to be with other guys. Basically, I wasn't enough to keep you from being curious about other dudes, like Sam Baker and whoever else. I wanna know if four years and however many other guys has changed that, Lisa. Can you be satisfied with me?"

Taking a cautious seat next to Terence, Lisa folded her hands in her lap and looked out toward the front window. "I don't understand your reason for asking, Terence, but yes, I can be satisfied— no, more than satisfied being with you. I love you! I always have—"

"But that didn't stop you from wanting to experiment with other brothers—"

"Terence, that is not fair! Do you *really* wanna play 'Who's slept with whom?' 'Cause if what the girls around campus say is true, you've always found someone to get it on with when we were apart."

Terence rested his head in his hands. "Lisa, I'm a red-blooded male. If I can't be with my honey, I'm gonna eventually have to get with somebody. It was you who put me in that position."

Frowning vehemently, Lisa jumped to her feet, seemingly talking more to the TV than to Terence. "Terence, why would you wait until now, after all we've been through, to complain about the past? You could have shut me out a long time ago. Nobody made you take me back when I got tired of those other guys."

Terence searched Lisa's eyes. "These last few days have made me look at life in a new light, Lisa. And maybe part of that new light is the belief that I'm worthy of a long-term commitment from the woman in my life. You're not my mother, Lisa; I don't have to be grateful every time you come back. I think I've gone so long without expecting anybody to value me as a person that I forgot that. So I gave you a free ride. Well, the free ride ends today, babe."

Lisa crossed her arms and began to trace a circle in the floor with her right foot. "Terence, we can't all be blessed with your talent for loyalty, for settling in life. I'm sorry, but I think my parents were right. They always told me to make sure not to marry the first guy who came along. They always encouraged shopping around. "

Terence hissed a sigh through his teeth. "You ain't sayin' a word. I knew *they* never liked me."

"It's not that they don't like you. They just wanted me to go as far as possible in life. I'll admit, in their eyes, that meant marrying 'up.' They enrolled me in Jack and Jill, the Greek auxiliaries, and tried to steer me toward sons of doctors, businessmen, or politicians. I guess by the time I got to Highland, I decided I needed to experience some of those types so that when I settled down, I'd be at peace about what I was missing out on."

"Lisa, I know the story, heard it from you many times. What

you ain't answering is, why I should expect you to be at peace now, when you weren't a year ago? Is it the fact that I'm goin' to achieve my goal of becoming an engineer? If Jerry Wallace hadn't talked to the cops about the Ellis mess and rehired me at Technotronics, would you even know my name right now?" He paused at the sight of tears sprouting in her eyes. Now his felt moist as well. "Dammit, Lisa, I'm not tryin' to hurt you. I just want us to be real with each other. Talk to me, babe."

Lisa wasn't meeting Terence's eyes anymore. "Terence, I can't give a definite answer yet. Of all the guys I've dated so far, you're the only one I could spend the rest of my life with. I know that."

"But there's still plenty of other brothers you might meet down the line, huh?"

"Who says it *has* to be a brother? I don't think I should rule out entire races of people like that, Terence. I don't know when I'll be ready for marriage, but right now I want to work on our relationship. It's the best thing I've experienced so far."

Terence trained a skeptical eye on his girlfriend. "You're putting a lot of conditions on my value, Lisa. Do you hear yourself? I'm the best 'so far.' That's damn flattering. Listen to me. Have you decided on those job offers yet?"

Annoyance lacing her tone, she sighed. "I have until a week after graduation to give my answers. I *was* leaning toward going with Johnson & Johnson, out in Rockville."

Biting his lip and avoiding eye contact, Terence decided to do what he felt best, regardless of the pain it was already inflicting on him. "I thought the job with Merck, in Jersey, was your dream job? The pay was better, you were going to be able to get into a management position more quickly. What's tipping you toward staying in this area?"

Lisa wiped a tear from her eye. The message was clear. "What do you think?"

"Lisa, maybe it's best if you take that offer with Merck. I wouldn't want you to miss the best opportunity over me. There's no guarantee about where we're headed."

Wrenching herself away from him, Lisa stood again, her dark eyes burning a hole through Terence. "So it's like that, just like that?" She paused and looked around the room, as if she expected someone to burst out from nowhere and talk some sense into him. "Terence, do you know what you're doing? Are you sure about this?"

He stood and moved to her, propping her up as she collapsed into him. "Lisa, hear me. I love you, you know that. You have to understand, I'm doing this for you. We have to be strong. You need to decide, once and for all, if you can live with the fact that you'll never find a perfect man, that you'll eventually have to take me or someone else for what we are. And I'll have to figure out how to get sincerely interested in another woman, if you decide I'm not the one you can commit to. It's the only way. We can't go on the way we've been. I'm sorry . . ."

As he loosened his grip, Lisa flitted away from him and retreated to the kitchen. Before he had time to weigh the pros and cons of going after her, she emerged with her jacket and purse, speaking in a clipped, hurried tone. "All the food is ready. More spaghetti's on the stove, garlic bread is in the oven. I turned everything off, so if it gets cold, just pop things in the microwave. There's enough of everything for you to share with the other guys or save some for your granny when she comes by after graduation. You don't have to ride home with me, I'll be fine. Good night, Terence."

As she broke for the door, Terence grasped her left wrist lightly, afraid she would escape before he could soften the blow of his comments. "Lisa, baby, I—"

Shaking loose his grip , Lisa lowered her eyes and continued to the door before turning back to face him. "Damn you, Terence Davidson."

His hands in the air, Terence took one step in her direction. "Why?"

As she yanked the door open and walked through, Lisa's terse response was a whisper. "Because you're right."

≈≈≈

It was almost ten on Friday night, and Monica Simone was cutting an insistent path through the lower level of Union Station.

Graduation would be tomorrow, but she wasn't going to be around for it. She held a still-warm ticket to Manhattan in her left hand and gripped her oversized beige Coach bag against her hip with her right hand. Several men passing by slowed their roll to consider approaching her, but they were just as quick in moving on when they glimpsed the salty expression clouding her striking facial features. This sister was not to be messed with, not tonight.

Bursting through the opening in the railing that separated the shops and newsstands from the Amtrak boarding platform, Monica had her ticket punched by the attendant and strode over to a bank of plastic chairs near the loading area. Setting her bag next to her, she took a seat, crossed her legs, and began to pump her right leg up and down impatiently. Anybody could tell she was ready to go.

Brandon desperately wanted to get right up on Monica before she saw him, so he did his best to get some help from the attendant taking tickets. Trying not to shout over the harried noise of the crowd, he leaned in toward the young brother. "Hey, man, I don't have a ticket. I'm tryin' to catch a woman friend. Can you help a brother out?"

The attendant, a sleepy-eyed teen who looked to be barely out of high school, eyed Brandon suspiciously. "What? I can't do that. No ticket, no admittance. Sorry, man."

"Brother man, come on, how you gon' do me?" Brandon flashed a twenty-dollar bill at the boy. "I'm trying to make it worth your while here. I got a woman in there."

Suddenly the boy looked at Brandon with startled recognition. "Hey, wait, I know you! Weren't you at that rededication ceremony at Ellis Center on Thursday?"

Confused, Brandon looked past the boy to catch a glimpse of Monica's busy legs. "Uh, yeah, I was an honorary board member this year. You used to attend the center or something?"

The attendant flashed a wide grin and shook Brandon's hand. "Yeah, dog, I almost grew up in Ellis. Your name's Brandon, right? You worked with my little brother, Billy Davis, in the science tutors program."

"You're Billy's brother? He's a great kid. Very talented little scientist, if I recall."

"Hey, man, go on in. I can look the other way for someone like you. God bless you, dog."

Shaking the young man's hand, Brandon slipped through the turnstile and wove his way toward Monica, keeping out of her sight all the way. When he was within a few feet of her, he slid into the next seat and waited for her to turn his way.

It took just five seconds. "What the hell do you want?" Eyes flashing, she looked at him as if he had just hit her with some lame come-on line.

Standing, Brandon towered over her, looking as deep into her eyes as she would allow. "Monica, the other night scared me. What we did, what happened, it—"

"Not here." Monica's response did nothing to release the tension percolating between them. As she gathered her bag and shot past the amused stare of the young attendant, Brandon followed closely on her heels. She stopped and allowed him to corner her just beneath the stairwell. She turned to face him, but her eyes held him at a distance. "Brandon, I'm going to say this once and once only. The other night was the first time I've slept with anyone in more than a year. You wanna know why? Because I was tired of being hurt. I held Victor off, avoided every dog on Highland's campus. I was saving myself until I met a real man, one who could share his emotions, love someone other than himself, and treat me with respect. I *thought* you measured up. You think I went out with you, slept with you, this late in the game, for the hell of it? I've tried to let you know how I feel. But what do I get in return? Judgment, like I'm a slut or something. Do you have any idea how it hurt to be called a waste of time?" She gripped her Coach and broke eye contact with him, the lingering pain in her voice saying more than the words.

Raising his right hand in despair, Brandon took another step into her personal space. "Monica, these last few weeks threw me for a loop. I didn't know what I was getting into. My grandmother used to tell me be careful what I pray for, 'cause I just might get it.

I see now what she meant. Even the best dreams and fantasies never measure up in real life. Everything comes with a price. It's taken me a while to accept that." He leaned in toward her, drinking in the smell of her hair and her Eternity perfume as she stared at the floor and toyed with her bag. "Monica, I don't know how this will work out, if at all. But I don't want to wonder how it would've gone if we gave it a chance. Please don't leave town tonight. I know you don't want to. Tara told me everything, about your plans to stay out of town until I was gone, and about those phone calls you've been getting from your ex back in Manhattan. But you don't want Victor."

He hugged her quivering body against his. "Your apartment's still waiting for you. Tara said your subletters don't move in for another two weeks. If you stick around that long, I'm sure I can. You know you want to." He gave her a look of longing.

The ice slowly melting from her face, Monica sighed and reached out, pinching Brandon's cheeks as if he was a cherubic infant. "Maybe I'll switch my ticket. My internship at home doesn't start for another three weeks. But Brandon, I don't do long-distance dating. After this, it's over. *Fini.*"

Brandon grinned. "*Fini* this. You and I both know *tu me veux.*"

"Okay. *Je t'aime, beaucoup.* Happy?" Monica's mouth crinkled into a mischievous smile. "But I promise not to take advantage of you anymore. I'll keep my hands to myself. No more *coucher.*"

"I like your terms. Friends?"

They remained rooted in that spot for several minutes, staring deeply into each other's eyes while the sounds of departing trains and the smell of Cinnabon pastries and Sbarro's pizza permeated the station. None of that mattered right now. With Monica in his arms, Brandon couldn't focus on anything else. One last time, he allowed himself to wonder how much simpler life might have been if he'd stepped to Monica the first time he saw her. Would she have paid him any mind? Would they have adapted to each other's morals and lifestyles? Would they have survived the many pitfalls that ruined Highland relationships on a daily basis? The odds were low on every point, so there was no use torturing himself over what might have been. Right now he was holding what had once been the idealized woman of his dreams. She had turned out to be a living, breathing, flawed but precious human being, no different from anyone else.

He would tell her about Brandy later tonight; that way each person's baggage would be on the table, and they could start with a clean slate. He'd learned so much from Monica. The next time a woman took his breath away, he'd no longer cower in fear or delude himself with religious excuses for his timidity. He'd remember Monica, if only for an instant, and spur himself into action, until one day he'd achieve that perfect match, the woman who would turn him to jelly and share his principles. One day it might even be Monica herself. But whoever it wound up being, Brandon knew the imprint this lady had made on his heart would never be erased.

Interrupting his meditation, Monica placed a slender finger to his freshly balmed lips. "I hate to go back on my promise, but do you think you can handle a *little* temptation, Mr. Choirboy?" Her teasing smile was loaded with promises.

Feeling his heart burn with a passion he knew he would have to control, Brandon pulled Monica's smiling face within an inch of his own. "I'll take my chances."

❧❧❧

Somebody was smiling on O.J. today. His doctors had expected him to be in the neck brace for at least two weeks, but when he'd climbed out of bed this morning for graduation, he knew he was ready to remove it for good. His father had helped free him of the scaly bandage, and so far the old neck was holding up just fine. O.J. took advantage of this as he bobbed and weaved through the buzzing crowd of family and friends that packed the backyard of the house. Lined up against the house was a row of card tables filled with baked and fried chicken, a turkey, ham, roast beef, and every soul food side dish known to man. Brandon's and O.J.'s families manned the tables, dishing out healthy portions and taking time to get acquainted with their sons' friends and classmates. Making his way through the crowd, O.J. coaxed another loaded plate of ham, collard greens, and dressing from his Aunt Junetta before dancing his way back to the table with his father and the Griers.

Rev. Grier laughed at O.J.'s hearty appetite. "Boy, somebody has sho' 'nuff been healed up in here! Look at your boy eat, Peters!"

Pastor Peters shook his head in exasperation at his legacy. "He gets that from his momma's side of the family, not from me. You see what a beanpole I am!" Peters ran a hand over O.J.'s newly shaved head. "You can cut those waves out of his head, but you'll never take away his love for vittles! I shoulda known my son would turn out with a healthy appetite. When I started courtin' his mother, the first thing her family did was have me over to eat. Don't you know my wife's brothers and father ate me under the table! Questioned my manhood over it, they did! O.J., you never had a chance, son!"

As the men coughed and chortled in amusement, Carla tapped O.J. lightly on the shoulder and asked the question he'd been waiting for. "So, have you talked to Keesa yet?"

Halting his fork over the stacked plate, he shrugged absent-mindedly. He was still coming to terms with the reality of Keesa's wrath. "They booked her on assault-and-battery charges, Carla. I asked the police not to bring the assault-with-deadly-intent charge. I confirmed her account about the mind games that Nico Lane and them played on her, how she had been deluded into thinking I badmouthed her in public. It's not formal yet, but it sounds like they're going for a suspended sentence, probation, and mandatory psychological counseling."

"What about the baby?"

"I haven't talked to Keesa, but I hear from the authorities that she and the baby are fine. I've left all my info with the authorities so I can take a paternity test when the baby's born this winter."

"And if you're the father?"

"I guess I'll cross that bridge if I come to it, Carla." O.J. looked off beyond the throng of celebration, his upbeat mood temporarily stalled. "But I will take care of my responsibilities. Believe that, there are enough deadbeat dads around without me adding to the problem."

Rising from her seat, Carla pecked O.J. on the right cheek. "I'm proud of you, O.J. I know you're going to emerge a better man from all this. I have to go. Look, please stay in touch, Okay? I love you."

Before he could crook his neck to watch her leave, Carla was gone. He knew it was best this way. There was no turning back now. He had the opportunity of a clean slate awaiting him in Atlanta, once he had squashed any leftover conflicts from his free-wheeling high school days. Carla was too good a catch to wait around on him; in Chocolate City it would only be a matter of time before a better man, one who was already where O.J. knew he needed to be, would snatch her up.

"O.J., hey, man! Good to see you, looking like yourself! Are you feeling okay?"

Startled by the man's sudden approach, O.J. whipped around to find Milton "the Bishop" Hobbs staring down at him, his well-groomed goatee shining in the sunlight. To his right, Brandon and Monica were posed like fashion models, their eyes full of laughter and their bodies joined at the hip. Slowly taking Hobbs's extended hand, O.J. stifled a confused smile. "Hey, Bishop, fancy seein' you here! I'm doing all right, good as can be expected! Keep me in your prayers, though. A brother can always use 'em!"

Glancing around the busy crowd, Hobbs nodded to another acquaintance. "Well, it's good to see you're doing better, O.J. I'll be praying for your continued recovery. Look, brother, you take care. Somebody over there's callin' my name!" Slapping O.J. on the back, Hobbs shook hands with Brandon, his eyes moving between the Choirboy and Monica. "Well, I expect I'll see you two lovebirds next week, since you're staying around a few extra days, Brandon. Thanks for the invite, man. I'm gonna holler at those folks over there and get going! You got all my numbers, right, man?"

Brandon nodded in recognition. "I got them, man. I'll be in touch. Later."

As Hobbs made his way back into the crowd, O.J. fixed his friend with an inquiring look . "What possessed you to invite the Disciple? I thought you fell out with Hobbs and Gilliam. I know they came through for the center and all, but—"

"O.J.," Monica interrupted as she played with a button on Brandon's rugby, "I think Brandon finally learned to live and let live. He has better things to do with his time than argue with Milton. Like spend time with me."

Smiling, Brandon placed a hand on O.J.'s shoulder. "Thank you, babe. O.J., I guess you could say I'm at peace with the fact my relationship with God is between me and he, nobody else. As long as that's the case, I don't have time for petty arguments about small details. There's too much living to do to waste time bickering. "

Rising slowly from his seat, O.J. turned to face his friends, his arms crossed over his chest. "Truer words were never spoken, friend. Hopefully, you and I'll be able to talk more about spiritual stuff someday soon. This brother needs a few months, though."

"Well," Brandon said, pointing over his shoulder at Terence, who was reclining a few feet away on a lounger chair, "I got one brother who's ready now. My family and I are taking T to church with us tomorrow. After that he's hollerin' something about going to the temple with Matthew X next week. At least it's a start for him."

Larry and Sheila burst into their midst, trailed closely by Terence. The couple had spent the better part of the afternoon tearing up the dance floor, which was actually a small section of the yard that had been designated for couples who wanted to cut a rug. They had been joined by little Andre Evans, who was napping up in Larry's room now, various Highland students, Sheryl Gibson and her date, and Brandon's brothers, who had drawn a lot of interest from the curious Highland sisters in attendance. Balancing a Seagram's cooler in his right hand, Larry saluted his friends. "All right, it's officially time for the men of 122 Moore to strut their stuff! We got 'U Will Know' by Black Men United coming up next on the sound system! This is gonna be our song, boys, you know what I'm sayin'? What we did for Ellis, what we've done for one another, we need a song to tie it all to!"

As the bass of the stereo boomed with the song's opening notes, O.J. playfully pushed his boy back a few steps. "Please, brother, ain't you heard of giving glory to God? We need a gospel song up in this place!"

Ignoring O.J.'s taunts, Terence began clapping his hands loudly, drawing the attention of the surrounding crowd. "O.J., either you with us or against us, bro! What up?" As the soothing voices of Tevin Campbell and El DeBarge crooned the opening lines, Brandon, Terence, and O.J. fell under the spell, joining Larry in front of the serving tables and swaying back and forth in fits of rhythmic passion. As the voices of Black Men United washed over one another, the brothers took turns imitating the singers. By the time the chorus came, the crowd could do nothing but hold their aching bellies as the men screeched, bellowed, and belted in unison with the recording. "Stand up tall and don't you fall," they roared, "and you will know!"

As he moved about more freely than he'd been able to for the last week, O.J. felt the warm, loving faces of his friends and family and allowed himself to relish the unique bond he had developed with the men surrounding him. He would leave town tomorrow a changed man. Hard times, including teacher certification, facing down his church, and mending fences with old conquests loomed ahead of him like a stormy cloud. But he knew, in that instant, that he had the strength to survive and even overcome those obstacles and more. Fate had pushed him to start with a clean slate, and like the friends around him, he was going to make the most of his.

READING GROUP GUIDE

This Reading Group Guide is designed to enhance your group's discussion of *Between Brothers,* a suspenseful coming-of-age story that moves from the halls of a historically black university to the streets of Washington, D.C., with great insight into the joys and perils of discovering what really matters in life.

1. In some ways Monica is Brandon's forbidden fantasy—beautiful, alluring, and experienced. But after he gets to know her Brandon finds his assumptions about Monica weren't always right. How is the Monica of his dreams different from the reality? Is Brandon attracted to her because of her reputation or in spite of it?

2. After Keesa attacks O.J., he doesn't reveal her identity immediately. Why does he turn Keesa in? How much responsibility does he have for her actions?

3. In the process of defending the Ellis Center, Terence, O.J., Brandon, and Larry are forced to reevaluate their priorities and make decisions about the truly important things in their lives. Discuss how each of the men changes and the decisions they make. What would have happened if they had not been involved with the Ellis Center?

4. Faith plays a large part in the lives of Brandon and O.J.; only Brandon's faith has supported him, while O.J. feels his has betrayed him. By the end, however, O.J. has reclaimed his faith, and Brandon begins to question his. How does this happen? What does each of the men realize about his faith?

5. In order to derail the Highland students' plans to save the Ellis Center, Nico Lane exploits their vulnerabilities through sabotage. Without O.J.'s, Larry's, or Terence's weaknesses, Nico and Eldridge's plan to close the Ellis Center could not have come so close to success. What are these weaknesses? Nico and Eldridge manipulate others into doing their dirty work; who is more responsible: the person who suggests an idea or the person who carries it out? Do we see this with Keesa? Rolly Orange?

6. The Ellis Center plays an important role in the community but cannot save a man like Nico from returning to the streets. What will make the difference to children like Pooh? How essential is the involvement of the Highland students and others from outside the neighborhood?

7. Larry lives in the shadow of his father's achievements and is following in his footsteps by running for student body president and choosing the "right" girlfriend. How does Larry deal with his father's legacy in the end? Explain his decisions to drop out of the election, leave Ashley, and work at his father's firm for the summer.

8. In some ways Terence, Brandon, O.J., and Larry have formed a bond greater than just that of housemates; their relationships with each other are brotherly in a I-don't-always-agree-with-you-but-I-got-your-back kind of way. Discuss the differences among each of the men. Are they like a family? Is it their different strengths and weaknesses that allows them to save the Ellis Center?

9. For much of his time at Highland, Terence faces an uphill battle to stay in school; of the four housemates, he has the most to lose from Nico's attempts to close the center. Why does he feel he can't tell his friends about Nico's threats? How does Terence's relationship with Lisa affect him?

10. Sheryl is the heart of the Ellis Center, and without her commitment the center would have likely failed. But she isn't able to see through Rolly Orange and his financial mismanagement until the end. Why can't she see how wrong things are going? Why do you think it is the students from Highland University and not the board members who step in to save the center?

WHY I WROTE *BETWEEN BROTHERS*: A SPECIAL NOTE FROM THE AUTHOR, C. KELLY ROBINSON

Between Brothers grew out of my desire to paint a literary picture of the black men I grew up around, came of age with, and continue to know today as family members and friends. In 1997, when I started putting together the outline and building the characters, it seemed there were very few contemporary novels featuring well-rounded black male characters. I stress "well-rounded" over the word "positive" because that's probably too simplistic a term. We all walk a line between the dark and the light, and no man or woman is one hundred percent virtuous or one hundred percent dysfunctional.

I felt the best answer to the controversy over black male depictions in literature was to present a story that could entertain readers while reminding them just how diverse and complex we are. I reflected on the different types of guys I've known, and came up with four personality types that cover the spectrum: the choirboy with high morals, the smooth operator who oozes charm, the bootstrapper who makes his way despite constant obstacles, and the sinister minister who sometimes uses his gifts for selfish purposes. I felt everyone could relate to these characters and would be reminded of someone they know. I also felt female readers might get some insight into what drives these personality types. I wanted to tie these diverse characters together somehow, which led to their being housemates attempting to help their community. In the end, I hope I have created an uplifting story that expands the scope of portrayal of the young black male while providing suspense, romance, and humor.

A Conversation with C. Kelly Robinson,
Author of *Between Brothers*

Q: How much does the story mirror your own college experience?

A: I really don't consider this to be a "college novel." In reality it shows the growth of four men who happen to be in their last year of college. However, the story's urban northwest D.C. setting and the Highland campus life were inspired by my years at Howard. When I thought about how to tell a story set amid the stunning diversity of "African America," Howard and D.C. in general made perfect sense. What I loved about Howard was that it brought together young African-American, African, and Caribbean students from all walks of life. Though there were many cliques, I found I could move among them without being stereotyped or marginalized.

My personal experiences at Howard aren't mirrored directly, but I did draw from some of the most striking aspects of campus life—like the highly charged campaigns for student government, the ever-present tension among students and community residents, and the complex social scene—to provide context for the overall story.

Q: Who are some of your favorite authors or influences?

A: I've always had an interest in literature, but I have to split my influences into two groups: those authors I admire from the perspective of a student and those I admire as an emerging writer. In the first class I would have to place Richard Wright, Ralph Ellison, Toni Morrison, and Charles Chesnutt. My more contemporary favorites in the second group include suspense novelists like Scott Turow, commercial writers like Tom Wolfe, and such storytellers as Bebe Moore Campbell, Walter Mosley, Valerie Wilson Wesley, Eric Jerome Dickey, and Colin Channer. This is not to mention the vast pool of talented writers my age who have hit the scene in recent years.

Q: You initially self-published a version of this book under the title *Not All Dogs*. Some mistook the title as a pure defense of black men. Given that the actual story line appeals equally to men and women, whom did you view as your primary audience?

A: My goal was always to write about men that female readers could invest in. I hoped to get more males interested in reading fiction, but I knew that could be an uphill battle. So I tried to be true to my instincts as a storyteller, my knowledge of what it means to be a young black male evolving into manhood, and my observations of the society around me. In the end, I hope female readers will feel they have taken an entertaining, insightful trip with men they know and love. I believe that as more males get into fiction they will read this book and feel they've found someone who is telling their story.

Q: Was writing a lifelong dream for you? Do you have a *Between Brothers* sequel penned yet?

A: Because I have worked to control a stutter since a young age, writing has always provided me with a certain freedom the spoken word could not. In high school and college I excelled in English and Literature and have won awards and other notice for personal essays, so writing was definitely precious to me. However, I come from a practical family full of "traditional" professionals, so I never considered a writing career until I completed the first draft of *Between Brothers* and was encouraged to seek its publication.

I don't have a sequel yet, though my head is full of ideas. My next project is a romantic comedy that takes place in Chicago among a group of twenty-something professionals. It's really like taking a group of Larry or Brandon's peers and showing what their lives are like four years later. The problems and dramas involve less physical danger but are more complex emotionally. That's the main thrust of my writing, an ongoing depiction of the dramas of middle-class black America.

Q: What is the most important message readers should take from *Between Brothers*?

A: When I was writing the first draft of the book, a CD that kept me company was Eric Benét's *True to Myself*. When it's all said and done, I think this story is about each character's struggle to discover what that means. Each man examines himself and readjusts his path to fit what he finds, in ways that will eventually make him a better husband, father, brother, and member of the community. I like to think that inspires readers to do the same.

About the Author

C. KELLY ROBINSON holds degrees from Howard University and Washington University in St. Louis. An MBA by training, his work experience includes Price Waterhouse, Emerson Electric, and NCR Corporation. He is also a former volunteer with Big Brothers Big Sisters, Mentor St. Louis, and Student Venture Ministries. He and his wife live in Dayton, Ohio, where he is working on his next novel. Visit his website at www.ckellyrobinson.com.